Praise for Celia Brayfield's novels:

For *Harvest*

'A good read but far from trivial. *Harvest* is a brilliantly textured "proper" novel about the women who surround and love, ever so painfully, a manipulative media man. A literary romance featuring the sophisticated English abroad in France' Fay Weldon, *Mail on Sunday*

'Cunningly plotted, extremely well written and compulsively readable' Beryl Bainbridge

'The authentic tang of human emotion at every level' Claire Rayner

'A cleverly plotted, witty black comedy, modern storytelling at its most enjoyable. Packed with insights – some acid, others poignant, all with the ring of truth. The throwaway observations made me laugh out loud' *Literary Review*

'Grand guignol in a gîte – shockingly readable' *New Statesman*

For *Pearls*

'Long, absorbing, its grammar impeccable, its theme the sufferings and eventual triumphs of a pair of beautiful sisters. Ms Brayfield knows what she is doing and what she does she does well. Her Malaya is exactly rendered, her women sound and act like real women' Anthony Burgess, *Independent*

'A triumph – Celia Brayfield's first novel is a complex and delicious amalgamation of glamour and sensitivity, sensuality and betrayal, sweeping from war-torn Malaysia through the England of the Beatles. A rich, multi-faceted story, her plot is a masterpiece of construction, her prose literate, insightful and frequently witty' *Rave Reviews*

'From a sudden crop of British bestsellers with feminist undertones – sisterhood is powerful in this passionate page-turner' *Time*

'A great adventure of our times' *Le Meridional*

Celia Brayfield has spent most of her life in suburbs, being born in Wembley Park in north London and moving to west London at the age of twenty. There she brought up her daughter as a single parent, led a successful campaign against a local road scheme and read John Updike's *The Witches of Eastwick* – all experiences on which she has drawn for *Getting Home*. The historic Bedford Park estate in Chiswick, the world's first garden suburb, became her model for the Maple Grove area of Westwick. She is the author of four bestselling novels, *Pearls*, *The Prince*, *White Ice* and *Harvest* as well as *Bestseller*, her acclaimed guide for fiction writers.

Getting Home

CELIA BRAYFIELD

WARNER BOOKS

A *Warner* Book

First published in Great Britain in 1998
by Little, Brown and Company
This edition published by Warner Books 1999
Reprinted 1999

Copyright © Celia Brayfield 1998

'Centrepiece' lyric by Harry Edison and Jon Hendricks ©
Renewed Andrew Scott Inc.
Lyric reproduction by kind permission of Carlin Music Corp.

Map artwork by Glynn Boyd Harte

The moral right of the author has been asserted.

A CIP catalogue record for this book is available from the British Library

ISBN 0 7515 2284 8

Typeset in Garamond 3 by M Rules
Printed and bound in Great Britain by Clays Ltd, St Ives plc

Warner Books
A Division of
Little, Brown and Company (UK)
Brettenham House
Lancaster Place
London WC2E 7EN

For Chloe

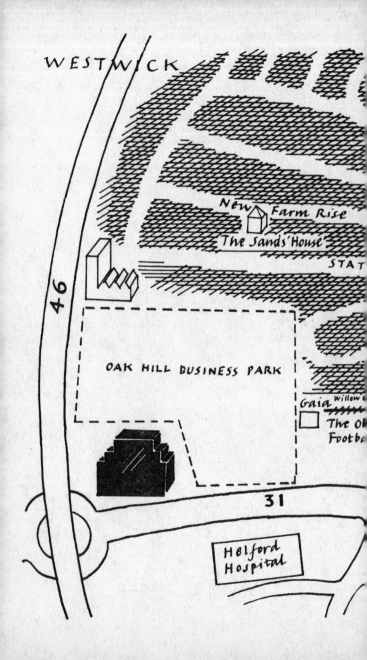

WESTWICK

46

New Farm Rise

The Sands' House

STAT

OAK HILL BUSINESS PARK

Gaia   Willow

The O
Footba

31

Helford
Hospital

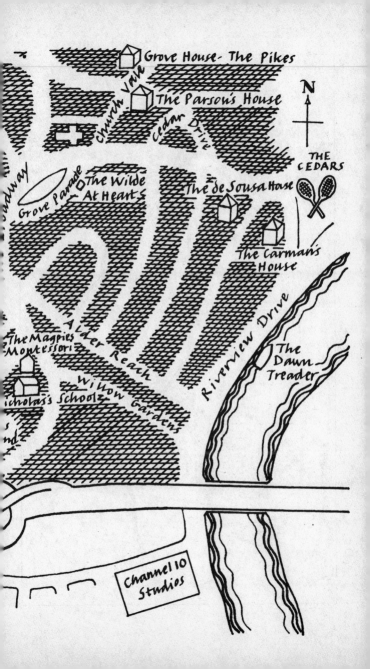

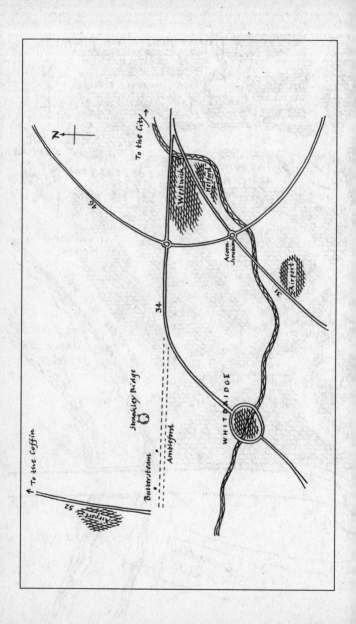

The more I'm with you pretty baby
The more I feel my love increase
I'm building all my dreams around you
Our happiness will never cease
But nothing's any good without you
Cos baby you're my centrepiece

I'll buy a house and garden somewhere
Along a country road apiece
A little cottage on the outskirts
Where we can really find release
But nothing's any good without you
Cos baby you're my centrepiece

'Centrepiece':
Lyrics by Harry Edison and Jon Hendricks

CHAPTER 1

The Healthiest Place in the World

The sun rose upon Westwick with respect. The pure glow of dawn approached the tree tops, discreetly penetrated the canopy of leaves and invited the sleeping community to wake up and enjoy the day.

The light falling through the cherry trees on New Farm Rise dappled the empty street. The white porches were virtuous with fresh paint; the cropped grass blades prickled in the damp earth. Stephanie Sands woke at 5.38 am, anxious because her husband was away but content because he was going to telephone at 6.00, her son was sleeping and her garden was growing.

All Stephanie could do was grow things. In thirty-two years she had obediently acquired other skills but felt no joy in practising them. Stephanie had raised plants, she made gardens and now she was raising a family. She had not considered that what one person grew another could then cut down.

That innocent morning in early summer, Stephanie

went out to her garden, barefoot in her bathrobe, taking the telephone. The air was cool and sweet, nourishing as milk. She breathed deeply. Her young crab apple tree was blooming, its branches thick with dark red petals, casting long ruffled shadows across the grass. All around, her life was as good as she could possibly have made it.

Half a mile away in Maple Grove, the leaves of the old trees smothered the tentative early sunlight. A grey glow revealed the empty gardens. At the corner of Church Vale and Grove End, a front door opened and a fat black dog hurtled down the front path. After it came a call hoarse with the universal terror of a citizen of the suburbs, the fear of annoying the neighbours: 'Moron! Come back here!'

At the end of the path, the animal cannoned nose first into the white gate. Westwick architecture was big on story-book details: picket fences, Dutch gables, Rapunzel turrets, hanging balconies. The dog yelped, fell on its rear, rolled over, crushed half a lavender bush and bounded back up on its paws, its blubbery body agitated by its frantic tail.

A man in running shorts appeared on the porch. He was lean and long-legged, and if his shoulders had not sloped he would have looked athletic. Gently, considerate of his neighbours, he shut his front door. Then Ted Parsons turned his back on most of the disappointments of his life, opened the gate and jogged into the street.

Start slow. No problem with that. The dog stormed ahead, joyfully delinquent, oblivious of other people's turf; Moron the labrador, named by his son. It takes one to know one. No, that was unfair, Damon was not that bad. Ted had two secret vices and fairness was one of them. The time was 5.55 am.

His blood was sluggish and his legs were still cold. There was a band of pressure around his chest. He had a flashback to the age of 14, stumbling after the rest of the boys on shaking knees, hoping at least that no one would notice him. Well, that had been football and this was life. In the real game Ted Parsons was a player, and those scrappy kids who years ago stuffed mud down his shorts in the changing rooms, where were they now?

As he turned into The Broadway, he felt his stride lengthen and the blood begin to pump. 'It ain't how you start, it's how you finish,' he said aloud, rounding the graveyard wall of the Church of St Nicholas.

St Nicholas's had a white bell tower with fretwork flashings topped by a little green copper cupola. A cocktail of creole, gothic and renaissance, it marked the southwestern boundary of Maple Grove; if Westwick was the most desirable neighbourhood in the whole conurbation, Maple Grove was its green shady silent heart.

St Nicholas's stood on the site of a much older place of worship dedicated to St Werberga. It was quite a few centuries since Werberga had been a good commercial name. Jackson Kerr, the developer who had caused Maple Grove to be built, had commissioned a new church and arranged the rededication of the parish in 1912. All that remained of the old building were some blistered head-stones set back against the churchyard wall for the convenience of the grass cutters. Moron halted and cocked a stumpy leg to piss on one of them.

Ted set off along The Broadway. He raised a hand to Mr Singh, who was taking down the shutters of the Kwality Korner Store. He considered his route: north-west through the New Farm estate or south towards the river along Alder Reach?

Gemma Lieberman lived on Alder Reach. Gemma Lieberman might be in the shower, drops of water rounded on her olive skin, drips falling from her nipples. Or she might be in bed, warm and tousled and . . . lonely. His thighs drove him on like pistons. Or she might be standing in her kitchen eating toast, in a T-shirt that did not quite cover her backside so that gorgeous dimpled half-moon portions of flesh were almost asking to be grabbed.

He turned south. Anyway, the New Farm area had a bad association – that dingbat of an architect. Who could understand a man like that, what went on in his head? Young but dumb. Big project, mega profit, quantum leap in your business profile – or putter along with the con-tracts you've got and in two years' time you'll be dead. Was that such a difficult choice? Ted Parsons shook his head. New Farm was off the map now. Here be losers. He turned into Alder Reach at 6.07 am. Knowing what to expect, Moron followed his master with reluctance.

In New Farm Rise, Stephanie Sands felt the dew between her toes. Aphids were crusting the buds on her *Souvenir de la Malmaison*, crawling three-deep around the sepals, insolently waving their antennae. In a well ventilated jar in her shed she had been collecting ladybirds to combat the aphids. Now she fetched the jar and, careful of their tiny legs, pushed the ladybirds with her finger-tips on to the encrusted stems.

'Feeling lucky, punks?' She watched the ladybirds advance on their meal. 'You don't know what this is, do you? This is a rose named in memory of the Empress Josephine. If you little beasts give it a break it's going to be pink.' Oblivious of their doom, the aphids kept their wings folded and crawled up the stems on microscopic feet. '*Souvenir de la Malmaison* has been in cultivation since eighteen thirty-something and I have wanted to grow it all my life. I am not growing it to feed you guys. This is not a soup kitchen, you've made a big mistake. Now get off my patch or you're toast.'

Was that the telephone? She was talking only because she was anxious. People said Westwick was exquisitely peaceful but in the early morning in summer the birds made such a racket you could miss the piping of a tele-phone.

Below the bird calls, to Stephanie's ears, her garden emitted a kind of green noise, the continuous bustle of vegetation going about its business, leaves reaching up for light, roots siphoning water, tendrils casting about for anchorage. This morning, however, she was not listening with her imagination. She could hear from the far dis-tance the thin growl of cars streaming into the city on the 31. Close by, the thrush in the flowering crab was hopping from twig to twig, trying out his throat. Yes, the telephone was switched to ring. It was 6.13 now.

Get a grip, woman. When Napoleon went to Egypt, did Josephine fret if his letters did not come? No, she pinned up her hair and went out getting into trouble with Therese Tallien. So why should I worry if my husband doesn't call from wherever he is? He called yesterday. The lines from Eastern Europe are always bad. Business is like war; men have to think about glory and fortune and victory, not their wives being pitiful back home.

She rubbed her eyes, then wiped away the crushed aphids she had smeared on her cheek. Napoleon had his army; Josephine had her roses. In her office, she used to keep a postcard of the Empress's coronation portrait by David on her pinboard. One day there had been a new partner, and he had stopped to look at it. 'She had your nose,' he had said.

'It was fashionable then,' she had answered.

'It's in the classical vernacular, fashion's got nothing to do with it.'

'My mother's always trying to get me to have it – you know – done.'

'Are you having lunch with your mother?' He had rushed that. Afterwards, when she knew him well, she realised that Stewart did not normally rush. He was a measured man, and she never dated people at work. Something got hold of them both that day.

She kept the postcard. Perhaps she wanted the poise of that long-necked figure bowing her head in a diamond coronet. Perhaps Josephine was an obvious role model for a gardener; otherwise she was not at all an obvious role model for Stephanie, who had no ambitions to be known as a woman who would have drunk gold out of her lover's skull. On the contrary, when people described her as a sweet woman she was well satisfied. She saw herself as a unexceptional, lucky to be married to the last good husband to be found in the wild, and ambitious only to raise a family. Which was more than the Empress Josephine had done for Napoleon, for all her *Souvenir de la Malmaison.*

The first ladybird opened its bright wing cases and took flight. One after another its companions followed, soaring away down the border, spurning the feast before them for the freedom of the air. Stephanie shook her head and strode over to the garage for the malathion spray. The aphids would die and to hell with the environment. It was 6.24 am. She was doing morning car pool.

Approaching the Lieberman house, Ted Parsons ran with the resolve of Jesse Owens at the 1938 Berlin Olympics. A triangle of sweat darkened the back of his vest, his feet in their battered Nikes pronated with a flourish. He ran his fingers through his hair in case it was sticking up instead of flowing aerodynamically off his temples.

Alder Reach was deserted. His footfalls echoed on the ground. Even the scratch of the dog's claws resounded in the still air; Moron was gamely keeping pace. Ted fixed a sportive gleam in his eyes and a relaxed half-smile on his lips. He was passing her house. The curtains upstairs were still closed. The bitch.

Topaz Lieberman bit the end of her pen. What were Stalin's aims in negotiating the Nazi–Soviet pact of 1939? Did he believe that by allowing Hitler to occupy first the Sudetenland and then the rest of Czechoslovakia the Western Powers had bought off Germany, who would then turn her expansionist ambitions east? Should we infer from the secret part of the agreement relating to the division of Poland between the two powers that Stalin's intention was that the Nazis should invade that country and thus provoke Britain and France to abandon their policy of appeasement? What are the implications of the second secret clause in the pact restoring the Baltic states of Latvia, Lithuania and Estonia to the rule of the Soviets?

'You know what?' At the far end of the living area, her sister ripped the laces from one of her boots.

'Don't talk to me, Flora, I need an A for this essay.'

'I just thought you'd like to know that That just ran down our street again.'

'So?' Inside the mind of Joseph Stalin, Topaz was reluctant to be recalled to the life of her family.

'So – third time this week. He's doing it on purpose, isn't he?'

'Mum has a life too, you know. I mean, she is a woman.'

'Yeah, but does she have to have a life with That?'

'She doesn't even like him, she called him a sleazebag.'

'That dog's going to die on him.'

'The dog's obese. Animal companions should have regular exercise.'

'People like That shouldn't be allowed to own an animal.' Flora glared after the figure on the street outside, sighed resentfully and began to rethread her boot laces.

In the marriage area of the house, the wind chimes, hung by their mother to ensnare any passing *chi*, clashed loudly. The youngest of the Lieberman girls backflipped into the eating area and landed in the splits. 'Molly, for God's sake!' hissed her sisters, neither raising their big oval eyes from their tasks.

In the deferential daylight of Maple Grove, Allie Parsons looked into her dressing-room mirror. Ravening free radicals were destroying her dermis, her collagen was mutating, the studio lights were baking her complexion like pie crust. Stress! Red veins coming up on her chin, that was stress. And she was allergic – that black stuff puffing out under her eyes, yeast allergy. Crostini, for God's sake. Ted knew what bread did to her skin. God, he was proud enough of her career in public.

Did people still have dermabrasion? She grimaced. Six weeks of a scabby face – forget it. Come the end of the series she would restore her facade somehow. Possibly just the eyes. Or one of those laser lifts? Maybe the Channel would pay. But, if they paid, they'd have to know. Ted would pay, he owed her.

She clipped back her hair, ignoring the regrowth. On the dressing table among the pots and bottles and tubes and jars was a packet of suppositories. Allie Parsons extracted two, stabbed them with her nail scissors, squeezed, smeared the contents under each eye, followed with pink Vitamin-E enriched hydrating gel over the rest of her face, wiped her hands on her robe and reached for the vanity vits. Co-enzyme Q? DHEA? Super-C? All of them.

That little smart-ass who was standing in on the weather desk, having the nerve to put up a feature idea about some spa. She should just shut up and get the pollen count right for once. Kids died from asthma. *Family First* was a tight team, no room for attitude problems. Facial aerobics, lower lip over upper, repeat five times.

On the bridge which carried the 31 over the river a black limousine glided among the slow-moving lanes of commuter traffic, bringing Chester Pike back from the airport. Chester flew to St Louis twice a week. He took a laptop, but the truth was that now he had no need to sit crunching numbers every fallow minute. He had thrust through to the stratosphere, he was cruising. Guys like DeSouza could do the figures. Chester should have liked that but he did not; he felt passive, he felt out of control, he felt uneasy.

That morning he also felt nauseous. Sitting on the group board announcing a projected profit increase of only 3.9%, seeing twenty-nine guys and the two women look at him with eyes like ice-picks; that had been bad. Initiative fatigue, loss of focus, failure to control the process of market change – he felt the accusations wheeling over his head like buzzards. Plus, after the flight his knees were stiff, his shoes were pinching and someone had sandpapered his eyeballs.

He saw a jogger in the distance and thought of Ted Parsons. Great guy. Great instinct for land resources. And a great operator. Years the Oak Hill site had been rotting away in a swamp of lapsed titles, lost deeds, zoning regulations and God knows what else. Ted had just gone in there with a flame thrower.

The beauty of it was that it had just been sitting there under their eyes, a wasted piece of land in the armpit of the 31 and the 46. He remembered it from his first years in Westwick: an industrial blemish on a residential landscape, carbon-stained cooling towers of the old plant standing bleakly over the derelict admin building. The kids who smashed the windows and sprayed graffiti on the walls must have come out from the city; Westwick kids did piano lessons and tennis squad for fun, not recreational vandalism.

The driver braked to an infinitesimal crawl to negotiate a lane closure for resurfacing. Chester grunted with irritation and checked his watch. In Singapore they'd have done the work at night and had the whole thing finished in a week. Every second of wasted time annoyed him, although he had nowhere to be for three hours.

One day the county, being head leaseholders of Oak Hill, had woken up and demolished the buildings, sold the rubble to an infill site in Birmingham and put up a razor-wire palisade. What remained now was a desert of stony earth, scattered with hub caps and rusting mattress springs, ragged banners of plastic blowing around the thistles. Plus a brand new lease and a royal flush of planning consents held by the Oak Hill Development Trust, directors Chester Pike, Edward J Parsons and A L DeSouza.

As his driver swung smoothly down the slip to the Broadway, Chester saw things as they would be two years down the line: a twenty-storey, mirror-faced high-rise, the low-rises including the Channel Ten studios with the blue and green logo on the roof, parking for ten thousand vehicles and there, right at the entrance to the Grove, the faux-alpine wood-effect eaves of the biggest Magno hypermarket in the country. Magno Oak Hill was going to be the most modern, most productive shopping environment in the entire continent. Strong location was the bedrock of Magno's corporate culture. They were brainstorming in St Louis right now. And next year Chester would sit with the group board at that never-ending black table and announce projected year-on profits of 300.9 per cent.

The car cruised down The Broadway and glided into Maple Grove. Chester belched disconsolately. He felt suffocated. The huge trees blocked the horizon, the little cutesey houses said little cutesey lives – the kind of place it was OK to live in during your first marriage. In his mind, Chester Pike was out of here. He was out of Westwick in a duplex on the river in town, out of the wife-and-kids life and in his own life. Two more years, that was all.

His electronic gates opened in welcome. His was the largest home in the neighbourhood, and the only one to have a name: Grove House, engraved in copperplate on brass, polished daily by the housekeeper. No longer feeling his pinching shoes, Chester let his vision carry him up to the bedroom, where his wife was half awake. He kissed her cheek, and when she flinched in surprise and asked, 'Good trip?' he answered, 'You betcha.'

Along the river, Ted Parsons took things slower. Plenty of time for stamina training on the home stretch. Waddling stiff-legged at his side, Moron looked up at his master with gratitude. The sun hung above the willow trees, a pale disc of light. A faint breeze drew the last wisp of mist off the water and shook the yellowed leaves of the trees. In the thin brightness of morning, looking back under the bridge towards Helford, an old church spire punctuated the curve of the river. Cut out the cars on the bridge and you had a village picture postcard.

He passed the houseboats, wondering how people actually lived in those things. At least a quarter of Ted's heart would have liked to know first hand, but he stifled it. At least half his heart was spellbound by the river at sunrise, and he ignored that also. It was all just romance, and, as his father had often warned him, romance is death to enterprise.

The brown water tossed the sunlight against the blistered black hull of the *Dawn Treader*. The yellow iris buds at the bankside swelled in the warmth. The ropes creaked as the hulk tugged at her mooring. In the upper berth of the second cabin, Sweetheart listened to the water and thought about the riverbank fairies. If they came out at night they must be going to bed now.

Sweetheart saw the queen of the riverbank fairies in a nightgown of all colours, like oil spreading on water. But it seemed likely that she wouldn't like the way nightdresses got up around your neck while you were sleeping. Sweetheart frowned. Pyjamas did not seem quite right for a queen. But if you were a queen you could have anything you wanted, anything at all. It was a problem.

Daddy would know. It would be very good to go into Daddy's cabin and get into the big bed and have him explain all this, but, since they had been on their own without Mummy, getting into the big bed was not allowed. Sweetheart sat up and scratched the back of her neck to stir up her brain and get an answer. Daddy was definitely still asleep, because you could hear a mouse think in the *Dawn Treader* and all she could hear was the water.

Maybe Daddy would change the big bed rule if she did something to make him happy. He was almost never happy these days. Sweetheart climbed out of her bunk and checked on her father. Then she went into the galley. She filled up the coffee machine and switched it on, peeled a banana and put it on a plate, found a clean glass and poured out some juice. Another problem: when Daddy smelled of wine in the morning he liked to have headache tablets with his juice, but they were in the cupboard with the special lock children could not open. Sweetheart scratched her neck again. Daddy had fixed the cupboard up on the wall with a screwdriver.

The telephone was silent. Stephanie put the handset back on the console to make sure the batteries were charged. The red light was on, the thing was plugged in. It was 6.42, he had definitely said he would call at 6.00. Stewart had also said Kazakstan had almost no infra-structure, there were probably only twenty telephone lines out of the whole state.

She heard her son coming downstairs. Max reacted when he could see that she was anxious. He would say nothing – her son did not waste words – but instead of noise and eagerness the five-year-old power pack would start running down and a resentful apathy would start stealing his good nature. She opened a cupboard, her mind still on the telephone. Maybe Crunchy Nut Cornflakes would distract Max. Maybe she'd have some too.

Halfway up Riverview Drive, Moron was lagging behind his master. The dog was wheezing miserably. Ted Parsons checked his watch: nearly seven, he'd done more than his time. They could slow up as soon as they passed the DeSouza house. 'Good boy, Moron,' he encouraged the animal. 'Good boy. Keep it up.' Moron was getting silvery about the muzzle. Ted was getting silvery about the temples. Adam DeSouza had gone grey at 28, but for a lawyer that was a plus.

Belinda DeSouza hugged her pillow with both her downy brown arms. Carlos Moya to serve against Becker. Championship point. At Flushing Meadow the crowd is silent in anticipation. Moya steps up to the line. His thighs strain against his white shorts. A lock of hair like a black ribbon ripples in the wind as he raises his racquet. The ball is in the air. Every cell of his body is dedicated to winning this point.

The ball is falling. Moya's eyes narrow against the brilliant sun. Impact speed of his racquet is estimated at 110mph. Then he sees her. The dark woman in the simple white dress in the front row. Or maybe the yellow suit with the ruffled blouse. Restless, sensuous, Belinda rolled over, trying to decide. The suit – it made her look thinner.

Moya sees her and he sees Becker recoil from the ball. As if from far away, he hears the umpire give out. The sheen of her full lips, the smooth softness of her throat, the unfathomable depth of her eyes, what tragedy is hidden there? He has to know. He must have her. In a dream, Moya sends up the second ball. Winning no longer matters. There is a bigger prize than the Open.

An uproar breaks out in the astonished crowd as the umpire calls double fault. Compelled by her mysterious allure, barely pausing to shake Becker's hand, he feels himself drawn across the court to her seat. 'Wait!

Please . . .' The ushers are already clearing the stand. She turns back to look at him, a look which stabs his heart like a knife. 'Me?'

Or maybe 'I?' Damn. The goddamn dialogue again. Why did her fantasies always fall apart when people had to speak? Belinda had pulled the quilt off her husband. He was waking up. His arm fell heavily over her waist, snapping off the image of Carlos Moya awed by her beauty. Damn. Catapulted by irritation, she got up and shut herself in the shower.

'Good boy, Moron. Not far now.' Riverview Drive led into Elm Bank Avenue, where sun gleamed on the two brass plates outside the Carman practice. Josh Carman was always lecturing Ted about overtraining. It was OK to walk. Cool down, not walk. His goal now was to get home and get on the road before his wife finished her face. This was never before 8.00 am. There was plenty of time.

A brave ray of light slipped between the master-bedroom curtains, filtered through the thick air, silhouetted a full ashtray, touched a pair of smeared spectacles and streamed over the cover of the May issue of the *Journal of Paediatrics*. In the bed, Rachel Carman rolled away from the light towards the body of her husband.

She considered that sex was indicated at this time, given the facts about testosterone secretion cycles and behaviours affecting the duration of the marital bond.

There were noises from the boys' rooms, but the bedroom door was locked. Manually, she verified that Joshua had a viable erection and that she was sufficiently lubricated to permit intercourse. She rolled her husband on to his back, kneeled over him and inserted his penis.

Gaining consciousness, Joshua Carman weighed the facts about hormone secretion cycles and the link between orgasmic experience and self-esteem in women. Sex would be indicated at this time. He thought of the stimulation achieved by handling Rachel's breasts against the effect of inhaling her morning breath, typically a distillation of Marlboro Lights, Famous Grouse, garlic and jalapeno chilli. He tried to remember if he had locked the bedroom door. He computed the possibility that he could convince Rachel that he had ejaculated if in fact he lost his erection. Then he held his breath and reached out with both hands.

Rachel positioned her mammary tissue within his grasp. This was quite good. She grunted to encourage him. Was it possible that the sensory messages from her nipples were overriding those from her vagina? Or was Josh losing it? If he was going to fake again, she'd have to go along with it. Raising doubts during intercourse was inappropriate. The door handle rattled.

Unexpectedly, Josh had an orgasm, a non-event of half a dozen spasms and an estimated 2ml of semen which sneaked up so fast he didn't even have time to vocalise. Damn. And Rachel was only just warming up. He'd have to get her off orally. Surprisingly, his olfactory system suggested that the Scotch and chilli were in the bloodstream in sufficient concentration for some molecules to be present in the vaginal mucus. Was that biologically possible?

A small boot kicked the bedroom door. 'Ma!'

'Go away!' Rachel's voice rasped her dry throat. She was going to cough.

Violent kicking. 'Ma, Benny's hungry!'

'Get lost, you little creep. It's too early.' She was going to come. She was going to cough. She was going to come first. It was all a question of focus.

'You have to get us pop tarts.'

'Will you *fuck off*?' Her pelvic floor was well congested. A bronchial spasm propelled a huge load of mucus towards her pharynx. Josh pinched her nipples. It worked. She fell off her husband and into the pillow, coughing but satisfied.

The door shuddered from renewed kicking. 'Get us pop tarts! We're starving.'

Dr Joshua Carman got out of bed, unlocked the bedroom door, grabbed his sons by the hair, cracked their heads together, threw them on the carpet and yelled, 'You little bastards, get your own fucking pop tarts.'

Rachel sat up and reached for her cigarettes. 'God,' she clicked her lighter. 'Kids – they're just so manipulative.'

Josh took the packet from her and shook out a cigarette for himself. 'Do we have an eight o'clock today?'

Ted Parsons cut down Orchard Close, at the end of which a pedestrianised area, which an amateur might have called a path, led between the gardens into Maple Grove.

Being screened by some immense chestnut trees, this route enabled him to walk without being observed.

The path meandered. Part of the special charm of Maple Grove was that all the streets curved. This also had been decreed by Jackson Kerr, the father of the community. Most authorities attributed Maple Grove to its architect, Tudor Wilde, whose inspiration it had been to take the steep-pitched roofs and homely gables of old Dutch farmhouses and reproduce them here in red brick and white weatherboard.

The Maple Grove Society held annual lectures on Tudor Wilde, and the Wilde At Heart bar in the Parade kept his name alive and the Art Nouveau tiles he had commissioned on the walls, but in the view of Ted Parsons it was typical of the chattering classes to credit the artist with the achievements of the entrepreneur. The man who really made Maple Grove was its developer, Jackson Kerr, who had dreamed of great profit bred by mating rural charm with urban ease, and ordered that his streets should wander peacefully like straying cows.

Ted squared up and sprinted the last fifty yards to his gate, which he reached at 7.23 am.

Aboard the *Dawn Treader*, Sweetheart watched her father pick up one of his headache pills. His eyes were almost closed and the way he was leaning his head on his hand probably meant he was feeling bad. The question would have to wait.

He had the pill on the palm of his hand and he was

looking at it as if he expected it to move. 'Sweetheart,' he said after a little while, 'did I have these in my gym bag?'

'They were in the cupboard.'

'Didn't I lock the cupboard?'

'Oh yes, it was locked all up.' Sweetheart started twisting her hair. There were these things that you found out were wrong only when you had already done them.

'So how did you get these?'

She had lost the word. 'Ummm . . . with the screwy thing.'

'What screwy thing?'

In the end she had to show him. He stood there and looked at the medicine cabinet on the floor, the step ladder, the holes in the wall, the screws she had kept carefully in the top of the coffee tin and the packet of paracetamol on the draining board with two capsules removed and 98 remaining.

After a while he began to say something like, 'You'll make someone a fine carpenter if you live to grow up,' but he started throwing up towards the end and had to dive for the sink. He stayed there, running the water, for a long time.

'Carpenters are nails. Screws are some other thing.' Sweetheart could not see his face. She really hated him to cry. 'Don't be sad.'

'I'm not sad.' He took some of the big breaths that made your stomach go in and out. 'I'm going to be late for class and you are going to be late for school.'

By 7.45, Ted Parsons had showered, shaved, dressed and was driving down The Broadway towards the 31, feeling optimistic because he had avoided speaking to his wife, and his kids had avoided speaking to him. So far, a perfect day. No, a good day. Perfect would have been Gemma Lieberman naked at the window.

Ahead of him he saw Adam DeSouza run the red light at the junction of Alder Reach. Waiting, he could look down the side road in his wing mirror. A bunch of kids on bicycles. Gemma's kids? What kind of mother actually let her kids bike to school in this day and age, at risk from paedophiles and drunken drivers?

The houses in Alder Reach did not appeal to him. Pseudo cottages with half-timbered facades, they nodded to the Wilde style but lacked its generosity. Romance had been the downfall of Jackson Kerr. Leafy, clean, peaceful and only 20 minutes to Central Station by train from Westwick Green, before it was even half built Maple Grove became a model for the world. But uglier homes were cheaper. The beauty of the river was worthless, the notion that the land was damp and vulnerable to flooding was costly. Five years and four hundred houses towards his dream, Kerr and his Maple Grove Company had gone bust, and there went the neighbourhood.

Another developer threw up Alder Reach on plots which Kerr was forced to sell at a knockdown price. For a few decades, Westwick was abandoned to the two species who will always colonise cheap land – artists and immigrants. Grove House, Kerr's own home, was cut up into six apartments. Maple Grove was satirised in popular revues as the haunt of Bohemian poseurs.

Time passed. The city bellied westwards. Westwick Green was no longer the railway terminus, merely another stop on the line. The airport was built by the 31. Time blew new merchant adventurers to the same shores, Ted Parsons among them. The foundation of his fortune, such as it was, had been laid in retrieving the vision of Jackson Kerr, evicting the occupants, painting it up, contriving a bathroom for every bedroom and selling it on for healthy profits.

When the euphoria of those early days was past, Ted took note of Kerr's history and identified the mistakes. Pride and passion between them had brought the dream down. A man would be a fool not to take the lesson offered. The green light flashed on and Ted Parsons drove on to the city, confident that pride and passion would never threaten him.

Stephanie planned the school run to start at 8.10. Max had his shoes, his shoe bag, his painting overall, his reading book and his lunch box. He was sitting on the stairs doggedly tying the laces on his new trainers, his little round legs boyishly decorated with scrapes and bruises. It was 8.12, they were due at the school at 8.30 and Stewart still had not called. Since Westwick was one of the most notoriously clogged nodes of traffic in the whole circulation system of the city, she had got into the habit of turning on the TV in the kitchen for the morning road report, reasoning that since they had to tolerate the noise of the helicopter overhead, they might as well get the benefit of its viewpoint. Sky High, the traffic reporter, a forceful black woman in a silver jumpsuit, fascinated Max.

To buy more time, Stephanie had cut a bunch of lilac and was tying the stems.

'Mum, don't give me that,' commanded her son, getting up and heading for the door.

'Don't you want to give your teacher something nice?'

'No.'

'But I thought you liked her.'

'We're late.'

'Well, if you like someone it's nice to give them flowers.'

'No it isn't. It's weird.'

'Max . . .'

It rang. The telephone rang. She grabbed it, so eager that her finger missed the talk button three times.

'Hello, darling . . .'

'Stephanie, I need to talk to you.' Stewart's partner. Maybe he could make only one call, maybe he'd asked Marcus to call her.

'Are you going to be at home this afternoon?' Marcus had been born without social skills. She hated talking to him on the telephone, getting the words out was like pulling teeth. And it was worse when he was embarrassed.

'Did you speak to Stewart this morning?'

'Ah – no, no, not today. Listen, can I come over at around four?'

Disappointed, she agreed then, seeing the time, swept

Max and his educational impedimenta into the car and hit the street. In Elm Bank Avenue she picked up Ben and Jon Carman, who had obviously been fighting so at least they were quiet. In Church Vale she pulled in behind the studio car waiting for Allie.

'It's eight-twenty, Mum.'

'Clever boy, telling the time.'

'It's a digital clock,' Ben Carman sneered, kicking the seat in front of him.

'Mum, we're going to be late.' Max was that kind of child, exceptionally anxious to do everything right. She did not like to go into the Parsons' house in the morning, Allie had a way of creating force fields, and at this hour there was always an invisible ring around her house repelling all intruders.

The door inched open and Chalice Parsons began to dawdle down the path, dragging her bag on the ground. Twice she turned round as if she expected to be called back. The ribbon from her wispy fair hair fell on the ground. When she got to the car, her bag fell open and two chocolate bars, a packet of frankfurters and a pencil fell into the gutter. Chalice burst into tears.

At The Magpies the sun had dried the dew on the climbing frame. Miss Helens came out and took Chalice firmly by the hand. Stephanie gave the lilac to the teacher herself. She knew enough about embarrassing mothers never to want to be one.

The plan had been for Stephanie to be a full-time mother until her children were of a proper age – maybe eight or ten or twelve – but when they came to Westwick they found that full-time motherhood was not quite the thing. A Westwick wife needed a job, the sort of job that embellished her husband's career, attracted tax breaks on the home and enhanced their family life, like Allie, of course, or Rachel Carman running her mother and baby clinic or Belinda DeSouza with her ski apartments or Lauren Pike with her counselling. So Stephanie was the sole proprietor of The Terrace Garden Design Studio, which allowed her to spend her mornings dreaming up treillage and water features for her neighbours.

Around 11 am, she had to wait for the ink to dry on a scheme for a pergola for one of Lauren Pike's friends. Why did Marcus want to come round? It was a very small question, compared to the much larger consideration of why Stewart had not called, but her imagination, a healthy and well-maintained faculty, could not offer an answer.

When the doorbell rang, and a courier from the florist next to Stewart's office delivered a bunch of lilies the size of a wheatsheaf, with a card from her husband offering all his love, she forgot about Marcus completely. She put the lilies in a vase on her desk then went to polish the green apples in the pewter bowl on the sycamore dining table. The Magritte apples were her shrine light when Stewart was away.

Outside, hidden in the carmine blossom of the flowering crab, the thrush stood, cocking his head. Above, he had four hungry nestlings and an expectant mate. Below, a colony of unsuspecting snails was bingeing on young hosta leaves. Every cat in the street was asleep indoors. The nearest hawk was hovering over the verge of the 31. In case any other birds were listening, the thrush sang a few notes to let them know that this was the greatest place in the world to build a nest, and it was his – all his.

CHAPTER 2

Annual Death Rate Under 6 Per Thousand

The streets of Westwick were quiet. The trees were rooted in the broad bands of mowed grass which lined every road. Vehicles moved about slowly, like idle fish in a pond. In wide, straight streets like Riverview Drive, exemplary traffic-calming features had been installed, humbling the cars to bump ridiculously over ridges of cobblestones. It was still Westwick's role to be a model environment.

The vehicles of Westwick were the breeder wagons. The Carmans ran an Espace, the Parsons family looked down on the world from their Discovery, the De Souzas had the Volvo as long as Stockholm Sound. Stephanie and Stewart felt a little juvenile with their five-year-old bottom-of-the-range Cherokee but agreed that they were not quite ready to trade up to a seven-seater which cornered like a floating wardrobe.

As Stephanie coasted into New Farm Rise, a breeze brushed blossoms from the cherry trees. Pink petals sprinkled the roof of a foreign vehicle outside her house, a 3-series BMW, the classic singleton transport, owned by Marcus, her husband's partner.

'Steph, I need to see you.' Marcus was better with drawings than words; anything without dimensions made him insecure. She had given only passing thought to why he might want to see her. Perhaps Stewart's visa needed to be amended. Perhaps Marcus had a job to discuss – since she had left the firm he occasionally sent a private client to her, someone whose landscaping needs were too small for the department at Berkman & Sands.

She saw Marcus get out of his vehicle and she saw a police car pull gently to the kerb behind him, a woman officer at the wheel. While she was scanning her memory for neglected parking tickets, the officer approached Marcus; they seemed to agree about something. Stephanie had the first tremor of anxiety. She pulled up in front of her house and was aware of the two of them standing around awkwardly while she let Max out of the back of the car.

'I am WPC Clegg.' The officer gave her a cold, strong hand to shake. Firmly buttoned and tightly belted, she stood square on her heavy shoes, employing routine eye-contact. 'I'm here about the same matter as Mr Berkman, so shall we all go in together?'

In the breakfast room the sun had drawn out the scent of the lemon geranium, *Pelargonium crispum.* The calico blinds were fresh and spotless; the long sycamore table, for which Stewart had paid a month's salary with joy, was pale and handsome in the sunlight and the silver bowl of

green apples was positioned exactly where he had determined it broke up the space most effectively. When
Stewart was away all the rooms felt neglected.

'You're getting the place in shape?' Because he was so
afraid of being misunderstood, Marcus ended his state-
ments with a rising inflection, always asking, 'you got
that?'

'It's coming along,' she agreed. 'I can't believe we've
been here two years.'

They let her make the coffee, and the hiss of the hot
water and the rattle of the spoons amounted to a clamour.
WPC Clegg had an air of impatience. She marched about
the room without looking around, as if concerned not to
waste time. Marcus perched awkwardly at the end of the
table. Something of great weight was lying in the air.

'So, on this lovely afternoon – what brings you out to
Westwick?' Stephanie put the tray on the table, wondering if she should have taken the initiative in opening the
subject.

Marcus drew in a deep breath. 'Look, Steph, we're
here . . . look, you've got to understand, there isn't any
easy way into this . . .' His high forehead wrinkled with
distress. The police officer shot him a look of annoyance.

'It's about your husband, Mrs Sands.'

'About Stewart?'

'Yes.' Relief made Marcus hiss a little. Stephanie
looked around for Max, but he was oblivious in the playroom, watching Pepe LePew.

'Well – ah – has something happened?'

'Yes. Yes. Something has happened.' Now he was
sweating.

'So – is he dead?' It seemed best to work down from the worst possibility. Stephanie was perfectly certain that her husband was not dead; she had not felt the shudder in the cosmos which their separation would have created.

The officer intervened. 'Normally, Mrs Sands, you would have received a visit from an officer alone, but in this case since the authorities had contacted Mr Berkman . . .'

'Could we cut to the chase? Is he injured? Has there been an accident?'

'No, nothing like that, Mrs Sands. As far as we know, he's fine. Would you like to sit down?'

They seemed to expect it, so she sat, and the others took chairs also. Her brain had stalled, no thoughts were coming. Her imagination, normally so good with disaster, was paralysed. The police woman took charge of the conversation, her manner implying that Marcus had unjustifiably attempted to usurp her role. 'I expect you know that your husband was with a trade delegation to the former Soviet Union,' she began.

'He called me from Kiev the day before yesterday.' What could have happened in two days? Sex? Drugs? A Mafia massacre? International fraud? Some Kafkaesque diplomatic incident? The idea of Stewart related to any of these was impossible. She felt interrogated; when did you last see your husband?

'I understand from the Foreign Office that it was quite a high-profile delegation to a place called . . .' she took an extra breath to tackle the pronunciation, 'Kazikistan?'

'Kazakhstan. It was a government invitation – the new government. They were talking about developing a resort on the Caspian Sea.' We do talk, my husband and I.

'That's right.' Clegg clearly did not like to be corrected. 'We understand the visit was well publicised within the province, a public relations coup for the regime there.'

'He told me all that. Is he accused of something? Is it spying? Stewart? I thought that sort of thing didn't happen any more.'

'Fortunately, what has happened seems to be clear. Fortunately because sometimes in these situations what has actually happened isn't clear for quite a few days . . .' She spoke as if incidents were staged purely to annoy the police.

Seeing Stephanie's face now breaking up in distress, Marcus cut in bluntly. 'Steph, it's a kidnap.'

'Kidnap.' A word, at last. Her mind turned it over, trying to make it fit into their life, like Max trying to fit the cylinder peg into the triangle hole in his shape sorter. It did not fit. 'So – why . . .'

'By what the FO tell us is quite an organised group who have already communicated with an embassy in Moscow. The French embassy.' Marcus was breathing hard from emotional exertion.

'We know they are all in good health.' Clegg cut in. 'At least, that's what was said.'

'What do they want?'

'It isn't clear yet what their demands are. As far as we know, that wasn't part of the message. They're not a group known to our intelligence and the FO find the action unexpected because this certainly isn't a war situation, or even one of conflict. I've been told Kazakhstan has been quite stable although is has a common border with Chechnya and obviously certain elements cross that border even though there's no more fighting in Chechnya now.' She recited this information with flawless authority, as if these distant provinces with explosive names had been the subject of her doctoral thesis. Stephanie pictured her lecturing a squad of armed muggers from the same great height of certainty. Did she know martial arts? Could she lay a man out with one supple high kick?

They kept talking, the officer calm but vague, Marcus very abrupt, both of them so intent on reassuring her that she began to feel panic because it was so obviously expected. It was a brittle emotion but enough for tears to start leaking from the corner of her eyes.

Marcus got up and shot away to the edge of the room. A twitch of something – regret? sympathy? – showed on the woman's face, but when she saw that Stephanie had tissues she kept talking. 'For the moment, Mrs Sands, it's going to be a question of watching and waiting. The French are handling negotiations very well. We've been told their experience of these situations is quite extensive although as matters progress our people may opt to take an independent line . . .'

Was she using bland language deliberately? Marcus, who would have said 'terrorist' without any hesitation, was halfway through the door now, glancing worriedly towards Max as if he had just remembered that they had the child.

Not knowing what else to say, Stephanie asked, 'What was the communication? What actually happened?'

'The message came by computer.' Clegg blinked and one side of her pink mouth was dragged out of line by momentary humour.

'An E-mail,' confirmed Marcus.

'An *E-mail*?' Her husband was lost in that infinite anonymity. She felt a flash of terror. In cyberspace nobody can hear you scream.

They seemed relieved that she had forced them to disclose this detail. 'That's right, Mrs Sands. Unexpected, certainly. I did query it and it seems that very few agencies in the former Soviet Union are linked up and able to do that. It should give the FO some valuable leads.'

'And . . . but . . .'

'They listed the passport numbers and scanned the photographs. It's been downloaded if you'd like to see it. It was in English. Kind of English.'

'Hadn't I better see it? Won't it be in the news tomorrow?' Terrifying enough to face the fact in her own home, much worse to share it with faceless, prurient millions.

'There'll be no media announcement unless you sanction it, Mrs Sands. And the FO advise against it, for your own sake as well as because they want to play this down. You would be surprised if you knew how many of our nationals are held around the world; the families often feel they want their privacy. And it may all be over by tomorrow. If it isn't,' the officer leaned forward, making an important point, 'you'll need some peace to get used to the idea.'

'I've had a visit from a Foreign Office official already, Steph. They'll be keeping in touch with us daily until he's home. He said these groups are often after access to the media and it is their policy to deny them that if they can. With a roadside ambush, which it seems this was, that's quite possible. Of course if this were a hijacking, it would be more difficult.'

'Yes, I can see that.' Her arm felt unreal as she poured more coffee.

'I'll give you his card.' Marcus laid it on the table in front of her, a white rectangle bearing the word 'Liaison' and some numbers. The name was Capelli, with three initials before it. 'His office handles anything that involves the relatives of nationals abroad. He'll be calling you pretty soon, I told him what time we'd be here.'

'Mrs Sands, is anyone with you at present?' She was winding up the interview, reaching into a pocket for a pen, ready to note down whatever was required from this assignment before moving on to the next.

'Only my son.'

'So – is there anyone you would like us to call for you?'

'I wasn't sure, Steph, I thought maybe your mother.' Marcus's shoulders were sagging in apology, his elbows rigid as if nailed to his body. 'And then there's Carl and Betty.' Stewart's parents had moved to British Columbia where his brother sold helicopters. 'I don't know what to do here, Steph.'

Marcus came along with Stewart, a fixture in his present and his past, partner in his business, keeper of his history. She had never asked herself if she liked him, that was a leading question. They were different. Marcus was entrepreneurial and Stewart was visionary, Stewart was relational and Marcus was mathematical. What Marcus decreed Stewart would dream and what Stewart dreamed

Marcus would cost, present, put in hand and see through to the last drop of paint. The business was the sum of them both and their prosperity the alchemy of their characters. When Stewart once asked, 'Are you ever jealous of Marcus?' she had been utterly surprised.

Marcus and Stewart could talk together, but otherwise talking was not Marcus's thing. Their city friends, collectively called The Crowd, tolerated him but there was mutual admission that he did not fit in. To Marcus, the long Sunday morning telephone calls fixing brunch wasted his time; he came, he ate, sometimes he smiled, once he made a joke about blessed eggs Benedict. Occasionally a woman came with him, and he appeared proud of it, but women were not his thing, or perhaps he was not a woman's thing.

Marcus did not like surprises. That much Stephanie had in common with him. Now she saw he was as helpless as driftwood, tossed every way around by this flood of the unexpected. 'You were kind to come, Marcus.'

He caught the officer's cold eye. 'They traced you through me, you see. Because we did the visa application through the office.' He wanted her to do what had to be done and what he could not do. Like speak to Stewart's parents.

They expected her to act now. She looked at her watch. 'Carl and Betty won't be up yet. I will speak to them this evening. I'll call my mother – she should be back by now.' Her mother's life was now ruled by golf and her stepfather. They did not like to play in the late afternoon because the shadows were tricky and working people started to get on the links.

'I can't think of anything else,' she said to the police-woman.

'You'll find it's a lot to take in,' she replied, moving towards the door. 'There's a very good Victim Support organisation in Westwick. I'll leave you their number.' She picked a card from a pocket in the cover of her note-book and left it on the console in the hall.

'If you need anything, Steph . . .' Marcus did not know how to get off the doorstep.

'I'll call,' she reassured him. 'You were good to come, Marcus. I appreciate it.'

She walked down the front path to see them off; it seemed only polite. The departing cars made whirlpools of blossom petals, then the street was quiet and sunny again. She felt dread drenching her heart; trouble had found its way to her door. Things like this were not sup-posed to happen in Westwick. The schools and the gardens and the history and the ten-minute run to the airport were part of the story, but the real reason she had set her heart on living here was that it was safe. Or had seemed safe.

The telephone rang right on cue as she shut the door. It was F A W Capelli, Liaison Officer at the Foreign Office, a brisk, even voice, not too young, reeling out words which, when she tried to repeat them afterwards, seemed to have no meaning. 'We expect things to move rapidly at this stage. The usual pattern is either an immediate resolution or possibly quite protracted nego-tiations,' she heard him say. 'Controlling the time-scale is an important advantage, so we will be doing our utmost to bring things to the swiftest conclusion possible.'

After he had hung up, she went to sit with Max. She would have liked to hold him, and draw some strength from the solid little body, but he never liked to be held. She watched him watch the TV, oblivious of the danger to his father. Would she have to explain to him? Stewart was not due back for another week, at least.

'How strange,' her mother said when Stephanie called her and tiptoed through the facts. 'What did he want to go to such an out-of-the-way place for?'

'They were invited. All the biggest developments are in those kind of places. You remember the hotel they built in Poland?'

'Business. Oh yes. Are you all right, dear? Is there anything you want me to do? There is a committee dinner this evening but I suppose I could—'

'No, no. We're fine. There's no need to put yourself out.'

'I could come over tomorrow . . .'

'No, please. You stay where you are. We'll just have to wait and see how things develop. I'll call you tomorrow.' She hated to have her mother visit because she transplanted so badly. As a house guest, she was fidgety and unpleasable. From the height of her own motherhood, Stephanie was coming to understand that after the divorce her mother had painfully built a life for herself. It was admirable; many abandoned wives of that generation recited a daily litany of resentments and dedicated their lives to trashing men. Her mother had swallowed pain and waged war on hardship with a show of smiling serenity. She had painted a bright facade on her shame and presented it with such conviction that when another man had appeared he had taken her at face value as an elegant, independent woman; so there she stayed, petrified in competence. Only her daughters knew how fragile she was, how thin her veneer of calm. Her second marriage was a support to which she was clinging in terror. Sometimes Stephanie felt that her daughters reminded her of her dark years.

She made food for Max. She talked to him, her hollow happy words falling into the silence like water from a fountain. The sun poured over the table-top. The buds of her *Souvenir de la Malmaison* were blushing and swelling. Time is vague to a five-year-old, a long time could be two days or two weeks. He would never know about this. Stewart would be home before the time when it would be necessary to tell Max anything. It seemed wrong to be forced to make this monstrous calculation. The whole thing seemed wrong.

'Ted – Chester.'

In the corner of Ted's office stood a tree in a tub, a tree which was meant to be living but had died. Its shrivelled brown leaves rustled spookily in the current from the air-conditioning vent. Ted swung around in his chair to get the miserable sight out of his eyeline. 'Chester!' He responded with maximum cheer.

'Ted, people here are looking at a site on the Thirty-four extension past Whitbridge. Adam'll fill you in – it's between two little places, Butterstream and . . .' there was a pause and a crackle on the line, 'Strankley. There could be something out there for us.'

'Got you. I'll take a look.'

About a year earlier, the BSD had stopped saying 'our people' when referring to the site acquisition division of Magno; it became 'people here'. At the same time, he started to talk about 'us'. Ted anticipated the day that Chester would say 'my people' and mean Tudor Homes. BSD was Adam's name for his boss. He had told Ted it was an old Afrikaaner acronym for Big Swinging Dick.

Ted keyed 'Butterstream, 34X past Whitbridge' into his notebook and felt a tremor of premonition. Chester had nominated a notorious region. The extension of the 34 past Whitbridge had mired the Department of Transport in a public enquiry into the highway's route across an area known as Strankley Ridge.

Ted folded his arms and sat on the edge of his desk. He had three things on the walls of his office: a large abstract painting selected by the suite's decorator, forty-two brightly coloured rectangles in lines on a white ground; the original 1910 advertisement for homes in Maple Grove; and a map. On the map he traced the 34, which branched west from the city's orbital highway north of the 31. The 34 ought to have run in a straight line to meet the 52, leading due south from the Coffin. Instead it kinked southwards, as if avoiding the horror ahead.

Geographers first called the imploded industrial conurbation of five towns grouped along the coal seams and canals of the northwest the Coffin. It was a good name for a feature which was coffin-shaped, and distinguished by exhausted fuel, redundant industry and mass unemployment. People said a young man leaving school in the Coffin had a 60 per cent chance of remaining unemployed all his life.

The Transport Department wanted to extend the 34 logically to meet the 52 running south from the Coffin, through smiling irrelevant farmland, thousands of pointless pigs, millions of acres of unprofitable wheat and oil-seed rape, unviable villages, uneconomic copses and unfeasible water meadows. People did not like the idea. On a long chalk escarpment named Strankley Ridge stood a Neolithic stone circle which had become the focus of protest against the plans. It was an archaeological site entangled in protective legislation more hostile than razor wire.

The original path of the 34 veered to the southwest of this region, grazing the hallowed university town of Whitbridge. As Whitbridge University became a world-renowned centre for information science, the 34 swiftly became a principal artery of commerce, encrusted with bright plastic-cladded parks of modern enterprise. Ted visualised the earth thick with cables, the air crackling with radiation, a dementia of polarised ions streaming in all directions like the commuters through Central Station at 8 am and 6 pm.

The Coffin had no gaudy industrial parks. After riots, the government had targeted parts of the Coffin for urgent programmes of urban renewal. The putative investors demanded fast access to the 34 corridor; the pension funds which owned the farms in the way had been induced to sell.

The government had not moved fast enough. The high-speed trains hurtling to the city from Whitbridge had already tempted a small herd of maturing yuppies to move into the abandoned countryside dwellings. The husbands commuted every day, the wives colour-washed the farmhouse walls and limed the old oak beams, the children grew sturdy and freckled on honey sandwiches and country air. With all the cunning their MBAs suggested, these settlers were now fighting the road scheme, and with them ranged a motley army of native inhabitants, Green party anoraks, Iron Age researchers, a famous actress and two hundred eco-warriors who were encamped close to the stone circle on Strankley Ridge. This was the neighbourhood Chester Pike had selected for a new Magno supermarket, and where a supermarket appeared homes sprang up like mushrooms.

The face of one of the protestors, a veteran of several earlier demonstrations, had caught the eye of the media. Radiant as a dirty seraph, his photograph accompanied every report on the inquiry's progress. He appeared on TV shows next to fashionable comedians who were entranced by his innocence of shower gel and the name of the Transport minister. They called him Crusty and, to some sections of the population, he was a hero. Ted remembered that his daughter Cherish had his picture on her bedroom wall, in pride of place between the wet-eyed seal pup and Leonardo DiCaprio.

As he closed his notebook and sped out to his meeting, Ted's shoulders sagged in apprehension. He felt the shadow of public attention. He sensed his wife's sorcery looming close. Sixteen years he had shared his life with incubi like Crusty, ephemeral monsters summoned by the media to ravish the public mind until the day a fresh demon appeared to supplant them. Ted was forming the idea that his wife too was a creature of that half-life, and had just taken mortal shape to entrap him.

He was afraid of these gremlins and of the process which spawned them, he had an instinctive fear which nagged from his subconscious and would not be silenced by reason. Jealousy played a part, for he saw that his wife had the gift of calling up the devils and giving them names, and was rewarded for it. He had blamed those rewards for changing a fond girl to an ice queen whose contempt blasted to dust his naïve dreams of a family. It seemed as if some evil breath emanated from Channel Ten through his wife to his home and himself. Every time he and his children were rounded up for a magazine photograph a little of their lives drained away, while the media thing got stronger and tightened its grip on them all. Straying towards Strankley Ridge felt to Ted like yelling into the mouth of the dragon's cave.

He left his office, and his dead tree, and the sickly thicket behind his secretary and the senescent creepers in the atrium – an atrium, at last! Littered with dead leaves as it was, the atrium still thrilled him. If a man had an atrium could the Fortune 500 be far behind? He took a cab to the offices of the Oak Hill engineers, which also had an atrium, verdant and flowering, where he met Adam deSouza. They delivered the brief for a feasibility study and it went well, without hard questions, just a short assent to the limits of the specification.

They went to lunch. Agile with high confidence, they slid into the discreet corner of their chosen oyster bar.

'Whitbridge,' Ted began as their order arrived on a

bed of crackling ice. 'The Thirty-four extension. Chester talked to me this morning.'

'The inquiry is expected to go on another couple of months, maybe three.' Adam's joyful gaze ran around the platter of oysters nestled in ice, assessing the molluscs for plumpness. He ate such dishes ritually in order of size, saving the biggest until last.

'As long as that?'

'Tsk. Waste of public money. Only people getting rich there are my colleagues, I'm afraid. The site we are interested in is about a mile further down the thirty-four, at Strankley. We are looking at it seriously. The result isn't really in any doubt, it's a question of the timing. Government's just playing along and changing the window dressing for the sake of public opinion.'

'I guess. It's the press I don't like.'

Adam chose his first specimen and lifted it off the ice with due ceremony. 'Me neither. Not that we've anything to hide in any way.'

Ted's unease suddenly returned, twice the size it had been in the morning. 'We don't want too much interest in Oak Hill . . .'

'No harm, no harm.' Energetically, Adam anointed the oyster with lemon juice.

'It could look . . . it's the *history* of the site. We've agreed that the cost of investigation is prohibitive, I know, but looked at a certain way . . .' He was not getting through.

Adam was intent on his food. Three oysters down he registered a distressed silence in his companion and ruled, 'That's why we undertook Oak Hill as a separate

enterprise and set up the Trust. The Whitbridge thing
will be a straightforward Tudor Homes show. No obvious
connection.'

'Strankley Ridge – it's a feeding frenzy for the media:
Crusty, the inquiry, all of it. When the media get inter-
est, people start digging around, *might* do a Dun and
Bradstreet on us . . .'

'They're very stupid, the media. Easy to get them in
hand. Don't run away with the idea that there's anything
like old-fashioned investigative journalism still going
on. We'll allow for a few sweeteners here and there.'
Adam swallowed his fifth choice, threw down the shell
and picked up the next. 'I'm feeling good about Oak
Hill after this morning.'

'Adam, I've got to say this, I haven't felt good about
Oak Hill from the beginning.'

'Your idea, as I recall.'

'I agree, I agree absolutely.' Adam suddenly stopped
feeding contentedly and fixed his companion with a glare
as flinty as the oysters' shells. 'I put the site up for consideration. But now . . .'

'There's no risk. You heard the guys this morning.
Natural biodegradation processes would have reduced
toxic residues to undetectable levels. We're in the clear.'

'But you and I know—'

'What you and I know is for ourselves alone, Ted.
What *do* we know, anyway? One set of experts says one
thing, another says another. Who's to say what the actual
truth is, really? What's eating you, all of a sudden?'
Adam was icing Ted with his flat, blue-eyed stare.
'Trying to rattle my cage?'

'Adam, I wouldn't dream—'

'Good.' He went back to the oysters. There were two of his portion remaining.

'But I can't see any benefit to Tudor in becoming a side-show to a media circus out at the Thirty-four extension.'

'Absolutely not. Not what we'd care for at Magno, either.'

'Not that I'm afraid of the media – for Oak Hill I'd like to see a supplement in *Architecture Today* and a five-page spread in *House & Garden* when we're at the stage of getting a designer in for our show homes. But we don't belong on the evening news.'

'Quite agree.'

'But if the BSD says go . . .'

'No harm in taking a look.' Adam now spoke encouragingly, as if a very disadvantaged child had suddenly discovered how to tie its shoelaces.

'Get a good price if we buy now before the inquiry reports.'

'That's certain.' The lawyer's large, pink, thoroughly manicured hand was poised over his last oyster, the largest, the juiciest, the plumpest, the most invitingly wet. It was time Ted stopped talking. 'The commissioners aren't obliged to report immediately, either. Law provides for them to take due time to consider the evidence. Could be another two years. In a way, the more kerfuffle that fella – what's his name, gets on TV nowadays . . .'

'Crusty.'

'The more fuss Crusty and his chums kick up, the better for us.'

'Two years, eh?' In the end, Ted allowed himself to feel encouraged. He reached for his first oyster as Adam downed his last. Nowadays oysters seemed to be smaller and thinner and less velvety in texture, but perhaps it was his advancing sophistication. Oysters made him think of the sea, and how he would like to sit somewhere in a fisherman's bar and share them with a smiling woman while the sea salt was still on them. One day.

Back in his office the map was looming over him, with an intrepid marker at Oak Hill. Tudor Homes was still a small concern. There was another marker the other side of Helford where he had a smaller development almost finished, and half a dozen query flags around the outer city limits to fill up space and make the thing look busy.

Ted did not care for maps, either. The logic of a map was ruthless. His map showed him the roads snaking over the land, and the businesses following the roads, and the homes following the businesses, and the area between the city and the Coffin gradually ceasing to be country and becoming conurbation, just as earlier the five dying cities in the north had grown into each other and become the Coffin, after which their industries had become extinct and the colonnaded public buildings had become soot-blackened graffiti-soiled shells and whole districts of homes been deserted by those lucky enough to be able to leave.

Anyone with any knowledge of history would be aware that the two cases were not comparable, that the demographics in the final quarter of the twentieth century were quite unlike those of its beginning. This was not Mexico City, this was not Los Angeles, this was not the end-of-the-millennium suburban nightmare, but no argument he could construct stopped the map staring down at him, swarming with black specks of housing development like flies swarming on a carcase.

They all had their little bit of floor, the Cappuccino Crew at The Cedars. Every Friday, there they were, same women, same clothes, same places – it just killed him. And they all drove past the security cameras into the car park and fought for the parking spaces nearest the path to the door, when their reason for coming to the club was to get some exercise. Rod Fuller enjoyed naturally ocur-ring irony. It put the flint in his eye and the curl in his lip and spun his handsomeness into something super-naturally fascinating; even in these black days, it comforted him to notice the random stupidity of life.

The regulars had claimed their territory. There was Arty T-Shirt right at the back, although she had nothing to be shy about with those legs. Beside her was the Jade Princess, who ran to a different drumbeat but balanced like an angel, and in front of them in all-black stood Catwoman, hypermobile and flaunting it with a leg on the barre. Blubberlugs in Day-Glo pink worked at second row centre with her little black eyes clamped on his backside like leeches. Next to her was Butter-wouldn't-melt-in-it, who came in with all her jewellery but worked like shit, and in front of her, as usual, the black hole in the front row, Sporty Stripes, fiddling with her hair and dropping the combs and retying her shoes and adjusting her bra and doing everything a woman could possibly do to avoid working up a sweat.

'Hi, team,' he greeted them. There had been a debate about what to call them – they said 'girls' was sexist and 'ladies' was bourgeois which was some joke, but he could hardly run in with 'Hi, women!'

'Hi, Rod,' they answered. Catwoman shook out her feet.

He strapped on the mike. 'Earth to class.' His throat was sore. 'Earth to class, ready to go.' Management told him he ought to yell more, but he never knew what he should yell. The other guys could do the verbals, it wasn't his style. He had to save his voice. In five years he'd be working again, auditioning again. Shin splints he would live with but his voice was sacred; not that he was that kind of actor, but he *had* played Anthony.

Last night's booze sloshed up his oesophagus as he began the warm-up. His eyeballs were sore and there was a pain like an iron bar through his back teeth. The mirror told him he was dehydrated, eyes like 'The Scream' but great definition. When he reached down for the floor his head swam and he nearly fell over. I can't do this, he told himself. I cannot drink any more. I will not. If there's anything left at home I'll throw it overboard. Ambition's made of sterner stuff. I will not go on like this.

Five minutes into the running, whatever was left in his stomach started a break for freedom, but he held it down. The Cappuccino Crew were flying, endorphin high, even Stripes was smiling. They noticed nothing.

Rod taught at another gym in Helford, another world where the floor was dirty, the class smelt of stale sweat and talcum powder, and they took twice as long to learn new moves, and twice as long to start smiling. Here the floor was sprung maple, cleaned twice a day. He had to ask them not to polish it. The Cappuccino Crew smelt like a first-night bouquet. They had the things only wealth-in-depth could buy: the nose jobs done just right, the posture from ballet lessons since infancy, the serenity created by never in their lives looking at a bill that would not receive the immediate application of the family gold card.

Some of them worked hard, the fast-track women who refused to slow down, concentrating all their high-percentile IQs on keeping beautiful. The rest just cheated, knowing they could buy it all whenever they wanted, flat gut, bouncing hair, peachy skin. They got blow-dried and made-up for class, got sweaty, got show-ered, got blow-dried and made-up again. They sat around the terrace with their coffee, bored to their bone-marrow and looking for trouble. He found them spooky. Perhaps that was why he was the way he was these days.

At the first break he begged some water off Arty T-shirt; did she actually blush? She looked a mite strange this morning, red-eyed and messed-up in some way, but who was he to talk, with his two pissholes in the mud.

His gut heaved again when he went down for the press-ups so he let them off with ten and walked around correcting positions during the floor work. Did his breath smell? Another reason not to talk. Blubberlugs giggled when he showed her how to hold her pelvis right for abductor raises. Mistake, mistake.

Arty T-shirt got up and ran out halfway through the abs. Instructors' guidelines said to check her out. 'I'm OK,' she said, wiping her face with her towel. 'I'm sorry. It's just personal. Don't worry.'

Blubberlugs filled him in, lying on her mat propped on her elbows like a little cow walrus. 'You heard the goss about her? Her husband's gone missing somewhere out East. You've lucked in, Rod.'

'Keep working,' he told her, trying to find the stretch tape in his bag. The music master tape for the whole class, he had to get it done. One day. One day he would never have another drink. One day he'd have to make a decision about his wife. One day he'd find Sweetheart a new mummy. One day, one day.

'No shit, he was kidnapped by terrorists.'

His right Achilles was burning as if someone had scraped it with glowing charcoal.

'Uh-huh.' Was this for real? True, there was something in the zeitgeist today, some bizarre buzz in the air, he could sense it even through the insulating fog of alcohol. 'I said, keep working, don't stop now.'

'You're a sadist.' Blubberlugs was trying to catch his eye.

'You're lazy.' Had he actually said that or just thought it? His brain was so scrambled he couldn't tell. She was grinning, anyway, thank God.

'It's true, it's not a joke,' Stripes dragged herself to sitting, for once moved to contribute; this must be serious. 'He was in Russia on business and the whole delegation got kidnapped. She just heard yesterday.'

'That's bad.'

'So now's your chance,' Blubberlugs suggested, flopping on her back and rolling her eyes at him.

'Another two sets,' he ordered, getting on the podium for the authority. He heard groans. 'Come on, hit the floor. Ten weeks to the beach, team. You'll thank me then.'

'Couldn't I thank you earlier?' Blubberlugs suggested, lubriciously eyeing his shorts.

Dear lady, he thought, if only you knew. 'Keep it smooth, don't jerk it, not too high, work the abs not the hip flexors. Try and pull your belly-button to your backbone, flatten out the stomach, no tension in the shoulders, keep the chest open, don't forget to breathe.' Forgetting to breathe, now that was a temptation. He saw Sweetheart in his mind's eye, the perfect joy of being five years old, streaking into school, waving over her shoulder. My heart is in the coffin there with Caesar, and I must pause till it come back to me. 'And eight,' he counted, 'and seven . . .'

'You just hate rich women,' Blubberlugs taunted, fingers straining half-heartedly towards her thighs.

'Not especially,' he answered, and wondered what he had said, and why.

Money crusted over The Cedars like clotted cream coagulated over the surface of the bowl. Every vehicle in the car park was brand new, top of the range, accessorised and alarmed to the roof. Rolex watches were found in the lost property basket and they were never claimed. Every child in the tennis squads had orthodontics worth a socialite's champagne bill. Every palm in the gym had its leaves wiped by hand every week. The Cappuccino Crew bought the new shoes as soon as his sponsor issued them. His sponsors were impressed with The Cedars, more impressed than with his silver for the single men's event in the World Aerobic Championships the year before last.

'Rod – you lucky boy, another private client.' As he checked out, the receptionist handed him the appointment card.

The card read: 4pm, Mrs E Parsons, 4 Church Vale, Maple Grove, Westwick. There was no telephone number. One private session paid enough for one week's groceries, or a new pair of jeans, or a party dress for Sweetheart, or one twenty-sixth of one term's fees at The Magpies. He liked training women, too. They were harder to motivate, but easier to pace; he could usually save his legs. His schedule was getting packed, two classes a day, four days a week and the private clients on top.

'She's a big TV star,' the receptionist assured him vaguely, too young to be aware of the universe of daytime television. 'She comes in sometimes but she's more of a social member. Play your cards right we'll be seeing *you* on TV.'

'Yup,' he agreed. Just five more years.

CHAPTER 3

Weekly Lectures

'That's it? That's the saddest-looking fish you could find?' Allie Parsons had an indefinable accent, the faintest clip on her words; it could have been Scottish and it gave a patina of sense to whatever she said.

She prodded the trout's speckled back with a finger whose nail felt annoyingly unstable. Eleven people cringed back from the Channel Ten conference table, leaving the fish exposed to the storm of her wrath on a tin foil catering platter.

'We thought he definitely looked the most unhappy. I mean, his mouth turned down more than the others.' Speaking alone in the trout's defence was Daniel Flynn, also known as The Himbo, co-host of *Family First*. His eyes almost crossed with the effort of composing his pleading. 'I mean, all fish look kind of miserable, don't they? Like they know they're dead and they're going to be eaten or something.'

'Precisely – they all look pissed off.' Allie glared at The Himbo as if he were a new wrinkle in her mirror. 'On behalf of our viewers – our three and a half million viewers, Daniel – we are testing the pledge made by Magno Hypermarkets to replace any unsatisfactory item purchased in the store unconditionally, however wacky or deranged or psychopathic the reason the customer gives for bringing it back – yes?' She was exasperated to see Maria, the stand-in weather girl, nod brightly.

'So,' she proceeded at a sarcastic pitch, 'we decide to buy a fish and return for the most ridiculous reason we can think of: we're going to take it back because it looks unhappy. And all you had to do, Daniel, was to pick the most pissed-off looking fish in the store – and you're telling me that's it?'

'I thought his eyes looked so sad,' the trout's advocate argued wretchedly. 'If you take a look at him,' and he reached out for the fish and bent its head around to stare his accuser plaintively in the face, 'his eyes are almost mournful. Haunted. Like he was going to cry any minute. I mean, he's really quite tragic. None of the others had sad eyes.'

'And you expect me to go out there in front of millions of viewers and tell them that this, *this,* is a sad-looking fish?' She poked the trout again, the loose nail snagging on a fin. 'The saddest-looking fish they've ever seen? I mean, yes, it looks sad. Absolutely, this is a sad piece of merchandise.' Between finger and thumb, she picked up the fish and exhibited it to the room. 'It's just not sad in the way we need it to be sad, is it Daniel? And who has to make this sad fish work? Who always gets to make the story work around here? Me.'

She threw the trout back on the platter, sending it skidding down the table to collide with the coffee pot.

The team arranged their faces in expressions of contrition, sharing covert eye-rolls as they did it. The weather girl, catching on, buried her nose in her chart folder.

Eviscerating The Himbo was a ritual. Allie did not work with competition; the only woman on the *Family First* team was her secretary, and if she could she would have hired a male for that job. Her preferred co-host was a dumb but nice-looking heterosexual boy, emasculated in a style-free hand-knit.

Allie graciously allowed The Himbo to report the poodle grooming classes, the phallic potatoes, the European Commissioner for women and the environmental stuff. For herself she reserved the bleeding hearts, the transplant babies and the miracle makeovers. Politicians and film stars were shared, but Allie asked the questions and The Himbo reacted. She hired a new Himbo on a year's contract every September; by March his agent would be snarling like a stoat in a gin-trap. In July The Himbo would leave, usually without trace, although one of them had actually made good in a cable kids show.

The producer cleared his throat to summon courage. 'I think on camera, Allie . . .'

'You're telling me it'll work on camera? That fish will look sad on camera?' Now the finger of damnation was pointing at her producer's heart. 'Is that what you're trying to say?'

'Not exactly, Allie, but I think you'll find . . .' He was a grey, thin, untidy man and it was ten years since he had won an award for investigating the child sex gangs staking out the city train stations. His star withered him with a flick of her wrist, as if she were throwing him bodily away, casting him on the scrap heap already piled high with ex-producers of *Family First*. Par for this post was eighteen months. Producers were not like Himbos, producers were dangerous, and so Allie's producers were fired in fusillades of writs and left to weep in the smouldering debris of their careers. If he was lucky, an ex-producer of *Family First* could end his days in radio. Small-town radio.

'What you're telling me is that it'll work on camera because I can make it work, is that right?'

'Allie, you're—'

'Don't tell me what I am.' She had the bee-stung lips of Manet's 'Girl at the Bar of the *Folies Bergère*', and they surged back into a snarl. She began stalking around the edge of the room. 'I know what I am, thank you. I am not whatever the tabloids call me. I am not what people in this industry think I am. I am not a star, I am not a prima donna, I am not a superwoman, I am not a killer bimbo on speed, I am not Joan Crawford on a bad hair day, I am not an armour-plated, nut-crushing bitch.' One by one as she approached them, the nine men and two women sentenced to contracts on *Family First* turned around, kept their faces blank and said inwardly: oh, yes, you are. 'Yes! I may have a few awards on the office wall. Yes – this show has topped the ratings every year since I took it over. But all I am is a broadcaster,' she proceeded in a calmer tone. 'A trained, experienced broadcaster, a professional. That's all that I am, and *because* I'm a goddamn professional . . .' At the end of the table was an unoccupied space and she turned to grip the table edge and glare around the room. 'I'm carrying you guys. I carry you, every day. Every day somebody in urgent need of a brain transplant screws up and every day you all look at me and expect me to ride up like the Seventh Cavalry and save the show. Well, I won't do it. Not this time. You screwed up, you sort it.'

'Hey, Allie . . .' The Himbo had a good nature, but not the ability to understand that this was not a universal blessing. 'Allie, hey – it's only a fish. If it's a problem . . .' The group winced as she turned her eyes on him.

'The fish is not the problem, Daniel.' Stalking back towards him on her stilettoes, she pushed up her jacket sleeves, getting down to work. Today's colour was pro-consumer cerise. 'No, the fish is not the problem, Daniel. You're the problem. You're a problem because you have lower intelligence than vegetable life. You're a problem because you are a complete dickhead and I am stuck with you until the end of the series.'

Papers were strewn over the head of the table, and from among them Allie seized a sheaf of newly opened mail, letting a couple of slit envelopes fall as she did so. 'You know what this is? All of you, you know what this is? This is my personal mail, and today – let's see . . .' She made a show of scanning the letters. 'Today, apart from the fan stuff and the woman complaining about the dog story, I got twenty-eight applications for your jobs and *of* those . . .' Theatrically, she began picking out individual sheets of paper and tossing them into a pile beside the trout. 'Seventeen were for your job, Daniel. Seventeen guys out there want your job today. Maybe eighty or ninety want your job this week. It would be a safe bet that at least eighty men will beg me for your job this week, Daniel, they will *beg*. And you can't find me a sad-looking fish.'

In as far as a man can when he has benefitted from multiple applications of self-tanning gel, The Himbo's face turned grey. 'I . . . do you . . . are you . . .'

'I'm asking for a better fish, Daniel.' Now the voice was pitched low, grinding like a glacier. 'Just get me a better fish. You've got half an hour.' She turned and left the room. Her secretary, well rehearsed, shovelled the papers into her briefcase and followed. The smell of make-up lingered in general reproach.

'Whew.' All around the table, people stretched, sighed and loosed their collars. Daniel got up and went to the window for the illusion of fresh air; there were no opening windows in the Channel Ten building. 'Wow. I never thought she'd chuck an eppy over the fish.'

'Does she often behave like that?' The weather girl felt like going over to lay a comforting hand on one of the rumpsteak-like protrusions under The Himbo's shirt but hesitated, uncertain if that would be politically wise and not willing to consult her copy of *Machiavelli For Women* in public.

'Krakatoa's always smoking round here. You never know what'll set her off.' The senior researcher was already reaching for the telephone. 'Only that something will. That one was off the scale. Wowee.'

'I couldn't believe her language.'

'Well, my dear, you'd better starting expanding your understanding of the universe right now because the truth is out there and it's worse than that. Is that Magno Hypermarkets? This is *Family First* at Channel Ten, put me through to your public relations office, it's urgent.'

'My-name-is-Maria,' the weather girl catechised, blinking hard. 'Do-you-feel-terms-of-affection-are-appropriate-in-the-workplace?'

The secretary returned. 'Allie says get a selection in and she'll choose the one she wants herself.'

In her dressing room, Allie sat uncomfortably on the edge of a chair with her hands spread on board. 'You've got an hour,' she told the waiting make-up artist.

'It's more like two to strip and reapply,' the cosmetician ventured.

'Then hurry,' was her reply.

Fumes of solvent filled the room. Allie crossed her legs, wriggled in her seat, twisted one ankle behind the other, and sighed. She was used to suffering for her profession. Taking off the jacket meant the risk of ruining the manicure when it was resumed, so she had to keep it on and sit upright to stop it creasing and hold her arms right away from her body in case of accidents.

Her vacant eyes were turned up to the monitor showing Israeli bombing-raid debris on CNN but her mind was running on Stephanie Sands. On hearing from Lauren Pike that Stewart Sands was a kidnap victim, Allie had gone directly to New Farm Rise with a bouquet of *Casablanca* lilies, anticipating an exclusive for *Family First.* Instead, her Westwick friend had pulled the delicate flower number, the fluttery fingers and the wispy hair. 'I couldn't, Allie, how could I? Go on TV and talk about Stewart? I'd die before I got two words out.

Besides, the Foreign Office wouldn't like it, I know they wouldn't.'

Allie retired, offended. What right had Stephanie to be drifting tearily around after that chubby kid of hers when she was a kidnap wife and belonged on TV? She imagined Stephanie on the studio sofa, dabbing tears off the end of her nose. So demure, so big-eyed and soft-voiced and . . . *decent*. Boss would eat her up – maybe literally, she must be gagging for sex by now. How long had it been, two weeks? There was something wrong with her, there had to be. She really should get that nose done. The fucking woman could weep over a dead daisy, so what was her problem with *Family First*?

Allie chewed her top lip. Other people's stupidity offended her. Didn't the dear girl realise that this was it, her Andy Warhol portion? Gardens for kiddies, who'd remember that? Kidnap victim husband, now that was cool, that was great. She could not turn this down. She was holding out, that was all. Money. Money or spite. Allie never understood it, but sometimes this thing happened and people got malicious or perverse and just refused to give her what she wanted. But she'd keep working on it. Geography was destiny. A story that big just a short spit from her own doorstep – it had to be.

An hour and a half later, two crates of assorted fish packed in ice were carried into the studio kitchen under the supervision of the senior wet fish buyer and the public relations director for the south-eastern division of Magno. Allie Parsons was invited to leave her dressing room, where the manicurist had just completed the operation of stripping off, reapplying and revarnishing her acrylic nails in cerise to tone with the jacket, and select the fish with which she wished to appear.

It was a new Allie Parsons who emerged, one who greeted the outsiders with flattering squeals of joy, as if they had chosen to leave their offices and entertain her. 'My, oh my, what a *magnificent* catch,' she cried, clasping her hands in admiration. 'And you did all this for us? I'm overwhelmed, I really am. Now you must tell me,' and she took the fish buyer seductively by the arm, 'which one of these gorgeous creatures would *you* choose?'

'Well, the tuna is on promotion this week . . .'

'Tuna . . . just a tiny bit in the luxury bracket for us I think.'

'What we need is a medium-sized whole fish with a sad expression,' the senior researcher interjected anxiously, seeing the entire feature transmuting into something else, the shooting ratio for the series rising even higher than it already was and his date for the evening left waiting in fury by her phone.

'Hey – look at this f-a-a-ab creature, isn't he beautiful?' Allie picked up an enormous lobster by the tail. 'Is it still alive? He won't nip me will he?' The extended f-a-a-ab was her catchphrase; on screen, she made a point of using it within the first three sentences of her opening speech. She was getting increasingly annoyed that no comedian had yet done an impression of her.

'Our lobsters are all freshly killed.'

'Or what about this? What *is* this?' Delicately she held up a big flat white fish, draping it reverently over the corner of the tray as if it were a length of cloth of silver.

'Turbot. Our turbot are farmed in the North Atlantic, enabling us to offer them at about half the price of wild turbot.'

'Oh my, that's just *f-a-a-ab* . . . Now, everybody, let's really think *fish* here . . .'

And so the drama continued, until after forty minutes Allie was presented with a pair of lobsters and the fish buyer had departed in a state of high satisfaction, also leaving behind a very average herring which, in objective truth, looked more cheerful than the trout first chosen. Thinking fish had determined that a fish was definitely an ocean-swimming creature, so trout were out. The Magno Hypermarkets public relations director left a little later, having summoned an assistant to oversee the operation in her absence.

The Himbo set out across the city with the herring, the assistant and a camera journalist griping about the afternoon light. He was filmed attempting to return the fish to a Magno Downtown store on the grounds that it looked unhappy. At another Magno, he was filmed returning a packet of detergent because he did not care for its perfume. Lastly, he was captured in the Magno at Helford taking back a packet of cornflakes because they were too yellow for his kitchen decor.

The herring passed the night in the refrigerator in the studio kitchen. In the morning, at the suggestion of the public relations assistant from Magno, it was washed, patted dry, touched up around the gills with a little red lip gloss and coated with hair gel to restore its healthy fresh-from-the-ocean shine.

'And now,' The Himbo primed the watching millions

with his extraordinary natural sincerity, 'a fishy tale for our Watchdog feature. Every week on Watchdog *we* put a consumer claim to the test for *you* . . .'

'And today,' standing in front of the studio audience, Allie brandished the herring above her head. 'With this fish,' she confided to Camera Two, 'we set out to test the claim of Magno Hypermarkets that they would exchange *any* unsatisfactory merchandise, however crazy the reason the customer might give for bringing it back, with *no* questions asked. We gave Daniel this fish and told him to take it back to Magno Downtown because it looked miserable and it was making him sad . . .'

The audience moaned, 'O-o-o-o-o-h,' in sympathy, their sensibilities tenderised by a warm-up man who had told blue jokes for half an hour before the show started.

'And after that,' Allie gracefully deposited the fish on an Italian ceramic platter decorated with hand-painted lemons, and picked up the detergent, 'Daniel took back this washing powder to Magno just because he didn't like the smell . . .'

'A-a-a-a-ah,' sighed the audience, here and there breaking into lubricious titters, for it was a feature of *Family First* that The Himbo should appear virile enough to stir a housewife's loins and bring sunshine to her day even through a veil of Prozac in the depths of winter and the pit of the menopause.

'And *finally*, at our local Magno store here in Helford, he took back these cornflakes,' and she held them up with both hands and shook the carton, 'because the colour clashed with his kitchen curtains.'

The sign above the stage which read LAUGH was illuminated and the audience guffawed obediently until the floor manager patted the air for them to quieten down. 'So Daniel . . .' Allie turned to The Himbo with an adorable wide smile. The rush of live television – there was nothing like it. 'Let's see how you got on . . .'

Needing powerful distraction, Ted Parsons picked up the phone. He changed his mind and put it down, then picked in up again, punched a number from the memory and gulped a breath.

'Listen,' he commanded the answerer, 'I have to go out to Whitbridge tomorrow afternoon. What say I pick you up when your kids are out of school and we enjoy the country air for a couple of hours and find somewhere to have a drink in the evening . . .'

'Oh hi, Ted,' responded Topaz Lieberman in a pleasant tone.

'God, I'm sorry – you sound just like her.'

'You always say that.'

'Sorry, sorry. Is she there?'

'Mum's outside with a customer. Maybe you could call again in a few minutes?' She meant that her mother would under no circumstances call him back. So young and so brilliantly oblique. At least Topaz had always been on his side.

'Is she tied up tomorrow afternoon? What d'you think she'll say?'

'Uh – well, I'd leave it a few more weeks if I were you.'

'Still mad, huh?'

'Well, kind of.'

'You mean yes.'

'Yes, I do.'

'Her plants have died, you know.' He was looking at a dead parlour palm in the window of his office, its leaves browner and dryer and more shrivelled as the days passed. 'We had a contract. She was supposed to maintain them.'

'That's too bad. There are other contractors – let me give you some numbers . . .'

'You said she had a customer?'

'Don't sound so surprised. We have customers.'

'I'm sure you do. How did the exams go?'

'Challenging, but I suppose that's how they're meant to be.' She knew he was not really interested.

'Maybe it's best not to tell her I called.'

'OK, if you want. Take care now. Have a good day.'

She hung up with a brisk click. Ted dawdled his receiver into place, as if it were possible that the line would come to life again and he would hear the voice he wanted to hear. He found that he very much wanted to hear that voice. It echoed from his memory, low and even, the chuckle of a wide river running over warm rocks, the drone of a fat queen bee. The hairs on the back of his neck prickled.

He got up and walked around his office. For the billionth time, he admired the design of Jackson Kerr's 1910 advertisement for homes in Maple Grove. A woman had started it all. Women were always responsible for men's dreams. Ted saw Jackson Kerr as a buccaneer on the seas of enterprise, a bold adventurer who made his fortune dealing in hides and cloth, married a Westwick girl and decided to settle down. He bought her father's house and the houses next to it. Grove House, Maple House, Elm Bank House. Kerr knocked down Maple and Elm Bank, creating, with their orchards and the paddocks, 24 acres of prime building land on which he planned a thousand houses, two schools, a library, a theatre and a church, all in the shade of the great trees of the arboretum planted by the venerable C E Crisp, president of the National Horticultural Society and owner of Elm Bank House for 36 years.

Ted's mind ran back to Gemma. I was a landmine and she stepped on me. I was a chrysalis and she split me open. I was wine and she poured me out. Now I cannot go back to what I was.

The map loomed over him. The palm was dead. The family picture on his desk had been taken when Chalice and Cherish were still babies, before his hopes were blighted and withered. On the street below throbbed a gridlock of taxis. He was not going to have a good day. The purpose of existence seemed exceptionally unclear.

Stephanie snapped off the television. How could people be concerned with fish when her husband was missing? It was a measure of her mental distress that she was even watching such junk. She thought of morning TV as some kind of voodoo capable of turning normal women into underclass zombies. The fact that Allie Parsons was the cult's high priestess and a national celebrity bothered her. Not that she would ever say so.

Westwick had a lifeboat mentality. We're all in this together, said the women tossed together on the stormy sea of parenthood, we must get along if we want to survive. Nobody argued in public, nobody criticised to the face. In private, and behind the back, gossip was to them what poison was to the Borgias – essential, compulsive, sadomasochistic rapture.

She knew they suspected her because she held back, but Stephanie had made up her own code, some Mary Poppins nonsense of treating others the way you want to be treated yourself, and found that she was stubborn about it. Besides, honour demanded her loyalty to Allie, who had been her mentor and was her friend. They went back to their student days.

Alexandra Azarian, as she had been then, was one of those girls who could never look clean or combed, never wear anything untorn or unstained, never get to a class accompanied by a pen and never hand in anything on time. Her hair had been black, thin and ratted into clumps, and she had a nose which although small was hooked like a parrot's beak.

At that time, Stephanie stood at the edge of adulthood as a doe stands at the edge of a forest, in terror of the open space ahead. She was a good student, because being conscientious kept her doubts to a manageable proportion. If her mind was free for an instant to think about her future she was overwhelmed by an uncertainty as fierce as madness. So she found the incompetence of Alexandra Azarian impressive.

They had coincided partially — since Allie had dropped out after six weeks — in an art history module. Stephanie was fascinated to witness her sigh and flounce through the lectures as if Ucello had developed perspective expressly to irritate her, asking questions such as, 'So what was Michaelangelo's *purpose* in leaving the "Pieta" unfinished?'

One day she vanished without formal explanation, although later when Stephanie saw her outside a bar the media students favoured she came over all bright with friendliness and explained. 'My parents wanted me to drop that course, it was such a waste of time, don't you think?' There was a rumour of an affair with her lecturer, although the idea of that exceptionally embittered academic actually performing sex was quite wild.

After a while, it seemed that she had disappeared altogether. She had not been popular, she had dated no one, no one was quite sure if she graduated, indeed she had changed course so often that what she might have graduated in was uncertain. Her most memorable quality had been a blitheness, a dizzy conviction that nothing really mattered, that consequently she could get away with anything.

Years later, at some corporate day at a race meeting, Stewart had pulled out a chair for his wife next to Ted Parsons and the cry of 'Oh my God, isn't that Stephanie? My, oh my, oh *my*!' had gone up from the far side of the table. This vibrant female had jumped up and come around to demand a hug, and Stephanie, compelled to rise and put herself between the little thin arms, had politely covered up her mystification with a muzzy smile until Allie posted a bulletin for the marquee at large: 'We were at uni! I haven't seen you since we did the Florentine school! Isn't this just great?'

She was immaculate, she was flaxen and her nose was straight, and she was also quite accustomed to the *dramatis personae* from the first act of her life failing to recognise her when they made their next entrance. Stephanie was not curious, but some cataclysmic event had turned the grub Alexandra Azarian into the gorgeous butterfly Allie Parsons. As they became friends, she assumed she would be told.

'You must do something *green* for us,' Allie said with non-specific fervour, and a few months later Stephanie's garden for an inner-city play scheme won an award, and her newly designated friend redoubled her applications of flattery and enthusiasm until she agreed to appear on *Family First*. Stephanie hated the entire experience – the exposure, the make-up, the business of reducing her lifetime study to fifty meaningless words. The subsequently increased respect of her clients, colleagues and even her husband she considered utter hypocrisy. The episode was such a trauma that her only clear memory was of the screen Allie Parsons, a more assertive, more defined, more brilliant incarnation.

Every man's fantasy, every woman's best friend – that was the Channel hype about their daytime star. It was almost true. Even among friends, Allie was always on, always up, always shiny. For Westwick women, sensitive to the allegation that motherhood had softened them, slowed them, blunted their intellects and weakened their wills, she was something of a role model.

Other women slobbed out when appropriate. Sunday morning would find Stephanie, Rachel and Belinda in their kitchens in leggings and sweatshirts with their brains running in neutral. Even Lauren possessed a pale green towelling tracksuit for homey evenings. Allie never took off her little suits, never switched off.

Part of her genius was understanding that no moment of public attention was wasted. Even her reaction shots were nano-performances. The eyebrow flash, the chin-dip, the magical close and pout of her rounded lips – the mouth of Manet's barmaid was topped up with collagen every six months – and men all over the region basked in her fascinated attention. *Family First* had the highest proportion of male viewers in the 10 am time slot.

The studio hairdresser came to her house every week to cut and maintain her hair the colour of butter – near-white, mountain-meadow gourmet butter. Most of it was razored into something neat and feathery like Peter Pan's cap; just this thick lock at the front flopped over her forehead, convincing the most slatternly of women that they had something in common.

As months passed, and then years, Stephanie under-stood that the time lost between Alexandra and Allie was not to be retrieved. She found that in any area not connected with her profession, Allie had an impenetrable vagueness. Her children suffered from it, since she forgot most things a mother needed to remember, down to their shoe sizes and what time school came out. At The Magpies Montessori, little Chalice was often the last child in the playground, howling with misery in the arms of an exasperated teacher until the Parsons' au pair appeared at the gate, or Allie herself drifted in, enquiring, 'Oh dear, am I late?' without a trace of guilt.

Almost the first lesson in the ways of Westwick was never to rely on the Parsons household for anything, for it would assuredly let you down. Allie seemed to exist fully only at the Channel Ten studio. Outside she was in a half-life. She told no stories, she seemed to have no memories, she certainly gave nothing away.

Direct questions were feinted aside. One day when Allie had been particularly down on Ted, Stephanie had asked, 'Where did you two meet?' and Allie had shrugged and said, 'Oh, you know, where do you meet your husband? It sort of doesn't make any difference, don't you think?' And then she looked up with a great swimmy smile, adding, 'I think women friends are more important, I really do. Isn't it great that we've been friends for so long? We should be girlie about it, shouldn't we? Exchange rings or make bracelets for each other or something. Would you wear it, if I gave you something?'

Stephanie had been dumbstruck. At the time of friendship bracelets she had made no friends, because their man-shorn rump of a family moved often, forcing her to move from one school to the next before any attachment had time to form roots. She had resigned herself to having missed those pleasures, skipped a stage of development and matured without the pleasure of feminine intimacy. She felt less of a woman because of it. Before Max was born, she had hoped for a girl baby to restore the missing female-to-female bond.

The relationships with other Westwick mothers suited

her underdeveloped heart, with their carefully managed distances and tacitly agreed exclusion zones around husband, money, sex, and the imperfections of their children. Not until Allie proposed that bond did she understand what a deep wound she had covered over. The next day a bracelet was delivered, two thick bangles of silver linked together with a ring which carried a silver tag inscribed A on one side and S on the other. Although it felt disloyal to Stewart, Stephanie wore it often. When Allie called her to say that she had heard of a house in New Farm Rise on the market at a bargain price, Stephanie got a sense of personal validation she had felt only once before, on her wedding day.

'But you must come on the show and talk about Stewart!' Allie had said. Stephanie recoiled in fear. Trauma was a shame you kept hidden, she had learned that from her mother.

'No,' she replied, 'I couldn't do that.' And her friend's eyes, which were normally an indeterminate colour which could be blue when necessary, had turned black with suppressed rage.

CHAPTER 4

Ladies' Discussion Society

'You're *so* brave . . . but you look great, honestly you do. Is there any more news? What an ordeal for you.' Effervescing with sympathy, Allie picked her way around their table on the terrace at The Cedars. 'And Max!' she cried, removing her sunglasses for emphasis. 'Tell me, how's he taking it? I suppose he can't understand. My God, how terrible. How you must feel. I – well, I don't know how I'd feel if anything like that happened to me. Not that Ted ever travels. It's been two weeks now, hasn't it? *Has* there been any news?'

'Nothing.' Irrational, but for a second Stephanie felt disbelieved. 'That man from the Foreign Office calls every morning but they haven't heard anything.'

'Agony, it must be just agony.'

'Yes.' Stephanie squirmed. She had spent the previous night tortured by her imagination, which insisted on producing pictures of Stewart as a limp corpse with a bullet hole in his forehead. The pain still felt shameful, she did not like to admit it to her friends.

Relaxing, Allie unbuttoned her jacket – scarlet for

politics, today's interviewee had been a transsexual mayor. Belinda deSouza, Lauren Pike, Rachel Carman and Stephanie moved their chairs to make space for her in the shade of the big white calico umbrella. In physical terms, there was enough space already. It was the size of the ego which they needed to accommodate.

'Such an ordeal,' murmured Belinda, refixing the combs in her thick dark hair.

'I can't imagine what you must be going through.' Truth to tell, Lauren could not imagine much at all, but Stephanie knew she meant well.

'Stress is the killer.' The mere thought made Rachel reach for another cigarette. 'Come see me any time, honey. Happy pills, we got 'em. Seriously, the stuff on the market these days, nobody need worry 'bout a thing.'

'You're so kind, Rachel.' Besides the shame, Stephanie sensed the element of entertainment in her drama. These women with lives from which wealth had removed all life-threatening incidents were avid to be her spectators.

Allie shook her head, marvelling at the terrible suffering before her, a mannerism copied from Princess Diana on her first landmine campaign; she watched its effect reflected in the glass of the terrace doors. 'The Internet kidnappers. Oh my. My, my.' Jealousy was making her feel nauseous. She reached for the day's menu. 'Terror on the Web. What is this world coming to? I didn't even know they had the Internet over there. Didn't we ban exporting computers to Russia? Is the tuna on today?'

Order was part of the beauty of life in Westwick. To everything there was a season, or a day of the week, or an effectively time-managed hour. Duties, pastimes, pleasures, they were all scheduled. Your life was an orbit, you were as predictable as a planet, your movements were cosmically ordained, your role in the universe was secure, destiny was predetermined, thought was unnecessary, $E=mc^2$ took care of everything.

This major conjunction took place on Friday at midday, when Stephanie, Lauren, Rachel and Belinda lined up for Rod's Bunbuster Workout at The Cedars Health and Racquet Club and flopped into lunch afterwards. In summer their table was upwind of the barbecue, not too close to the door and in full sun when there was full sun. Rachel and Belinda brought their racquets and stayed on afterwards for their game. In case there was a pollen surge, Lauren kept her Ventolin on the table. They kept a chair for Allie, who looked on the event as an important research exercise, keeping her in touch with what ordinary mothers were thinking.

They called themselves friends. In the virtual relationship of parallel parenthood, in ante-natal class, playground and PTA, they had spent so much time together exchanging information essential to their children's development that it was only seemly to erect the facade of friendship around their association.

Allie waved over a waiter. 'There has to be tuna, it's so delicious, it's what I ought to be eating and you always have it. And a green salad, no dressing. Has everyone else ordered?' They nodded. The waiter departed with a worried frown. Allie let her eyes follow him, drift on to the corridor leading to the changing rooms and take in the sight of Rod Fuller departing in his leather jacket. She put on her sunglasses again in order to be able to keep watching undetected until he passed the reception desk and disappeared. Such a hunk. And dumb, so dumb.

The normality of it all cut Stephanie so deeply that she started to cry and put down her Snapple. Belinda reached out with her freckled arm and hugged her around the shoulders. 'Bear up, sweetie. We're with you.'

'If there's anything we can do, you must tell us.' Lauren dispensed a taut professional grin, her gold necklace winking in the sun. 'We're all here for you, you know that.'

'Can the sympathy, for Chrissake. You'll make it worse.'

'Rachel, I don't mind, I'm fine, really.'

'Trust me, he's OK. Stewart isn't the sort to get into trouble, it'll all be over soon. I'm prescribing a decent glass of wine, a plate of comfort food and don't get stupid and call your mother.' Rachel was their jester, licensed to voice the thoughts and do the things they dared not. People were inclined to smile at the mere sight of her, a little woman with surprised eyebrows, chubby cheeks and bubbly black curls. Given her addiction to clothing in Day-Glo colours, she needed to invoke the gravitas of her profession frequently to maintain a level of respect.

She waved over the waiter. 'Now the Pinot Noir has the most iron, but I know you girls want to stick with your Chardonnay, so what say we have a bottle of each?'

Allie propped her chin on her hand, indicating thoughtful consideration, once more checking the effect with her reflection. Yes, it worked. 'Now, what are we going to do with you this afternoon?'

'Max . . .'

'We'll take care of Max.' Rachel dunked a potato skin, dropping sour cream on her Day-Glo bosom.

'I thought I'd just carry on as normal. I don't want him to feel that anything is wrong. Max has swim squad today.' Stephanie did not like to say that she yet to discover any argument, bribe or threat strong enough to get her son to agree to play with Ben and Jon Carman.

'Great, so he'll be dropped off here and you don't have to pick him up until five. Let's do something, come on, what's it to be? How about a little retail therapy? Or shall we see if we can get a court?' Rachel refilled her glass. Lauren murmured things which were not quite advice, indeed were not quite anything, but sounded pleasant. Belinda mentioned the new linen shirts at Bon Ton on the Broadway. Stephanie sipped and smiled and listened and let the cooing sympathy and the wine wrap around her trembling heart and soothe it. An hour slipped past.

'So,' Allie had bright round eyes which most people thought were blue, 'what's it to be? You wanna burn some plastic?'

'You're so dear . . .' Stephanie felt her throat seize. She would not cry, they wanted her to cry. 'You're such wonderful friends, I just don't know . . .'

'Yes you do,' Rachel informed her, picking up her racquet. 'You definitely don't want to play tennis because you hate it. You want to go shopping.'

'I don't hate tennis, I just hate losing.'

'Don't we all?' Belinda was tying back her hair, annoyed because Rachel was drunk, and actually played better when she was drunk. 'Go shopping, go on. Spoil yourself.'

Shopping or tennis. Was it the wine or was this pathetic? Remove my child, remove my husband, and my life is down to shopping or tennis? Where were the art galleries of yesterday, where the boutiques and the bookshops and the brasseries and the *caffe latte* with conversation which swallowed up city time so sweetly? Where was the city, and its friends?

From the day she met Stewart, their friends started to merge into a single entity. Singles, couples, her sister, Marcus, they rolled themselves together and became The Crowd, fit only for immature amusements, French movies and late parties. She married Stewart, and they had Max, and each passage was a warp factor thrusting them into a different dimension. It was not just a single-couple thing, because most of The Crowd were coupled most of the time, but a matter of interests. The conversations became shorter, they could not mesh their minds.

When Stewart had told The Crowd they were moving to Westwick, she had seen a mixture of envy and resignation on their faces. One of them, the one who for a time Stephanie had dared to designate her best friend, had asked sharply, 'How do you think you'll like living out in the suburbs?' 'A whole lot,' she had sassed back, and broke the back of the friendship right there.

Allie brushed unseen crumbs from her red jacket and reached for her phone. 'Shopping it shall be,' she said. 'I'll just call in and tell them where I am – unless . . .' Yes, there it was, that stricken look in Stephanie's eyes. Pathetically easy to make that woman feel guilty. 'Unless there's something else – Stephanie? A massage or something? They might have a therapist free – shall I ask?'

Stephanie looked from one concerned face to another. They wanted to know that they had cared for her, these women whose primary role was supposedly caring for their husbands and their children, who flocked around her distress, soft and anxious like fluttering doves. She had to make a decision.

'I'd like to stay and watch Max swim,' she told them. 'Truly. I'll be fine. Don't worry about me. Please.'

They got up and went their different ways, but Allie remained at the table, and, when they were alone, reached out with her little hand for Stephanie's arm. 'You'd feel so much better if you talked about this.' Her eyes were now violet with sincerity. 'Believe me. I know how you feel about TV and of course I understand, but listen to me just one minute. You have no idea how powerful it is to speak out and be heard by all those people. It's really, really therapeutic. If you could only just share . . .'

Suddenly, Stephanie found herself dry eyed, clear headed and unashamed.

'No. I can't, Allie. I can't stand people knowing. This is private.'

'But if you knew, if you really knew – people out there, the people who watch *Family First*, they've got such big hearts, Steph. I am amazed, truly, every day,' the hand now on the heart again, 'at how wonderful people are, how they empathise . . .'

'I'm sure they are wonderful, Allie, but I couldn't do it. Please, I have to go now – I'm late for Max.'

After she had gone, almost running off the terrace, Allie sat alone and looked at her phone. Then she called the *Helford & Westwick Courier* and explained to owner, editor, advertising manager and sole reporter that they had a victim of international terrorism in New Farm Rise.

A hopeless light from the low grey sky made it seem late in the day, although it was only just after two when Ted Parsons filled the Discovery with gas and the CD player with the new Three Tenors, Classic Duets and The Ultimate Opera Collection, and set off for Strankley Ridge. It took an hour and a half to struggle out of the city. Another forty minutes behind a convoy of articulated trailers brought him to the outskirts of Whitbridge, where a five-mile tailback led to the contraflow around the works for the new orbital highway.

Patiently he inched the Discovery forward. '*Vesti la giubba* . . .' When Domingo sang, resignation was heroic. 'I am just an actor, the show must go on.' He sang along, his other secret vice. Lusting for Gemma Lieberman was not really a vice; if God had not meant her to inspire lust, she would have been born into a family of Taliban priests. The engine idled, his mind ran in neutral. When the road was finished, the transport people estimated that one million people would make this journey every day.

Already, three hundred people took this trip every day and never returned. Every day, three hundred people moved out of the city. An excellent statistic, discovered that morning in the property pages. They would need houses, this daily three hundred, and Tudor Homes would build them: unique, exclusive, double-garaged homes. Triple-garaged homes, that was the way forward now. Ted Parsons tried to take satisfaction in the thought.

He navigated the last excavation then drove on down the small roads which awaited upgrading. Tree branches overhung the highway, etiolated limbs from doomed hedges no longer considered worth trimming. Driving west across Strankley Ridge, he passed the site of the Neolithic stone circle. There was a banner lashed to some bushes, reading NO MORE ROADS, and another accusing the Transport Minister of masturbation, and a working model dragon made of old car body parts, thirty feet long with flashing red eyes, posed in the act of eating an inflatable plastic planet. Behind this installation Ted glimpsed some dirty tents and a phalanx of security vehicles.

Cruising downhill, he reached the valley bottom, where the road wandered between the settlements of Butterstream and Ambleford. As he descended, he saw the land to which Magno had staked claim, a flat apron of meadow intersected by small streams and bordered by a derelict railway track. Adam's foresight was recognisable here; the green lobby, forceful in country areas, could be distracted by assurances that freight would travel by rail not road and would turn their attention to the uncooperative rail network companies while the trucks rolled.

He parked by the Quaker Meeting House in Ambleford, and felt spots of rain on his face as he set off, map in hand. The village had one street only, the road itself, running dead straight between two rows of buildings like a main street in a cowboy town. His route led away from it, through the back of the village, past stone-walled country gardens already exuberant with roses, down an overgrown track pitted with horses' hooves and out along the field's edges, respecting the green wheat. His mother had been a country girl. 'Walk on the irons of the field,' she used to say to him. 'The farmer won't thank you for treading down his crops.'

There was no wind. Raindrops still fell singly. A thousand shades of grey surged slowly across the sky, swallows flying black against the light. He turned uphill and disturbed a huge settlement of rabbits, who scampered madly for their holes, leaping over each other in panic then leaping again for good luck. Moron, he remembered with guilt, was patiently waiting out his years on the end of a rope in their yard.

On the skyline stood three gangling old beeches, oddly slender for their obvious age, the tallest in the middle. Each trunk kinked at the same point thirty feet above ground as if a giant had reached down from heaven to gather them, clamped his fist around the trunks and then changed his mind. The canopies did not spread until much higher, leaving a few contorted branches below. Three trees on a hill suggested crucifixion, but Ted had trained himself to disregard omens.

When he reached the top, the rain had conceded. In the clouds a few triangles of aquamarine appeared and there was more light. Ted rested his map against a beech trunk and outlined at least five tracts of land which could each support a development of small, spacious closes leading to quality homes. His preference would be for the far side of Ambleford, since overlooking a supermarket was unlikely to appeal to the end-users, and just high enough up the valley sides to avoid the problems of water without sloping uneconomically.

Run-off fertiliser from the wheat made the grass at the edge of the field fine and thick like the first hair of a lusty infant. His city shoes slipped as he descended the hill. Another memory of his mother came back to him, of walking with her on a hot day through a field of tall yellow flowers which threw golden shadows up to all the soft parts of her face, under her chin and around her ears and in the smiling hollows of her cheeks.

As he walked the sky cleared and a silvery light washed the landscape. The wheat was blue-green in the sun but there were no poppies. His mother had worn a sunhat decorated with wheat ears, cornflowers and poppies, but modern herbicides conceded no territory to flowers. Ted regretted not changing his clothes. His suit imprisoned him, slapping his wallet against his ribs at every step, dictating a walk when he wanted to run like a boy and leap like the rabbits.

Back in the village, he bought a Coke at the general store and leaned against his car to drink it. Melancholy circled, wheedling him like a beggar. What are you here for, it demanded, and why, when you are here to hunt profit, are you thinking of your mother and your dog? Where is your focus, where is the progress? This is what you did when you were twenty. Why waste your costly time on walking in fields when a lower-paid man could do the job? I know you, you can't lie to me; you came out here wanting to be alone in a field. You are not old but you act like it; you should not be tired but you also act like that. You are heartsick, but why? Is it that woman? Or you, you sickening yourself with your own weakness, frightening yourself with your own imagination. You lost your nerve yesterday with Adam. He has you marked now. Chester is a heavy hitter, and Adam will become a heavy hitter, but you will be stuck on the reserve bench all your life because your mind is disobedient, it runs around after pleasure and beauty and shiny bright ideas.

Down the valley floated the sound of a church clock striking six, the church in Butterstream without doubt, since Ambleford had only the unadorned Meeting House. Ted rubbed his eyes, and when he opened them a miraculous procession was approaching along the road.

First came a dog, some kind of crossbred agricultural dog with eager, naughty eyes and a long coat so caked in mud that its colour was undetectable. Tongue lolling, it ran diagonally to and fro across the street.

Behind the dog came a police officer on a motorcycle at the lowest speed he could achieve, his engine idling, his feet skimming the ground. His leather jacket was smartly fastened and his eyes were fixed on the middle-distance, indicating that what followed was his affair only because it constituted a matter of public safety.

Behind the police officer came another dog, quite possibly a parent of the first one, older but just as dirty.

Behind the dog walked a horse, a heavy-set coloured animal and the filthiest horse Ted had ever seen, mud and dust sticking to every inch of hide including its snarled black-and-white mane, which hung to its nose and streamed almost to the ground over its shoulders. On unshod hooves, carrying its head low in order to see its way, the horse meandered more or less in the centre of the road.

At the horse's shoulder walked a young woman wearing enormous mud-encrusted boots on the end of bare legs. She smiled, an echo of the triumphant grin of Crusty, and smoked a small hand-rolled cigarette as she walked. Her hair was matted in dreadlocks and her print dress, under an old blanket wrapped squaw-fashion, was unbuttoned to reveal multiple navel rings.

The horse was harnessed, by a split leather collar and yards of orange baling twine, to the shafts of a cart, on which sat another woman, much fatter with a shaven head and a steel bolt through one eyebrow. With one hand she held the flapping reins and with the other petted a third and even older dog sitting on a cushion at her side.

On the cart, a dwelling had been erected in the style of a covered wagon, with black polythene stretched over a barrel-shaped frame. As the vehicle progressed it swayed from side to side, a jaunty pennant made from an old yellow fertiliser bag waving at the rear. Various pieces of equipment hung clanking from the body, among them a ladder, some shovels, a rusted Hibachi barbecue and a child's pushchair.

Behind the cart skulked a fourth dog of unrelated

breed, skinny and greyhound-like, and at a proper distance crawled the last unit of the procession, another officer on a motorcycle, sun twinkling from the chrome. He smiled around him at the people who appeared at doors and windows to gape at the spectacle, his cap pushed back on his head in self-satisfaction.

Ted observed that all the performers in this tableau enjoyed their roles, that the women were delighted with the degree of outrage which they offered the village and the officers were well pleased to be protecting their community by escorting such a dire menace safely on its way. The inhabitants of Ambleford also seemed gratified to have been visited by a manifestation of the great public drama of the Strankley Ridge inquiry. Ted himself felt satisfied to see his fears actually made flesh before his eyes. If Adam had seen this, he thought, he would hear me better.

The air became still again. The mother-of-pearl light of the early evening softened the pink of the roses and warmed the plain stone walls of the Meeting House. The cooing of a dove echoed between the hillsides. A grinning youth drove his tractor down the main street and collected the girl from the general store as she locked the door. Ted climbed back into his vehicle, in no hurry to get home.

A traffic jam gives a man a dangerous sense of impotence. '*Ecoute-moi*,' sang Sumi Jo as he waited stoically in the tailback to a crash, '*Rapelle-toi! N'est-ce plus ma voix? N'est-ce pas ma main que cette main presse? N'est-ce plus Manon?*'

In the last roadhouse in the 31 corridor, with a cup of

coffee-flavoured liquid on the table, Ted pulled a piece of paper from his briefcase and wrote a letter. 'I can't go back to what I was,' he wrote. 'I am like wine in a bottle and you poured me out. I don't care what you do with me now, whether you drink me or throw me away. But you have to know what you've done. I'm not asking you to forgive me. I know this is stupid.'

The roadhouse offered every convenience necessary to support human life: vegetarian hamburgers; fragranced plastic flower arrangements in the toilets; a post box and a vending machine for stamps.

Mrs E Parsons had such poor muscle tone that it seemed biologically impossible for her to stand upright. Her blood pressure was high for a woman her age, her resting heart rate was fast, her BMI was low but body fat was surprisingly high. Grip strength was poor, stamina was poor, flexibility was below average, peak flow rate average. Rod assessed her build as endomorphic, query disguised by an eating disorder. She gave off the sour smell of a body which was never used. Spod city, absolutely.

To touch she was like an oven-ready broiling chicken, cold and flabby and rather light for her size. He considered tactful approaches to suggesting she should have a bone scan.

'I have so much stress,' she told him. 'Media is a real high-stress profession. You know, deadlines, pressure . . . and I carry my show, I just am the whole thing. It's a real responsibility. Sometimes when I leave the studio I'm so tense I feel like screaming.' The hand to the forehead, the fingers to the bridge of the nose, anguish mimed so as not to smudge the make-up. A miniature woman, everything undersized.

'What I would recommend is a programme of three sessions a week to start with, building to four . . .'

'Oh God, I'll never have the time . . .'

'And I'd suggest concentrating on aerobic work to begin with, to give you a base level of general fitness, plus I'd like to do some Pilates exercises with you to work on posture and flexibility. Then in time we can start thinking about strength work.'

'I'd hate to get muscles. I hate that look.'

'Tone. Just toning. Tone is essential in the abdominal area to hold your spine correctly, and toned muscles work better and protect you from getting injured.' The same lines every day. When you are in the theatre again you will have to say the same lines every day; look on this as training for yourself.

'I can't possibly do three times a week.'

'I could come to your office. I do that with quite a few of my clients.'

Horror flashed in her eyes and she groped for an excuse, finally fixing on, 'But you don't know what my schedule is like.'

'Would you say it was heavier than Oprah Winfrey's schedule?'

'She was *fat*.' She got up from the bench and pinched a little white skin at her midriff below the pristine sports bra stretched over her chest – surgically enhanced chest; they stood out like grapefruit halves.

They were out on her patio, where the bushes in tubs were yellowed and the soft summer air had a faint ammonia tang. The end of the garden was fenced off with a Versailles-style trellis. He made out rabbit-hutches, and some kind of fat dog which was tied up, and occasionally yelped at them. 'Be quiet,' she ordered it, sounding irritated.

'We could include power walks, just around the block here or over in the park. He could come along.'

'He's my husband's dog,' she told him, with emphatic distaste. 'I can't really walk in the street, in public. Not in my position.' The example of Jackie Onassis came to his mind but he let it go. He was feeling tired now, and the right Achilles was flaming, and the management had issued a disciplinary notice about using original music for classes instead of the synthetic tempo-adjusted bilge which cleared the copyright laws.

She suggested going into the kitchen for a drink. Was he kidding himself or was there something a little off about this? She had a preening manner, and a way of over-emphasising her words which made simple state-ments sound suggestive. Her interest in her health was clearly recent. All her kit was skintight and brand new, but that was not unusual in Westwick.

'Having children can raise the stress levels of working women so much that their health could be at risk,' she told him, finding an item from that morning's show still retrievable in her memory. 'They did research some-where, California I think. Even if they have only one child, the stress hormones just shoot right up. And I have three kids.'

'Uh-huh,' he agreed, wondering about working men with children.

'Shall we have that drink now?' she suggested, heading back to the kitchen where unwashed plates covered all the surfaces. 'Do you think I need massage?' she asked, wiggling her rear as she peered into the fridge. He retreated to the far end of the room. 'My shoulders get so-o-o tight . . .'

Her shoulders were habitually dragged forward, the left lower than the right, with marked torsion through the middle thoracics. It was a mess. Actually, the whole body was a mess, right down to the prolapsed metatarsal arches and the bunions. 'Working on your posture and the way you use your body will help realign your spine and stop that tightness from building up.'

'I just love massage.'

'Of course, massage is good for releasing tension, loosening you up, helping the muscles work through their fullest range of motion and recover from training so building up strength faster.' Mistake, mistake. Even before he had finished speaking she was perking up hopefully.

'I thought maybe shiatsu, or something? To get my energy moving. I have no energy, I feel kind of bleaghh, you know? Would you do that, massage?'

'It isn't something I do, no. Fitness training is all I'm qualified for. Pilates technique works on the alignment of the whole body, it would definitely release the kind of tension you have.' She gave a pout of disappointment, and more little ridges appeared in her make-up like sand waves on a beach.

'What age are your children?' He had noticed the detritus of pink plastic shards and dead cyberpets around the edges of the room.

'Oh – young. Really young.' She cracked a can of diet drink and poured it into two smeared crystal glasses. 'They need so much, children. They drain you. So you don't think shiatsu?' Now she was fetching ice. 'You know, you look familiar to me . . . Of course, I've seen you at The Cedars but I'm sure I know you from somewhere else.'

'I'm an actor,' he owned, knowing what would follow.

'An *actor*,' she repeated, seeming pleased. 'Of course. Weren't you in . . . what was it . . .' Yes, his instinct was correct. There was her hand trickling over his when she gave him the drink, and her eyes heading his off at the pass.

'You won't have seen anything I've done. A lot of theatre, just a few little things for TV. My high spot was an educational video of *Julius Caesar*.'

'Shakespeare. Well for heaven's sake.' His personal space was invaded, indeed it was almost colonised, she was too close and she was lingering. 'I can see that. I bet you could really fill out a toga.' Sweat broke out at his temples and a drop ran down his cheek.

'It was modern dress. I had a suit.'

'Look,' she said after a few moments, mercifully taking a step back. 'I'm sure you haven't watched my show, *Family First*, you know, it's all sort of family oriented so why would you? But, you know, every series I have a co-host, you know, a *man*.' It was as if she had named a rare, magical, mythical animal, seldom sighted. 'We'll be looking for someone new next year – starting late September. Screen experience, a good presence, intelligence . . . You don't have to write scripts or anything, they do all that for you. Why don't you think about it? Do you have an agent?'

'That's very kind.' He never knew how to get out of these things, or for that matter how he got into them. 'But I have a family. I've booked myself out for a few years, while my daughter is growing up. I can't really commit myself to anything. We lost her mother a few months back so I'm all she has, really.'

'Oh, I do know, those early years are so precious. But I've got children, and I manage.'

Clearly, no need to fear sympathy, but all the same he kept his eyes down and tried to look stupid, and probably succeeded, because her lack of interest was total. Speaking lightly to indicate that she cared nothing either way about the outcome, she continued, 'Think about it, why don't you?'

He promised to do that. For her own good, he manoeuvred her into booking three sessions for the following week, anticipating that she would call and cancel.

Sweetheart, he remembered while buying frozen peas at Mr Singh's, had once pointed out the Parsons girls to him at the kindergarten. That evening, over his famous *linguini primavera* with sweetcorn, he asked her opinion. 'Their mummy is on TV,' she said. 'She never comes to school except once on Sports Day she gave the prizes.'

'What are they like?'

'The big one is a total bubble-head but she left because she's older. The small one cries all the time. She says her mummy will take her away because she hates it. And their brother is going to be in prison, Topaz says.'

'You don't like them.'

'No. They've got stupid names. Nobody likes them.' And she giggled and shovelled down another forkful. 'Will you come to Sports Day, Dad? You can win everything.'

'That's why I don't come. It's not always smart to win everything. Sometimes it's smarter to give someone else a chance.' The worst thing about parenthood was it made you sanctimonious. The real problem with Sports Day, and every other social event he attended as a father, was the loneliness – the mothers avoided him as if he carried a flesh-eating virus, the few fathers talked over his head. He did not understand why. Gemma said it was all down to sex and something to do with projection and envy in the case of the fathers, though he saw no cause for a man with a new Range Rover *and* a new Mercedes to envy him, running a seven-year-old Toyota.

'Will you make a cake?' she persisted. 'Everybody liked the one you did last term.' Carrot cake with cream cheese frosting, only a tiny bit collapsed at the centre. Not bad for an amateur.

'The Carman boys didn't, they said it was disgusting.'

'They never eat anything home-made.' She stabbed the air with her fork as if to impale the Carmans, left and right.

'Don't wave your fork around, it's bad manners.'

When she was asleep he went up on deck to put the remaining frozen peas on his swollen tendon and watch the stars twinkle to life in the creamy summer night. Lights twinkled along Riverview Drive, and up Alder Reach, and all over Westwick, where husbands were coming home to their wives; granted, Westwick husbands, when they were not travelling, seldom made it through the door before 10 pm, but it was domesticity of a kind, along with brothers and sisters arguing over TV. Families all together under one roof, most of the time, at least. In the North Helford Hospital and Home for Incurables, his wife was drifting towards the end of her life on a river of morphine. Her eyes were open but unseeing. She was nourished by a plastic bag of soluble chemicals, and a vibrating waterbed coaxed her blood through her capillaries and stopped her getting bed sores. He could not go up to Mr Singhs to buy wine and leave Sweetheart alone. So here he was again, alone on deck, watching Venus blinking at him over the willows.

CHAPTER 5

Masquerades

In Westwick there was no smoke without a barbecue. Smoke rose above Riverview Drive. The first barbecue of summer was a rite which belonged to Adam DeSouza, who had dreamed of *boerewors* sausages with gravy every day since he had left Cape Town and, in his reasonable and ruthless way, had made Belinda's existence unbearable until she transmitted her persecution to the proprietor of Catchpole & Forge, Family Butchers on the Broadway, who petitioned his wholesalers and placed a regular order.

The women sat on the terrace with wine and the men stood over the fire with beer. Above the funereal wall of *Cupressus leylandii*, which preserved the DeSouza's privacy, the evening star was faint, depicting Venus in affliction.

Allie Parsons crossed her knees, feeling the toxins trapped in her cellulite protest. The appalling interlude of the weekend lay ahead; there was no filming to be done, no conference to attend, no story to cover. She would be incarcerated in her home. Ted would take the girls to The Cedars while she washed about the rooms like driftwood, turning over magazine pages. Of the popular press, Allie cared only for one genre: the magazines full of lovely homes, devoted couples, photogenic children and courageous triumphs over personal disaster.

It was over a year since Allie Parsons, host of *Family First*, had invited readers into her lovely home to reveal how her son Damon had beaten alcoholism. She questioned the value of that exercise. Damon had been 15 then, with menacing feet the size of telephone directories.

'Kids grow up fast these days,' observed The Boss, the Channel's chairman, appraising her with less approval than she had anticipated.

'We were so young when we got married,' she parried. 'We made so many mistakes. Damon's a good kid at heart. The young have so much stress these days. I was thinking of a feature on it – exam pressure, suicides, you know.' But The Boss had merely smiled.

A cloud of smoke from the barbecue blew towards the women. 'My husband is a pyromaniac.' Belinda flapped her hand at the fumes. 'I think his ancestors must have been those people who burned each other in wicker cages.'

'Sun worship, that's what that was about.' Rachel flicked ash into the rosemary bush, confident that her ancestors were guilty of nothing so barbarous.

'They're all just boy scouts with their camp fires if you ask me.' Examining the futility of men was Allie's favourite pastime in these deadly nights when couples gathered together to excavate acquaintanceships in which the seams of affinity were running dangerously thin.

'You could be right. Did I tell you, he wants us to go on a wilderness weekend?'

'A what?' Allie was alerted. Another feature?

'A wilderness weekend. You go off into the woods with a backpack and a Swiss Army knife . . . oh, stop, Allie, I know what you're thinking. Adam would never do it. The firm wouldn't let him. Besides, he's not insured.'

'I was thinking maybe another couple, if it's a thing people are getting into. So go on. You set off into the wilds . . .'

'With a ton of mosquito spray and your Discman and a bottle of Bolly . . .' prompted Rachel.

'Yes. And you sleep under the stars and tune into nature.'

'That's it?'

'That's it.' More smoke belched from the barbecue, and they all waved it away.

'No tennis?' Rachel was horrified.

'No tennis.'

'He's crazy. You're sure Adam isn't leading a double life? I mean, maybe he's got a second family somewhere and he just forgot which wife he was with. You'd die if you had to go two whole days without tennis. I give you that as my professional opinion.' Rachel's deep, rough laugh reverberated from the walls of the house. She laughed alone. Women in Westwick kept cold houses and seldom laughed at jokes about adultery.

The essential facts of the DeSouza marriage were common knowledge. Belinda had brought her condominium in Jackson Hole to the union, while Adam, as an immigrant, had been required to resit his bar exams and was therefore ten years behind his peers and trapped in a corporate job. Until his capital contribution to the family wealth outweighed that of his wife, Adam was a man who had been bought and paid for; other wives envied Belinda the power balance of her house, and wished her husband might stray to a strange bed to even the score.

'So, go on. You drive out miles from anywhere . . .' Allie leaned her chin in her hand.

'Well, that's it. You just go off and sleep in sleeping bags, pee in the woods and get ants in your hair.'

'And what's the point of it?'

'There isn't a point. He just wants to go fishing and make camp fires and be a boy scout.'

'But is it always a husband and wife thing? Is it supposed to get you back in touch with each other and revitalise your relationship or something?'

'Well, maybe . . .' Belinda shrugged. Rachel scowled. Allie tried a pleading look. Of course, they – the elite, the favoured, the wives of Westwick – did not need to pee in the woods in order to rediscover their husbands, but it might be a valid exercise for less enlightened women. 'But I mean – what's to revitalise? If he's a jerk when he's washed and shaved, am I going to like him any better when he's wearing designer stubble and muddy old Levis?'

They nodded. A blanket of smoke rose from the barbecue and rolled over them. They coughed. 'Sorry, ladies.' Adam brandished the tongs in apology, his smooth round cheeks shining with pleasure. 'It'll burn down in a minute.'

Rachel tossed her cigarette butt into the hedge. 'Did you hear what the first chicken said to the second chicken?'

'Not another chicken joke.' Belinda could look very like Katharine Hepburn, with her square jaw and square smile and thick mane disciplined with combs. Now she did Katharine Hepburn looking down her nose at Cary Grant.

'The first chicken said to the second chicken, "Why did the man cross the road?"'

'And . . .'

'And the second chicken said, "I don't know – why do men do anything?"'

They laughed and the men heard the laughter. 'The girls are enjoying themselves,' Adam remarked fondly.

He smiled frequently, his thin lips disappearing in a beatific crease which made his rounded cheeks plump like cushions. He stood over the barbecue with the tongs poised, impatient for the charcoal to glow, his blue butcher's apron tied around his waist area with a manly knot. Adam was a big man, not a fat man, well covered all over, his straight silver hair barbered boyishly short, a picture of substance and prosperity. Joshua Carman felt small beside him. Josh was small and round like his wife, with little, nimble-fingered, restless hands so delicate they could almost take a blood sample from a sleeping patient without waking her. He rolled a beer can nervously between his palms. 'Ya know,' he offered the gathering, 'there's an enzyme in beer which has been proven to counteract the carcinogenic properties of burnt meat.'

'Should I infer something about my cooking here?' Adam demanded. His sense of humour ran shallow while Josh's surged deep.

Standing up-wind, Ted Parsons cracked another beer and let his mind drift away from the pantomime. What amused him was that DeSouza, for all his childhood under African skies and his undeniable intellect, had never considered positioning the barbecue so that the prevailing breeze fanned the charcoal and carried the smoke away from the house. As it was, the apparatus shielded the fire basket, flames were half-hearted, and by the time the food was cooked the women were tired, drunk and smoke-cured like a row of Black Forest hams.

'How'd it go this week?' Carman was talking about the Oak Hill project. There was no need to name it, it was number one on all their action lists.

'Pretty good. The study'll be with us in two months and then we can go back to the county and get a start date.' It was Ted, through Tudor Homes, who moved things forward for the Oak Hill Development Trust. Adam worked for Chester, Chester controlled Magno. The payoff for Carman would be the health care contracts for Magno Oak Hill and Channel Ten, which condemned him to starve for two more years at least while the trust directors would get their snouts in the trough as soon as the feasibility study was done. Josh defined starving as being unable to justify buying a second home.

'No hassles?'

'We're not expecting any.' Adam at last speared a *boerewors* and lovingly laid its succulent length on the grill.

He felt that the brief he had prepared for the consulting engineers was his masterwork. It had emphasised concerns about the water table and gravelly sub-soil and segued around the site's history so elegantly that the only areas of potential difficulty were effortlessly blocked out of the picture. Only a very curious mind would choose to forage, and he had delicately indicated to the engineers that they were not getting paid to be curious. 'The access thing exercised a few minds, I think, but we've handled that and everyone's happy.'

'And the BSD is cool?'

'The BSD is cool,' Ted confirmed.

Adam moved on to lay out the steaks. They smiled around the fire, the contented bondmen of Chester Pike, who spent weekends at his place on the coast and left the neighbourhood lighter for his absence.

'So nobody's fingered the problem?' Josh savoured the forbidden aroma of the sausage.

'Problem?' Fat began to run and a burst of yellow flame consumed it, highlighting Adam's white teeth.

'It's not a problem.' Ted shifted uneasily on his feet. He never followed Carman's humour. He had argued for his co-option to their talks because the man – no, the couple – had tentacles around certain areas of the community, making them good hostages against local trouble, but a medic did not think the way people in business had to think. He was afraid that one day Carman might rediscover his conscience. For that matter, he could still remember where his own was buried. 'There's no problem,' he said again. 'We've hired the biggest firm of consulting engineers in the country. On what we're paying them, I think if there was a problem we'd know by now.'

'So everything's cool?'

'They raised the question of a new access road, because the Thirty-one is already at capacity traffic-wise after the interchange with the orbital.' Adam smiled again and turned the sausages.

'We anticipated it,' Ted told him. 'Crap about vehicle emissions, World Health Organisation guidelines. Acorn Junction is a black spot. They figured a significant increase in the traffic might get us into trouble, but a new road down from the Forty-six will handle it, and we've got a choice of two or three routes well away from the conservation area so they don't see a legal basis for objection.'

'Suppose some environmental weirdos—'

'Relax, Josh. This is Westwick. We have no weirdos, none of any kind. There's too much oxygen, they can't breathe out here. Have another beer, lick the big C.' With his free hand, Adam passed him a bottle and took another for himself. For a moment, Ted felt uneasy. Every now and then DeSouza got gung-ho about something about which Ted would have preferred to be cautious. There was his own weakness again; not agressive enough, testosterone-deficient. Until he met Gemma Lieberman. But all that was past; she hadn't answered his letter.

With jaundiced eyes, the wives watched their husbands standing over the fire.

'Eat football. Drink football. Breathe football. Screw football. When we can clone people, do you think we'll bother with men?' Rachel felt irritable. She was hungry and she was down to two cigarettes, and since the men were drinking she'd have to bully Josh into going down to Mr Singh's.

'Oh my, there's a thought.' Perplexed, Belinda considered cloning Carlos Moya. She had a purgatorial vision of a tournament of Moyas eternally slamming balls at each other without ever getting two games ahead, and herself eternally waiting for the wild victory sex session without ever knowing to which player she should give her allegiance.

'I think I'd clone Rod the Bod.' Allie had been growing dangerously bored. She sat up, suddenly revitalised. 'But maybe we could get some genetic engineer to block the gene for saying "and another sixteen sit-ups".'

'And graft in another half-inch between his eyes. I thought he was a clone already. Those quadriceps can't be for real.'

'What do you mean, you think he uses steroids?'

'Let's hope not, for your sake.' Rachel blew smoke into the air. 'He'll be no use to us girls if he does. Steroids induce penile atrophy. Believe me, I saw it when I was a junior registrar.'

'He doesn't look to me like he's got penile atrophy.' Allie raised her voice a little, hoping to bait her husband.

'I'm with you there. That is one well-packed lunch box.' Belinda giggled with her hand over her mouth. She was learning, but was still not quite up to speed with this kind of conversation.

'Uh-huh,' replied Allie. 'What do you suppose it's like to fuck something like that?'

Belinda and Rachel exchanged glances. 'How's the personal training going?' Rachel swigged her wine expectantly.

'Hey, please. Oh no. No, please. I mean, I wish I *could* say we did more than a zillion step-ups but believe me . . .' Allie had one hand on her heart and the other, still holding the half-empty glass, waving away the suggestion. 'In my position – career suicide, I'd be crazy. I mean, I'd *love* to, you know, he's such a studmuffin. I'm sure it'd do Ted good, to feel he had something to compete over. They're so aggressive, aren't they? That's how I'd choose to revitalise *my* marriage, if I could. But I can't. Impossible. There it is.'

And she dunked her nose in her glass, hating Rod Fuller for coming around twice a week, behaving with blatant decorum and virtually running out of the house at the end of her hour. He wouldn't even stay to shower.

The men heard the women laughing again. Their conversation was inaudible, but Ted could read Allie's face. He heard mirth, he saw smiles but he sensed anger, and malice. Someone had pressed her button tonight.

His wife's face was extraordinary. True emotions never appeared there, supposing that she had any true emotions. Her face was a screen, on which she projected whatever she felt was appropriate. Unless she was alone with the family, a doll-like vacancy underlay all her expressions. She might be anything – curious, offended, in a fury – but nothing penetrated the bright-eyed mask.

Only the most sensitive observer, and Ted had developed the sensitivity over the years, could detect her feelings. For instance, nobody ever guessed that she hated him. He knew it because he felt it, and of course because in private she told him so, but in public Allie merely acted as if he did not exist. She never looked at him, never spoke to him, never joined any group including him, never touched him. This was done without emphasis, as if it were as involuntary as breathing. If he had to be with her for any space of time, he began to feel that he was fading away to nothing. It was quite possible she had hated him even before she married him but he, carried along by her radiant energy, had never understood that. Now she was angry, and when she was angry she would strike. Probably at him. He felt fear trickling like sweat down his ribs, and despised himself for it.

The two genders had to eat together. The Carmans squabbled over who should buy cigarettes. When she discovered that there was no chicken, Allie recoiled into a sulk and picked at a spoonful of rice. Adam made an attempt at general conversation.

'Garden's looking good,' he nodded at his wife.

'Yes,' she said, pinching the pleats in her skirt. Belinda was no gardener. She knew that their plot was charmless and had hired Stephanie to induce some beauty in it the previous year. There had been a number of conversations which Belinda had not understood, and a scheme whose cost had horrified Adam, and in the end for the sake of friendship no bill had been sent and no work commissioned.

'Yes, where are the Sands tonight?' Josh liked Stephanie. Precisely, he liked her legs, the more for the fact that she never seemed to realise how much of them she was showing. He packed a chunk of steak into his mouth and reached for a napkin to stop the blood running down his chin.

Rachel pushed away a half-empty plate and lit up from the fresh pack. 'Don't you *know*?'

'Know what? Nobody tells me anything. I was going to ask him to take a look at our porch.'

'He's been kidnapped out in the Ukraine or somewhere.' Evidently this was an event which put Stephanie in a social exclusion zone.

'Kidnapped?' Josh's eyes popped over the next forkful of meat. 'Who by?'

His wife shrugged. 'Terrorists. At least, that's the story.' She turned away to blow smoke over the shrubs.

'When? Was it on the news?'

'No,' confirmed Allie sourly. The *Helford & Westwick Courier* were taking their time. 'No media. In case the terrorists want the exposure. Stephanie's being stupid. It's been two weeks at least.'

'They should hire a PR firm like decent people.' Josh was indignant. 'If that's what they're after, why not give it them? If you asked Stewart right now I bet that's what he'd say. Hell – put 'em on TV, put 'em on CNN every half-hour. What's fifteen minutes of fame when a guy's life is on the line?'

At the end of the table, Allie Parsons sat still, licking her lips, testing the mood of the party like a snake tasting the air with its tongue. Rod Fuller had refused her, Stephanie Sands had refused her. Worse, when Stephanie did go on TV – in Allie's mind it was inevitable – she would then be gilded with public attention, just as Allie was, except that her spotlight might be brighter. Allie was jealous and her venom rose.

'The poor woman.' Ted had stopped eating. 'I had no idea. And the boy's only small, isn't he? How's she taking it?'

'Well . . .' Belinda thought about Stephanie's pleading eyes and felt uncomfortable. The truth was the woman was devastated, but it was wrong to expect any of them to respond to that. People had lives, after all. 'OK, I suppose. They're just hoping it's over soon and he'll be back home.'

Allie noted her husband's concern and prepared to strike. 'A kidnap – that's some story, isn't it?'

Idly, Rachel picked up her lead. 'Yeah, it's almost too fantastic, isn't it? I mean, things like that don't happen, do they?'

'I guess if you choose to do business in Eastern Europe that's the sort of risk you take.' Ted considered that anyone who chose to do business more than a hundred miles from his own front door was crazy. OK, two hundred miles. Strankley Ridge was about one-twenty.

'But does he *really* do all that travelling? I mean, it's none of my concern, I don't know anything about these things, but he's been away an awful lot this year.'

'Don't look at me,' Josh took a piece of bread to wipe his plate. 'Generations of Carmans dedicated themselves to getting out of the Ukraine. How can we relate to anyone who actually wants to go over there?'

'I don't know.' Allie raised her eyes to the dark sky as if heaven was due to send down an explanation. 'It's always seemed to me – hasn't it seemed to you? – that there was something . . . I don't know . . .'

'They're very quiet.' Belinda was scanning her memories for abnormality. 'And they don't seem to have any family. I mean, they do, of course, but they're never around, are they?'

'You never know with people, do you?' Allie continued. 'I mean, she's fair-haired and he's fair-haired and their little boy is quite dark, isn't he?'

'Most of the characteristics of light-haired people are carried on recessive genes.' If there was to be a witch-burning, Rachel would put her bunch of faggots on the pile.

'You know she actually wanted us to cut down that hedge?' Belinda pointed to the barricade of foliage, indicating its blatant necessity.

'Lauren Pike says she went round there once past eleven in the morning and she was still in her nightdress.'

'It's odd, don't you think?'

'So what are you saying here, Allie?'

'Nothing, I . . . *you* had some problem with him, didn't you?' This was to Adam, who now sat withdrawn from the discussion, wrapped in a film of regret for the gravy. Back home, the maid always made the gravy. He had no idea how.

'With Stewart? A problem? As I recall,' he belched gently, 'he and that partner of his were going to tender for Oak Hill. I was all for it,' he spread his hands, palms upwards, there was nothing to hide. 'Then they backed out. For no good reason that they ever gave.'

'As you say, it was odd.' Ted felt justified in confirming that much. 'And embarrassing, frankly. We were about ready to go for the planning consents when they withdrew. But they're kind of young. For something as big as this. And I think it was all resolved to our advantage. I'm happy with the people we've got now. It's a bigger firm, and, looking back, Sands and his partner were perhaps a bit out of their league.'

And so it lay on the table before them, a proposition in four parts: one, that Stephanie and Stewart Sands were strange; two, that Stewart's absence was related to the state of their marriage; three, that their child was not his child; and four, that whatever evil befell them proceeded from their strangeness and irregular lifestyle, and was therefore their own fault.

In this region of shadows and bends, logic itself was elliptical. The forum considered the proposition proved, and restated it often in the days that followed, outside the schools, the church and the synagogue, in the changing rooms at Bon Ton, queueing for the Sunday roast at Catchpole & Forge, foraging the ready-meal counter in the Magno at Helford.

The night was silent. Sounds in the houses were muffled by lavishly interlined curtains and double-glazing. There were no noises on the streets. Only in the very far distance, probably out on the 31, the siren of a police car could be heard.

The party strained their ears and reminded themselves where their children were.

The siren rose as the car turned into the slip down to the Broadway, then cut off. The Carmans relaxed because their au pair was babysitting Ben and Jon. The DeSouzas were sure of Wendy, who was sleeping over with Chalice

Parsons, and reasonably sure of Freddie, who was at a party but not often in trouble.

Ted Parsons was despondent, because his heart already knew the truth. Westwick's police station was over in Helford, where all the community utilities were situated, on the far side of the 31. He was good friends with the chief constable, and a good contributor to the police benevolent fund. When Damon was picked up locally the station called the house. The siren meant he had been picked up in the city. In another ten minutes – thirteen if the lights on The Broadway were against them – the car would be in Church Vale.

Allie also knew the truth as it appeared to her, and looked steadfastly at the ground, because the trouble with Damon was all Ted's fault. Belinda began to clear up the plates.

'Time we made a move, I think.' Allie stood up to ward off any argument. 'I need my beauty sleep. Lovely food. It's always lovely food, you're such wonderful cooks. You *must* come to us soon. Very soon.'

'Steph, you must come for lunch.' Marcus's invitations always sounded like commands. She arranged for Max to play with Chalice Parsons in the afternoon, put on the black suit she had for client meetings and took the train from Westwick Green.

'The thing is, Steph, our insurance only covers us for three months. That's if it isn't a war situation. Then we aren't covered at all. There was a lot of yelling from the assessors but that Capelli guy told them. I can keep paying Stewart's salary a couple of months beyond, but if things don't resolve soon I'll have to take another look at it. You see what I'm saying here?'

She saw what he was saying. In the autumn there would be no more money. But Stewart would be home by then.

When she got back to Church Vale there was no answer from the Parsons' house. Stephanie passed two demented hours running between her house and theirs before Allie drew up in the studio car, casually imparting the news that her help had taken all three children to Helford Hospital because Cherish had thrown Chalice head-first downstairs. 'They don't think she's broken anything, thank heaven. It's not the first time.' With a little chuckle which implied that there were professions in which stupidity was an advantage, she added, 'I think she might be not too bright.'

'You mean the help?' Stephanie asked, weak with anxiety but momentarily entertaining the unspeakable opinion that when children came so close to murdering each other defective parenting might be involved.

'Chalice. I don't know about the girl yet, she's only been here a couple of weeks.' The Parsons' household suffered a rapid succession of domestic employees. Allie complained savagely if things were not done but seldom got around to telling the help what to do, much less to paying them.

Stephanie telephoned her mother. Lately they had spoken almost every day. 'Marcus says the insurance runs out in three months. Stewart should be home by then, shouldn't he?'

'Darling, do you think it's wise to count on that?' She

was dismayed at her daughter's tone of otherworldly certainty.

'I just hope he'll be home soon. I know it shouldn't be different, being alone now, when he travels so much, but . . .' Where Stewart had been there was a void. His clothes were not there to wash, his food was not there to cook, his telephone calls never came. His absence was fearful. She thought of him all the time, which made things worse. Nobody liked to put to Stephanie the possibility that her husband might not return at all.

'I know, darling, I know. You just have to keep busy – that's the secret.' Stephanie's mother was moved to confide what she considered an intimacy. 'That's what I did after your father. I made myself so busy I didn't have time to think. The golf club saved my life. And then, of course, I met your stepfather.'

'I suppose it couldn't hurt to build up the business a little.' It would take a moment for her mother to register that thought. Her concept of a woman's work was as a dating strategy; she had always had difficulty in understanding her daughters' careers.

'What business?' she said vaguely.

'My business. You know. Designing gardens. You're right, who knows how things will turn out? We've so little saved.' There was a stifled intake of breath on the telephone. Stephanie's mother thought at once of her own savings, and feared the day that her daughter might need support.

'Don't worry,' Stephanie followed with regrettable bitterness. 'If we're really stuck I can always rent out the house for six months.'

'Good idea,' her mother said warmly.

Angered, Stephanie went to work with commitment which surprised herself. Previously, she had run her business on social principles – nice clients only and not too far from either home or school. Now she seized every commission that came her way, especially the well-paid ones. She flattered clients, padded costings, rethought her pricing structure and sharpened up her invoicing. Her telephone rang all morning, her fax spouted paper, her desk became mountainous with briefs and sketches and piles of catalogues. She felt more secure but also disloyal.

With the house cluttered and the day full, the emptiness of her life still echoed. After six the phone fell silent. After Max was asleep, she sat up working, her desk a pool of light in the dim, silent house. Work was not enough. As the hours passed, her sickening fears accumulated until by midnight she was strung out with terror and unable to sleep. She held out against asking Rachel for pills, and against acknowledging the mistrust of her so-called friend which underlay her resistance.

She was certain that Westwick would nurture her – wasn't that the purpose of a community, to support its members when they needed it? She volunteered – to serve on the members' events sub-committee at The Cedars, to research air pollution for the Old Westwick Society, to run the cake stall at The Magpies Sports Day. She drew a project management chart of cakes promised, cakes to be frozen, cakes to be collected, cakes for which recipes had to be found. Then the phone rang all evening. On the empty sycamore table, baskets of paper appeared.

She volunteered to host the next meeting of the Old Westwick Society in the duly apologised absence of their chair, Lauren Pike, who was away on a psychologists' course. Then she forgot, so that, when the doorbell rang suddenly one afternoon, her heart raced. She jumped up from her desk and ran downstairs. Stewart was found, he was safe, they had come back to tell her. She ran to the hall, but there on the front path stood Clara Funk, secretary of the Society, clutching the velvet lapels of her baggy coat, and there beyond her on the street was Jemima Thorogood, another society stalwart, chaining her bicycle to a lamp-post. Stephanie's hopes crashed like an elevator in a disaster movie. It took strength to smile welcome.

'I hope we are not too early.' Mrs Funk peered about her as she came into the house. Patrolling the pavements, sitting beside her husband as he drove their old car very slowly around the streets, she was a familiar Westwick sight. People said she had lost all her family in concentration camps.

'Not at all,' Stephanie muttered.

'You did not forget?' demanded Mrs Funk.

'Oh no. Everything's all ready.' Only half a lie; the sitting room was orderly at least and with Sports Day imminent there were already six cakes in her freezer.

Across the road, the old Land Rover driven by the chairman of the environmental sub-committee was disgorging the balance of their quorum, two more grey-haired women, a humourless young man from the Nature Triangle Working Party, the prematurely aged ex-army man who served as their treasurer and two town-planning students working on theses of suburban development.

Stephanie asked Mrs Funk, 'Can I take your coat?'

It was a rhetorical question. Even in high summer, Mrs Funk kept her body layered with clothes, the rusty velvet coat fastened with straggling tassels over sweaters and scarves. The Funks had come to Westwick from Czechoslovakia at the end of World War II. Mrs Funk lived in layers of clothing as if she felt the need to protect her body from curious eyes. In winter, a black chenille beret sagged over her crag of a nose; tonight only a flowered wool scarf was tied over her staring brown hair, and she picked at the knot with gloved hands.

Energetically, Stephanie brewed tea and coffee, defrosted a cake, found pencils and checked on Max, who was absorbed in the adventures of Roadrunner. Under cover of these activities, she called up the draft of her paper on particulates and environmental health and printed it out.

Apologies for absence were received from Mrs S Appleyard, Dr R Carman, Mrs F Delingrand, Mrs R Lloyd-Richards, Mrs L Pike, Mr E Parsons and Mrs P Salmon. The minutes of the previous meeting were adopted with only two paragraphs of additional notes on the question of the proposed new street lights along Riverview Drive from Mrs Funk.

The lack of progress of the planning application for the Oak Hill Business Park was noted with lengthy approval. Support was readily pledged to the Grove Parade Traders' Association against new parking regulations. It was agreed that Willow Gardens, which unluckily led to a narrow stretch of tow-path, just negotiable by car, which was the only passage from Westwick to Helford that did not involve a junction on the 31, was becoming a rat-run for motorists and the secretary agreed to write to the Planning Department requesting a barrier on the tow-path and speed humps on the road.

The results of the study of the colony of red ghost moths discovered at the Oak Hill Nature Triangle were noted, although the chair of the environmental sub-committee pointed out that the return of this rare lepidopterous native should not be taken as an indication that there had been any reduction in the toxic vehicle emissions concentrated at the junction of the 31 and the 46, which remained above World Health Organisation recommended maximum levels. Reinforcing these concerns, Mrs Sands presented her paper on particulates and the incidence of asthma, and it was resolved to forward this to the Environment Department with a request for immediate action to reduce the emissions.

Mrs Funk spoke eloquently against the encroachment of bars and restaurants into the commercial sites of the Broadway previously occupied by useful small shops and the committee resolved seriously to consider the question of opposing the renewal of the licence of the Wilde At Heart. The date of the next meeting was set for one month's time, and the place the small room in St Nicholas's church hall, Mrs Sands to liaise with Father Strudwick and the St Nicholas Players. Mrs Sands was thanked for her hospitality and delicious coffee fudge sponge.

Mrs Funk left last, and in the hall she suddenly reached out for Stephanie's hand. 'I have heard terrible news about your husband,' she began.

'Not terrible . . .' protested Stephanie.

'Yes, terrible,' Mrs Funk affirmed righteously, her cloudy eyes wet with emotion. 'A terrible thing. You are a brave woman.'

'Not really . . .'

'*Yes*, really. I know. I know what it is to be brave. To have to be brave like you are. So. I say well done. And I say, if you are feeling alone, come and see us. Erich and I. You know where we live. Promise me, come and see us.'

'Yes,' Stephanie was embarrassed. 'Oh yes. Of course I will.'

'Promise me,' Mrs Funk demanded again from halfway down the path. 'We know what it is, remember.'

'I promise,' Stephanie lied, trying to look bright-eyed and cheery. The telephone rang in the kitchen. 'I must go now.'

Breathless with emotion rather than running for the call, Stephanie flipped the kitchen telephone off its bracket. The caller was a stranger, a man, his voice callous but young. 'Mrs Sands? I'm from the Helford and Westwick Courier. We've had some information that you've suffered a rather sad event just recently . . .'

'Who from?' she demanded, alarmed. Her arm, holding the receiver, was trembling. She leaned against the work-top for support.

'The police have confirmed it to us that your husband is missing . . .'

Damn WPC Clegg and her officious cold heart.

'We thought you might be able to talk to us about it, maybe give us some pictures, you and your family—'

'No,' she broke in decisively. 'I've already decided I don't want to do that. It's bad enough that this has happened without being exploited by the media. My son's only five, for goodness' sake.'

'People often find there's a lot of sympathy—'

'The Foreign Office advise me not to talk to newspapers,' she went on, knowing that there was no argument against this point. 'I'm sorry. I can't see any advantage to us in giving you what you want. I'm sure it would be nice for you, because nothing much goes on out here, but I have to think of myself and my family. Nobody else will, it seems.' And she rang off, clumsy with her shaking hand, before he could argue any more.

After that, the veneer of calm she had achieved through concentrating on the petty business of the neighbourhood was torn away. She sat down in the kitchen feeling defenceless, victimised, a pathetic helpless thing about to be torn apart by greedy predators. She wished Mrs Funk had not left. It occurred to her that no one else had made her a good offer of sympathy. When the telephone rang it was never a Westwick friend asking how she fared, alone with a five-year old and perhaps already a widow. The fact was she had heard less from her friends since the disaster than before.

In the city, when a bad thing happened and she couldn't talk to Stewart about it, she called one of The Crowd. A friend. The Crowd were friends for every need. Whatever your pain required, advice, psychobabble, a bottle of vodka, a night of talking, even comfort sex for those who found sex comforting, The Crowd would supply it. You had only to name your need.

She had expected the same from Westwick, but, she excused them, people here had more complex lives. They had children, they had husbands, Rachel had her clinic, Lauren her clients, Belinda her tennis and Allie her TV show. Her mind's ear heard Allie spelling out in tabloid sound bites the sensations which were still unreal to her: ordeal, anguish, heartbreak, grief.

Stephanie went out into her garden in the twilight. The jasmine was flowering now, the perfume was wonderful at night. She had imagined sitting out here with Stewart, while their children slept contentedly in their bedrooms above, all at peace at the end of the day. Her breathing was loud in the silence; someone should help her, but nobody was coming.

CHAPTER 6

The Vigilance Committee

'The search is continuing in the city of Astrakhan, just at the north of the Caspian Sea . . .' Mr Capelli paused to let her find the name on the map. Still true to his promise, he called from the Consular Division every morning at ten. He sounded young, but he spoke with authority and had the patience of a grandfather. 'On the estuary of the River Don. Got it?'

'Yes.' From the travel bookshop where they used to inform themselves for their holidays, Stephanie had bought herself a map, Soviet produced, captioned in bizarre English. She needed to reassure herself that this was not a fantasy. With nothing but Capelli's voice on the phone to ground her in reality, the word kidnap bounced off the walls of her mind. When she was alone her mood wavered violently between unnatural serenity and howling panic; without Stewart, her whole being seemed unstable.

'The new information suggests strongly that they are in the city. We've been aware of nationalist elements there for a while. Can you see the border with Chechnya is relatively close? The war may be over but our reports suggest that things are hardly settling down. There's been some migration by people whose allegiances were with minor factions. Kazakhstan is oil-rich, predicted to be richer than Kuwait by the year 2015. That's their incentive.'

Mr Capelli was her greatest comfort. She had discovered that he would talk on as long as she cared to listen, always fluent, always informed, always eager with phrases like 'our consular case report' and 'our counter-terrorism policy department' which imparted the reassurance that there was a magnificent official machine working full-stretch for Stewart's benefit.

After ten minutes, she felt foolish asking questions just to keep the flow of his confident voice rolling and brought the conversation to an end. On the map the Caspian Sea curled around like an evil foetus in the womb of central Asia, its head crested with grey to indicate land below sea level. Her imagination offered pictures of flooded streets and pestilent swamps and Stewart dying of diseases long eradicated in the developed world.

To stabilise her mind, she turned the map sideways to read the scale, put her ruler against the page and calculated that Astrakhan was 400 kilometres from Grozny, the name faintly familiar from half-heard news bulletins. To the north, Volgograd was the same distance. She had last heard Stewart's voice from Volgograd. Her calculator told her that 400 kilometres was 250 miles. On the facing page was a map showing population density, on which the region of Astrakhan was coloured burnt siena, indicating 10.25 inhabitants per square kilometre. There were five million Kazakhs in the total population. On the next map the whole area around the Don was coloured light green for arable land with meadow, permanent grassland and grazing.

She was sitting at the little desk in an alcove outside their bedroom which Stewart used for household business. He was a major empty desk man, generating surfaces which were blatantly bare, boasting spaciously of decisions actioned and paperwork eliminated. A screen, a space, that was it. The mouse and the keyboard were concealed in a nifty drawer, the fax and phone had a hidden shelf, the cables were invisibly integrated.

Stephanie was for clutter, up to a point. In fact, quite a high point. She was also attached to paper. It was, after all, derived from vegetable matter. Baskets with documents lapping over their edges felt industrious. Well-stuffed files were a testament to security. You never knew when you were going to need a list or a letter or a certificate or something.

She conducted the business of The Terrace Garden Design Studio among slithering, fluttering mounds of paper, and Stewart administered everything else from this naked desk. They were one of those fraternal couples who looked alike and thought alike, so this pocket of disharmony in their relationship was exciting. They made much of it, this little interface of yin and yang. She crowed when his system crashed. He laughed when she could not find her driver's licence. She gave him Dr Solomon's Anti-Virus programme for his birthday. He gave her a magnetic badge reading 'hedgehog on the information superhighway'.

He ran the household accounts on a spreadsheet which he had taught her how to enter several times. She had the instructions written down on a piece of paper inside the cover of her organiser. Or maybe on the pinboard. Or the pending tray. Or if not there, down the back of her desk where things which fell off the pinboard might be found. When he went away, which he had done more than they were comfortable with in the past year, she preserved their mail casually in a willow basket to demonstrate that life was perfectly viable without the computer. When he came back, he updated the system and threw the papers away.

Somehow, in the six weeks Stewart had been missing, treacherous paper had crept on to his desk. Here was a note she had written herself about ferns, a catalogue of children's clothes, the leaflet from a new moisturiser, a couple of cards from her Rolodex. Here also was the morning's mail, and among it something she had read once and hidden under the rest until she was ready to read it again, a letter from Marcus. 'I am sending on to you a note from the partnership's insurers . . . you should be aware that in this situation we can continue to pay Stewart's salary at the full rate only until next month and at 50 per cent for a further three months afterwards. Our cover does not extend beyond that time.'

Marcus was a pig. Everything was money to him, his heart was a balance sheet, his veins ran dollars. He should be lying filthy and unshaven chained to the wall in some windowless concrete basement crawling with cockroaches, and Stewart should be here at this desk, the bridge of this enterprise, their family.

The letter ought to be filed. She wanted to burn it. It would poison the house. People did not write such letters unless they had legal significance, it had to be kept. In the end she devised a compromise, screwed it into a ball and threw it into the waste bin, planning to recover it when she felt better. You're crazy, she told herself. Without Stewart you're going mad.

She went back to the map. How had they travelled 250 miles? In a car with a gun to his head and a jittery finger on the trigger and potholes in the road? The Beirut hostages had been taped up like mummies and nailed into crates like coffins. Why had she ever agreed to see *Pulp Fiction*? Horrible muddled visions were filling her empty head when the doorbell rang.

In the morning, doorbells in Westwick rang for service calls – the dog walkers, laundry deliveries and Derek and Dave reporting with the summer bedding for her clients, who abhorred contact with the soil. Stephanie did not see herself as mature enough to need such services. From behind the curtains of Max's room she saw Lauren Pike on her front path.

'I thought perhaps it was about time I came round.' Being trim, immaculate and blonde, Lauren was not a natural for the role of Hera in the neighbourhood Olympus. Allie had once compared her to a West Highland Terrier, game for anything in her jolly little way. As was required of the wife of the BSD, Lauren had grand manner to assume for the right occasion, and Stephanie saw that this visit was such an event. Lauren had put on a suit, and carried a folder.

'You know we've started a victim support scheme,'

she opened, tight-jawed. 'We get names passed to us by the police. When your name came up, since I know you, it seemed the natural thing. But, listen, you can send me away if you want. I'll quite understand. I mean, you might prefer to talk to someone you don't know. It can be easier. Or you might be perfectly OK and not want to talk to anyone. We're just here to offer support if you think it's something you'd like.'

'Oh. Oh – well, how wonderful.' Stephanie felt quite feeble with relief.

'You're sure? I wouldn't be at all offended, really . . .' Lauren stood resolute on the doorstep, unwilling to risk the offence of intrusion until positively assured.

'Lauren, I'm quite sure. You're a dear, kind friend to take me on. Do, come in. I'll make us some tea.' *At last.* Another sign of madness; she had started communicating in two modes, verbally with the rest of the world to whom she said what was necessary, internally with a voice that said what she thought. *At last.* All these days she had been standing in pain, and all around her people had been brightly correct, concerned to distract her, comfort her, make her strong. She had begun the conspiracy herself, frantic to betray nothing when what she really wanted to do was lie on the ground and scream. Weeping through a box of tissues under Lauren's guidance might be almost as good. Bless this excellent social ecosystem, this community that contained everything necessary for life to flourish.

They sat in the garden. Lauren took the centre of the bench and kept her legs parallel and away from the wood for fear of splinters. Her ankles, girlish perfection when in tennis socks, looked brittle and fussy out of them. She pulled the hem of her dark blue skirt even. Navy blue, Stewart had once said, was the pink of Maple Grove.

'There hasn't been any more news?'

'I'd just finished speaking to the Foreign Office when you arrived. They've narrowed it down to one city.'

'That's encouraging, isn't it?' Brightly, she opened the folder and Stephanie glimpsed Nile-green sheets of fuzzy recycled paper. 'So they're being good about keeping in touch then. Do you think this man feels disappointed when they've got nothing to tell you?'

'Yes, maybe.'

Lauren uncapped her fat Mont Blanc pen, then put it down and reached for her cup of tea. She had asked for peppermint tea with sweeteners. In her own home she had loose-leaf tea in spherical silver infusers. Her hand paused over the cup; she seemed unable to decide what to do with her tea bag. 'And how about Max? You've explained it all to him, I suppose?'

Stephanie sighed, feeling she had been cowardly here. 'Sort of. They have such a vague sense of time at this age, don't they? I'm not sure he can really understand.'

'I should know – how old is he, exactly?' There were forms in the folder, and Stephanie noticed that the prissy way Lauren had chosen to sit aslant the bench enabled her to hide what she was writing.

'He'll be six in November.'

'And does he ask after his father?'

'Well – you know Max.' Felix, the youngest of the three Pike children, was in the same class as Max at The Magpies. Between the two boys existed an absolute void of empathy; as far as Stephanie could discover they did not dislike each other, merely recognised, with the cruel sincerity of infants, that they shared absolutely nothing beyond the same class environment for thirty hours a week. 'He's just like his father, really. A boy of few words. He never asks for anything except to watch *Rug Rats* on Saturday morning.'

Lauren raised her Ventolin and took a shot. She did not approve of *Rug Rats*. 'So his father didn't communicate very well?'

'Oh no, I wouldn't say that at all. Stewart's a talker, definitely. That's why he tends to do these trips – the early client contact is his responsibility because he's naturally just very persuasive when he's talking about something he believes in. But when there's something on his mind, you'd only know because he won't talk about it.'

Lauren was not writing anything. She fiddled with her inhaler, turning it end over end on the table top; she had her head on one side with a small fixed smile and seemed to be widening her eyes like a pair of zoom lenses. Stephanie had never witnessed this performance before. 'And you feel Max imitates Stewart?'

'Not exactly – I think they're quite like each other, that's all.'

'So Max accepts him; there weren't any difficulties with that?'

Shaking her head, Stephanie felt uneasy. Now Lauren was fussing with her folder. She had clearly been hoping for some disclosure which Stephanie had not made. Her speech was flattening under a ridiculous artificial modulation. 'And how long is it that you've been married?'

'Almost seven years. Our anniversary's this month. Isn't that corny – a June bride?'

'Most people would say it was very nice.' She was writing now, taut strokes of the pen putting hieroglyphs on the form. 'Seven years, did you say?'

'Yes.' Disbelief – she actually sensed it and she was sure she was right. 'I was there when we got married, you know. I've got pictures to prove it.' This was not working out as Stephanie had hoped.

The zoom lenses and the weird grin were Lauren's professional manner, intended to convey a superior, enlightened sympathy. 'Oh yes, that's your wedding photograph in the dining room, isn't it? I remember it. Very pretty dress. So – about you and Stewart, how were things before he went away?'

'The same as always. Just normal.'

'Just normal.'

'We didn't have any problems, if that's what you mean.'

'No problems.' Her eyes were almost popping now.

'Why?' Distinctly, Stephanie was aware of feeling harried.

'Why?'

'Yes – Lauren, I'm mystified. Why would how things were in our marriage be significant? Or how long we'd been married. It's not as if I could arrange for him to be kidnapped because he kept leaving the toilet seat up or something.'

'Stephanie – you've lost me. Nobody was suggesting . . . look, perhaps this wasn't the best idea.' She snapped the folder closed in disappointment. 'Let me give you our helpline number; if there is anything you need to talk about you can ring. Any time, it's twenty-four hours. People take turns to be on call. We can put you in touch with a trained counsellor in your area if later on perhaps you feel you can't cope or you'd like to see someone. OK?' Now she was on her feet and preparing to go, almost squeaking with the desire to be elsewhere and leave this embarrassing interlude behind.

In the hall she stopped and said she needed to use the bathroom, and put her folder and her pen on their claw-footed Empire console. It was one of the symbols of the early Stewart and Stephanie days, dragged home in five shards from a junk shop after their honeymoon and kept in a cupboard for two years before Stewart took a month to fix it together and Stephanie added the lightly dis-tressed paint finish and metal-gilding on the carving.

Stephanie opened the folder. The form was headed 'Helford & Westwick Victim Support'. She ran her eye down it, deciphering words in Lauren's large, loopy script. She read: 'Son/stepfather rel?' The word 'denial' stood out. 'Withdrawn' could be distinguished. She heard the lavatory flush and closed the folder.

'Shall we see you at The Cedars later?' Lauren had recomposed herself as if she kept poise in a handbag com-pact ready to freshen up during the day. 'It's our class today, isn't it?' Bunbuster was the kind of word which did not fit in Lauren's mouth.

For a merciful moment, Stephanie had no breath with which to reply. Options rushed past – smile, agree, comply? Smile, evade, withdraw? Challenge, demand, protest? To her surprise, she caught the last set by the tail.

'Lauren, could I look at that form?'

'It won't help you,' was the tart reply, and the form was picked up with ceremony to invest it with official status. 'They're just for us. They're confidential.'

Stephanie caught her nervous gaze and held it to the point of rudeness. Lauren's irises were chalky and opaque, the blinds were down on the windows to her soul. Under her make-up, she was colouring but she would not be stared down. In the end, Stephanie said, 'Lauren, this is me – please, can we talk about this like women? I've looked at it already. Of course you're entitled to write what you want, but I don't understand things like "stepfather". Stewart's parents have been married thirty years, he has no stepfather. I'm concerned that you're recording stuff that isn't right. And I'm concerned anyway – I don't know what that conversation in the garden just now was all about.'

Lauren was now a colour close to that of Maple Grove brick, and blinking emphatically. Her small chest heaved as she redoubled her self-control. 'I'm so sorry that you saw that,' she returned on gracious autopilot. 'That really should not have happened. We – we get our information passed on from the police and someone has obviously made a mistake. And of course, I was *misguided* to take your case, I can appreciate that now. Do, please, forgive me. I'm really not experienced at this yet. Let's just say I was wrong and put it behind us – we musn't fall out, must we?' And she extended her hand, evenly tanned from daily tennis, and Stephanie found herself shaking it although she felt like stabbing her fingers into the opaque grey eyes which were now cast down in suitable repentance. *Fuck you, get out of my house.* 'No harm done,' were Lauren's final words before she marched out to her car.

Stephanie shut her door and leaned on it, in shock. It was a moment or two before she could focus. A woman she had considered a friend had grabbed the first opportunity to call her a liar and rummage in her life for the evidence. Her family life. She felt violated. Lauren's parting chatter echoed in the hallway like a bad smell, the slick patter of social superiority. She had distant memories of her paternal grandfather, promoted from the ranks on the eve of D-Day, rhapsodising about the officer class and their behavioural ideals, and of her father and the smokescreen of phoney gallantry behind which he bounced cheques and had affairs. These status tricks, these too she had intended to leave behind when they moved to Westwick.

She went out into her garden – her Prozac, her opium, her safe oblivion. The first time they had left Dad, her grandmother had taken her into the garden, away from the screaming and the stuffing of suitcases. It had been raining. Tiny pools shimmered at the centre of each lupin leaf. There was a fairy ballroom at the bottom of each one, her grandmother explained, where orchestras played and dancers whirled and the daylight twinkled through the water like the sparkle of chandeliers.

Topaz Lieberman felt she did her best work before dawn. At the business end of the kitchen, she cleared a space for her books around the computer by moving things which had invaded the desk to their proper places: the basket of clean washing on to the ironing board, a tray of seedlings to the conservatory, the telephone to its wall bracket, the cat litter sack to the utility room, the midnight blue satin bra and a pair of green snakeskin high-heeled sandals to the stair from where they might or might not progress back to the drawers and cupboard in her mother's bedroom over the following fortnight.

She wiped the screen with anti-static cloth, angled the keyboard as she liked it at 35 degrees to the screen, paused to throw away three mouldy nectarines in the bowl because the sight of them bugged her, powered up and began to write.

'Joseph Stalin: His Path To Power.' Click click, mark and underline. Line, line. 'Three men fought for the leadership of the USSR in the power vacuum created by the death of Lenin on 21 January 1924. Lenin, although in his early fifties, had been a dying man since his first stroke in May 1922. In his final hours Stalin, general secretary of the Communist Party, was asserting himself as never before at the Party conference.'

The silence was unreal. When the cat came in from the garden, the cat flap crashed in the quiet; knowing better than to disturb Topaz at her work, the animal bolted furtively upstairs to a welcoming bed. In the distance, a single car roared along The Broadway from Maple Grove. Peace, order, sterility. The parable of Switzerland and the cuckoo clock. If one of those ants stopped moving, would you really care? Topaz allowed herself a nanosecond to yearn for the tumult of Bolshevik action, for ranting and storming, the thunder of boots in corridors, the roaring of mobs in streets. She slipped the encyclopedia disc into the CD drive and scanned in a photograph of the young, lean-jawed Joseph Vissarionovich Dzhugashvili (a name indicating Jewish ancestry) in a peaked cap and worn greatcoat.

'Stalin's Leadership Strategy.' Her slender, tapering fingers rattled the keys with enthusiasm. Click, click, mark, underline. Click click, bullet points. 'Strategic alliance against Trotsky. Line. Suppression of Lenin's critical testament. Line. Proactive moves against Trotsky. Line. Identification with famine relief measures. Line. Popular policy objectives. Line. Trotsky isolated from military.' The man was just awesome. The way he wasted Zinoviev, just incredible. She scanned in a contemporary cartoon of a floored Trotsky defenceless before the massed bayonets of his opponents.

She stopped when it was light, closed the file, poured herself a long glass of milk and went into the on-line banking service. No change. On the Gaia business account the balance was just enough to cover the loan interest due in at the end of the week. On the personal account they were overdrawn already with ten days to go until the end of the month and Molly down to captain the school under-14s in the county finals on Saturday, which meant fares and snacks and entry fees. There was the tax money in the savings account, her major achievement of the year, but Topaz's spreadsheet told her that it was not enough. The Liebermensch were barely hanging on by their fingernails.

She closed down the computer, laid the table for

breakfast, pulled another load of washing out of the machine and pinned it up on the line outside. The cat had been at the trash again, rubbish was blowing over the tangle of vegetation her mother designated a physic garden. From among the stinking fronds of wormwood she pulled half a letter.

The letter had been torn in two while still unopened in its envelope, the method of dispatch her mother used to favour for bills before Topaz had educated her. This was not a bill. This was a handwritten letter, which suggested to Topaz a person of an earlier generation, probably also of a sentimental temperament. The other half of the letter was still in the garbage, stuck to a crescent of pizza crust – *Fiorentina*, Mum's usual, spinach and three cheeses, alleged to send a donation to the Florence Rescue Fund with every order. Gemma never could get the difference between low-fat and vegetarian.

Topaz took the letter indoors, extracted the halves from the envelope and taped them back together. As she suspected, the signature was 'Ted' and the text was the kind of pathetic mush people were reduced to when hormones were in control. Hormones mystified Topaz. Her own never disturbed her mental balance, they would not dare. Hormones had stuck her mother with three kids and no money to raise them, not really a viable life choice. Looking at other people, Topaz had concluded that hormones produced the kind of distraction which definitely blocked the path to power. Look at Clinton. And surely it was no coincidence that Stalin's greatest years were right after Nadia Aliluieva killed herself at the age of 30.

She put the letter in her bag and went upstairs. 'Wake up, Flora.' She shook her sister by the foot, pinching the boot-calloused toes. 'Don't forget it's your day for ironing today. Come on, Molly, time to get up. You're to eat your cereal this morning, don't think you can throw it down the sink and I won't know because I will.'

'Coach doesn't want us getting fat,' mumbled Molly from under her pillow.

'Coach cares about cups and medals, doesn't care whether you're crippled at thirty. You're just another body to him, he has no appreciation of adult female metabolic requirements. You'll be out of his life in a couple of years and he'll be starving a new team. Women who eat a diet deficient in essential oils and calories risk premature osteoporosis, you know that.'

'No I don't,' was the defiant response. Topaz thought of what a labour camp could do for her sister's attitude, but contented herself by dragging the Polly Pocket quilt off her prone form and warning, 'And tidy this room up before you leave. Flora, you make sure it's done. And don't forget to wake Gemma.'

While she rode over to the Magno store at Helford and labelled apples for two hours before school, she considered the question of the letter. Her mother's business was carrying too much debt, it was sick. Actually, so sick they couldn't sell it, although it was doubtful that her mother had marketed the enterprise sincerely. The stock turnover was virtually non-existent, because most of the plants they ordered died. While Gemma had a contract with Ted Parsons' company she brought in enough money to keep the household afloat.

Topaz asked herself why in the world her mother had suddenly elected to walk out on the job. It was quite typical of her to contract an inappropriate involvement, and, obviously, some kind of lover's tiff had taken place, but in Topaz's reasoning these considerations were trivial and easily resolved.

Denouncement, that was the right strategy. And purge the opposition. Flora had a field camp meeting today in any case. And little Courtenay Fuller was coming back with Molly, and she was the mushiest creature in the universe. Luck had always smiled on Stalin, too.

'Mum,' Topaz began that evening, as soon as Gemma was standing contentedly in front of the stove stirring the rice, sipping from the glass of wine in her free hand, 'I found this beautiful letter in the garden.'

She unfolded the repaired page and held it carefully out of her mother's reach. At the far end of the table, Molly and Courtenay looked up from their improvements to Polly Pocket's Pony Gymkhana.

'How dare you read my letters!' Gemma exclaimed, putting down her glass and lunging for it as Topaz had anticipated. Gemma Lieberman was built to lounge rather than lunge. Wearing platform sandals and a long aubergine-coloured dress elaborated with ruffles and fringes and trailing cuffs, she was not dressed for quick movement. She dragged a lettuce off the worktop and scared the cat with a clatter of falling utensils while Topaz drifted serenely away behind the little girls without looking as if she had moved. 'Give me that,' she demanded, knowing her daughter had won again. 'It's private. You had no right to look at it.'

'I'm sorry, Mum. I thought it might be important. I've never seen a real love letter before. I didn't know people still wrote things like that.'

At the word 'love' the attention of Molly and Courtenay was riveted on Gemma. 'I said, give it to me.' Gemma lunged again and her hair, which hung like unravelled rope to her waist, snagged in a door handle. She yanked it free and held out her hand, demanding the letter.

'You tore it up,' Topaz protested in her calm, deep voice, 'and it wasn't even opened. I thought you must have made a mistake. I mean, people don't write love letters nowadays, do they? I thought you might want to keep it, it might be precious. I mean, supposing you both died and you never knew he loved you – wouldn't that be tragic?' The little girls were wide-eyed at the notion.

'Come on, Topaz. You just think it's tragic I'm not getting a paycheck from Tudor Homes any more.'

'No, I don't. It's like . . .' Topaz struggled for the words. Emotional stuff was so hard to express. 'It's like you said about love being sort of energy, like breath or something. I thought you couldn't really want to just block it out like that.'

'You don't know what you're talking about. This has nothing to do with love.' Gemma had a good sense for her eldest daughter's strategies, but she could not decently accuse Topaz of having the mentality of a pimp in front of Molly and her friend. Nor could she claim that love was entirely out of the picture; Ted had been kind to her, a response for which she had not been

prepared. 'Look, you've got it wrong.' She opened negotiations in a reasonable tone designed to give the lie to
the usual allegations of irrationality, 'That letter isn't
precious and it is *not* a love letter. It's something I will
never want to remember from someone I want to forget,
and the kind of letter I hope you never have to deal
with when you're an adult. Which is why I threw it
away. Now put it back in the rubbish where you found
it. I promise you, that is its proper place.' She was
pleased with that, it struck the perfect note of high
parental piety.

'You're upset about it,' Topaz countered.

'I'm upset that you decided to get hold of it and read
it, Topaz.'

'I thought it was a sweet letter. He writes some lovely
things, really quite poetic. Are you sure you don't even
want to read it?'

'You ought to read it, Mum,' Molly observed, her eyes
huge with curiosity. 'Supposing he died and you never
knew he loved you.'

'It's trying to persuade me to do something wrong,
Molly, so why should I read it? If I don't want to be persuaded, I can just throw the letter away and then there's
no danger.'

'Can I see it? What does it say that's so lovely?' Molly
persisted.

'Oh, that'd be *so* sad,' sighed Courtenay, combing her
micro-pony's luxuriant mane.

Gemma smouldered at her eldest daughter, indicating that she considered Topaz irresponsible for raising
adult affairs in front of infants. Topaz iced her mother,

conveying that a parent had no right to let personal feelings interfere with her responsibility to provide for her children. Hadn't the brothels of the Caucasus funded the Bolshevik victory?

'You're treating me like *Boule de Suif*, Topaz, and I don't deserve that.' Gemma shoved her hair off her face and skewered half of it into a bun with a handy satay stick.

With ceremony, Topaz folded the letter. 'You might change your mind one day and want to know what it says. If you don't want to keep it, I'll keep it for you. In my room. So if you ever want it, just ask me.' The entire household, even including the cat, knew better than to invade Topaz's room.

'Fine,' Gemma shrugged her shoulders, hitched up her bra straps and turned back to the rice pot. Holding the letter with reverence, Topaz moved towards the spiral staircase incongruously introduced into the kitchen area sometime in the seventies when the house's previous owner knocked out all the internal walls at the ground floor level. She took her time; Stalin knew when to be patient.

'My dad says love is the answer.' Courtenay turned back to her game and mounted a tiny plastic horsewoman on her horse.

'My dad said if love was the answer he was glad he didn't hear the question,' Molly cantered her tiny plastic horse up to a tiny plastic gate, 'but he's a crazy person and they can say anything.' A tiny plastic refusal occurred. 'Bad pony. That's three faults.'

'Make him do it again,' Topaz advised from the stairs.

'You should never let a horse get away with a refusal, you know that.'

In the deep of night, the telephone rang in the Parsons house. Ted was still awake. He had been sleeping badly. 'We've got your son again,' the caller told him, in a portentous man-to-man tone.

'Oh God,' he responded.

'Yes,' the caller affirmed, sucking in an accusatory breath.

'Has he been charged?'

'Not this time.'

'I'm most grateful.'

'Yes.'

'Is there damage?'

'Damage? Damage, John?' the caller demanded of someone across the room. The answer was drowned. In the background his son was bellowing like a distressed bullock.

'Some damage, yeah. A vehicle involved.'

'He stole a car?'

'Nah – vehicle was one of ours,' the caller confirmed. Then, without being asked, added, 'We'll bring him over. Ten minutes.'

Ted and Allie slept in a super-king-size bed whose lavish latitude, covered in riotous rose chintz of an authentic nineteenth-century design, looked magnificent in photographs and suggested marital bliss of a high order. In reality it enabled the couple to sleep together with no fear of physical contact. Ted trekked around the bed to wake his wife. Gently, he put his hand on her shoulder. Violently, she reared up from her pillows and hit him.

'Your fucking son,' she yelled, sitting up and grabbing the quilt around her. 'That piece of shit. Why doesn't he just run under a truck?'

'I didn't know you were awake,' he apologised, tasting blood from the inside of his lower lip.

'Get out of here. Get out on the street. Stop them waking the fucking neighbourhood.'

He took cash from the safe in the dressing room and filled his wallet. A few minutes later he was fully dressed, and waiting at the roadside ready to begin damage limitation when the squad car appeared. Whispering, which induced the police officers to lower their voices in imitation, Ted got the party into the house. The neighbourhood, he calculated, was less likely to wake than Cherish and Chalice. Poor sleep patterns seemed to have been passed on in his genes.

Damon, now unconscious and heavy as a horse, was manhandled to the sofa in the family-size eat-in kitchen, and the officers assembled around the oak farmhouse table to begin the paperwork.

The charges were to be assault with a weapon, criminal damage, resisting arrest, using insulting language, possession of marijuana and damaging a police vehicle. 'He followed a woman out of Filthy McNasty's bar in Helford.' The senior officer related the events with fatherly regret. 'Asked her to come home with him and pulled a knife. Four guys from the bar saw it and piled in. Bar windows are out, he threw a table. Glass injuries, broken bones. They got the paramedics out, he attacked them. Terrible language. Tore the buttons off one of my officer's uniforms with his teeth. Parked his lunch in our car, just to finish things off nicely.'

'I'm so sorry.' Ted wanted to crawl under the table and scream.

'So're we. Can't take it off the road tonight, we're a car short already.'

No, he wanted to be a long way away, say up on Strankley Ridge with the rabbits and no representative of any other mammalian species, especially not *Homo supposedly-sapiens*.

Among his minor weaknesses, Ted counted a tendency towards honesty. Devious went against the grain with him, but he would do what had to be done. He rubbed his eyes and nerved himself. The first time Damon had come home in a squad car, the arresting officers had patiently talked him through the routine. Now he was getting suave with it. 'What can I do?' was the opening move. 'Let me get an idea of the level of damage we're talking about here.'

He had the charges down to drunk and disorderly plus plain assault, and was about to explore the possibility that the bar owner would prefer restitution of a direct and personal nature to waiting on the deliberation of the Criminal Compensation Board when Allie appeared in the doorway. She was fully made up and wearing a pink silk kimono which ended above her knees. The famous lock of silky blonde hair fell over eyes now blue with innocence.

'Oh dear. I am *so*, so sorry.' She perched on the sofa's edge to smooth her poor boy's troubled brow. 'He's just under so much stress with his exams, you know. There's so much pressure on children these days, it's just too much for them, don't you think?' She crossed the kitchen and got some glasses from a cupboard. The three officers were mesmerised by the flicker of sinews in her calves. 'Have we offered you something? Or are you still on duty?'

It was established that the senior officers were about to go off duty, while the youngest was driving. Ted invited them to sample a bottle of fifteen-year-old Island malt which an associate had given him that very day. It transpired that the senior officer's ancestors were from Skye. His wife enjoyed *Family First* very much and looked forward to baking the Cake of the Week. The Lemon-and-Lime Mousse Gateau had not risen as it should, although it had tasted superb all the same.

'We're doing Chocolate Pecan Brownies this week.' She invested the promise with as much glamour as if they were planning to confide the secret formula of Coca-Cola. 'It's such a great recipe – I'm sure they'll be just perfect. Of course, we have a professional caterer test all our recipes, but we had to change the firm we used a while ago because we were getting complaints. You must let me send you some tickets for the show – it's so good when we get a really smart audience in, the whole thing just gets wild.'

The senior officer was gratified to have his opinion validated.

'And this poor girl.' Allie pouted in sisterly compassion

for her son's victim. 'How is she? She must have been petrified. He's a big boy now.'

'She was pretty mad,' the junior cop contributed. 'She was saying all kinds of things.'

'Mad?' Allie's eyes widened with hope. 'You mean – she's not quite right?'

'She's right enough if you ask me,' answered senior officer, draining his tumbler which Ted solemnly refilled at once. 'Works in some law firm. Hot stuff. Spouting this act and that case.'

'Oh – not a secretary, then?'

'Trainee, she said. Mind you, these women tell one story to us and when you get to court it's another thing.'

'Terrible shock for a young woman. I'm sure she was nice looking.'

'Depends what your taste is,' the driver replied, watching with a sour face as his superiors lowered the level of the precious malt at an astonishing rate. 'Didn't reckon much to her myself.'

'A woman can always make the best of herself,' Allie observed brightly.

'She'd done that. She was having a night out, no question.'

'The *poor* girl,' Allie sighed, and the drinkers drank, ingesting also the impression that daylight would reveal Damon Parsons' potential victim as a stupid, unstable young slapper unlikely to cross-examine well.

At 5 am, after an egg-and-sausage breakfast enthusiastically cooked by Ted, the officers left, leaving both whisky bottle and Ted's wallet empty. In exchange, the senior officer handed over Damon's weapon, a rusted Swiss Army penknife chosen for the implement for getting stones out of horse's hooves.

'Get him off there,' Allie commanded Ted when he returned to the kitchen. She was walking up and down the room, jittery with anger. 'That sofa'll be ruined if he pisses himself.' And because her husband did not react immediately she picked up an empty glass and threw it at him. It hit a worktop, fell to the Provençale tiled floor and shattered.

'I can't carry him,' he told her, aware of his cut lip now smarting from the whisky.

'I didn't ask you to carry him. Let him lie on the floor, for God's sake. Disgusting thing. Disgusting. Look at his shirt, for God's sake, look at it. I'll kill you if you get that on the covers. He's an animal, he should lie on the floor.'

Fearing the rising hysteria in her voice, Ted slowly rolled his son on his side and eased his bulk, legs first, down on the tiles. 'Lucky he stayed in the area this time. At least the cops know us.'

'If they hadn't banned him at the Wilde At Heart he'd never have got into this state.'

Wearily, Ted stopped himself contradicting her. Damon had been able to get into this state wherever in the world he was since the age of ten.

'He'll have to go back to that re-hab place.' She was approaching the knife, which lay on the table with the blade open.

'He won't stay. He checked himself out after a day and a half, remember?' From the corner of his eye he saw that Cherish, in her Forever Friends pyjamas, had appeared silently in the doorway.

'Must you be so negative? If that place isn't secure, I'll find a place that is. Find somewhere that locks 'em up. God knows where you think I'm going to get the time to run around the country looking for a place, but I'll do it if you won't. He's not bitching up my life as well as his own. I'll have him locked up – why not? He's a fruitcake. A secure mental hospital. What they call it? Sectioned? It'll be for his own safety, he'll kill himself at this rate anyway.'

'He's not mad,' Ted protested, keeping his distance and trying not to look at the knife in case she followed his glance. 'He's just dumb.'

'You'd know, would you?' she demanded, getting into a well-worn groove. 'Where were you when he was screaming his guts out round the clock from the day he was born? Out to meetings, out to lunch, out to dinner – that's where you were. Your usual table, sir. May I recommend the fucking Krug, sir? And I was locked up with him in this fucking house. Don't tell me he's normal.'

He breathed easier as she walked past the knife. Too soon. She heard him. Quick as a lizard she whirled around, seized it and ran at him.

Cherish let out a screech of utter fear. Ted dodged the blade and grabbed for the arm which held it but the whisky had made him clumsy and she was too quick for him. 'Get out of here,' she screamed at the child, waving the knife furiously at father and daughter in turn. 'You fucking little bitch, you had to get up, didn't you?'

Cherish let out scream after scream. Blonde like her sister, she was undersized for eight and pitifully thin. The exertion brought no colour at all to her little grey face.

On the staircase behind her, Ted saw Chalice appear, trailing a quilt. Another scene.

'Alex,' he said, hoping her real name would connect her with reality if only for an instant, 'the girls are upset. Let them see you put the knife down so they'll know everything's OK.'

'Everything is not OK,' she protested with bitter sarcasm. 'Their brother is dead drunk, their father is dead beat and their mother will be on camera after two hours fucking sleep.'

He tried to hold her gaze but her eyes were flickering around the room, looking for further cause for anger. They found nothing. 'Huh.' She exhaled viciously. 'Hah.' In another few seconds, quite playfully, she tossed the knife into the sink. 'Go on,' she told them, roaming the floor once more. 'Go on. Go away now. All of you. Just – leave me alone.'

'I'm going to take the girls upstairs.' When it came to moving, he did not have the nerve to turn his back on her but retreated step by step towards the door. He gathered Chalice in his arms, hustled across the hall to get Cherish by the hand and made himself climb the stairs to their bedroom at a normal speed.

Chalice was trembling and teary. Cherish was stiff with fright, her white limbs were actually rigid as she lay in her bed. Neither of them could speak. There was a storybook, a present from his mother, and he read from it with all the animation he could summon, but his daughters lay in their beds and stared at the ceiling. Outside, he knew, the sun was over the horizon and the day was already light. No one was going to sleep.

'*Nessun dorma*,' he sang softly, '*che*—'

'That's the football song,' Chalice said, rolling her shadowy eyes around to watch him.

'Yes,' he agreed. 'Do you like it?'

'Singing is for dick-heads,' she replied, in perfect resonance with her mother.

He fell silent and closed his eyes, thinking of Damon, grunting in beery oblivion on the cold kitchen floor. Certainly, it was true that the boy had changed their lives. Allie had conceived him as soon as she had landed her first screen job and, in the drama of that career breakthrough, failed to notice the signs until she was so far advanced that the pregnancy could not be terminated, for all she insisted and demanded and ran from one clinic to another with her gold Amex card.

It was then that she first entered the state of cold rage which was now normal, from which she never emerged. And it had been he, Ted, God help him, who had tried to soothe her fury by calculating that the programme's Christmas break fell exactly a month before the baby's due date. 'You could only be off screen for a few weeks,' he had pleaded. 'I could drop the baby on the studio floor and carry on working,' she retorted. 'I suppose that's what you want?'

Damon had been born by Caesarean on December 23, much more premature than expected, destined to spend the first month of his life in hospital until his lungs were fully mature, a sad creature with loose, mottled red skin over his tiny bones. Allie, in contrast, made an excellent recovery, to no worldly purpose as her show was axed before her stitches healed.

For ten months she had no job. Her mood descended to a burning apathy, while the baby screamed to the limit of his growing strength. Night or day, he seldom slept for more than ten minutes at a stretch. 'He's a high-energy kid,' Allie announced, 'like me. He can't switch off.' She went to a spa for a month. The nurse who moved in to care for Damon suggested that the boy be assessed for evidence of brain damage. Nothing conclusive was ever established.

Allie got another job, and another, and came home later than her husband, and continued to act as if her child did not exist. Each year Damon grew bigger, noisier, more aggressive. At five, a paediatrician asked to see Ted alone, and suggested mother and child might be emotionally mismatched. 'How can we be mismatched?' she demanded. 'I'm his mother.'

At school, Damon failed consistently. His IQ was low. He made no friends. At eight, his headmaster suggested a psychiatrist. 'I never had any friends,' Allie told him, 'he's independent, he doesn't need friends. There's nothing wrong with him.' At twelve, Allie sent him to an exclusive academy for over-privileged under-achievers, where three years of one-to-one educational support left him able to read and write, but often unwilling to do either. After he was expelled for urinating on the principal's car, Allie decreed that he should attend the St Nicholas High School, on which the *Family First* crews descended whenever they needed playground shots. Channel Ten sponsored the new computer system.

The first time Damon got drunk was the first time he had his mother's attention. She watched him with delight, she fairly flirted with him. Looking back, Ted could have sworn that she actually tempted the child to drink.

Ted suspected that his wife had maintained their sex life, and given birth to their daughters, entirely for the sake of her publicity profile. After Damon she had her next pregnancy terminated, something he discovered only when the fee appeared on his credit card statement. Cherish was born in the summer break after Allie's first year as host of *Family First.* This time she went directly from labour ward to spa. There were day and night nurses, and then nannies, who lived elsewhere and often resigned. After Chalice, sex ceased.

She was different with the girls. Designer babies were in vogue the year Cherish was born, models carried them down the runway at Calvin Klein. Allie cuddled her baby on camera throughout a report on breastfeeding; Cherish, who was bottle-fed like her siblings, had to be sedated for the event. The Catholic Broadcasting Union gave *Family First* the award for Most Outstanding New Show On TV. The readers of *Woman's Life* voted Allie their top TV personality. The following year, she was The Women's Caucus Working Mother of the Year.

The girls became her accessories. They were her living dolls, always being dressed and painted and posed for the world to admire. Their room was filled with gigantic toys, life-sized stuffed animals and a fantastic playhouse created by a fashionable sculptor. A lurid circus mural coloured the walls. Gushingly, Allie praised her daughters for looking pretty and being underweight. They were listless, unresponsive children, prone to nightmares, afraid of many ordinary things and frequently ill.

Ted felt he was as good a father as any, and better than quite a few, but he had nothing by which to judge himself. Wealth had moved him into a new dimension. His own plain, milk-and-biscuits childhood was a redundant model. His own mother would have dissociated to atoms rather than raise her voice to his father, much less a knife.

Allie alleged that he had abandoned her with Damon, so he tried to pay his daughters extra attention and found that she blocked him. He was not to give them food in case they got fat, or play games with them in case they got hurt, or watch TV with them in case they absorbed whatever it was about him that was so hopelessly unsatisfactory. 'You're a man,' she condemned him. 'You can't possibly understand.' The simplest childhood pleasures were booby-trapped; from one of his country surveys he brought home tadpoles in a jampot and Cherish screamed in a frenzy of terror at the sight of them.

He was at first frightened by their frailty, and now alarmed by it. Guiltily, he compared them to the Lieberman girls, who seemed so sturdy and individual. Gemma said bluntly that Chalice and Cherish were abuse victims. He yearned to talk to Gemma; she did not want to talk to him. There had been no answer to his letter. Had he expected one? Sitting with his wretched daughters, tasting blood in his mouth, anticipating the threat of a new day, he could not remember his mood at the time.

CHAPTER 7

Hot and Cold Water to Every House

'She's impressive.' Marcus masked his face with the menu. 'Of course, I made it clear that the job was only on a temporary basis, until Stewart's . . . uh . . .'

Stephanie made an encouraging face at him. *I'm hurting all day, Marcus. I am suffering without my husband; be nice to me, please.* The restaurant was not designed to induce relaxation. It was the kind of place that executives in creative professions favoured to express their cutting-edgeness. The tables were jagged slabs of glass and the lights grew up from the floor on snaky metal stalks. The other clients were brash women with shirts clinging to their ribs and men with bristly hair and pastel jackets. 'This must be *the* place,' she observed brightly.

'Yup.' Marcus was still in hiding. 'Look, believe me, I didn't want to do it. We need another architect. Business is coming in. The home market's pretty exciting. Things are hotting up right now.'

'When is she starting?'

He gulped air. 'A week today.'

It was a Monday. Monday, Stephanie recalled, was the day when you scheduled your tough bananas. Monday was the day for no more crapping around, the day when you chose to grit your teeth, bite the bullet, get your shit together and just do it. 'So – you need his desk. And you'd like me to take his stuff home?'

'That's not why I asked you to lunch . . .'

Yes it is. She dragged out a smile. *But – aha! I too have my agenda.* 'I was going to ask you, actually.'

'Uh?' He blinked like a startled rabbit.

'Yes. You've sent me a client or two . . .'

'The least I can do, Steph.' Magnanimous, avuncular.

'Why don't you give me my old job back?' There, she had done it, the proposition was out in the open. She felt she might have coloured up but the place had black mirrors so it was hard to tell. The waiter arrived to take their order, giving her time to get composed. 'I heard your landscaper is leaving after the summer.' Was it smart to give that away? Yes, of course it was; her business reflexes must be stiff from disuse.

'Steph, have you thought about this?' Avuncular no more, he was giving her his pleading look, begging mercy for his pitiful insensitive chromosome, the look that said: don't hate me for hurting you. Stephanie was well acquainted with that look. People hated to hurt her, which meant eventually they hated her for being hurt.

'Yes, of course I've thought about it, Marcus. I need a job. I've got to be realistic, we don't know how long it will be until Stewart comes back.'

'But your own business—'

'Means I spend half my time chasing invoices and the other half chasing deliveries. I need a proper job. Corporate accounts, not the back-yard jobs. You know what I mean.'

'But your little boy?' Had he forgotten Max's name? It seemed likely, he had that beamed-up look in his eye which meant he had mentally removed himself from this distressing conversation.

'Goes to school full time in September. I was planning to go back to work then in any case. We have childcare already.' Let him choke on that 'we'. This is your partner's family, your best friend's family, your only friend's family. The truth was her plans had been for another baby, but now Marcus was wriggling on the hook she found herself unwilling to give him an advantage.

'Look, Steph, we're a young firm, our clients expect absolute commitment. This is the nineties. The bottom line is: I can't hire someone with small kids. That's it.'

Stephanie said nothing, waiting for it to dawn on him that the small kid in question had not been a flaw in Stewart's professionalism, but it did not happen. Instead, their food arrived and he waded into his soup as if the matter had resolved itself naturally. In the silence, she looked warily at her salad; it had been splattered with a viscous white dressing that resembled semen, as she remembered the stuff.

'You had any news?' he asked at last, gulping the final spoonful.

'No,' she answered flatly. 'The FO call every day.'

'What do the people want?'

'The kidnappers? They've made no demands.'

'Do we know he's . . .' He paused, watching her entangle rocket leaves with her fork as if she had exceeded the time limit for the task.

'Alive. Yes. They put pictures over occasionally.' She had them around her desk, harshly lit blurred images of Stewart sitting on a stone wall with his two partners in misfortune, some sort of tree casting a shadow behind them. Apart from Max, the pictures were the only comfort she had. The rest of her life, at that point, was just auto-anaesthesia. The reproduction in the photographs was poor and the eyes were just sockets so the heads were horribly skull-like. Except for the characteristic way Stewart had his hands, with the right holding the left wrist, the figures could have been anyone.

'It's crazy,' Marcus said without deep interest. He might have been criticising a new building regulation. 'What's the point?'

'Yes,' Stephanie agreed, resenting the wasted afternoon, the work not done, the effort of persuading Rachel to have Max, and of coercing her son to play with the Carman boys, for the futile purpose of appealing to Marcus's supposed humanity.

They disposed of the remainder of the meal quickly and returned to the offices of Berkman & Sands, where Marcus's secretary apologetically showed her her husband's possessions already packed into three storage crates. 'And he had some personal files in our system.' Her voice was muted, as if at a funeral. 'I copied them on to a disk for you.' The disc was labelled 'S Sands – Personal' and decently preserved in a perspex case.

They carried two of the crates down to the car park

and loaded them into the Cherokee. As Stephanie went back for the last crate, Marcus reappeared from his office to see her on her way. He followed, letting her struggle with the load.

'You're still running the Jeep?' he asked, bright-eyed in the gloom of the car park.

'Of course. Why wouldn't I?' Stephanie was puzzled at the question. She heaved the crate into the vehicle. Marcus had his hands in his pockets.

'Things must be pretty lonely,' he observed, suddenly looking animated.

'I have my work,' she reminded him.

'Well, if you need anything, give me a call, huh?' And he patted her backside. His hand, as if moving automatically and having nothing to do with him, removed itself from his pocket, drifted sideways and made contact with her flesh in the feeble fashion of an essentially cerebral man pretending sensuality in order to get sex. She wanted to slap him, but she was still holding the crate. Marcus then walked away to the exit, mumbling a preoccupied goodbye.

His touch lingered like slime on her skirt. Stephanie roared the Cherokee out into the street. She was shocked, she was disappointed, she was so angry at Marcus it felt like spontaneous combustion.

Waiting out the old familiar gridlock leading to the 31, she felt the grip of the future squeezing out her breath. Max would go to a new school without his father. He would pass his next birthday without his father. Tomorrow, she would look for a job – any job. Never trust a man who wears short-sleeved shirts. Damn

Marcus, what was the matter with him? He knew they needed help. Bearing up under the new weight of responsibility for Max, she felt murderous towards the man who called himself her husband's friend and yet abandoned his child and made a move on his wife. And let her carry crates. When they had considered christening their son, Stewart had proposed Marcus as a godfather. She was glad now that they had let the fast-running tide of new parenthood carry the idea away.

Back in Westwick, she detoured to Elm Bank Avenue to collect a resentfully silent Max from the Carman home. At home she carried the crates of Stewart's possessions into the house and up to the study by herself. *I'll beat this, I'm stronger than people think.*

While Max was in his bath she sent off a stack of faxes confirming arrangements for a planting which she had to do on Thursday.

Smouldering anger at Marcus kept Stephanie awake into the night. She sat up sorting through the crates, trying the points of pencils Stewart had sharpened, following the lines of his sketches with her finger, turning the pages of catalogues in the hope the they would exhale the smell of him. She looked at the disk labelled 'S Sands – Personal' but it seemed inert, not capable of offering the kind of comfort she needed.

Tuesday, in Stephanie's sentimental calendar, was always a pretty day. She put Marcus out of her mind and prepared to have people to dinner on Wednesday. Lately, people had not been asking her to dinner. The good families of Westwick shuttled around each other's houses in the energetic exchange of hospitality which gave the neighbourhood a reputation for village atmosphere and kept the mascarpone and truffle oil turning over at Parsley & Thyme, but this year, with a tragedy in the house instead of a husband, she was definitely out of the loop. There had even been strong suggestions at The Cedars and The Magpies that she was now 'too busy' to serve the Events Committee and the PTA, and could decently resign.

'Perhaps people feel awkward, darling, with a woman on her own,' her mother had suggested brightly. 'They don't know how to react to you, they might think you don't want to go out. Take the initiative, invite them. You're so good at dinner parties – I'm sure they'll respond.'

This summer was happening as usual for her friends, but not for her. The realisation skewered her painfully. Her mother's enthusiasm, as usual, foamed over her like a tidal wave. 'You really think I should?'

'Yes, darling. Don't forget, you get out of life what you put in. Don't you have that helicopter thing to raise money for?'

The Helford Hospital Helicopter Ambulance Appeal had indeed instituted a series of fundraising dinners, themed by national cuisines. The hostess made a small charge, the guests each cooked a dish for the buffet, the company had a delightful evening and took away a comforting sense of civic participation.

Of course I should entertain, she argued with herself, writing invitations on hand-laid cards. Just because I am by myself for a while there's no reason not to live normally. Stewart would want me to do exactly what we always do. It will make me feel better. A little party. Something to look forward to.

For a theme she chose French, because it seemed easy to her and she was aware that the culinary illiterates could buy their contributions at Parsley & Thyme. Josh and Rachel, the DeSouzas, that couple I've just been doing a terrace for, and those people with the rose garden, Allie and Ted . . . Her hand hesitated over the P pages in her address book. The Pikes. Perhaps not, not after that victim support business. It might be childish to bear grudges, but she did. They would not be offended; Chester was always travelling and his status set them above the rest of community.

She looked at the final list and saw herself partnerless among the couples. Should she ask an extra man to balance the genders? Not Marcus, after yesterday. Not one of The Crowd: he would stall the conversation by expecting to talk about films or art or politics. No, better to be as she was, just by herself.

'You must by psychic, Stephanie dear. I was longing to see you.' Allie made it sound as if she was utterly ravished by the invitation. 'But will you be all right, by yourself? So clever of you to choose French. We'll bring a tart or something.'

On Wednesday, Mr Capelli from the Foreign Office tried a joke. 'It's a pity,' he suggested, 'that Mr Sands wasn't travelling in the Yemen. Foreigners who are kidnapped in the Yemen seem to actually enjoy the experience. Beautiful country, interesting culture, very good food and the kidnappers always save the best for their guests. Arab tradition of hospitality, I suppose. The only real complaint we've had is that they seem to think all Westerners drink whisky so they tend to give them too much.'

Stephanie was thrown. Needing inspiration, she gazed at her pinboard. The Empress Josephine was said to have been a natural diplomat. 'How interesting,' she suggested.

'Yes, isn't it,' was the enthusiastic response. 'Of course, when we have your husband safe home, Mrs Sands, we will know more about the Kazakhs. They might be just as good. We hope they are.' *And pigs might fly. Get my husband back, idiot.*

The part of entertaining that Stephanie enjoyed most was setting the table. She got busy laying out her antique linen napkins on the beautiful pale wood, polishing her fingermarks off the silver sphere salt and pepper mills, cutting trails of ivy for a centrepiece. The glasses – wedding presents – made her a little sad.

The rose garden people, who were new to the neighbourhood, brought a redolent *daube de boeuf à la Provençale* and murmured awed appreciation of Stephanie's roses. Joshua Carman brought a bucket-sized pot of his celebrated *cassoulet* with his own hand-decorated label, and looked daggers at the *daube*. The terrace couple came with an immaculate home-made *tarte aux pommes* which must have taken an hour in the slicing alone.

The first indication that the evening was ill-starred came with the DeSouzas. Belinda shamefacedly offered an identical *tarte aux pommes* in a box from Parley & Thyme, saying, 'I suppose this is French, isn't it?' in the guilt-trippy way she contrived whenever made to feel like an immigrant.

Last of all came the Parsons, with the unmistakable colour and rumple and averted eyes of a couple who had fought before they set out, bringing the third identical *tarte aux pommes* from Parsley & Thyme, but considerably damaged. In fact, it looked as if someone had sat on the box. 'That'll be OK, won't it?' Allie watched while Ted produced the battered contribution, as if resentful of having to consider such trivia.

'It's fine,' Stephanie reassured her, swiftly taking the box to the kitchen where she could mask the damage unseen.

'We haven't seen you in a while.' Ted followed her, needing more than ever to place the maximum space between himself and his wife. The fight had been about the party, which Allie had alleged was part of his conspiracy to wreck her looks and diminish her to a *hausfrau*. Unwisely, he had recalled that she had accepted the invitation.

He leaned against the worktop, looking as if he felt stupid. 'How's it going with Stewart?'

'Still the same. No news. I'm keeping busy.'

'Good, good.' There was always something indistinctly wretched about Ted. His shoulders were too high and his chin too low and his arms held too tight to his side, as if something was crushing the joy out of him. If he could smile and open out his chest, hold his head up and get rid of the pinched look around his eyes, he would look vigorous, almost handsome. Tonight he seemed exceptionally pathetic. Stephanie took pity and poured him a decent whisky, which he downed as eagerly as his poor dog snarfed biscuits.

'My!' Rachel Carman's sharp shiny eyes ran over the scene in the dining room, comparing it unfavourably with her own. 'We are formal.'

'Stewart and Stephanie were always formal,' her husband reminded her.

'You mean they *are*,' Allie corrected him, flashing Stephanie a glance intended to show support, as she followed Ted into the room.

'Can I introduce Sonia Purkelli? And Ray, her husband? They've just moved into Cedar Close.'

'And we have the most *divine* rose garden.' Sonia Purkelli was a little gushy, a fault on the right side that evening since she babbled sweetly on while Allie and Belinda, unable to relax, perched unnaturally on their seats throwing brittle interjections at no one in particular. Josh poured wine down his throat with silent dedication and Ray Purkelli, a skinny, leathery man, sat blinking like a lizard, getting the measure of the new neighbours.

'Your table is charming,' Ted told Stephanie, warmed by the whisky and wondering what life would be like with a wife who could do charming, and cared if you were unhappy.

'Isn't this delightful?' he said as they took their drinks to the tables in the garden and he looked around at the green, scented harmony as if amazed that plants could be beautiful. The grass was soft under his feet, a growing carpet. Moron, he thought, could lie on it in real comfort.

'Would you like me to open some more wine?' he asked. 'I see old Josh is in training for the Olympics again.' It was a neighbourhood joke that wine-drinking was Dr Carman's Olympic event.

Stephanie laughed. 'He says it cleans the arteries, doesn't he?'

Pulling the corks, Ted reflected that her laugh was pretty, light but throaty like the call of some gentle bird. His wife screeched. Gemma Lieberman laughed like melted chocolate bubbling on a stove, but he would never hear that laugh again. He filled his own glass first. 'You're so organised,' he muttered, looking at the invitation list and the cake chart and thinking of the knee-deep flotsam of checkout magazines in Allie's study.

'I'm busy now,' she explained. 'I have to be organised.'

'Are you lonely?' he asked.

'Of course,' she answered. In her mind, Ted and Allie blurred into one entity; she felt it was as safe to confide in him as it would be in his wife. 'I miss Stewart so much. Somehow . . . I don't know,' she paused, weighing the exact burden of her pain, 'it's having to keep things normal for Max, and not having anyone to talk to, I suppose. Anyone who's in the same situation, I mean.'

'I know how you feel,' he returned. 'I get lonely myself.'

'But you've got Allie, and the girls, and Damon . . .'

'No.' He had downed a couple of Scotches at home. Evenings with Allie went better that way. 'They're in the house, of course, but we're not a family somehow. I guess everyone knows about Damon's problems?' She nodded, leaving off activity for an instant and leaning against the fridge in a manner which was more taking than she realised. 'But even before that, I don't know what it was, exactly. It's hard to explain. Sometimes I feel loneliest when we're all together.'

There are men to whom a declaration of loneliness to a person of the opposite gender is an invitation to sex. Ted appreciated this, Stephanie, despite her experience with Marcus on Monday, did not. Ted began to wonder if Stephanie might be a little bit sweet on him. He carried plates in and carried plates out and watched her taking care of her guests, a glow spreading across her forehead where little wisps of hair curled like vine tendrils, and felt he ought to take care of her.

He refilled his glass, and noticed that although she was pale-skinned the sun had flushed her nose and cheeks the colour of shortbread. Abandoned with a little boy, a terrible thing for a young woman. Someone should look after her, he thought. She should not be working in the sun and opening her own wine. He filled his glass again. In the kitchen, she camouflaged the battered *tarte* with whipped cream while Ted looked on, dumb with drink and enchantment.

'For dessert, ladies and gentlemen, we have three French tarts,' she announced brightly, evoking some laughter. Ted found he had boundless admiration for a woman who could be so elegantly suggestive. Ray Purkelli started to speak and disclosed a career in marketing automobiles. The men at once paid him close attention and the atmosphere settled at last. People were smiling. 'Let's have coffee outside,' Stephanie suggested, going out by herself with the cups. Ted followed, empty handed, noting the remarkable length of her legs.

She put the cups on the table on the terrace and started striking a match to light the citronella flare which supposedly deterred night insects. A sudden zephyr blew the match out.

'Here.' In his severely mellowed state, Ted considered that this fooling with phallic objects was an obvious overture. He stepped forward with a manly lighter. 'Let me.'

'Ted, you've been so kind.' Unmistakable, he concluded. She was giving him the green light. He dropped the lighter, put his hand over hers and pulled. He thought he pulled with a light but masterful force. In truth he pulled quite violently, overbalancing them both so they fell on the bench. He launched a kiss which landed near her ear.

'Ted!' His lips were still puckered and he had screwed up his eyes as well. She saw he was going to fire again. His breath smelled of whisky. She felt his arms holding her rigidly around her waist. 'Ted, stop it. People will come out any minute.'

Laughter billowed distantly from the French windows to the dining room. 'No they won't.' He opened his eyes. She was a silhouette against the windows and a squirming burden in his arms. 'They're having a good time. We can have a good time too.'

'No we can't. Don't be silly, Ted.'

'You don't mean that.' But his arms slackened and he allowed her to pull away from him. She jumped to her feet at once, feeling all the wretched, messy, embarrassed terror of a male in rut which she had forgotten since her college days and had hoped never to feel again.

'Of course I mean it.'

The cold consciousness of his mistake rose up like vomit in his throat. 'But I thought . . .' He contracted his limbs and felt his head drop into his hands and his elbows dig into his knees and his spine collapse into a defeated curve. 'Never mind. Oh God. I was wrong.'

'Yes, you were. I love Stewart – whether he's here or not. And Allie's my friend, for heaven's sake. I *like* you, Ted, but that's all. How could you imagine . . .'

He barked in irritation, 'Why do women ask those kind of questions all the time? How do I know how I could anything? Your husband's gone, you said you were lonely.' She noticed him swaying on the seat and realised that alcohol was the major part of the equation. But something in his inflection had troubled her, and called back the memory of Lauren Pike's clipboard.

'What do you mean, my husband's gone?' Hateful, that word gone.

'He *is* gone, isn't he?' A suspicion floated up from the boozy depth of his mind. 'Oh God. I thought, I mean I understood . . .'

'What? What did you understand, Ted?' She felt quite unsteady herself. Were they both drunk?

'Nothing. Nothing. It doesn't matter.'

'It does matter to me, at least I think it does. What do you think has happened, why Stewart isn't here?'

'Look, let it go, Stephanie . . .'

Her mood had shifted violently. 'If it's that serious I

can't let it go, can I? Tell me or I'll tell Allie you made a pass.'

He let out a sarcastic, B-movie laugh. 'As if she'd care. I should think she'd be thankful.' But the name of his wife was like a whip lashing him into line. He curled up even smaller and cradled his skull in his hands before mumbling, 'The word is he ran off, Stephanie. That you'd been having . . . uh . . . problems and . . . uh . . . he was seeing someone else maybe. And all the kidnap stuff is just—'

'Lies?' she finished in a disbelieving tone. 'My God, is that really what people think? They think Stewart left us?'

'It's just what was around . . . you know, the word,' Ted pleaded, trying to summon some authority for his error. 'People don't really pay any attention to that stuff . . .'

Except you, dear Ted. She did not say that. Westwick training was hard to break. All she did was fold her arms and stand over the miserable man she had counted among her friends until ten minutes ago, feeling like fainting but not daring to sit down in case he touched her again.

'Hey – did somebody say coffee?' Josh Carman crashed across her fern bed, missing the lily pool by a few inches. He carried a full glass of wine. The rest of the party followed but, to Stephanie's relief, were sober enough to keep to the terrace. At that moment she felt she could have torched anyone else who damaged her garden with the citronella flare.

The party had now become a monster beyond her control. People sprawled and chaffered and roared with laughter at nothing at all. This was unusual, for early nights and sober mornings were the mid-week style in Westwick, if, indeed, husbands could be extracted from their schedules in time for dinner at all.

The thrush in the crab tree hopped restlessly from branch to branch, unable to roost in peace. Women grew flirtatious, except Allie, who sat in poisoned silence with mineral water and tightly crossed legs. Men up-ended bottles and hopefully looked around for replenishment. In the normal way, Stephanie would have felt justified in fetching the brandy, but now all her hospitable instincts were frozen. Who are these people, she wondered, watching the Goya-esque faces in the candlelight, who called themselves friends and slandered me behind my back?

The night was close, but she found she was shivering. The scent of her jasmine was intoxicating, but it made her feel sick. Perhaps Ted was exaggerating, he was drunk after all, and now devoting his ungovernable libido to teasing Rachel. But she judged him a straight man and on the prosaic side of imaginative. Besides, how many bitch sessions had she sat in on herself? 'We're always here for you,' those women had said. Here to think the worst of her, and of Max. *Thanks, girls, at this point in my life I really needed that.*

Stephanie sat still and said nothing and wondered how long it would be before the riotous company realised that their hostess had been wounded. She waited in vain. The party broke up merrily after midnight and left with enthusiastic promises to have her over *soon*.

On Thursday, miserable and hungover, she drove over to a job at the opposite end of Church Vale from the

Parsons' house, one of the largest properties in Maple Grove, whose owners had excavated a swimming pool at the end of their garden. Getting the approval from the Maple Grove Society for things like this was in the league of getting the Biblical camel through the eye of a needle. Over in Grove End, a family had actually torched their own house in order to be able to rebuild it without the old servants' staircase, which the Maple Grove Society had insisted they preserve.

Stephanie suspected that her client, a character actor with a great career in psychopaths, had hired her to landscape the addition as part of his political strategy. Ingeniously, she had resurrected a Tudor Wilde design for a pergola with climbing roses around a brick-paved terrace, submitted it with copies of the original, schmoozed Jemima Thorogood most tastefully and been gratified to get the Society's consent with only two pages of modifications.

So far, the job had gone like a charm. Derek and Dave did not always work well with construction teams, but this time there had been no cause for flouncing. The bricks were laid, the uprights were raised, the crossbeams were being bolted into place as she watched. 'Good work, team,' she commended them. 'I'll be over with the plants in the morning.' Derek and Dave did not always plant successfully, either. Pruning, clipping and mowing were their major talents; they slashed and burned with enthusiasm. At digging, mulching and planting they were erratic; watering and spraying were activities which they could not be trusted to perform without supervision. They did not do nurture; their thing was destruction.

Back home in the evening, she set about stowing the stuff from Stewart's office in the study area he had arranged for himself. She sat at his desk, his beautiful desk with the flush-fitting keyboard drawer and the integrated ducts for the three plates of spaghetti linking the PC, and considered it a tribute to him to fit everything very neatly into its logical place.

Stewart sat here every Sunday evening. Flashy masculinity was not her husband's way; he did not care to drive fast or spend Saturday afternoons roaring at sport on the TV. What he liked was the dull business of being a man, reading the financial pages minutely, balancing their cheque books, getting into long dreary conversations with other men about world events which they could not, in all conscience, have any real knowledge of but would still chew over with the colossal gravity of global experts in the area. After the noisy, unstable life which her father had created for their family, Stephanie had felt like a little ship anchoring in a deep harbour when she met Stewart. Now she felt adrift, and sensed a storm brewing.

Here he had finally been forced to accept paper. Here were the household files, from AIR MILES to WILLS, their insurance policies and birth certificates and handbooks and guarantees. She got teary looking at his precise italic writing on the labels. There was space behind them. She pulled back WILLS and there, beside his will and her will in their matching plastic pockets, were two letters with her name and Max's name on them.

'My darling,' hers began, which was enough to get her tears falling fast, 'you will only be reading this if I'm not around any more. I want to tell you forever that I love you. You and Max are all that gives my life meaning . . .' She read on, her blurred eyes roaming over the page, fixing on *joy* and *always* and *care* and finally resting on *regret*. 'The only thing I regret is that I haven't left you both better provided for. Finding our house was a dream come true, but as things have turned out the element of illusion seems to have been more than we imagined. I'm sorry for that.' The passage lodged in her memory because she did not really understand it, but she had to weep for some time, and in the flood of her sadness she did not pay it specific attention.

At the Church Vale job on Friday, displaced rage seized her as she set about planting her scheme. Her energy was demonic. With Derek and Dave standing wilting over the supplies of water and manure, she worked full tilt into the heat of midday, installing the roses, beginning with the flashy scarlet *Danse de Feu* over the steps and ending with the rampant white *Iceberg* by the pool house. She broke fingernails and raised blisters on her hands. The sun brought out a sore on her lip.

'Such a waste.' She threw down her spade at last. 'All the boring ones with no scent. And he'll never keep that *Iceberg*, it gets black-spot.' Dave nodded in sympathy. The client claimed to be a martyr to hay fever and had insisted that they use only scentless varieties of rose.

'What can you do if people have these allergies?' Wearily, Derek turned off the hose. 'We're giving him what he wants. The customer is always right. At least he agreed to have the mint walk.'

They were all very taken with the mint walk, one of Stephanie's best solutions to the problem of fragrance without pollen. It was to be a part of the paving, a decorative band of cobblestones interplanted with creeping aromatics, tiny, fragrant little leaf mats which would tolerate occasional bruising as people walked on them and released refreshing perfumes into the air.

'Yes,' she agreed, picking up her spade again. 'The mints – where are they?'

Dave looked at Derek. 'Haven't they come?'

Derek looked at Dave. 'Don't look at me, I've been here with you all morning, I don't know.'

'Well,' Stephanie said reasonably, 'I know I confirmed the delivery, so they should be here. Why not check with the housekeeper?'

The mints had not been delivered. A call to the nursery established from a hysterical assistant that the driver delivering their plants had fallen asleep at the wheel and crashed on the 31 when still two hours away from the city.

'Hell,' said Stephanie, and she stamped her foot. The boys flinched. Stamping and profanity were quite out of her character.

'Steady,' suggested Dave.

'Don't steady me,' she retorted.

'Hey, enhance your calm, Steph,' Derek cautioned her. 'Don't lose it over a few little mints.'

'I'll lose it if I damn well want to,' she asserted. 'This job has to be finished today. Where are we going to get two dozen prostrate mints in Westwick on a Friday afternoon?'

They were temporarily silent, then Dave said, 'There's that mad place down in Willow Gardens.'

'What mad place?'

'Gaia – you mean Gaia, don't you? Sort of nursery place with the falling-down fence and that woman with huge hair?'

'That's the one.' They giggled. 'But she does have some unusual things; she might have what we need,' Dave allowed. 'Although the place is kind of crazy.'

'Well, call them up and ask,' Stephanie ordered, starting to feel tired. 'If they've got them I'll go over and get them right now, while you start sweeping up.' Talking to the boys about missing Stewart was pointless; they seemed to think that sex was the problem, and cruising the Wilde At Heart on Saturday night would fix it.

Dave pulled out his phone and made the call. 'Yess!' he reported quickly. 'She's got mints.'

'Tell her I'm on my way,' Stephanie directed, heading for her car.

CHAPTER 8

A School of Art

Cleanliness had been the business of Westwick for more than a century. Long after the river became a scummy, soup-thick vein of liquid waste, its tributaries still ran clear down Alder Bottom and Hel Vale; long after the city had smothered itself in stench and smoke, fresh breezes blew about Oak Hill. There had been laundries there, the highest land convenient to the city; old prints showed the slopes festooned with lines of white sheets drying in the clean air, billowing vineyards of purity whose weekly harvest was carted back to houses in town.

History fixed things so that the cleanliness connection became almost karmic. The washing machine was invented, the laundries disappeared, the streams were buried in storm drains. At Oak Hill a power station was built to blacken the air with its emissions. But coal tar was a by-product, which made soap manufacture cheap, so by the thirties, barges were fetching tons of Goodie & Hazard's Daybreak Household Bars and Acorn Shoe Cream from their Helford works, where the one-time laundry maids clocked in and thanked progress for rubber gloves.

The Channel Ten building on the river at Helford had risen from the rubble of an old soap warehouse, a fact which The Boss decreed should be stressed in the corporate image. 'Cleanliness is next to godliness,' he observed. 'This is a dirty world and people like to know we've got God on our side.' The windows were enhanced with turquoise metal grilles; the boardroom had a fine view of the river and the helicopter pad built on the old wharf.

'Queue Here For . . .' read a signboard outside the studio reception. The intention had been that the name of the programme currently needing an audience should be inserted in a window at the bottom of the sign, but the reception staff never bothered and the window was left empty. People queued all day anyway, mesmerised like cult devotees by the charismatic glow of television. Mostly women, mostly unemployed, very young or very old, they shuffled heavy-footed as a chain gang through a race of crush barriers, getting hot in the sun or wet in the rain, leaving the forecourt studded with chewing gum and littered with cola cans and cigarette butts.

The Channel's workers, down to the lowest runner, disdained even to mention the queue. The idea that *their* programme, however mindless it might be, went out to this underclass was impossible. These poor, stupid, ugly, ill-dressed, tattooed, sociopathic cattle were just live set-dressing, not representatives of the real audience. They went as embarrassedly unacknowledged as sexually transmitted parasites. What primitive sub-species would wait in line all day for the sake of making up a studio audience?

The queue were misunderstood. They did not particularly want to be an audience; they wanted to see a star. They did not know that the celebrity entrance was through the gated and guarded scenery dock at the other side of the building. Only Allie Parsons ran the gauntlet out front every morning, and the geeking and gawping and twittering and truanting children asking for autographs lit her up like downtown Kowloon.

The end of the series was in sight. 'In the autumn,' *Family First*'s senior producer announced, 'we're going to be losing Daniel.' The Himbo grinned a wide, hard, desperate grin, like Steve McQueen at the end of *The Great Escape.* 'And we'll be interviewing co-hosts over the summer.' Each year, the agents heard him with less enthusiasm. 'That Parsons bitch,' one of them had said, 'I wouldn't let one of my clients work with her if she was the last pair of implants on TV.'

'We want to introduce some new features in the next series,' the producer announced to the team. 'We need ideas. Audience research says we should be moving away from issue-based items to a more human—'

'Real people, real lives,' Allie broke in with impatience. 'Feelings, not so much of the talky-talky junk. We need to put more of life on the screen, the tears, the pain, the anguish, the guilt . . .'

'The embarrassment,' suggested Daniel, insouciantly tipping back his chair.

'And the laughter, of course' Allie waved her hands about as if to sculpt the desirable emotions from the air.

'Love, warmth, stuff like that. What we need is more *heart*.'

'Gossip,' the senior producer elaborated, sensing a lack of response around the conference table. 'We want to do more gossip. We're going to be losing Watchdog completely, nobody goes for that consumer stuff any more. Environment will be restructured. Health Matters stays but we'll turn it around to focus on personal stories, my life with motor-neurone, that kind of thing. There'll be a style makeover every day, not just every week, and we're going to invite viewers to actually make each other over so you'll get say a kid giving her grandma the look he thinks she ought to have, or the secretary dressing her boss, whatever.'

'Are there still secretaries?' asked Maria, the one-time weather girl, with delicacy. Miraculously confirmed as a permanent researcher for the next series, she was staking out her turf.

'Plus - this is the big one, folks,' Allie recaptured their attention with a sweep of her pen, like a conductor gathering up an orchestra, 'we're going to start a lead feature strand focusing on real women with real problems, stories, tragedies.'

'And there'll be a tarot reader on the sofa with Allie giving the spiritual perspective on every guest's dilemmas.' The producer nodded to his star with pride, inviting admiration for her selfless sacrifice for the sake of the programme. There was a silence. 'Humanity, that's what this is about,' he urged, 'Next season. I don't want anyone coming in here with an idea that hasn't got a human face on it. Now, if that's clear . . .'

'Dumbing down,' said the junior researcher, throwing down his pencil with disgust. 'I thought we were dragging our knuckles in the dirt already.'

'Lightening up,' the producer pleaded. 'Our audience are hard-working, decent people. They deserve to be entertained.'

'If they're so hard-working,' Daniel enquired, smirking at his own acuity, 'how come they're watching TV all morning?'

'We shouldn't act like it's a crime to be unwaged. And working in the home is a viable life choice for women with small children,' put in Maria.

'Yes, Daniel, you should really watch your attitude,' Allie endorsed her. 'Let's not forget the men who choose to be active parents,' she added, trawling the table for eye-contact. 'I think men who're committed to their role as fathers should have *special* recognition, don't you?'

'Ah – wit, information, gossip – the very stuff of life,' recited the senior researcher, with the earnest face he always put on to camouflage irony.

'Is that Shakespeare?' breathed Maria, projecting admiration.

'Mark Twain,' he condescended.

'Mark Twain! F-a-a-a-b! That is such a great idea. The Skywalker who fell to earth. What has he been doing since *Star Wars*? Do we know who his agent is?' Allie prided herself on being a great motivator.

'And we need ideas now to work on over the next few weeks,' the producer reminded them. 'Blood costs, as we know. These bleeding heart features are bitches to set up. There'll be more work in the field. Our first show in the new format has to really knock their socks off.'

'Aren't we doing those lesbian mothers at sixty?' Allie sat up in alarm.

'Ricki Lake has them on an exclusive.'

'Fuck.'

'In vitro, actually.' Daniel was undeniably demob happy.

Allie threw herself back in her seat in a spasm of despair. 'Your penis will be in vitro if you don't can it, Daniel.'

'If I can it, will you buy it?' he threw back.

'I have an idea,' Maria announced, pulling a folder from her neo-Prada document case.

'Maria's got an idea for the new series,' announced the senior researcher, wondering if this pushy meteorologist would be willing to advance her career horizontally. Shagwise, *Family First* was tundra and permafrost.

Producing a clipping from the *Helford & Westwick Courier*, Maria cleared her throat, her voice rising with nerves. 'There's this woman – she's thirty-two, one son, sounds very our market and she lives locally – whose husband has been kidnapped in the former Soviet Union . . .'

'When was that exactly?' Allie faked vibrant interest.

'A couple of months ago.'

'Oh.' Subtly, Allie switched off her vibrancy and sketched a coma of boredom, miming *old story*.

'He was on some trade delegation with four people – Western businessmen – and they were snatched by nationalist guerillas in this remote region and there's been no news, no ransom demand, nothing. The poor woman must be just distraught . . .'

'It's not one of those places nobody can pronounce and nobody knows where it is, is it?' The producer gave her a weary smile. 'Foreign stories are a real turn-off.'

'But she lives right here,' Maria urged him. 'Right here in Westwick. And in October, the United Nations commission on terrorism is due to report,' she extracted another newspaper clipping, 'so I thought why don't we get this woman on the show with the head of the commission, and just have her ask what he's doing to get her husband back?'

'Great,' said the producer, thinking tabloid.

'Really great,' said the senior researcher, thinking blow job.

'Absolutely great,' said the junior researcher, thinking that it might not be totally impossible for him to get a news contract next year after all.

'Isn't that a little tacky?' Daniel demanded joyfully. 'Some poor inarticulate housewife fronting up to a UN statesman?'

'It's putting a human face on international relations,' said the deputy producer, anxious not to be left out. 'I think that's just what *Family First* ought to be doing.'

'Melanie Griffiths!' Allie blazed a delighted smile at Maria. 'That's who you remind me of! I've been trying to think of it all morning – Melanie Griffiths! In *Working Girl*. With the clippings and everything. Isn't that just a f-a-a-a-b thing, everybody?'

But the team had picked up the ball and was running too fast to be distracted. 'So where exactly does this woman live?' the producer asked.

'Westwick,' Maria confirmed, rasping her voice down

to counter-tenor so she sounded as little as possible like Melanie Griffiths. 'Somewhere called New Farm.'

'Leafy Westwick, eh?' The producer tapped his teeth with his pen. 'Great. Allie – could you do some net-working here? You must be neighbours.'

Twelve stern faces were now accusing Allie of failing to get a story. 'If I had time to get to know my neigh-bours . . .' Petulantly, she shuffled papers, playing for time. Then she launched the last offensive. 'Catch *up*, guys. I mean, come on. We all know her. She's even been on the show – it's that wispy woman who did the dumb garden for children a couple of years ago, remember? The one who got all those complaints about toxic paint and allergic leaves and stuff?'

'Leggy,' muttered the senior researcher.

'And of course I've talked to her, but . . .' she laid one hand to the heart region of her chest, 'she's so fragile, and just devastated by this whole thing. Really, my instinct is to protect her. I've tried talking to her, of course I have, but she's just not the type, you know what I'm saying? She'd dry. I think she'd be a disaster, frankly.'

'If she's so fragile, won't she just crack up and cry and stuff?' Daniel was learning the pleasure of settling scores. 'Make 'em cry – isn't that our motto?'

'She didn't dry when she was doing that garden thing,' the senior researcher remembered.

'Oh, but I really had to coach her,' Allie parried. 'She did OK in the end, but not fab. And this is different, she's just all in a heap right now and she withdraws, you know what I'm saying? Withdraws and clams right up. I just can't see it working . . .' She opened her eyes wider than wide, trying to evoke the terror of inarticulate silence which gave every talk show worker sweaty palms at three seconds to transmission.

Maria braced her shoulders, resolved to seize her day. 'I hope I'm not out of line saying this, but maybe if she was approached by someone she didn't know . . .'

'Good idea,' the senior researcher nodded with vigour.

Allie was cornered. It was clear that she now had only two options: get Stephanie on to that sofa or give away her job. 'I will try again,' she promised, keeping her hand pressed to her breast. 'We are kind of friends, you know, the way you are through your children. I can talk to her again – but it ain't gonna be easy. No, no. We should think about this. The child's from a previous relationship, I'm not sure they're even married . . . Do we want the show to get into that kind of morality?'

'What we want is for our viewers to know how it feels when terrorists kidnap the man you love,' the deputy producer gave no quarter. 'I don't see the moral thing matters. Who's to know, anyway?' His implication was that Allie was the only person in the room with a direct line to the gossip magazines.

'The viewers would really empathise. Serial monogamy's the way of the world.' Three months into his second marriage, the senior researcher smiled down Maria's neckline; yup, Melanie Griffiths it was.

'Oh, well.' Allie handed her files to her secretary and prepared to leave. 'If that's everything?'

Outside the building, she waited by her studio car until Maria appeared, on her way to lunch with the senior researcher. 'Great idea, Maria,' she waved the girl over. 'Can I say something to you? Kind of a woman thing?'

'Mrs Parsons, I do hope – I mean, is this kidnap story difficult for you at a personal level . . .'

'Not at all. Being professional means you just can't let that kind of stuff get to you. I just wanted to share something with you.' She lowered her voice but kept it cosy. 'I really believe in mentoring new staff, you know? I haven't had a chance to really tell you how thrilled I am you're joining the team. It's so important to me that we should all be really close and really work together, you know?'

Warily, Maria nodded. Allie put her arm around her shoulders and walked her along past the curious eyes of the queue. 'I notice you're still doing all that good-girl stuff? Smiling all the time, apologising when you make a point – you did it right then?' Maria wiped off her smile and rearranged her lips in a self-determined crimp. 'Now, you may have noticed television is still a bit of a boy's club, which is why no one will tell you this except me. That kind of making nice can really poison a woman's career. The boys just won't take you seriously. Forget assertive – hell, in this kind of office, you should really be aggressive.'

'So – you mean – I don't need to rethink my hair?' Maria copied the senior researcher's irony screen and tried baring her teeth just short of smiling.

'Humour!' Allie punched her playfully at the shoulder. 'All right! That's just what I mean!'

She raised her arms to the heavens, what-can-a-poor-woman-do? 'Be one of the boys, speak out, blow your own horn, don't be afraid to scrap a little. All that good-girl routine went out with padded shoulders. OK?'

'Oh yes,' agreed Maria, confidingly, 'padded shoulders are just so David Bowie, aren't they?'

'Excellent! You got it,' Allie affirmed, mystified. Then she recoiled into the depths of her car, waving goodbye to the multitude. 'Have a good summer!'

CHAPTER 9

Plenty of Greenery

The sign at the corner of the Broadway and Willow Gardens read: GAIA – Discover The Green World. Stephanie passed it every time she took the 31. In this region of coach-painted, craftsman-lettered shop signs, it was conspicuous, painted unevenly on a blistered board in the rambling script which is charming on French bistro menus but crazy anywhere else.

An invisible taboo hung over this road. Stephanie had never been to Gaia before, although normally she could never resist an unknown nursery. Even though she ordered her plants from wholesalers, she still cruised garden centres like a New York singleton working parties; the lure of a specimen she had never met before was all-powerful. Subliminally, however, she had received the idea that there were reasons not to buy here, reasons which proceeded from the moral consensus of the neighbourhood, reasons which therefore did not need to be defined. Swimming heedlessly along in the tide of Westwick opinion, she had passed by Gaia until now.

It lay between sports grounds and builders' merchants in the wide strip of dead land alongside the 31. Nobody had ever tried to build here because the road was so close. North of the Broadway the ground sloped up to the derelict Oak Hill site; to the south this disregarded portion extended right down to the river banks. The football fields and running tracks of St Nicholas's High School occupied the riverside half. Adjoining, the Helford Harriers shared a club house with the Old Nicks football team. A golf driving range disfigured the next plot, screened from Gaia by a utilitarian windbreak of poplars.

This pocket of territory had been some kind of nursery as long as anyone could remember. The land had once been part of the New Farm; it was rich and heavy, benefiting from natural irrigation, and as the farm had retreated and the city advanced these fields had been the last to be sold. The farmer had leased them to a commercial seed grower who raised lurid blankets of poppies each summer. Fifty years ago, when the city was still small and the 31 was a generous highway humming with boxy new Fords, the seed grower sold to a market gardener and the poppies gave way to cabbages. Then the county bought it to raise the trees to plant the streets of Westwick, leaving the double row of poplars as a shield against the amplifying emissions from the 31. On good land, and serving a neighbourhood which was garden-conscious and rich, Gaia should have prospered. Stephanie saw as soon as she turned in the gate that something had gone wrong.

The gate itself was propped permanently open and hung from a drunken post by a single rusted hinge. In the weedy gravel car park there were only two other vehicles: a tinny Mitsubishi pickup and a dead-looking grey Lada slumped low on its suspension. A giant willow sculpture of the goddess herself lurched over the entrance, with bindweed racing up her calves.

Inside a ragged hedge, a hand-lettered signpost directed Stephanie through the outdoor beds where the stock straggled in containers between paths of pinkish gravel. This was going to be a waste of time. With rising irritation she took a rusty cart and pushed it down the unweeded paths towards 'Perennials H–M'. A slime of algae glistened on the ground. Land cress was sprouting lustily in the pots but the growth of the plants for sale was retarded for the season.

Striding impatiently, Stephanie noted that plants had fallen over, plants had lost their canes, plants had taken on bizarre colours, grown twisted leaves on stunted stems. In the tree area the junipers were sickly and yellow; killing a juniper required real talent. She saw stagnation, and neglect and disease; her mood was souring to despair when, at the end of the enclosure, she also saw the mints.

The mint bed at Gaia was storming. Billows of scent rose in the humid air above the rank stems of *Mentha rotundifolia*, already three feet high with velvety leaves as big as babies' feet. Energetic runners had thrust out of the bottoms of the pots and taken root in the ground, fat buds with red-veined leaves sprouting from the nodes. Searing yellow blotched the pineapple mints, and the row of white-striped eau-de-cologne mints reeked like a new designer fragrance.

The state of the plants in the neighbouring frames seemed even more pathetic next to this herbaceous frenzy. Irregular watering might have been a cause, although a hose lay along the path, and the earth was spongy with moisture.

In her mind, Stephanie already saw great aromatic cushions of vegetation spreading over her new paving scheme. The choice overwhelmed her. A greyish specimen with woolly leaves like the pelt of a prehistoric mammoth? Or the pennyroyal, so lush it would soon be ankle-deep? Or her old favourite, the Corsican mint, tiny heart-shaped green leaves sprinkled with pinhead-sized pink flowers? She toyed with the merits of a mixed planting instead of a bold statement. The pink flowers settled it. She picked out two dozen of them, inhaling their sharp scent as she settled them in the cart.

Neglect depressed Stephanie, she liked to see things flourishing. At the end of the enclosure stood a once-handsome gothic glasshouse streaked with rust, with another sign reading 'Please Pay Here'. She was surprised to find the conservatory plants in superb condition, with palms swaying to the roof and a banana in purple flower. There was a desk, and a till, not new but definitely operational because it was humming. A careless litter of documents covered the counter. It was impossible not to notice some overdue bills. Clearly, Gaia was not prospering.

She looked around, impatient again. Just an hour left to get the planting finished before she had to pick up Max. The glasshouse was quiet and there was only vegetable life to be seen.

'Hello?' she called, hearing her voice evaporate among the still leaves. 'Hello? Is anyone here?'

There was also a brass bell, such as the hotel managers have in old Western films. She hit it smartly. The humid air muffled the ringing. She hit the bell again, twice. 'Hello!'

'Oh – hi!' Unashamed, a woman emerged from behind a screen, one hand grabbing wild corkscrews of honey-brown hair off her face, the other making vague gestures as if a hairclip was going to be conjured from thin air. 'I didn't mean to keep you, I was just on the screen chasing an order. Oh, Corsican mints – aren't these to die for? I haven't even priced them, let me just check the list . . .' Leisurely, she began to shift through the papers on the desk. No hairclip having materialised, the ringlets fell back in her eyes. Her free hand wandered to the pen pot on the counter and pulled out a topless ballpoint.

'I'm in a hurry.' Stephanie had her Visa ready. 'I have to pick up my son from school.'

'Oh, I knew I knew you.' The woman looked up again, clearly more interested in conversation than commerce. 'Isn't he at The Magpies?'

'Yes – look, I really have to run—'

'Don't worry – take them, pay me tomorrow. I'll have figured out the price by then.' She twisted some hair into a topknot and used the ballpoint to skewer it.

'I can't possibly do that—'

'I bet you could if you tried. Go on. Hell, you could just leave me your Visa number and I'll give you a call and tell you how much. Or you could call me. Take one of our cards, the number's on it.'

The cards were scattered on a soapstone lotus dish, under a coating of dust. The woman's smile struck Stephanie as over-eager. Her small face was widest at the high cheekbones and her eyes were deep-set, slanting and dark like black olives stuck in a loaf. She stood with her hands at the back of her rounded hips as if she were pregnant and had backache. A washed-out purple T-shirt, riding up under her overalls, revealed a roll of olive-skinned midriff. Her bare feet were in muddy Birkenstocks. Stephanie tried not to look at the belly area. No, she wasn't pregnant. It was just the way she was built and the way she was standing.

'Look, I know you. I must do, my girls went to The Magpies too. I trust you. Take 'em – they're gorgeous. I'm just dying to sell them to somebody. Please . . .'

'I couldn't possibly,' said Stephanie. She was becoming angry now. 'I really have to go.'

'Ah! I've got it.' From the bottom of the pile of papers the woman pulled out one sheet, which sent a dozen more cascading to the ground. She ignored them and squinted at the page. 'Let me give you a bulk discount here – ten per cent, OK?'

'That's very kind.' Stephanie spoke through grinding teeth. *Hurry up.*

'You must be making a feature of them. A seat or something?' Keying in the price and calculating the deduction, her finger looped uncertainly over the numbers. Her hands were large but elegant, with strong wide knuckles. She seemed casually keen to develop the conversation.

'An aromatic walk at the end of a terrace, an edging of

cobbles with these little things tucked between the stones so they'll give off a scent when people step on them.' Stephanie heard her voice getting clipped. *For heaven's sake, hurry.*

'Hey, great idea. So we can sell you some rocks? Did you see I have some four-inch granite cobbles out there?' She waved a generous arm at the door to the exterior.

'I'm OK for rocks,' Stephanie confirmed with desperate calm. 'All I need is the mints and to get out of here in time to fetch my son from school.'

'They won't mind if you're late. I used to show up late all the time for my girls. Look, you're getting some moss thrown in here – you want me to scrape it off? Isn't that bizarre, when we're so close to the road? I always thought moss needed pure mountain air.'

Stephanie felt dizzy. She felt a blast of rage. She felt her face breaking into hard portions like river ice breaking up in spring. Nothing computed. She wanted to finish this planting, she wanted to fetch Max this instant, she wanted people to stop bitching about her, she wanted a real job, she wanted Stewart back right now, she wanted her beautiful safe sun-dappled life back again just as it had been before. She needed these things, she should have these things, she deserved these things and she could not have them. She was going to explode.

'Are you OK?' Something was showing on her face because the woman was immediately concerned. 'Would you like to sit down for a minute? Can I get you something? A tea? I've got some rescue remedy somewhere . . .' Stephanie shook her head. It was hot in the glasshouse, maybe this was just the heat. Her hands were together on the counter top, holding her Visa. She pinched herself at the base of a thumb, digging her nails into her flesh, knowing the pain would make sense.

The woman pushed past the loaded desk and came around towards her, holding out her arms. 'Please, I am so sorry, I didn't mean to upset you . . .'

'No, no.' Stephanie hated to be hugged by strangers. She felt the world was falling back into place. She took some deep breaths and stopped herself fending the woman off with a push. 'I should apologise. I'm a bit stressed right now, that's all. But I am OK. Can we just settle up? I really have to get going.'

'Absolutely. Absolutely. Look – ah – I can put these in the car for you but will you be all right to unload them?' Standing back on her heels, her muddy hands with their long, flexible fingers propped at her waist again, the woman was now eyeing her with curiosity. It was a frank instinct, tempered, Stephanie was amused to see, with the wish not to imply that another woman might be too weak or too prissy to handle plants herself.

'I have help,' she assured the woman briskly.

'Well – lucky *you*.'

'Nothing like that – they work for me.' Was that unjustifiably prim? She hated to be stereotyped as privileged just because she lived in Westwick. 'We're in the middle of planting up a job. That's my business, I'm a landscaper.' She quite shocked herself. In Westwick people were guarded; disclosure was unwise for it led on to intimacy. Back in the torrent of city encounters, she used to enjoy the pleasure of making acquaintances but she had learned new ways. Besides, this woman was over-eager for connection, but Stephanie reassured herself that she could still withdraw; actually, she was skilled at it, fading away from people she chose not to know so softly that they often put down her departure to simple timidity.

'A business?' Gaia's proprietor was outraged, her voice rising to a squeak. 'You are in *business* and you're letting me charge you retail? No, no, no! I would die!' In histrionic alarm, the fingers flew to her perspiring forehead and seized clumps of her hair as if to pull it out by the roots. 'Hold it right there! Right there! You can't let me do this! My father would kill me if he thought I'd let you just pay retail and drive out of here. Where's the invoice – have I given you an invoice?' She let go of her hair and started checking the multiple pockets of her overalls. 'I haven't even given you an invoice, I deserve to go to hell. OK. OK. You're in a hurry, I know. It won't take a minute.'

A calculator was excavated from a stack of catalogues under the counter. With a mauve felt-tip she covered a sheet of newspaper with figures, muttering percentages to herself. The calculator malfunctioned and she banged it on the edge of the desk; the pen ran dry and she put it back in the pen pot; she picked another which was also finished, then a pencil which was broken, then pulled the ballpoint out of her hair, then arrived at a total, swiped Stephanie's Visa, keyed numbers into the terminal, made a mistake, swore, voided the process and began again.

When the machine accepted its instructions it fell silent. Stephanie realised she was grinding her teeth and opened her mouth to stop it. *I don't believe this.*

'Everybody's shopping this afternoon,' the woman said, tapping her teeth with the chewed end of the pen. Stephanie sighed again. The conservatory microclimate was close. 'You're so calm,' she observed. They exclaimed with relief when the transaction went through, then the paper jammed printing the receipt. 'I *don't* believe it,' the woman hissed, hitting the desk with her fist.

'I do. You put the roll in the wrong way again.' A young woman with a deep voice and an air of nun-like transcendence was gliding towards them between the towering palms, the hem of her skirt undulating rhythmically at each step. In one smooth sequence of movements she reached over the apparatus, flipped open the casing, turned the roll, eased the edge under the roller, flicked out the wad of crushed paper, closed the lid and touched a key to reprint.

'Have you met my daughter, the electronics engineer? Topaz, this is . . .'

'You're Mrs Sands. Hello.' The girl had the same powerful hands as her mother, and very similar features although her hair was dark and cut as short as a lamb's fleece. Everything about her was economical and controlled. She carried a briefcase. All the buttons of her ice-blue cotton cardigan were fastened, running in an even line between breasts whose symmetrical masses were effaced almost to flatness by stern underwear. She had elfin ears, lying close against her head, decorated with tiny pearls. 'Nice to meet you. I'm Topaz Lieberman. I was really sorry to hear the news about your husband. Hope he'll be home safe soon.'

'What news? Topaz, what haven't you told me that I should know?'

Embarrassed, the girl glanced from Stephanie to her mother. 'We heard at school. Mrs Sands – I don't know if I have the facts right . . .'

'My husband was away on a business trip in Eastern Europe and he has been kidnapped.' For the first time, Stephanie found it simple to say, although she also felt pain at being an object of discussion in the high school. Announced to the chaotic Mrs Lieberman amid the bizarre proliferations of the Gaia Garden Centre, the facts sounded less monstrous. And there was something about the daughter, with her over-mature manners, her geeky beauty and habit of taking control; she promoted trust.

'My God, that's *you*? I heard about that. That's terrible. You're the one, and we've been gassing away about nothing here all afternoon?' Gemma was now looking at Stephanie with blatant admiration.

'Mother . . .'

'Excuse my daughter, she has feeling difficulties.'

'Mother, please.'

'She's been having remedial classes since she was ten but there's so much to make up. We may have to go for a heart transplant. Darling, will you mind the store for me while I deliver Mrs Sands's stuff for her?'

'Oh no.' Strangers, emotions, spontaneity – Stephanie recognised that she had become afraid of them all. Was this the herd instinct of Westwick, fleeing from everything new and unpredictable? 'That really won't be necessary. I'll be fine.'

'Let me help you get them in,' Gemma insisted. 'I'd feel better – I've wasted your time and been so insensitive.'

'No, please . . .' She was wavering. She was weak from chronic high emotion, her resistance was low.

'Look,' Gemma pressed her, 'I know you think I'm a crazy person but I'm great at planting, really. Even my daughter will let me have that, won't you dear?'

'Yes,' Topaz agreed, gathering up the spilled paperwork from the floor. 'Everything grows for my mother. It's a good offer, I'd take it if I were you.' There was a note of command in her speech.

And so they changed places, Topaz sliding gracefully behind the desk and seating herself on a stool. As they left she was opening her case and taking out books.

'Look, I'm Gemma. Gemma Lieberman.' One of the grubby long hands was offered in a sweeping arc. Clumsy in the Birkenstocks, she half-turned to walk sideways.

'Stephanie Sands.'

'You can hardly go around giving newscasts to every stranger who crosses your path.'

'It's been difficult.'

'I bet. My husband left – did you know that? Nothing like you at all, I mean, forgive me, actually he went to jail. But I just got so ticked off telling everybody all the time. Saying the same words over and over.'

'I'm . . .' Jail? Had she jumped at that word? In alarm, Stephanie groped for the correct response. 'I'm sorry that—'

'Please, don't be sorry. It's the best place for him. Please God, I should never have a worse problem than how to tell people. But it was such a drag. I felt like sewing it over my chest in sequins or something.'

Unexpectedly, humour like a sip of champagne bubbled up and tickled the back of Stephanie's nose. She actually chuckled. 'I know,' she murmured. 'It gets too much. I can hear myself saying the same things every day, all these useless words piling up. I just want to scream, but what good would it do?' Her disturbed feelings, added to the fatigue created by her hours of work in the morning sun, were now generating a silly weakness. Waking and sleeping, anxiety had been chewing her nerves for weeks. 'And you feel like you're being a burden to people. You're not asking for their sympathy exactly, but they feel they have to say something kind.'

'In the end, I took the Noël Coward line. "Nevair apologise and nevair explain."' With the ballpoint as a cigarette holder, she did The Master very well.

'I'll remember that.'

They climbed into their vehicles and drove in convoy to Church Vale. Stephanie was not surprised to find that the dead Lada belonged to Gemma. In the actor's garden, under the dismissive eyes of Derek and Dave, Ms Lieberman laboured with a will and the planting was finished in half an hour.

'There,' she said, wiping her hands down her thighs. 'All done. I feel better about being such a durr now. Look, I've got to get back, I promised Topaz I'd do stock-taking – but come see us again, huh? Not just if you need something – let's face it, we haven't got much – but if you'd like company or something. I know you're busy, but come anyway, huh?' And she ducked into the wretched Lada and rattled away.

That night, when she was alone with her sleeping son, Stephanie's thoughts turned back to Gemma Lieberman, and raised the question of the crime for which her husband was in jail. The distinction interested her beyond the scope of gossip. At that point in the history of the region, husbands from Westwick did not go to jail. It was one of the particular attractions of the neighbourhood for Stephanie, whose father had also gone to jail, if only for a ridiculously ineffectual attempt at fraud and only for six months.

CHAPTER 10

A Club for Ladies and Gentlemen

'Mr Fuller, this is always a sensitive conversation.' The doctor looked as if someone had stopped in the middle of pulling his entrails out through his nose. He was hanging his head and kicking invisible fluff balls off the mirror-polished floor of the twelfth-floor corridor outside the Intensive Care Unit in Helford Hospital with his mirror-polished shoes. 'To combat your wife's infection we could give her antibiotics intravenously as I believe we've done before.' He twitched the patient's file into his eyeline as if to refresh his memory. 'Which might very well be successful, although she is a little weaker now. And we have seen some of the drug-resistant strains here this year. Or, our alternative is to not intervene. Then nature will take its course and we can allow Mary-Sue to slip away from us.'

His wife's name was Mairi-Sui, but Rod felt it would be mean to correct the man when he was doing his best. Furthermore, at that exact moment, the moment he had been expecting any time over the last six months, his mind was void of words.

'It's always a very, very difficult decision to make with a PVS patient,' the doctor continued in an earnest tone which did not really camouflage his own opinion that the decision was in fact very easy. 'I would never say that miracles don't happen. If you asked me, though, I would have to say that they haven't happened in my experience of these patients so far.'

Rod found some words. 'Can you give me a moment?'

'Of course. Take all the time you need. I'll be on the ward another half an hour.'

At the far, far end of the corridor, where four red seating units were grouped alongside a dying *dieffenbachia*, Sweetheart was restlessly flicking her fingers, waiting. Rod wished he was a child of five, with someone he considered wise to make decisions for him. He made the long trek down the glassy floor towards her. The hospital had a special atmosphere, the air was hot and thick but its smell was dry, as if chemically desiccated. Sweetheart looked at him and he knew that she knew. He wondered if she ought to know, and what he had given away in his manner. This was a burden that he could hardly bear, let alone share with his child, delightfully precocious as she was.

'It's pneumonia again.' He sat down beside her, the person he lived for who he now had to exclude from the most vital part of his life for her own protection. This was not a child's decision. He had to make it by himself.

'Might Mummy die this time?' she asked, playing along so well that it cracked him up and he lost the words again for a while. He nodded his head. She put her hand in his and it was like holding a tiny bird.

'I've got to go back and see the doctor again,' he said when he could get the sentence out. 'I'll be back in a minute.'

In the sister's office, the doctor tried to put a good professional facade on his satisfaction. 'It's a very peaceful thing,' he said, keeping half an eye on the monitor screen while he keyed in some characters. Was there a code for death, one of those medical references framed to hide the facts from ordinary people, a string of numbers to signify the end of a life? Look, with a spot I damn him. With a slash and a sub-code for the circumstances – /DOA, dead on arrival; /DDR, during resuscitation; /DSI, secondary infection; /DMA, death by mutual agreement? 'I'll ask the nurse to make her tidy and then you can sit with her for a while. Do you know where the telephone is, if there's anyone you need to call? I'm afraid we can't allow mobiles in the hospital, they interfere with some of our equipment.'

He knew very well where the telephone was. He had spent much time there. Mairi-Sui's parents were the other side of the world, with five other children, three of them male. His own mother had never approved of their marriage. They were already getting his classes covered at The Cedars. Gemma would cancel his private clients. 'Be strong, honeybuns,' she enjoined him gently. 'Like you have a choice, I know. Do you want me to come up and fetch Sweetheart?'

'I don't know.' Did he have to be alone while his wife died? The weight of his daughter's body, the touch of her warm limbs, young and dense with life, was unbelievably comforting to him, but he never dared hold her for long except when friends were about to witness. Was it right to take comfort from a child? Did he already lean on her too much?

'You could ask her what she wants to do.' Gemma prompted. 'Maybe it's too heavy for her. I don't know. She's a good kid.'

'She sees people die on ER every week. This is her mother. I don't know.'

'On ER, when people die, what happens with their family?'

'Usually they get a great screaming entrance and then they're kept out of the way by the nice curly-haired nurse while speccy Doctor Mark does the flat-iron thing. If you see it. Quite often they cut to another story.'

'OK. I can't believe I asked that. Are we really sitting here on the phone trying to get the protocol for dying from a TV show?'

'I don't know, I don't know. I can't believe I answered you either.'

'What's your gut tell you? What feels right?'

'Nothing feels right, Gemma. What would feel right is having Mairi-Sui back with us. Nothing's felt right since . . .'

This was like his fog dream, when a shapeless fear smothered him and he ran in every direction without seeing where he was going, running into a wall whichever way he went, and each time he ran a little less far, so the walls where getting closer and closer but he could never see them because of the fog, even when he could put out his hands and touch the walls from standing still.

A drink would feel right now, a real drink, maybe vodka. No vodka: he had made a rule for himself to stick with wine. Crossing to spirits was the great divide, crossing Jordan the wrong way. Who could be a serious drunk if all they did was get sloppy on wine every now and then? Self-deception, the first sign of alcoholism. No vodka, no wine.

'OK, OK.' At the end of the phone, Gemma was slurping her tea. 'So – if Mairi-Sui could speak still, what would she want?'

'I don't know. Nothing ever happened in our lives until this, you know. I don't know what pain would do to her. She wouldn't want her to suffer, she never wanted anyone to suffer.'

'What would Sweetheart want?'

That was simple. 'To be with me.'

'Well, then – isn't that your answer?'

'I don't know.'

'Won't you feel better if she's with you?'

'Yes, but this isn't about how *I'm* going to feel, is it? I can't lay this trauma on her because it'll make me feel better. This is about what's best for Sweetheart. Or least bad, anyway.'

'OK, then, how about this. I'll decide for you. Keep her with you. Then she can't turn round to you later on and accuse you of keeping her away. It's too bad you'll have to feel better. You can't win this one; being a parent means always having to say you're sorry. And I'll close up here and come and sit outside and impersonate your mother if she was a good person and if Sweetheart gets upset or anything I can take her home. How about that?'

The fog was clearing. He did not want vodka. Maybe wine, maybe he could reconsider that, when it was over. Rod scrubbed his scalp with his free hand. 'That would be good, Gemma. Can you do that?'

'Of course I can. Hospitals, I've been there. I know hospitals. I can close up Gaia, nobody ever comes in anyway and if they do, they'll come back. Topaz'll be here in a couple of hours anyway. Tell me what ward you're on.'

With all the tubes and monitors, Mairi-Sui looked like one piece of equipment linked up to all the others, and a broken down, ill-designed machine at that. The nurses had disconnected most of the apparatus, which made her seem more human, but the real Mairi-Sui had vanished long ago. While most of his mind quaked with distress, a reasoning voice babbled on, calling his attention to the bloomless, parchment skin, the stringy joints, the sunken throat which aroused no memory at all of the pulsing creamy hollows he had once kissed.

They had smeared balm on her lips to keep them moist, not very accurately. He remembered her sitting at a mirror with her lip-brush, the poise of her wrist, the tip of the brush pecking at the petal skin. The body was not yet wasted but it seemed halfway into another existence. She could still breathe for herself, but it was just a function, harsh and mindless, nothing like the easy breath of life.

The humming of the waterbed was eerie. Sweetheart

had the CD player, the same which pumped out aerobic mixes for the clients. They talked about putting on something she liked, a hard choice because Mairi-Sui had loved Meatloaf, which seemed wrong, and the old R & B songs, which were going to make them cry. She had just finished a run of *Carousel*, but that was dangerous too; for a while every musical she had danced in that they could think of had sad songs in it. When Gemma arrived she found them sitting either side of the bed, holding the cold hands under the blanket, listening to 'Luck Be A Lady Tonight'.

'Welcome.' In the doorway of Grove House, Chester Pike balanced on his neat little feet beneath his eighteenth-century fanlight. 'Welcome, welcome. Good to see you, Allie, my dear. Ted. Welcome. Come along through.' Soon his guests would be announced by a porter thirty floors down and admitted by a manservant. Only two more years. Or maybe less. Things were moving in that department.

'So pleased you could come.' Lauren wafted her house-keeper towards them with two misted flutes of champagne. Twice a year the Parsons were invited to Grove House. At Christmas, when the Pikes gave two parties, A list and B list, the Parsons came to the A-list party, not because either Lauren or Chester considered that they deserved to but because they lived close enough to observe all the arrivals and departures and therefore knew that two parties were held and would know to

which they were bidden. In the summer, usually late in
the summer because the Pike's impulse to entertain them
was not strong, they were asked to dinner. 'Chester's so
hard to pin down these days,' Lauren would say to Allie.
'Twice a week in St Louis. I hardly see him myself. I've
told him we can't live like this. But I'll get a day out of
him, I promise.'

Ted fed himself some salted almonds from a silver
dish and took a short stroll up the edge of the blue
Chinese carpet. No kicking back or hanging out *chez*
Chester, let alone partying down. Every detail of an
event at the Pikes was choreographed, as if they followed
the prescriptions of some secret social manual. Their
affairs were so regimented they could have been staged
from a military entertaining handbook. Tonight was a
Summer Casual Dinner Grade II: four courses, catered,
but served by the housekeeper, with Lauren in floor-
length black linen and a plain gold link necklace. Grade
I would have been five courses, served by the staff, short
silk and diamonds.

Guests never saw the manual, so you had to guess
your grade in advance. Allie, trussed in strapless white
silk splattered with red roses, had over-estimated. Ted
was glad he had held out against her in the matter of a
black tie. Of such bitter little victories was marital satisfaction made nowadays.

'Hurmph.' Chester cleared his throat for conversation
and took up a position in front of his eighteenth-century
limewood fire-surround carved with swags of fruit and
dead game birds. 'Hurmph, hah. Oak Hill progressing,
yes?'

'Planning consent was granted yesterday,' Ted confirmed with pride. 'I got the word, informally. Old contact on the committee. We'll get the papers next week.' Fifteen years ago, Ted had let the planning committee chair, then merely the deputy surveyor for the county, in on a deal with a rambling, rotting mansion at the end of Riverview Drive, now undergoing its second facelift as a complex of luxury apartments with stunning river views. It was, he felt, one of the smartest things he had ever done.

'Splendid, splendid. So when . . .' Chester's impression was that the affair had hung fire forever. This business of waiting for permissions, which Parsons thought so important, seemed plain soft to him.

'We can move the day the papers are through. Contractors' boards will go up tomorrow; they've started work clearing the site already. The heavy plant will come up mid-week. They need a police escort for that.' The vision of giant diggers crawling up the 31 with outriders and flashing lights ought to appeal to the small boy in every man, Ted considered. And he was proud of his zap off the starting blocks with this one.

'Very good, very good.' Chester put his elbow on the mantelpiece with a view to leaning casually against it. He was not a tall man, certainly not as tall as the man who had carved his fire-surround, and the pose left his jacket seams straining. With his round body, little feet, undershot jaw and slightly popped eyes, Chester looked like a tortured toad. 'And how did you enjoy your trip to Whitbridge?'

Ted had prepared a report on the Strankley Ridge sites, and Chester had it, but clearly did not intend to waste time actually reading it. He knew the pattern; the BSD worked on capsule briefings. He had underlings to read for him.

'You were absolutely right,' Ted watched his launch flattery disappear into Chester's ego like water vanishing into sand. 'Magnificent opportunity, magnificent. When the Thirty-four extension is completed the region will be equidistant from the city airport and the new airport to the north. Rail link to Whitbridge due for upgrading next year. All the support services in place – schools, hospital, the new Magno at Ambleford. At least five prime sites in that valley alone. We can take our pick.'

'So your decision . . .'

'I've had a prospectus prepared.' Ted throttled back self-satisfaction as he announced this initiative. 'We could take a look after dinner.' And he glanced chivalrously to Lauren, seeking the châtelaine's sanction for this unseemly commercial note in her home.

'Why not now?' Chester blinked at him, the amphibian sighting a fly.

'Why not?' Ted echoed. 'Of course, why not. I'll just be a moment.' Don't rush, he counselled himself as he left the room and went out to the Discovery. No shuffling to impress. You are cool, you are in control. This is going well, really well.

Sprint, man, sprint, Chester urged him, watching silently at the window as Parsons loped towards his vehicle. This is taking too long.

'Have you planned your holiday?' Lauren enquired brightly of Allie, who hated holidays and hated planning them almost as much.

'We might borrow a friend's boat,' she answered, trying to convey that a small yacht was always at their disposal somewhere, 'though I do worry about the children on boats, don't you?'

'Nothing for them to do, is there?' Lauren sympathised.

Corporate syncopation was not Ted's thing, never had been. He was a loner, a maverick, an independent freebooter sailing under his own flag. Oak Hill was a breakthrough project for him, his first commercial development. Commercial was where the big money was; he was waiting for the out-of-place feeling to get normal, like the discomfort of having your teeth scaled, a friendly sort of soreness once you got used to it. Commercial was a different game, surprisingly different. He was pleased with himself for learning the moves, even making up his own moves, but he had fallen into a way of feinting passes at Chester to see him react and getting a bead on what he ought to be doing from that. Weaselling around the BSD was not what he had been made for; it went against the grain, but it was getting to be a habit.

Take Strankley Ridge. Left to himself, he would never have even looked at the site. Or maybe he would have looked, but only to reassure himself that his gut feeling was the right feeling. He was uneasy with building on green fields, it was that simple. With the big dick swinging over him now, he found himself having to construct a whole commercial rationale for his instinct. That instinct had made him millions, it had never been wrong, but tap-dancing around it with logic seemed to damp it down, it did not speak to him so clearly.

The prospectus was mouthwatering. *Ambleford Meadows*, it proclaimed over a photograph of the glorious sweep up the valley to the three skyline beeches. *Experience the best in luxury living; pre-eminent homes; a dream location convenient for two airports; glorious views; painstaking attention to detail; fast trains to the city; above all else, a Tudor home.*

The artist's impression of the houses themselves nodded to the hyper-realism of Andrew Wylie paintings, suggesting homestead values and the fruitful earth. Instead of the dull specification of room numbers and sizes, he had run the street names under the pictures: Beehive Lane; Quaker Wood; The Hawthorns; Beech Tree Heights.

'Isn't that attractive?' Lauren commented, looking around her husband's shoulder. 'I love the names.'

'Beech Tree Heights,' Chester repeated, turning over the glossy page. 'Impressive, Ted. I like it.'

'We're fine-tuning the costings.' Ted slipped that in before finishing on a high note. 'Our target market are young city-living professionals, middle-management, who've perhaps started families already and are looking for a real lifestyle package. In this location we can look to the north as well, for the people who don't see the urban renewal happening fast enough for their children.'

'Good thinking,' Chester told him, thinking that without the costings this was all froth and no beer. 'What's holding up the costing?'

'Survey.' Airy, Ted's tone was as airy as a galleried duplex. 'With a hillside site like this, I'd like to be quite happy about the sub-soil.'

'Why pick a hillside?' Damn. Trust Chester to put his finger on it straight away.

'Danger of subsidence down there in the bottom of the valley. Flooding, too. And the view, Chester. People will pay anything for an outlook. An extra thirty per cent on top of what they'd pay for the same house on the level.'

'Well,' said Chester, his bullshit detector trembling significantly, 'you're the expert. I'm hungry. Shall we go in?'

Lauren's decorator had carried the Jacobean theme through into the dining room, with a massive oak table on barleytwist legs and carved chairs which dug spitefully into the diners' backs. Ted looked without appetite at his plate of scorched vegetable matter in truffle oil. The smell of the truffle oil made him feel queasy. The feeling that Chester was not going to buy his elaborately designed evasion made him feel positively nauseous. His strategy to abort the project had been to choose a site whose development costs would be prohibitive, then let the BSD himself decide to pull out. Instead, the BSD was swinging around the corner ahead of him already.

Chester chopped his plateful to shreds and scooped it into his mouth. Lauren twiddled some leaves. Allie poked something solid to the side of her plate. 'Perfect,' Ted complimented his hostess, 'not too heavy.'

The housekeeper cleared the plates. Lauren asked her to take out one of the silver candlesticks and polish away a fingermark on its base.

'And how do you view this digital business?' Chester asked Allie, groping for an aspect of broadcasting capable of holding his interest.

'Oh, that's way in the future, isn't it?' she parried, 'We live right in the here-and-now on *Family First.* That's what I find so frustrating.' Chester and The Boss met on a few boards about the city. If The Boss was temporarily unaware of her potential, perhaps the word of another man would help. 'I feel I'm really too experienced for that kind of thing, it just isn't fulfilling. Of course, *some* things are fulfilling. We got great feedback on the Magno exchange promise, great.'

'Don't saw the meat, Theresa,' Lauren admonished the housekeeper, who was struggling to carve a saddle of lamb at the serving table. 'Just gentle pressure on the knife.' Then she twitched a smile at Ted to assure him that he must be family if she corrected her staff in front of him. Her right hand moved continually from entrée knife to salad knife to bread knife to white wine glass to claret glass to water glass and out to her Ventolin and back, as if she needed constant reassurance that the table had been set correctly.

'You get a such a boost when you can do something like the Magno report,' Allie ran on. 'You know you have really, really connected with the audience, you know?'

'Our people look after you all right with that?' Chester was expecting the answer he got.

'Oh yes. Yes, of course. They were just f-a-a-b.' She had an inspiration. 'I'd just love to be able to do that kind of feature on a bigger scale, you know? A prime-time show. After – what is it now? Five awards? I feel I've gone as far as a girl can go in the daytime.' She fairly sizzled at him over the rim of her glass, but Chester accepted flirtation from other men's wives as no more than his due. His wife took a squirt from her inhaler.

'Surely not,' he said, not smiling. A portion of organic lamb balanced on a hill of lentils appeared in front of him and he applied himself to it, leaving her to turn back to Lauren with, 'And you'll be away to The Hamptons this summer?'

'Oh yes, I can't wait. As soon as school breaks up. Very dull of us, I know, always going to the same place, but we love it so.' And she tried to catch her husband's eye up the table, but Chester had relapsed into a momentary reverie of distaste for things heavy, dark, old and uncomfortable, and yen for things light, bright and modern, and for a light, bright, modern woman, perhaps the one he had already met in St Louis, to sparkle among them. And no lentils, fiddly, a waste of time.

By 11 pm, the Parsons were home, wound-up and wakeful. 'That went well, I thought,' Ted ventured as they cast about the kitchen looking for cause not to go up the stairs together.

'Vile,' Allie said. 'That man is such a bore.' She meant that Chester seldom showed any sexual interest in her. She caught her reflection in the glass door of the oven and pulled up her jaw to keep its line taut.

'You get on with his wife,' Ted suggested.

'Only the way women do,' she flopped into a chair, pouting. She did not consider women of any importance unless they threatened her job.

'She can be very gracious,' Ted suggested, thinking about a small malt.

'Oh God, the lady of the manor act. Isn't it sick? God help the people she visits on her victim support thing. I think I'd rather be mugged than have Lauren Pike support me. She'd make me sterilise the Kleenex before I started crying.'

From Allie, this was mellow conversation. Perhaps a useful moment was approaching. Ted decided to pass on the small malt, since the fact that he enjoyed the occasional late-night belt was one of the myriad of his characteristics which unfailingly enraged her. He poured himself a Coke instead, and Allie allowed him to give her a diet one also. This was tightrope walking. Judging the business minutely, he handed her both the can and a glass; actually pouring the drink would be servile, handing the can by itself, on the other hand, would be too rude.

Snap, pour, drink, pause. So far so good.

'Do you think about the future at all?' he enquired, trying to find a casual segue into the subject.

'Of course I think about the future, Ted.' Snappish, but still amiable. They were sitting now at either end of the farmhouse table, splayed in the carver chairs among the disorder of the kitchen like a modern *Mariage à la Mode*. 'I must, must, must get out of daytime,' she added, kicking at the table leg in frustration. 'It'll be the end of my career if I don't. It's hardly a career at all, daytime TV. And past thirty-five, you're dead on the screen in the day. I'm a great political interviewer, surely they can see that? Besides, you get five times the money.'

'I was thinking more about – you know, the family,' Ted ventured.

'He's got to go back into rehab.' Her tone was suddenly belligerent. 'Tough love, that's all he'll get from me. I won't have him falling about round here.'

'I didn't mean Damon,' Ted explained. 'All of us. I was thinking, while I was working on this Ambleford thing. There are some lovely houses that way, and still cheap. We could get something three times this size, with land, ponies for the girls—'

'No thanks,' Allie responded briskly. 'I'd have to get up at five every morning to get to the studios and I'd look like death warmed up in a week. You never thought of that, I suppose. Anyway, I thought you adored your precious Westwick.'

'Oh, I do, I do,' Ted assured her. 'And I don't mean get rid of this house, not at all. Keep it. Just base the family in the country. I'll be spending a hell of a lot of time down there if the Ambleford thing goes live.'

'Oh – *I* see,' Allie said with a sneer. 'What you're saying is separate lives. You and the girls go off and play country living in some worm-eaten old farmhouse, I stay here and work my butt off and in a couple of years you file for divorce on the grounds I deserted the family. Is that what's on your mind?'

'Alex! Alex, please! What a monstrous thing to say!' Ted jumped up and acted as outraged as he dared, spooked because his intentions had been guessed for the second time that evening. 'How could you imagine I could even think of such an idea?'

'Because I know you,' she replied, unmoved. 'You're a

pathetic little man with a bag of slop for brains. You hate me – you must do, because I sure as hell hate you; you're too mean to divorce me because I'd get at least half everything as well as the kids. Well, thank God I got my share on paper, you can't touch it. And now you're so fucking stupid you thought you could manipulate me into giving it all away.'

'I don't see why . . .' Ted protested, running his fingers into his hair and pulling it in frustration. 'Look – I don't care about the money. Really, I don't. Money's only money, take all you want. This is just a CV marriage to you, isn't it?'

'Absolutely.' He was surprised that she made the admission.

'You could at least let me lead my own life,' he pleaded.

'No,' she said lightly, kicking the table leg again with one of her pointed pink suede evening mules. 'Don't be so god-damned selfish, Ted. Your life is my life, my life is my work. I can't have that kind of thing said about me. While I'm on *Family First*, we stick together. You're a joke, Ted, a lightweight, a dickhead. You and your stupid little deals and your stupid houses. Chester – you kiss his ass, you think he's the big "I Am", he's just a jerk, no style; he can't cut it. We can get divorced when it suits me, when I've moved on from *Family First*. Believe me, I can't wait.' She was longing to move up into the next level of life, wife of some hot big guy, anchor of some hot prime-time show, her cover of *Time* not far off. One breakthrough, that was all she needed; the job or the man, the chicken or the egg.

'Are you having an affair?' she demanded, as he expected her to.

'No,' he said.

'You're not even lying, are you? Well, I can't say I'm surprised. You're hardly a man, are you? Not many women could put up with you sliming them. Go on, have a fling, be my guest. I don't want you leching after every little whore in your office, getting into a sexual harassment suit. That would look good, wouldn't it?'

This was too much for Ted. All his hopes lay pulverised in fragments at his feet. He announced that he would take the dog out for a while, and dawdled along in the deep darkness beneath the old trees of Maple Grove, listening to Moron snuffling equably in the trim grass. If he were a proper man, he knew, he would be able to walk on to Alder Reach now, and find a warm welcome there. As it was, he would have to go back to his own desolate bed and lie there in the darkness, the man who made his fortune selling happy homes to happy families.

'Topaz, can I ask you something?' For once, Flora Lieberman was idling. Mooning about the living space ruffling up her mop of hair, picking up an apple, deciding she didn't want it, picking up a pen, not knowing what to write, scrubbing at her eyes and making them red, flopping on the sofa, getting up again, stretching up her dimpled arms to the ceiling, letting them fall heavily to her sides.

Her sister, chipping at her rock-pile of books, was becoming irritated. 'If we can deal with what's bothering you and get some peace around here – sure, ask me anything.'

'You remember Damon Parsons?'

'Lurch.'

'Yeah, that's him.' Damon's sense of balance was defective. At St Nicholas's High School he canted at his desk, lummoxed about the corridors and fell over on the sports fields. No lecture the staff could devise about the social divisiveness of stigmatising the disadvantaged saved him from his nickname.

'Is he still in school?'

Flora sighed. 'Unfortunately. He was sent away on some alcohol programme but when he came back they just put him down a year.'

'What about him?' Topaz already had the essence of the problem. All this sighing and avoidance – it had to be sex.

Of the three Lieberman sisters, Flora alone took after her mother. While Topaz and Molly were economically made, Flora was ample and unconstructed. Molly was an imp; Topaz had matured effortlessly from imp to dryad; Flora was in mid-metamorphosis from blob to goddess; her suddenly abundant flesh burst seams every day. She was struggling through the curse of full-out adolesence, randomly attacked by sweat, pimples, blubber, jugs and despair. To Topaz, she was a pain.

'He keeps following me.'

'Tell him to go away.'

'I have told him.'

'And . . .'

'And he just grins at me.'

'You can't be telling him right then. If you intend to communicate something, you're responsible for doing so in a manner which achieves understanding.'

'I don't think he can understand, Topaz. He's not right, you know? I think he's only in school because his mother schmoozes around with all that TV stuff and the head's just taken in by it. I mean, I've been in classes with him and he's not playing with a full deck. He's weird. He scares me.'

'That's not logical, Flora.'

'It is so logical. He's a huge thing and he could do anything. You know he smashed up the Wilde At Heart last year when he was drunk.'

Topaz considered. Unruly elements had to be purged. Society was healthier without their influence. Nepotism was a cancer which ate at the hearts of the people. On the other hand, her sister, with her flouncing flesh and feeble spirit, was colluding with her persecutor. Since they were not in a position to purge the offender at this point in time, only Flora's contribution to the problem could be addressed.

'Go and sign up for a martial arts class,' counselled Topaz, 'or self-defence for women or something. You need to empower yourself. When you cease to feel like a victim, you won't act like a victim and then you will no longer be a victim.'

'They make you fall about and hit people in self-defence.' Physical activity, beyond a little languid dancing, did not attract Flora. She regarded having to cycle to school as the greatest burden of their comparative poverty.

'How do you know until you've done it?' Topaz countered. 'But this isn't about learning to fight, Flora. You don't understand. It's about getting in touch with your inner strength, so you never need to fight anybody. You shouldn't be creeping around letting yourself be intimidated by a retard like Lurch.'

'No,' Flora agreed. If you asked Topaz for help, you had to take whatever she gave you. Her authority was total. Trouble was, there were things Topaz didn't understand. Like failure. Let alone fear of failure. And as for worrying that you'd chosen the wrong thing to fail at . . . Topaz could do things that most people found difficult without any trouble at all. If you said you were having problems, she just blinked at you.

'Otherwise,' Topaz added with supreme rationality, 'what we could do is get Gemma to go and speak to the school about it . . .'

Flora winced. Nothing in the world was more painful than having her mother intervene in her school life. Topaz went back to her books, confident of the outcome. For a short while the only sound in the room was the muted clatter of her keyboard.

'OK,' Flora sighed eventually. 'I'll do it. If you really think it will help.'

'They do martial arts at that gym in Helford. You can ask Rod to take you, if you like.' Topaz never took her eyes from the screen. Flora had once heard Rod Fuller say that Topaz had been born without doubt, and that this was a great advantage in life.

CHAPTER 11

Good Cheap Day Schools on the Estate

High summer came to Westwick. The lawns lost their lushness and the leaves on the tall trees hung limp in the dry air. Radiators boiled on the 31. Ted, Adam and Josh boasted to each other of their in-car air-conditioning. Moron found a wedge of shade on the terrace behind the house and lay there like a dead dog all afternoon. Damon Parsons took to bunking off school and sleeping among the weeds in the central reservation of Acorn Junction. The water level in the river fell, leaving the *Dawn Treader* half-beached among blooming pink willow herb.

The management of The Cedars posted a notice to its clients warning them that correct tennis attire might include a tennis headband of white or pastel towelling with a discreet logo, available from the boutique at only three times a reasonable price, but did not embrace aerobic sweatbands in bright colours, bandannas or surf wear; players wearing such apparel would be asked to leave the court, and members were requested to advise their guests accordingly. The mirrors in the studio steamed up during the Bunbuster. The studio manager gave Rod Fuller his third warning about wearing no socks with trainers.

The first blooms on her *Souvenir de la Malmaison* were stupendous but Stephanie had no time to admire them, for all over Westwick people saw stupendous roses in other people's gardens and wanted some for themselves, and some of them called The Terrace Garden Design Studio and demanded bowers and arbours and pergolas the day before yesterday, so Stephanie's phone rang more than ever and she asked Inmaculada, her baby-sitter, to work every afternoon. The aphids recolonised *Souvenir de la Malmaison*.

Her hair made her neck sweaty, however she braided it, twisted it and pinned it up. One day she grew violently impatient with it and had it cut.

She preserved a window in her diary for sports day at The Magpies. In good time she withdrew the cakes from the freezer, rounded up the promised donations, packed them all prettily in baskets, ironed her gingham picnic cloths and made up a basket of posies for good luck. It felt excellent to bustle about her kitchen while the neighbours dropped by with their batches of cookies. It felt decent and goodwifely and like living in a real community where people cared and looked out for each other. It felt like playing her proper part in weaving the social fabric, exactly the kind of experience for which she had wanted to live in Westwick. Her rankling indignance faded; gossip was natural, after all. And Ted had probably heard what he wanted to hear. Such a shame for Allie, to see her husband becoming the classic marital loose cannon.

The Magpies was housed in a gothic mansion on the edge of Maple Grove, a large, fantastical building more fit for the Addams Family than for fifty privileged infants on a regime of finger painting and flash cards. Sports Day was a matter of high tradition. Red, white and blue bunting was draped on the lych gate. The flat grass space which was the house's former tennis court was painted with white lines. Beside the finishing tape was set a table for the teacher deputed umpire, also responsible for superintending a deposit of the contestants' asthma inhalers. The refreshment table was spread in the shade of the last remaining maple in Maple Grove.

Stephanie got busy displaying her stock. 'I like your hair, it makes you look more assertive,' Lauren Pike told her with her *noblesse oblige* simper as she double-knotted Felix's trainers. *So I looked like a pushover before*, Stephanie concluded, smiling as if complimented.

'Did you know your son was in love, Mrs Sands?'

'In what? Who? What, Max?' Stephanie jumped as if she had been bitten, almost dropping Sonia Purkelli's magnificent sachertorte which was getting shiny in the heat.

'We see it all the time. True love can strike at any age. Aren't they sweet?' Miss Helens, principal of The Magpies, had a smile that was not really a smile, more an attempt to suppress excessive signals of pleasure. She stretched her lips flat against her teeth, pulled her mouth back into her chin and tucked her chin down into the pie-crust frill around the neck of her pink-striped blouse as if she thought smiling was not quite normal. Nevertheless, a glittery excitement lit up her blue-shadowed eyes as she poked a finger across the playground towards Max. 'With little Courtenay Fuller, there. Aren't they delightful?'

'God, Stephanie, what have you done to your hair?' demanded Rachel Carman. 'Shut up, Rach,' ordered her husband, steering her towards the centre of the front row of the spectators' chairs. 'It's cute, Steph, really. I like it.'

Stephanie followed Miss Helens' finger and saw her son standing gravely at the foot of the climbing frame attending a little golden-skinned creature who swung from a high bar like a pretty gibbon, her checked frock flapping from her shoulders.

'It's been going on for a fortnight.' Miss Helens smartly adjusted her manner to ameliorate what she perceived as maternal disapproval. 'They're charming together. She's quite a nice little girl. A good choice, I think. Brought Max out of himself a bit. Something to take his mind off things.'

Miss Helens was probably younger than she looked. She had allowed herself to become plump. More than any of the citizens of Maple Grove, she preferred to wear navy blue. She clasped her hands together in a prayerful attitude under her noble bosom and delivered archly voiced opinions on school affairs as if she were the dean of a great ivy-clad college, not the headmistress of a suburban kindergarten whose windows were obscured with cut-out animals and pasta collages.

In keeping with the dignity of her role in the community, Miss Helens did not teach. She left the finger-painting and flash cards to the assistants, but stood favouring parents with her conversation, framed in the gateway of her institution, which was now painted a wholesome cream, with short gingham curtains tied back with bows at every window, red for the reception class, yellow for intermediate, green for the seniors getting ready to move up to St Nicholas's Junior.

By and large, Westwick accepted Miss Helens's estimate of her value. Days at The Magpies might be devoted to the adventures of Fluff the Cat and Nip the Dog, and the goodness of sitting down and being quiet, as against the badness of showing your bottom and stabbing other children with pencils, but it was nevertheless a sacred place, a repository of virtue, a cornerstone of the community.

The principal's self-importance assured parents that in sending their darlings to The Magpies they were placing their tiny feet in orthopaedically approved footwear on the moving pavement of educational privilege which would carry them on through slick academic forcing houses and expensive boarding schools to the pickiest universities, and thence out into lives in which they would never have to talk to anyone with an IQ of less than 120 except in an emergency.

A junior teacher called the children to order. Stephanie watched the girl who was the object of Max's devotion as she scampered to the fireman's pole at the edge of the frame and slithered swiftly to the ground. Then she allowed him to take her free hand as soon as it was within reach and escort her into the school house. Max did not look back. Stephanie felt a stab of regret.

I'm not a smother-mother, she lectured herself, I will let my son do what he has to do to grow up, I will respect his independence. It's natural for him to form close attachments. I should be grateful he's so affectionate. And caring. Just like Stewart. She ate a deliquescent butterfly cake to neaten up the plate.

The festivities began with a display of Scottish dancing to a slightly dragging tape of jaunty accordion music. The children skipped along in pairs. Miss Helens tapped her foot in time. The sun shone. Adam DeSouza zoomed in on Wendy. The sachertorte glistened, the wings on the butterfly cakes drooped. Jon Carman tripped up his brother, who punched him in the face before a teacher could separate them.

The races took place after an interval for lemonade and refreshments. Courtenay Fuller won the egg-and-spoon race. In the three-legged race, Max was paired with Ben Carman. For some reason they did not finish, but from where she was standing at the back of the spectator seating, Stephanie did not see what happened. Felix Pike won the sack race, largely by knocking over the other competitors. Courtenay Fuller won the sprint, the somersault race and the hopping race. Max appeared fit to burst with pride.

'She cheated,' Wendy DeSouza informed Stephanie, handing over her pennies for a flapjack.

'I don't think so,' Stephanie replied. 'It looked like she won fair and square from where I was.'

'You would say that,' Wendy retorted, picking the raisins out of her purchase and flicking them into the flowerbed. 'Max is her boyf.'

'No he isn't,' declared Chalice Parsons, lurking spectrally behind her. 'She can't have a boyf. She climbs things.'

'Nobody your age can have a boyfriend,' Stephanie declared, struck with the horror of Max being termed a boyf. 'You're way too young. Do you want a cake, Chalice?'

'Ugh, no. Cakes are disgusting. They make you fat. When can you have a boyf? How old do you have to be?'

'Grown up,' Stephanie told her.

'Courtenay isn't grown up,' the child complained, getting into her characteristic hysterical vibrato. 'She isn't grown up and she has a boyf.'

'No she doesn't – they're just friends,' Stephanie announced, feeling sticky with innuendo again. Ridiculous, from a five-year-old.

'See,' Wendy carefully put her mutilated flapjack back on the plate. 'I told you. Max won't be her boyf now because she cheated.'

The vista to Max's adulthood was suddenly illuminated. My son is my son until he takes a wife. Of course, he would leave, and it would be her duty to let him go gladly, into a world full of little monsters like Chalice and Wendy, into another woman's house, leaving her own empty. She felt in advance the vacuum of his bedroom, the gape at the kitchen table. An empty house, except, please God, for Stewart. Please, God, because we love him, we need him, I'm going mad and I can't bear this. It has been ten weeks now; if this is some divine joke, it's not funny any more. It wasn't funny in the first place.

'Mrs Sands,' yodelled Miss Helens from the trackside. 'We need one more for the parents' race.'

Reluctantly Stephanie left the table and went over to line up with three other mothers and Josh Carman. Max was always severely embarrassed if she did anything to distinguish herself, but Miss Helens was not be refused.

Afterwards, she realised that three months alone had reversed some of the processes of coupled parenthood. She had been genderised, the presence of her husband and child had killed whatever was perceived as unmotherly in her, made her soft and slow and passive. Now she was changing, regaining her toughness and aggression. And her speed. At the starter's flag she tore away and was surprised to find herself along by the umpire's table and declared the winner, to black looks from Josh, who lumbered in behind her in second place.

'Well run, Mrs Sands! Such a pity your husband couldn't be here.' Miss Helens had a propensity for elephantine tact. Stephanie decided she could let it go.

'There's no more news, I suppose?' Miss Helens persisted.

'Afraid not,' Stephanie confirmed.

'You cut your hair,' observed Ted Parsons sadly, as if personally rejected once more. 'Allie can't make it. Something came up at the studio.' The brief and tepid look which Stephanie threw his way held enough promise of forgiveness for him to hover.

'I've tried to keep everything normal for Max at home.' Stephanie resumed her conversation, trying to shoulder Ted away into the press of parents. 'He is sensitive, of course, and he does pick up on my moods, but I haven't noticed any signs of stress so far. But you never know how your children are when they're away from you, do you? How has he been in school? Does he seem upset at all?'

'Certainly not. Nothing that we've noticed. He's reading marvellously and his number work is coming on. Delightful boy.' At five, Max had a reading age of nine, which made him the hero of his class as far as Miss Helens was concerned.

'That's good then, isn't it?'

'Indeed it is.'

Miss Helens clanked with gold bracelets, her puffy face defined with hard colours and thick lines, and gave the general impression of a lady colonel sportingly enduring brief secondment to an infant's school. Her manner implied that she solicited news of Stewart not from care for Max, nor sympathy for his mother, but because she claimed it as her social duty to gather such information and disseminate it as she saw fit.

'I must say, Max has been very calm about it all,' she told Stephanie. 'Perhaps a little quieter than usual, but that would be all. We keep them busy. It may look like play, but there is a structure to the day here.' She patted the back of her crisp, butterscotch curls, swallowing a snicker of disappointment that no news was to be offered to her about the most colourful incident in the community for some years.

'Yes.' Stephanie turned back to the stall and gave all her attention to her price list, trying to embarrass Ted into moving on and Miss Helens into changing the subject. 'Do you think I should charge more for the butterfly cakes? They're so popular.'

'Max always has been very good, considering. I suppose he is used to your husband being away.' Ted drifted to a seat by himself at the edge of the arena but Miss Helens was not be embarrassed. Stephanie found her sunny mood clouding. That was a significant choice of words. Time for more firefighting.

'Miss Helens,' she said briskly, 'I do hope you'll forgive me if I'm out of order here, but I've heard some very odd stories about Stewart and Max since this terrible thing happened . . .' Yes, the story had got even this far. Miss Helens was gulping like a goldfish and turning pink under her make-up. A demon landed on Stephanie's shoulder and suggested that she open up a broadside and blaze away on the evils of gossip, tittle-tattle and circulating malicious rumours. 'And just in case you had any doubts, I'd like to reassure you that we're just a regular little nuclear family,' she went on, struggling to keep her tone sweet. 'Just mummy, daddy and their son Max. No step-parents or anything. Not to imply any criticism of other family structures, of course. But we're just the simple blood-related fairy-tale thing. OK?'

An angel's voice in Stephanie's ear sternly pointed out the possible disadvantages to Max of annoying his head teacher. A questionable reference from The Magpies, no place at St Nicholas's High School, her son turned out into a wilderness of educational discrimination which would leave him disadvantaged for life if she gave in to this outbreak of maternal defensiveness. Miss Helens was no fool. She had experience. If she was signalling some subtle difficulty with Max it was probably for good reason.

'Your *hair*!' Belinda DeSouza growled, double-knotting Wendy's trainers with ferocity while Adam raked the scene with his camcorder. 'It's so modern. But it really suits you.'

'Of course, Mrs Sands,' Miss Helens pushed out her chest in maximum dignity, 'people will say things, I appreciate that. But I don't pay any attention. Here at The Magpies we are concerned only with the children. I assure you I was just thinking of Max and what a brave little boy he's been through all his troubles.'

Stephanie knew too much about the cruelty of infants. When she had been the child crying alone in the playground, she thought she had somehow invited persecution by not being good enough. Max was good enough. Actually, Max was pretty near perfect, healthy and clever and developmentally unchallenged. Such a plain, sturdy, four-square little boy that she had assumed he would escape. Stupid, stupid. Victimisation was part of life, you can't protect your children. Her heart plummeted. 'What troubles?' she demanded. 'Do you mean that he's been teased, then?'

'Oh good heavens no. Certainly not. Nothing like that.' But that was a hit. Miss Helens suddenly diverted her attention to Chalice Parsons, who was lying prone on the grass, receiving the occasional accidental kick from her classmates playing nearby. 'Chalice, dear, are you all right? Excuse me, Mrs Sands, won't you? Chalice, come along – we don't lie down unless we're ill now, do we? Are you ill this afternoon?' Limply, with a resentful glare, Chalice suffered herself to be helped up by a junior teacher and seated safely on a bench.

Stephanie was relieved when Max finally approached her with his new companion, saying, 'It'll be all right, I promise it will. I'll ask her. It'll all be fine, you'll see,' in the tone of phoney cheeriness which Stephanie recognised as her own.

'This is Courtenay,' he informed her. The announcement sounded much rehearsed. 'She is my friend. Please can she come back with us today?'

Three sentences. This was serious. 'Of course, if it's OK with her mother. Where is she?'

'She died,' was the reply, serenely spluttered through incisors only halfway descended. 'She got hit with a truck on her bicycle and she was ill for a long time and then she had to die. My daddy's coming for me. He'll be here soon. Max could come to our place but it's a boat and you might worry about him falling in the water.' Inclining her head, with her golden skin and little down-turned mouth, the child looked like a living icon.

Max gave his mandarin nod. Miss Helens breezed in with an explanation. 'Courtenay lives on one of the houseboats along Riverview Gardens. I'm sure her father will be along any minute.' When the children had gone back to play, she added, 'The mother died, some kind of accident. That's the story, I believe. He's very good with her, considering.' And Miss Helens' pale tongue flickered around her flat lips and her hands clasped each other more firmly, protectively clutching virtue to her belly.

The father. The story. Considering. Five words encoded her condemnation. An indignant sympathy caught flame in Stephanie's heart. She wanted to defend this bereft husband and father, whose honesty, morals and competence had been so casually impugned by a woman who had dribbled away whatever intelligence she had once possessed in queening over three- to five-year-olds. Inhabiting a nursery universe, Miss Helens' human faculties had been stunted to infant proportions.

'Ah.' Miss Helens almost clapped her hands with satisfaction to see her proposition proved immediately. 'And *here* he is at last.'

Abruptly, Stephanie turned and found herself in the face of the child's father, who almost ran into the playground and halted well within the boundary of her personal space. At foreshortened angles she took in warm breath faintly smelling of peppermint, a fresh shirt open around a smooth thick neck, damp dark hair flipped back from the forehead and very long eyelashes, pale at the tip so the eyes were starred like daisy flowers.

Fragments of physical perfection fell into place as she and he recoiled. She was looking at Actaon, Endymion, Narcissus, some youth of mythical beauty created to humble goddesses and drive mortal women mad. She was looking at Rod of Rod's Bunbuster. Around him the air thinned, colours were brighter but there seemed to be less oxygen. 'Oh.' Real words slipped away like fish; all she could manage were exclamations. 'Um – ah . . .'

'Mr Full*er*,' Miss Helens' face was now twitching with the effort of disciplining her smile. 'We were waiting for you.'

Mr Fuller. From the jumble of information spilling out of her startled mind, Stephanie picked out the name and occupation. Rod Fuller, Fitness Instructor. She also retrieved his photograph from the notice board at The Cedars, a morbidly lit three-quarter profile above a polished shoulder and a sculptural bicep. 'Rod the Bod,' Allie had giggled as they passed it, 'isn't he just awesome?'

'My client was late, I got here as soon as I could.' Now he was awed rather than awesome, and anxious that the explanation should be accepted. Not wishing to be suspected of ogling, Stephanie looked at the ground. Clover was invading the grass.

'Courtenay has been invited to Mrs Sands' house.' One of Miss Helens' hands tore itself away from the other to waft graciously in Stephanie's direction.

'That's – uh – very kind.' He seemed disappointed.

'Did you have other plans?' She hoped he did. This vibrantly physical but tongue-tied stranger in her kitchen, even for the five minutes sanctioned for the sake of politeness, was not what she needed right now. The leap of libido his nearness induced was scary. Jezebel, traitress, when Stewart is helpless, in danger and far away. And there was always the judgment of Westwick – glances like Ninja knives were already winging over from the few mothers remaining in the playground. The place had turned as jittery as a chicken run with a fox outside the fence.

'Not at all. I like to do her reading before she gets tired, but . . .' The child, now hanging upside down from her knees on the highest bar of the frame, suddenly squealed, 'Daddy!', windmilled her arms and hurled herself to the ground.

'Take it easy.' In a symphonic counterpoint of glutes, hamstrings and the sculptural biceps, Rod Fuller strode over and scooped up the wriggling girl. She put her arms round his neck and smacked a kiss on his chin. 'So you want to go to somebody else's house today?'

'Please-oh-please-oh-please, can I, Daddy? Please. You can come for me later, can't you?'

'I suppose I can.'

The remaining details of the pact were swiftly settled. The Carman twins were ordered down from the roof of the annexe, from where they had been throwing dried dog turds from the street at their companions, and made to wash their hands. Chalice Parsons was coaxed to her feet and given some tissues because she was crying. Max saw his lady love properly belted into his own infant seat. Stephanie drove them all away, stardust still tingling in her arteries from contact with the neighbourhood lust object who, she noticed, climbed into his small Toyota with a marked lack of energy, as if he had just had bad news.

Suddenly she had the feeling of looking down on herself from way up high, seeing a tiny woman with two minute scraps of humanity in her charge, unprotected on the surface of the earth, with a great wind gathering around them, about to blow them all away into the cosmos like motes of dust. In the hot Jeep she found herself shivering, gripping the steering wheel to stop her hands shaking. Stop it, she scolded her mind. You're just a blob of tissue in a bubble of skull, you count for nothing in the universe. These thoughts you're hounding me with are just sparks in a speck of jelly. Stop it. I'm not going to cry in front of the children, you won't make me.

Clara Funk was waiting for her when she arrived in New Farm Rise. 'Mrs Sands, I'm so glad to see you.' Her gloved hand gripped Stephanie's forearm. 'I need to ask your advice,' she confided. 'This letter about the parking at Grove Parade.'

For once, Stephanie was grateful for the interruption. It terminated her desolate fantasies and her fear subsided. People said the Funks had met in Auschwitz, although that was not an enquiry easily made during the small talk of an Old Westwick Society meeting. Mrs Funk might now be an eccentric old woman but once she had been young and courageous, a woman who had survived the second Antichrist, who had triumphed over such unimaginable terrors that Stephanie's puny anxiety retreated in shame.

Willingly, she settled her in a chair and made tea in a glass with lemon as she knew Mrs Funk preferred. Her guest sat stiffly down, piling her shopping bags under the table, unwrapped her scarf, and began a litany on the subject of the parking regulations.

'The last time they did this my husband was knocked down in the street and his leg broken,' she announced, looking suspiciously at the tea as it was set before her. 'Outside the church, too. Of course I understand the regulations are the regulations, but if they enforce them so strictly and make the cars go faster all that we get is more accidents. At our age it's a serious matter, a broken leg. It will never be better, not really. Three months it took to heal just enough so he could go out. It's ridiculous. Ridiculous and dangerous.'

Cautiously, she took a sip of the tea, pulled her deeply lined face into a mask of disgust, put down the glass and stirred in more sugar, the spoon tapping in her unsteady fingers. 'You, Mrs Sands, you are so clever,' All the sparse bristles of her eyebrows agitated with the effort of making her appeal. 'Won't you write a letter for me telling them there are better things the police can do with their time than take away people who are parking where people always park anyway?'

'Of course I will. No trouble at all.' Mrs Funk's written English was eccentric and barely legible; thus tasks for the Secretary of the Old Westwick Society often came to roost with other members. 'I've the template all set up from the last time we wrote to the police. Shall we write to the Transport and Planning people too?'

'Certainly, why not?'

'I'll do it this evening.'

'Well, thank you.' Having attained her objective without struggle, Mrs Funk was temporarily lost for a topic and went on stirring with her spoon, her yellowed eyes resting curiously on the children slumped in a carbohydrate stupor in the playroom. After a few moments Mrs Funk gathered her thoughts again and demanded, 'You know, of course, why they are doing this?'

'Aren't they always having blitzes on parking?'

'There is always something behind these things.'

'Do you think there's something behind it? I think they're just obsessive about parking because its the only problem the police have got round here and they've got to keep their offences quota up.' There were benefits to active membership of the Old Westwick Society, including the opportunity to discover from the area inspector that the Helford station had the lowest arrest and highest offence clear-up rates in the entire conurbation.

'Of *that* I would not be so sure, either, dear Mrs Sands.' Mrs Funk swelled with delight in her knowledge of Westwick's undiscovered crimes and became alert at once. 'They have all kinds of problems, let me tell you. Because the streets are clean doesn't mean nothing dirty's going on here, believe me, I know. No, why they are so excited with the traffic now is this Oak Hill business, don't you see? They will be bringing all kinds of heavy trucks down here, and the great big diggers and bulldozers, and they want everybody off the streets to let them through.'

'But they haven't got permission for that, have they? I thought it was still stuck with the planning committee?'

'No, it was granted last week. So there's nothing to stop them clearing the site and digging out for the foundations now. You see, I know how these things go. These big businesses, they don't take any account of little people like us. They spit on us. They think we're only crazy old women and stupid housewives, not worth their attention, not worth answering our letters. They just go right ahead, they *assume* they will get all the permission they need. There will be bulldozers coming down our Broadway any day now, you'll see.'

'I don't think so, Mrs Funk. I do know a little about town planning laws, you know. They're pretty strict. When I was working in my husband's firm I had to comply with them all the time.' Reasonable, perhaps, to be paranoid if you really have been persecuted in your life, but all the same she had a policy of not indulging Mrs Funk's complaints because too sympathetic an ear only inflamed the old lady more.

'We shall see,' was Mrs Funk's reply, complacent and not offended, for she was quite accustomed to these strategies for switching her off. 'This is the beginning. We shall see.'

'I'll write those letters this evening,' Stephanie promised as she bustled away to the playroom under the cover of motherhood.

In the long emptiness of the evening, after the disturbing Rod Fuller had collected his daughter and Max had gone obediently to bed, Stephanie composed the letter, and for good measure reviewed the Oak Hill saga in the minutes of the Old Westwick Society's meetings for the past two years.

The plans, she knew because she had been deputed to verify the fact, had been correctly submitted. Only three civic groups had lodged objections – themselves, the Green Party and the Westwick Nature Triangle. Not a formidable alliance, especially since the Triangle group was a conspiracy of anoraks forever locked in violent internecine conflict who could agree on nothing except that they needed a grant to improve disabled access to their rank little tract.

Stephanie considered that, were she herself in the position of sitting on the Planning Committee, she would probably approve the plans. After all, Stewart had been very positive about designing the development until he

changed his mind and decided it was too big for thei
firm. She could not share the passion of Clara Funk and
Jemima Thorogood against Oak Hill. In the irritating
manner of the elderly, they were opposing change for the
sake of it.

She sighed at the prospect of conflict to come, the
hours of Mrs Funk's rambling oratory, the inevitable dep-
utation of two irony-free officials from the Greens and a
vociferous delegate from the Nature Triangle spouting
statistics about the red ghost moth. Perhaps Stewart was
right, perhaps it was time for her to let Westwick look
after itself.

At 2 am, sedated by civic concern, she went to bed
and slept well.

CHAPTER 12

All in a Picturesque Style of Architecture

'Now most of us think that a holiday is all about fun in the sun and unwinding away from all the stresses of modern living,' Allie burbled to the camera. 'But a recent survey of holidaymakers revealed that four couples in ten admit they have worse fights on holiday than they do the rest of the year, and over fifty per cent said they found travelling very stressful. So since this is the last show before the summer holidays, we've invited a couples' counsellor along to the studio to tell us what we can do to make sure that the family who holidays together stays together afterwards . . .'

In the suffocating canicular doldrums of the year, Westwick was abandoned to plant life. The spikes on the horse chestnuts at the end of Orchard Close swelled viciously while their leaves showed rusty streaks. A Russian vine seethed over the DeSouzas' garage. The lawns scorched and thundery breezes blew dust into eddies at the street corners. A tomb-like quiet settled on the empty houses, where security lights switched themselves on and off, burglar alarms winked in empty rooms, cars rested silently in their garages. Sirius, the Dog Star, sparkled over the river by night and in the empty wind the dried sedges hissed along the banks.

The families of Westwick had their own methods of defence against the menace of intimacy in a strange place. Off Sag Harbor, Chester Pike went fishing all day, every day, while Lauren read Melanie Klein and the nanny took Felix and his siblings to the beach. In Tel Aviv, it was Josh Carman who took the boys to the beach while Rachel stayed in bed with a gastric virus. In Wyoming, Belinda DeSouza buzzed around her investment annoying the workmen carrying out low-season refurbishment while Adam sat indoors with the windows closed because of the flies and worked through the case of papers he took with him.

On Venice Lido, Ted Parsons ate an entire *Fantasia Tre Cioccolati* with three flavours of ice cream, strawberries, cream, amaretto, almond flakes, chocolate curls, praline wafers and raspberry sauce to show Chalice and Cherish that real Italian ice cream did not cause immediate death from obesity, but they drank Diet Coke and refused to eat. He splashed in the waves mewing like Flipper to show them that the sea was lovely and cool and wavy, but they would only dip their legs suspiciously in the pool. He explained to them the special beauty of a city which had grown up organically, a city through which the wealth of half the world had passed, a city with no cars, but they complained about walking and said the palazzos were dirty. He took them into St Mark's at sunset to see the rosy rays shimmering on the gold mosaic vaults of the roof but they said it was dark and scary and Chalice sat up in her bed all night gibbering hysterically, chewing the sheet and saying she wanted to go home.

Allie Parsons stayed to make a pilot for a new late-night talk show and series of staff training videos for Magno then went to the Edinburgh International Television Festival where The Boss was giving a lecture on Programming the Digital Revolution. The Boss chose to share a bed with a druggy-looking woman from a new youth channel who wore black leather trousers fastened with thongs. Allie stuck her nose in the air and tripped briskly between the conference rooms; her courage, as she saw it, was repaid by the earnest attention of a twenty-eight-year-old film school graduate from Western Australia who was trying to finance his script about Jesus the feminist.

Although he was far from being in the mood for hedonism, Rod Fuller forced himself to honour his contract to spend a week at a Club Med resort in Turkey. In the morning, while Sweetheart snorkelled, he took a yoga class in an air-conditioned pavilion on a cliff over-looking the sea; in the afternoon they slept; in the evening, while Sweetheart made shell necklaces, he took an unchallenging aerobics class on the beach. In the night he tried to stay away from the women, and very nearly succeeded until the day before he left, when a wily Brazilian colleague poured zombies down his throat until he agreed to let her verify his claim that he was incapable of getting an erection. She blamed the rum. They both reckoned this chivalrous and parted friends.

Stephanie's stepfather decided she needed a holiday.

'Don't you think she's kind of losing that bloom she used to have?' he ventured to his wife.

'Youth doesn't last forever,' Stephanie's mother returned amiably.

'She worries all the time,' he insisted. 'It's only natural in her situation. But she looks kind-of pinched in the face. The light's gone out in her eyes. She should get away.'

'I'm sure she'll take a holiday if she wants to. She seems to be making plenty of money,' the mother insisted, seeing how the land was lying.

'She can't go off and sit on a beach with Max all by herself,' her husband persisted, assuming that simple obtuseness was all that ailed his wife.

'Maybe one of her friends will think of asking her.'

'We should ask her to come away with us,' he said finally.

'If you like, dear,' was the answer. And so Stephanie and Max were invited to join the couple on their annual golf excursion, scheduled for their benefit at a family-oriented resort in Portugal.

Two days before departure Stephanie was offered her first commercial contract for years. 'I don't know what to do,' she wailed down the phone.

'Max can come with us,' her mother suggested patiently, 'and you can stay home and get on with your . . . work.' The accusatory pause. You seem to think this work stuff is so important.

'We won't *have* a home if I can't make enough money,' Stephanie pleaded. She heard her mother sigh.

'I can't believe Stewart left you in this position,' she said, muting the words a little to indicate that her daughter could ignore them if she wanted, but Stephanie was getting a taste for combat.

'What do you mean, Stewart left us?' she demanded.

'Nothing, dear. Just a form of words. People of my generation believe a husband ought to provide for his family.'

'Like my father did, I suppose?'

'Don't be spiteful, Stephanie. You were never spiteful.'

'Maybe I'm a late developer,' her daughter suggested crisply. It was the first time her internal voice spoke aloud.

'Daddy will be home when I get back,' Max said as she drove him over to her mother's house. It wasn't a question, but her son had a way of asking for what he wanted by making these sudden statements.

'I hope he will, darling,' she answered carefully, 'but there's no way of knowing. He's still kidnapped. And you're only going to be away a week, you know. Even if they set him free tomorrow it could take him almost that long to get home to us.'

'Kidnapped.' She heard him, on the back seat, kick his feet with anger. 'Are people rescuing him?'

'They're negotiating. It means talking to the people who've captured him. When people kidnap people it's because they want something, you see. So to get Daddy back, we have to find out what the people want. Or the negotiators have to do that.'

'They should hurry up. Then Daddy could come on holiday.'

The first two days without her son were like days without a vital organ; the shock knocked a hole in her short-term memory and she wasted precious minutes looking up the names of common shrubs she used all the time. The third day she stabilised, functioning but submerged in a cold depression. No husband, no son, no life except her own. And when that ends, this is how it will be. She wasted a morning crying.

'How are you bearing up?' enquired Mr Capelli, calling from the Foreign Office.

'I'm not,' she answered shortly.

'Because it's been suggested that – ah – there might be some benefit in meeting up with other families who are – in – or – well – ah – going through the same thing. Same kind of thing.' His fluent confidence had gone, he was embarrassed. Weeping kinfolk were obviously outside his terms of reference. 'And if – ah – you felt that was – ah – what you wanted to do, as it were, I could – ah – put you in touch.'

'Yes,' she told him eagerly. 'Yes. A support group, you mean. Are there that many of us?'

'Not so many,' he was conscious of the need for discretion. 'Six or seven, maybe. But one of the cases handled by a colleague here has made this suggestion. Lady whose husband – ah, partner – is being held in the Middle East. If you like I'd be only too happy . . .'

'Yes. Give her my phone number, please.'

Other people lived in this limbo also. It was a burden, a great weight of loneliness and fear crushing her spirit.

The idea of sharing it was a comfort. She turned up the radio and began a new job. The silent house was so threatening that she had closed the doors to empty rooms and liked the radio playing loud enough to be heard everywhere. Sometimes she had to leave the radio on all night.

Topaz Lieberman went to a Youth for Democracy Summer School even though it was a known CIA front and democracy was really the least efficient form of government. Flora Lieberman went to a martial arts summer camp. Molly Lieberman went to Hungary with the county junior gymnastic display team. At the Gaia Garden Centre, Gemma Lieberman hosed down the conservatory then lounged behind her mountainous desk rationalising that there was no point watering the stock outside since the mints grew whatever she did, and whatever she did nothing else would grow at all.

Gemma also hated a quiet house. On the evening of the first day when all three of her daughters were about their business, Gemma saw Stephanie disconsolately browsing the organic vegetable counter at the Helford Magno. She looked out of focus. Even in old shorts and a blue chambray shirt the woman was a pretty dresser in the trim, modest style of young mothers in French baby-wear ads, but today there was something disarrayed about her. Gemma decided to approach.

'So howyadoin?' Stephanie blinked in surprise. 'Remember me, the madwoman you bought the Corsican mints from?' Her thick hair was braided for coolness, and tied with black silk cord. It hung down over one

shoulder, tangling with the buttons on her loose orange
dress. There was a lot of movement in the dress; if she
was wearing a bra, it was not up to the job of keeping her
breasts still.

'Gemma,' Stephanie confirmed, coming back to earth
from the misty grey planet Miserable, where she seemed
to spend all the time that wasn't given to work. 'At Gaia.
Of course. You saved us with those mints. Hello.'

'Howareya?' Gemma disregarded the flicker of guilt in
the other woman's face and picked up a pack of oyster
mushrooms. 'Do you eat these things? What are they
like?'

'They're . . . pointless, I think.'

'No taste, no texture, why bother, huh?'

'I think people have them for stir-fries.'

'No taste, no texture but no real cooking necessary, is
that it?'

'Pretty much.'

'Mints take all right?'

'They must have done, the clients haven't complained.'

'I hope they've got someone to water them if they're
away.'

'No need, I put a watering system in the design
scheme. Automatic. On a timer. Always do it – you have
to have automated sprinklers. Even if they take out a
maintenance contract with the boys who work for me
they never remember the watering.'

'I never understand how people can do that. I mean,
why invite a plant into your life and then kill it? You
have something in your life, you give it what it needs,
right? I mean, it's only water. Pretty basic.'

'And it has to be a timer with a year calendar. They can't handle setting it month-by-month.'

'People are weird, aren't they?'

Companionably, they walked over to the fruit. 'These are so cheap,' Gemma marvelled, weighing a Guatemalan melon in her hand. It was chilled and had no scent. 'What did they pay the guys who picked them?'

'I know.' In her state of deepened melancholy, Stephanie was so tender-hearted that the world's injustices ate at her spirit like ulcers. 'I wish they wouldn't label the apples,' she remarked, picking up a ball-shaped red cellulose growth with a sticker reading 'Gala'. 'It's like they're just products.'

'There's no fun in shopping when you're on your own, is there?' Gemma rolled the melon back into the display.

This was not a Westwick conversation. Westwick conversations were as light as the thistledown which drifted over in the summer air from the Oak Hill Nature Triangle. Westwick conversations were as free of content as a fat-free yoghurt is free of fat. Actually, more so. Westwick conversations would no more court an issue than a Westwick child would ride in a car without a seatbelt. In Stephanie's increasingly robust opinion, Westwick conversations were not worthy of the name. She found herself breathing easier.

They drifted on to Magno's café, which attempted, with a blue and white plastic awning over the steel counter and plastic palm trees stuck on the tiled walls, to convince the supermarket's clientele that the store was as warm, human, entertaining, varied and nutritiously enticing as a Mediterranean street market.

'You're not going away, then?' Gemma blew on her coffee; they both took it black rather than get involved with non-dairy whitener.

'I don't like to. I keep thinking — suppose I wasn't here when there was some news of my husband?'

'They'd find you.'

'I suppose — I don't like to take the chance, you know? And I need to keep working. I mean, thank God I can. His firm — well partnership, he's an architect — isn't insured to pay his salary for ever. I've got to be a bread-winner now.'

'Tough, huh?'

'Mmn.'

'Tell me about it. I like your hair, by the way. It suits you.'

'Thank you.' Stephanie ran her hand over the nape of her neck, still not used to feeling bare skin. She found she wanted to ask why this woman's husband was in jail. The question was welling up like molten lava, not to be resisted. 'Why—' she began.

'He imported a foreign car without a licence,' interrupted the other, confidentially narrowing one eye. 'Actually, quite a few of 'em. It was his business but he bent the rules because he was crazy. So what he's really in jail for is being mad. Oh, excuse me, I shouldn't say that. Mad people have their rights too. Sanity challenged, maybe. Manic depressive, it used to be. Now its bi-polar syndrome. Molly was what tipped him over the edge, after she was born he made our lives living hell, which is not actually a crime. So in the end, I found out what he *could* be charged with, and turned him in. Now is parents don't speak to me because I made their son a lunatic and my parents don't speak to me because I made the girls' father a jailbird. But we get by.'

'My father was in jail,' Stephanie looked into the dregs of her coffee, realising that she had confessed this to no one since the something-to-declare conversation she had with Stewart after they decided to get married. 'We got by. I can see now, it was very hard on my mother. But for my sister and me, it was just a blessing to have a quiet normal life.'

'How is it with what happened to your husband and stuff?' For once it seemed a natural question.

'Hell. It's so frustrating, there's nothing I can do. Nothing anyone can do. I think I'm going mad, sometimes. This morning the guy from the Foreign Office said there was going to be a support group of people like me and did I want my name put forward.'

'There are that many people?'

'Seems so. So I said yes.'

'Good.'

They were silent for a little while. Stephanie slipped her feet half out of her white summer loafers and felt relaxed for the first time in months.

Gemma finished her coffee. She sensed something, the *hi* flipping about like a fish, sending destiny off in a new direction. 'Look,' she proposed, 'dya wanna go down the Wilde At Heart and do some serious bitching?'

Grove Parade faced St Nicholas's Church across the corner of The Broadway and Church Vale. Here the municipality had been induced to recreate a theme park market square, with old shop fronts glowing under the preservation orders around a red granite horse troug now planted with begonias.

Among these little emporia, the Kwality Korne Store stood out by its lack of pretension. The rest of th shops, battered as their margins were by soaring rent redoubling taxes, merciless parking restrictions and th relentless competition of Magno Supermarkets, turne bright-painted faces to the world and offered suc luxury goods as Magno customers did not buy in bi enough quantities to make their supply economicall viable.

Gemma and Stephanie took an outside table at th Wilde At Heart and indulged themselves with whit wine and salads. The long afternoon sun sparkled in th bottle-glass panes of Parsley & Thyme's bow window The boy from Catchpole & Forge was sweeping up th day's sawdust. The window designer of Bon Ton slippe a Max Mara beige silk shirtwaist over the single displa dummy and complemented it with a pair of pale pytho slingbacks. In Bundle's Baby Boutique, the assistant, he mouth full of pins, finished a window display of sunsuit and swimming costumes.

Outside Pot Pourri, Marcia the owner topped up th water of her stocks and sunflowers and her spanie Bedlam, lay on the hot pavement panting. Pot Pour had taken to staying open in the evening, hoping t make some guilt money from commuting husband returning late from the office. The bank of bouquet displayed in rustic baskets outside the period shopfron led one to expect Eliza Doolittle at any moment.

They exchanged fears and wishes and life-stories. They talked luxuriously about their children. They discussed hybridisation of fashionable plants and deplored it. They discovered that they both knew Rod Fuller, and Gemma told Stephanie the true story of his wife's death but did not open the topic of his drinking since the accident. They agreed that Sweetheart was the most adorable child in Westwick after their own and put this down to her Irish-Chinese-Anglo-Saxon heritage plus good parenting.

They finished their salads and, in holiday mood, ordered ice cream. The senior negotiator at Grove Estates put in the window the details of a new six-bedroom, five-bathroom immaculate family home in Cedar Close. People almost never bought homes from Grove Estates and this woman was the reason. She was small and thin with a pinched face which seemed on the point of creasing up with quiet weeping; she looked like a woman whose husband had just left her, and people came to Westwick for substance and space, stability and happy families. Greenwoods on the Broadway did three times as much business as Grove Estates, although their negotiators were almost caricatures of their profession, vulpine young men in striped shirts, mobile phones welded to their ears.

'This isn't just have-ovaries-will-talk, is it?' Gemma suggested. 'This is a moment. Something will come of this.' Stephanie opened her mouth to say she had to get back to work, then changed her mind and said nothing.

'You see, I have this theory about mothers,' Gemma continued, putting her feet up on an empty chair. 'That every now and then when two mothers are gathered together a moment comes along, and they have to say yes. We will have this. This is for us. Not for our children, or our husbands, or our families, or society, or God, or the highest good – we have no excuse for this, this is for us and we are going to have it, just because we want it.'

'Good theory, I like it,' Stephanie affirmed, surprised that now she was not even wondering what she might be getting into here sharing the deepest, darkest and dirtiest with this voluptuously undisciplined female whom the rest of Westwick shunned.

'What a moment is is an oxygen mask.' She pulled out the cord that tied her hair and dangled it from her upstretched arm, copying the air-crew cabaret. 'Just when you're gasping for life with the trivia and the banality and the socks and the pants and the schoolbooks and the total endless utter responsibility for everything, it comes tumbling down from the sky and you can breathe again.'

'But I like the little stuff,' Stephanie protested, truthfully. There was much security in knowing you were doing your best for your child, even in tying his shoe laces. Parenthood as the spiritual death of a thousand cuts was something she had heard other mothers complain of, but had never experienced. 'I enjoy it. Max is just . . . an angel, I'm so lucky. And I like looking after everybody.'

'Yeah, I like it too, and I love my girls to pieces and I like the nice warm feeling you get of doing the right stuff.' Gemma looked at the face opposite her and saw the slightest, most tentative gleam of vitality dawning in the harrowed grey eyes. 'But let's face it, that's all you get. Otherwise all you get for bringing up kids is abuse. If you're lucky. And if you're not, you're just wiped. People come along and take another little piece of your heart, and one day you won't be there any more, just the hole where you used to be. You'll be a disappeared one, a non-person. It's like you can make yourself a victim because you think kids are the purpose of life but everybody else thinks it's something else. So the purpose of their life actually is taking away yours. You're just the next best thing to dead meat, a herbivore in a carnivorous world. So that's why you need the moments. I mean – did Thelma and Louise have any kids?'

'I can't remember.'

'Betcha they didn't. If you're a mother you can't even drive off a cliff and get away with it. I tell ya.'

CHAPTER 13

The Tudor Theatre

The days after this meeting seemed lighter. Stephanie found she worked faster. Jobs which had stuck to her fingers were finished at last; things she had lost were found. She became aware that since Stewart had been gone she had drifted for long, grey hours in a kind of chaos which was born of unhappiness, with so little mental strength that a very simple task, like costing a planting or computing a slope, had needed long and laborious concentration.

She went with budding hope to the first meeting of the support group for the partners and families of kidnap victims, which was convened by a deep voice on the telephone at an anonymous uptown hotel, close to Central Station, at 5 pm, over coffee and finger sandwiches. When she arrived she found a woman of a species she recognised at once, the unsexed matron bred by the armed forces or the civil service, a flat-chested, crop-haired, long-skirted doyenne, posed in the centre of a small group and using her institutional good manners as a means of domination.

'And where is *your* husband?' she enquired, and fluttered with insincere embarrassment as she added, 'Or is it your husband? We've all got so much to learn about each other.'

'Kazakhstan.' Stephanie mumbled the still unfamiliar name. 'In Russia. What used to be Russia.'

'The former Soviet Union.' The matron made it sound like a correction. Around them the rest of the group, unified only in their willingness to be drones to this queen bee, nodded understanding. 'My husband,' the matron confided, 'is in Iraq, poor man. A diplomat. Very junior, actually.'

There were four others, their missing men had been on business in Namibia, studying the climate in New Guinea, backpacking in Indonesia and on a church mission to Algeria. 'And she has had *no* news,' the matron volunteered. 'Not a word since he was taken. That must be the worst, don't you think? I don't know how I'd cope with nothing at all.'

The scrape of cups on saucers was loud in the quiet room. Eating sandwiches seemed too gross, they went untouched. Soft, shallow smiles were traded. The matron mediated the exchange of information as she would have run an embassy cocktail party. No doubt she had used her leverage with Capelli to get this event organised for her own benefit. Stephanie felt cheated; she had hoped for the chance at last to rage against the unfairness of it all in good company. The horrible compost of her feelings was just too ugly to bring into her cultivated day-to-day life.

The matron and two of the others were seeing counsellors. Only the backpacker's partner had no children.

The others all had children in their teens. In time they
got down to where they all lived.

'Westwick!' marvelled the matron, as if personally
affronted. 'But that's a very nice neighbourhood, isn't it?'

'We thought so,' Stephanie answered, half smiling at
what she was saying. Five faces were regarding her with
rank envy. The matron was in a Foreign Office apartment
close by. Three of the others were from cities in the
Coffin, one from a much less favoured suburb to the east
of the city.

'Where is Westwick?' queried Algeria, sounding as if
the place had been chosen to distress her.

'Out near the airport,' Stephanie answered briskly.

'One of those lovely quiet places with old houses and
trees on the streets – it was the first garden suburb,
wasn't it?' The matron was giving no ground.

'That was Maple Grove,' said Stephanie. 'We don't
live in Maple Grove.'

'All the same,' said the matron, 'it must be very nice.'

After that the other five formed a bond which
excluded her, and Stephanie went home on the train in
tears again, having been condemned to suffer without
support as punishment for the privilege of living in
Westwick.

The next day her mother returned, bringing her son to
console her.

'Max is such a dear,' she said, settling in the garden as
if she had an important matter to discuss. 'Quite fell in
love with my grandson when we had him to ourselves.
Did I tell you what he said to the stewardess on the
flight back?'

'Yes, you did.' Stephanie observed that her mother was restless. She was looking around and twitching her toes and playing with her triple-strand pearls. Something was up. There was a sense of purpose about her. She usually cruised along with at least a facade of serenity. Since the necessity for action was what made her mother nervous, it wouldn't be long before she made her move.

'Oh well – but he was a dream. I suppose it is the annoying thing about children that they always act their best with other people.' Rejuvenated, her mother appeared now, with a good strong suntan to set off her Grace Kelly pastels.

'He's a dream at home too. And at school. Term starts tomorrow.' Another milestone in time, another cycle of the year begun, and still no hope of Stewart. Mr Capelli had lately been assuring her, 'things are moving forward very well in Kazakhstan,' but after nearly five months he was obviously running short of things to say.

Max had been inside his home all of thirty seconds before asking if Courtenay Fuller could come over. It was simple to amuse Courtenay, all she wanted to do was climb things; Stephanie's garden had one tree worth climbing, with one branch within reach. Between the three of them they had added a rope ladder and the children had begun some fantasy game requiring them to climb the tree and descend the ladder interminably.

It was the no-man's land of the year, the time when seeds are setting, fruit is ripening and late roses open in the mellow afternoon sun. Creation was gearing up for the great push of the autumn. In the city, working people were getting back to their desks with an obscure feeling of relief and drawing up masterful task lists. In Westwick, mothers were pairing football boots and naming hockey-sticks and laying in supplies of pens, pencils, ink, socks, calculators, geometry instruments, gym leotards, dictionaries and nit lotion, mobbing out the scruffy little school shop in Helford.

'How's the work going? Did you get much done while we were away?' her mother enquired with unusual interest.

'Fine. There's plenty coming in. I'm getting the hang of making it pay. It seems all the suppliers want paying in advance and all the clients want to pay six months late. I wish I was making enough to hire an assistant.' She resented time wasted chasing invoices, and besides, it was hideously embarrassing. On the other hand, there was a sum equal to a month's budget owing from a job she had done back in May.

'You've got that girl . . .'

'Inmaculada? Her English isn't up to it.'

'We'd always have Max for you, you know, if things got difficult one day.'

It was a three-hour drive to her mother's house. Not a tempting offer. Stephanie made an appreciative face over her tea cup. So much talking without saying; the pressure of words unspoken was getting critical. Impossible to think of telling her mother that half the neighbourhood was gossiping that her grandson was illegitimate and her son-in-law had abandoned them. Where would you start on a topic like that? All the same, it was seething unsuspected in her head like magma in a volcano, that and her pointless rage at the whole situation.

Four years of living here and that absurd Lieberman woman was the only one person she could actually talk to. The rest of the time it was stay cool, draw trellis-work, make peanut-butter sandwiches and find courteous forms of words to remind people you were still a human being, even if something bad had happened to you.

'Have you thought any more about renting the house out?' her mother asked before long.

'Why?' Here it was, the cause of the trouble. Stephanie made her eyes big and soft, and her voice low and soft, and tilted her head on her long neck like a polite giraffe, a pose of non-confrontational innocence which she had always found effective.

'We were thinking,' – she smoothed down her skirt, picking invisible threads off it – 'your stepfather and I, that you might like to do that. And maybe move in with us for a while. We worry about you, all alone with this terrible business dragging on. You wouldn't have to work so hard. Our place is so big. I think there's even an old tree house in the garden.'

Stephanie pasted on a bland half-smile and felt it set like concrete on her lips. Careful, take it easy, take it at face value, don't give offence. 'How kind,' she forced out, holding down the voice tone, then for the sake of simu-lating warmth, she put her cup down and gave her mother a hug. 'I'll think about it, really I will.'

'You've done wonders with the house,' her mother pressed on, gentle but pitiless, 'I'm sure it would rent well. Then you wouldn't have all these things to worry about – the money, or getting someone to look after Max . . .'

'I really will think about it,' Stephanie repeated, howling with horror inside, 'but I do like working, you know.'

'But you look tired, dear. More than tired, you're looking – harrowed.'

'Of course I'm looking tired and harrowed – wouldn't you in my situation?'

'I suppose . . .'

'Have you thought what might be happening to Stewart right now? Have you thought that he might be dead, he might have been dead for weeks?'

'Don't be angry, dear. We're only trying to help.'

'I know, I know. I'm sorry.'

When she was alone with the children, and her mood settled, she found herself keeping her promise. Probably the house would rent well, everything she and Stewart had taken such pride in, the lustrous sun room, the pretty terrace, the gleaming kitchen, the cosy bedrooms. Rental homes were never stylish, anybody would be thrilled to be offered their house.

Go home to Mummy. Give up, give in, revert to a child-state, eat without having to cook, sleep without having to launder. No more climbing into a suit to give a presentation then coming home and climbing into a sweatshirt to be a mother. Regular cheques, no more clients, no more invoices.

No more Westwick. No more acting sweet around Lauren Pike when you felt like stabbing her. No more hiding from Allie in fear of becoming a media victim. No more avoiding Ted in case he made another pass. Lately she had poured half her energy into these accommodations.

She was tired of it, she was sick of it. So why the silent scream at the mere idea of moving out?

This house is us, it is Stewart and me, and once it made me happy. Ecstatically happy, on the day we moved in. She remembered standing on the front path watching Stewart get Max out of the car and feeling joy streaming around them, gilding the scene like the October sunshine. She remembered going back to Stewart, holding on to his arm, laying her head against his shoulder, stroking Max's hot round cheek and saying, 'You can't imagine how happy I am,' and Stewart clumsily catching hold of her fingers. She remembered thinking, I must remember this: my husband, our baby, our home in Westwick – perfect happiness.

Needing comfort, she sat down at the sycamore table and called back the scene. She saw herself and Stewart carrying their baby, walking together up the path to the new house. She saw them opening the stiff door and letting their happiness blow them through the fresh empty rooms, and knew that they had felt bliss then, but now could not retrieve the feeling. Her memory held nothing but words and pictures when she urgently wanted the proof that she had once deserved to be happy.

Stewart had done what he always did in houses, a funny little dance, running his fingers around architraves and his toes along floorboards, as if communicating with the construction itself by touch. 'It's a dream, isn't it?' he said to her. 'A lovely family home in Westwick. You are a very clever woman, you know that?'

'I'm not. I was just in the right place at the right time, that's all.'

'I thought that was cleverness.' He asked the baby, now gazing wonderingly up from the crook of his arm, 'Isn't that cleverness, Maxie? Being in the right place at the right time so we get to buy a beautiful house in a beautiful neighbourhood we never even looked in because we thought we couldn't possibly afford to live there. I think that's very clever. My boy, your Mummy is a very clever woman.' The baby yawned fit to unhinge his little gummy jaws, and appeared to agree.

Stephanie had said nothing. People had on occasion called her clever, but she was afraid if she accepted that opinion she would have to do something to justify it. She had gone on into the garden, her own little Eden.

Presently, their furniture had been carried in, followed by Allie, their first visitor, who pushed a great Cellophaned bouquet of red roses with corkscrew willow twigs into Stephanie's arms with one hand and put a bottle of champagne down on a packing case by Stewart with the other. 'Welcome, my dears. Welcome to Westwick!' Stewart lowered Max for her to kiss. Somehow, people had an instinct to save Allie from ever looking awkward. 'Darling baby, always so good! I just came to see you over the threshold. Look at me, I'm still in my make-up – don't let me get it on you. I can't stop, I know you're in chaos and I'm waiting for the studio car. Gorgeous kitchen, do let me see . . .'

She darted inside like a bright parrot, still wearing the searing pink suit in which she had presented her show that morning. The greasy smell of her make-up was the first alien scent in the house. At once Stephanie felt useless; she was a head taller than Allie and twenty pounds heavier. They had no vase for the roses or glasses for the champagne; their possessions were sealed in crates all around her. She took Max while Stewart washed out the plastic cups she had packed for baby juice and popped the cork.

'It will be so, so good to have you as a neighbour.' Allie skipped up on a crate and sat on the end of the worktop, crossing the legs of which Channel Ten's publicist said a million men dreamed each day. 'Maybe we should do a new home feature – what do you think? So much social mobility these days, people relocating and stuff. We could film right here.' Stephanie did not realise she was shaking her head. 'Oh! I forgot, you hate all this media stuff, you're so, so shy. I am so insensitive, Steph, can you forgive me? Of course you must be rushed off your feet. And the baby, he must keep you busy too. Never mind, we can do something another year. You must come over, meet some more neighbours. It's lovely having you so close to us now. Darling, do forgive me, I gotta run now . . .' And she jumped to the floor and was clattering down the front path to her car.

'Just think – two years ago we knew nothing at all about daytime TV.' Stewart watched the car pull away, a pink sleeve waving through the window.

'And we thought people who did were just sad.'

'And then Allie Parsons came back into your life and we changed our minds. And now we're her neighbours and we owe her this, really, don't we?' With a sweeping arm, he indicated the huge space awaiting transformation at their hands. 'If she hadn't given us the tip that they were knocking the price down we'd never have looked at it. I'd never have believed we could afford to live in Westwick.'

'You negotiated them down. God, I was proud of you.'

'She told us they'd sell for less – I pretty much knew what we could get it for.'

Stephanie heard Max and Sweetheart shrieking joyfully outside and felt her own mood all the more leaden. Happiness was like water, it just slipped through your fingers, it had no substance. When it disappeared, there was nothing left, not even the memory.

'Mistur Parsons, you come arround to Sun Wharf today? Somzin' you might want to see.'

'What is it, Yuris?' Ted did not want to go to the Sun Wharf site, where Yuris and the Lithuanians were doing some architectural salvage. He wanted to stay out at Oak Hill: the contractors there were new and he needed to spend time with them, bringing them up to speed. Yuris had been his best foreman for the past ten years and could be trusted to get a job done well and on time with no trouble and no more than one site visit from Ted each week. Besides, Ted liked watching the diggers. And Sun Wharf, on the east of the city, was almost three hours away.

'We make start on second building this morning and is not what we zink.'

'What do you mean?'

'Different building behind front wall. Some kinda t'eatre or zomzin'.'

'Theatre?'

'Thaz right. You need see it, Mistur Parsons.'

'Yup,' he agreed, startled. 'I'm on my way.'

Three and a half hours later – the cause of the delay was a double trailer bringing ready-baked potatoes to Magno Helford which jackknifed and rolled over blocking all three lanes just after the Acorn Junction – Ted stood on a pile of rubble in Sun Wharf Lane and saw for himself.

The site had been a factory, at different times dedicated to bottling brandy and stitching mink skins but most recently in use as a sweatshop where two hundred Bengali women and children had sewn trousers day and night. After a pincer movement of the Immigration and Public Health authorities had closed the operation down the building had stood empty for years, the filthy windows boarded over and the roofs sagging and shedding their slates.

The inspector who had condemned the building after the raid gave the tip to Ted, and Tudor Estates bought the site for peanuts when the regeneration of the old docks was just something smart architects talked about and the concept of a brown-field site had not yet been named. Ted never had any intention of developing it himself. The cost of gutting and renovating an old building, the endless bureaucratic hassles, and the volatility of the market for dockland properties did not charm him. He bought the site to sell on when the market rose. That time was now at hand, and the cash would be better invested in Oak Hill.

Cleared sites sold best, but before demolition he put in a gang to strip ironwork and window shutters, collect the old slates and chisel out the corbels, cornices and fireplaces to sell on to an architectural salvage yard. Financially, the operation barely washed its own face but it put him in good standing with the planning authorities, and besides, he felt better about razing a building when he had first honoured the original craftsmen by saving their work.

Ugly, featureless and begrimed, from the outside Sun Wharf looked like three utilitarian brick boxes jammed together, the biggest in the middle. Yesterday, the gang reported that there was almost nothing worth saving except a few floorboards. Today, they had knocked their way into the central building through a bricked-up doorway and found a broad stone staircase leading below ground level.

'Come,' Yuris suggested, respectfully watching Ted to see he did not trip over the fallen laths from the ceiling. 'Firrst, look here,' and he turned his torch to the walls, lighting up what seemed to be a picture.

One of the men stepped forward with a broom and very gently brushed away the dust and cobwebs, revealing a lifesize mosaic panel of a dark-haired woman in rosy draperies, encircled by lilies and curlicues. Her dimpled feet in fanciful sandals were level with Ted's face. The next panel was a pert girl in knickerbockers with a bicycle. Opposite her posed a busty beauty laced into a black corset, bending saucily over a cage of doves. The stairway was lined with Edwardian chorus girls.

'I'm zinkin' how in hell do zis,' the foreman explained

as he led onwards. 'Mozaic. How take down. Zen we go on . . .' The plaster from the ceiling had crumbled, becoming a layer of powdery dust on every surface. The handrails were brass. The doors at the bottom of the stairs were mahogany with cut glass panels.

They passed through a wide room with a low ceiling and wooden counter down one side; the men's boots had trodden a track across the floor to another pair of doors. Ted stood in the middle of the auditorium, struck dumb by the visions in the beam of his flashlight.

Everything was as it had been when the last punter staggered cheerfully out into the night. Here and there crumpled playbills lay where they had been dropped. Beer mugs stood on the tables in the stalls, with chairs pushed back at all angles by the departing audience. A few sheets of music were still on a stand in the pit, the pages bearing alterations scratched in uneven ink. A mop rested in a bucket in a corner. There was so much animation in these objects, which had lain as they were posed for eighty, perhaps a hundred, years, that it seemed as if the gaslights might glow to life at any moment, and a ghostly audience of sailors and long-shoremen suddenly push through the doors and take their seats.

Walking tentatively forward in the darkness, Ted dis-covered that this had been a pocket playhouse, seating barely a hundred revellers, mostly in boxes in the higher tiers with plaster nymphs holding floriform gaslights to divide them. A shred of a curtain hung from the gilded proscenium. The boards where the players had their hour had rotted and fallen in.

'Strange,' the foreman commented, shooting Ted a sideways glance. 'I don't know what to do. I zink nobody knows this here.'

'It's dry.' Ted shone his torch up at the ceiling, again finding holes in the plaster but only blackness above. 'That's why everything's so perfect. There's two floors of building above us. Foundations must be dry. Water never got in.' The men of his salvage gang moved tentatively about, one of them finding an old briar pipe discarded on the lip of a stage box.

'You zee what I mean?' Yuris asked with anxiety. 'Eez perfeck. Perfeck. How take down, where we start . . .'

The romance of the find had its fangs in Ted's neck. His phone peeped and he turned it off. He passed through the secret door from front to back of the house and scrambled about backstage, finding rotting ropes and faded scenery, old machinery unrusted, greased and capable of working, an empty willow skip which fell to dry twigs at his touch.

The advantage to the developer in building a theatre was not obvious, unless perhaps such properties went for better prices at the beginning of the century. 'Why build underground?' he asked himself, and took the stairs again to pursue the mystery outside. The beauty with the doves, with her deep bosom and strong flanks, put him in mind of Gemma. In another way, the dormant vitality of the entire find seemed to speak of her, but he dismissed the notion.

'I neverr zink . . .' Yuris began, following eagerly.

'No more did I. God damn, I've owned this for years. I had no idea, none at all.' He had never surveyed the site properly, always intending to keep it only until it was worth selling.

Blinking in the light, he saw that the ugly street elevation was false, thrown up in front of the arched music-hall facade, with iron stairs from side doors leading to the workshops above. At the wharf side, where the land approached the river, it fell away sharply. Probably here the water had carved a bed for itself thousands of years beforehand. The neighbouring buildings had extra half-floors on the wharf side. His investment probably occupied an area where the slope was wide enough to embrace the auditorium.

Yuris followed him patiently while the rest of the crew sat down around their pick-up and smoked, waiting for his decision.

'Don't touch it,' Ted instructed them, and saw their hard, closed faces break up with pleasure. 'I'm going to get a few more people to see this. Board up the door for now and leave everything just as it is. Make a start on the other side, get some flooring there if you can. I'll be back.'

'Mrs Sands? Is this Mrs Sands?' Her heart jumping like a landed fish, Stephanie crushed the phone into her ear as she pulled into the slow lane of the 31 westbound.

'Miss Helens?' Something had happened to Max. There could only ever be one reason for a call from the teacher at 11 am. 'What's the matter? What's happened?'

'Hopefully it's not too serious, Mrs Sands . . .'

Hopefully? Then it was serious. Watch the road, watch the road. She stood on the brakes in time to avoid running into the back of an old Nissan crammed with people.

'What's happened?' she demanded, furious with the woman for prevaricating.

'He had a fall, Mrs Sands. Off the climbing frame. Of course, since we had the shock-absorbant surface put down it isn't nearly so hard—'

'*What happened?*'

'But he has hurt his arm quite badly so one of the juniors has taken him to Helford hospital.'

'Right.' Stephanie pulled out to the fast lane, wishing she had a hand free to let the hooting truck driver alongside her know what she thought of his impatience. 'I'm on my way.'

The speed control camera flashed as she tore up to Acorn Junction. There was no turn-off before then. She roared back eastwards calling in to her client to cancel their meeting, threw the Cherokee down the slip into Helford, hurtled along North Broadway to the hospital, wedged it into the last space in the car park, sprinted a quarter of a mile back to the building, found the emergency entrance and arrived breathless at the desk.

'Max Sands,' she gasped. 'Boy of five, fell off a climbing frame, hurt his arm?'

With maddening slowness the clerk put menus up on her screen. 'Ah,' she said, pointing with her ballpoint as if Stephanie could see. 'Should be up in X-ray by now. Take a seat, will you?'

'Can't I go up and find him?'

'You'll get lost. Just take a seat.'

'But how long—'

'We're very busy. He was lucky to have seen the nurse already.'

'One of his teachers is with him – they must need her back at the school.'

With a bad grace, the clerk leaned towards the security glass and indicated a sign halfway down the corridor. 'Go up to the fifth floor, turn left. There are more signs up there.'

In the X-ray department she found Max watching with interest through an open door as five nurses tried to hold a drunk homeless man down on the table. The nursery assistant who sat beside him snapped out of her coma of boredom as Stephanie approached and got to her feet.

'I'm so sorry,' she whispered, obviously intending that Max should not hear. 'I didn't see it. He's been awfully brave but I think something must be broken.'

'All right,' Stephanie murmured, wondering why she was reassuring the girl instead of the other way round. 'I'm here now. I'll take over. Hi, darling . . .'

'Mum.' Max acknowledged her with the face that hoped she was not going to make a fuss.

'Does it hurt?' she asked. The arm, the left arm, was packed in a plastic splint which he was holding carefully against his chest with his other hand.

'Not much,' was the stolid reply. She ruffled his hair and he flinched away.

After the tramp was finally strapped to the table and

dealt with, the nurses called in a patient in a neck brace on a trolley, a young man knocked off his motorcycle. Next came an old woman in a wheelchair, hit on a pedestrian crossing. Max's turn came after seventy-seven minutes.

Back in the emergency waiting area another hour slipped by. Stephanie went to the pay phone, cancelled her afternoon appointments and warned Inmaculada that the house might be empty when she got there.

Back on the ward, there was no sign of Max. The clerk reluctantly verified that he was with the doctor, and even more reluctantly pointed out the curtained cubicle.

'And you are . . .' The doctor was a thin young man with an unhealthy grey-white skin studded with raging post-adolescent acne. He looked up from a file as if she had no right to enter the sacred enclave.

'I'm Max's mother.' Stephanie always felt proud to say it.

'Ah. The mother.'

'So – how is he?'

As if to remind himself of the diagnosis, the doctor held one sheet of X-ray film against the ceiling light and then put it down and picked up another. 'I think we're looking at a break in one of the bones . . .'

I took biology, you can use long words. Stephanie smiled encouragement at him. 'Yes,' was all she said.

'Not, unfortunately, a simple break, although one that's quite common in children. I'm getting an orthopaedic surgeon to take a look, which won't be until he finishes his afternoon schedule, say around four o'clock.'

'So we wait here until four pm?'

'Well, in the waiting area. Now, Max, can I borrow your Mummy a moment to answer some questions?'

'Sure,' Max gave his mandarin nod.

'Good boy.' The doctor patted the good arm.

Take your patronising mitt off my child. Stephanie smiled and followed the doctor to a windowless, coffin-shaped little room off a corridor, which contained one table and two chairs. She took the seat he indicated.

'You're Max's mother?' The doctor asked, clicking his ballpoint. Was he 23? 24? Was it a sign of growing old when you thought doctors looked impossibly young?

'Yes,' Stephanie confirmed.

'And your name would be . . .'

'Sands. Stephanie Sands. That's Stephanie with a p h.' She noticed that he entered her name in a box and ran up the form with his pen to check it against Max's name at the top. She was getting to be paranoid about forms.

'And you were not there when this accident happened?'

'Well, it happened at school. I was on my way to work.'

'And what work do you do?'

'Garden designer.' It was shorter to write than landscape architect and besides she was not sure she deserved the grand appellation.

'And the father . . .'

'My husband's name is Stewart.'

'No, I mean, where was he?'

'He isn't at home at the moment.' She was too weary to get into the whole explanation. If this was a place where no one read the *Helford & Westwick Courier*, she was grateful. Besides, if they told the truth this squit would probably decide to call in a psychiatrist and a straitjacket as well.

'Do you mean not living with you at the moment.'

'No.'

'So you are a single mother, is that it?'

'No, we're married. He just isn't home right now.'

'Because I have here that you are a single parent.'

'Well, I'm not. Where would you have got such information?' Such care she had taken to correct Miss Helens, and she had not passed on the facts to her staff.

'From the young woman who came in with him . . .'

'She's just a nursery assistant, she obviously had the wrong impression.' *Damn Miss Helens to hell for this.*

'I see. So, is this a – uh – full-time employment?'

'Yes, it's full time.'

'So how much time do you spend with your son, Mrs Sands?'

'Time?'

'Yes, how much time?'

'Do you mean in hours?' *You are going to sweat for this, sunshine, I'm going to make you sweat for this.*

'I mean, how much time?'

'Well, rather more than most of the other parents at our very nice Montessori nursery school, Dr . . .' She leaned forward to read his name label. 'Dr Wallingham. I do the car pool in the morning Monday, Wednesday and Friday and since my office is at home I'm working there on those afternoons. I do the car pool in the afternoon Tuesday and Thursday, when we have tennis squad and swim squad respectively, and since I'm my own boss I can pick my own hours and so I pick a couple on those days to stick around and watch. And if something goes wrong at that very nice little school, as you see, I can be with Max in no time at all if I have to. And then unless he goes to play at a friend's house we're together all weekend.'

'Except when you go out, presumably?'

'I don't go out.'

He blinked. 'You are still a young woman.'

'Oh gee, thanks. But I gave up rave parties when I was pregnant and going down the crack den's so difficult with a toddler, you know.' He was still blinking, his pen hovering over the page. Stephanie stood up. 'Joke, joke,' she said, shrugging her shoulders but momentarily unable to smile. 'Don't you think I should go back to Max before he starts wandering up the ward picking up needles or something? I take it you have finished. You don't need to apologise or anything. Just don't put any more lies on paper, OK? And better cross out the ones you already have. I *will* sue.'

'I don't appreciate your attitude,' he snapped after her.

'Same goes here,' she threw angrily back over her shoulder.

By 7 pm they were home, Max with his arm in a better splint. The word of the surgeon was that the fracture was simple and should heal without any further treatment. They were both exhausted. Stephanie put a pizza in the oven and took Max to the bathroom where she set about undressing him ready for a shower. The nurse had already cut off the arm of his shirt but

Stephanie found she had to cut through the shoulder as well to ease it over the splint.

'There you are.' Sadly, for it was as cute a garment as her son would agree to wear, she dropped the ragged remains in the bin, and set about the trousers, the socks, the shoes and finally the pants. She ran the water in the shower, pulled out a clean towel, checked the temperature and helped Max to step in. His body was almost dappled with bruises, old and new. Square in the centre of his back was the print of a shoe, a trainer, every ridge in the sole clearly outlined in black and purple.

Since her personal panic button had been stuck down all day, Stephanie's head was full of white noise and she was perfectly calm. She made the shower gel foam between her hands and spread it over his rounded little shoulders, agreed that there was no need to shampoo hair after such a heavy day, made him giggle by spraying his little penis after he soaped it, wondered if that might be construed as sexual abuse, turned off the water and wrapped the dear body in the towel.

'So who else was on the climbing frame when you fell off?' she asked, trying hard not to sound crafty.

'Sweetheart,' he said at once. They had all adopted Rod's name for Courtenay.

'Sweetheart,' she repeated, still expectant.

'And some boys.'

'Which boys?'

'Ben and Jon.'

Of course, of course. Why had she been so blind? He never wanted to play with the Carman boys, never went willingly to the Carman house and now the connection was made she remembered the many times he had left there with the red-faced, rumpled look she should have recognised. 'So was it Ben who kicked you, or Jon?'

'It was Ben,' he said, yawning with unconcern. 'Jon stomped on me on the ground.'

She made no reply, knowing he would retreat from further questions. After a while he suddenly gave her a dark, pained, humiliated look that stabbed her heart, the first expression of real distress he had ever worn. 'They always do, Mum. They hate me. They hate everybody. Ben tried to push Sweetheart off too, but she was too strong. I hate them.'

'I wish you'd told me before.' He allowed her to hold him but lapsed into silence. Soon he was half asleep, and as she tucked him into bed Stephanie felt a pulse thumping at her temple and her hands hot and sweating, as if her anger was running through her blood and bringing it to the boil.

CHAPTER 14

A Natural History Society

'You're kidding me,' said Rachel. Her voice over the phone had that half-connected tone of someone doing something else at the same time. 'Ben and Jon? Look, this is just boys, you know? Boys being boys . . .'

'No,' Stephanie insisted, earnestly calm. 'Look, we're friends, I don't want to be having this conversation. He was pushed off the climbing frame and kicked on the ground. He had a broken arm and a bruise the shape of a shoe in the centre of his back. He says Ben pushed him and Jon did the rest.'

'Aw c'mon.' Was Rachel chewing gum? It sounded like it. 'They were just rough-housing. Play-fighting. Our tiger cubs. They do it all the time. You should see the things they do to each other.'

'I'm afraid it was deliberate, Rachel. I talked to some of the other kids, they all saw it. And I don't think this was just once – it's been going on for a while.'

'That Fuller kid? Hyperactive, gender-confused;

father's a personal trainer, for God's sake? Can't you see what's going on with her? She just wants to be a boy, Steph, that's why . . .'

'And I'd picked up the signs myself, Rachel. I'd been asking myself why Max always tried to avoid Ben and Jon. It's been going on for months.' Get the sleeping tigress here. Stephanie shook her mane, amazed at her own strength of purpose.

'Max has to plough his own furrow, you know, Steph. You shouldn't try to protect him all the time. He's a boy, boys fight.' Down the telephone came a loud, unmistakable slurp. Coffee. Rachel was putting down her breakfast there. The scrape of a fork was also detectable.

'This isn't fighting, this is bullying and I want it to stop.'

'What can I do about it? It's human nature.'

'You could stop whatever you're doing and pay attention to me,' suggested Stephanie acidly.

'Oh my, we are stressing out this morning.' Defiant clattering testified that Rachel was applying herself to her plate with enhanced focus. 'OK, tell me this, Steph – if it's being going on for months, why hasn't Max said anything before?'

'You know what he's like, he doesn't talk. It's pride as much as anything.'

'So, maybe Max was feeling a bit of a fool for falling off the climbing frame yesterday and decided to whine about some other child and get into a blaming thing to make himself feel better.'

'I had to trick him into telling me, Rachel. Then I

checked the story out. Don't take my word for it, come around and take a look. Call up Helford Hospital and get the X-rays. Meanwhile, I'm afraid I'm not coming to pick up your boys this morning. Max is my son and I have to protect him.'

'You don't have to fight Max's battles for him, Steph. Or teach him how to run away from trouble. Ben and Jon are my sons and I'm not going to fret over them, turning them into little wusses because that's what you think a boy should be. I think we should just leave our boys alone to sort things out between them. Now excuse me, I have patients waiting.'

She crashed down the phone. Stephanie stopped herself slamming her own receiver back in place, took three deep breaths, opened her office door and called Max, despising her phoney bright voice. This was not how Stewart would have handled things.

Stewart would have gone into his crumpled-forehead mode for a few hours then come out with icy dignity, grave concern, regretful intervention. She had seen it a few times when he and Marcus had disagreements. A real physical transformation. He could look as if he had grown three inches and aged fifteen years. Icy dignity. She pulled herself up and straightened her spine.

They drove in silence to Church Vale for Chalice then on to The Magpies. As she stopped the Cherokee, Josh Carman came out of the gate, looking blackly self-satisfied. Through the classroom window she saw Ben Carman standing on a table sounding off for the benefit of the infant audience gathered around his feet, his arms folded in defiance.

Could we have a word, Stewart would say. 'Miss Helens, could we have a word?'

The headmistress had an office, but showed no sign of leaving the playground. 'How *is* Max?' she enquired, eyes bright with unfelt sympathy under their turquoise swags. 'Such a brave little boy.' The rings glinted as she put her hand on his head.

'In you go, Max. Teacher's waiting.' She was expecting the don't-embarrass-me cringe but instead he walked off with a businesslike bustle which said that he knew very well that she had to do what she had to do and it was OK with him. Which gave her strength.

'Shall we go inside?' Stephanie suggested.

'Is that really necessary?' Miss Helens spoke as if confronted with some irritating, outmoded educational convention like rote-learning the names of all the capital cities of all the countries in South America.

'I would prefer to talk in private.' Icy dignity, steely politeness. With reluctance, Miss Helens retreated to her office.

Gingham curtains here even. The dinky plastic tables loaded with copies of *Pre-School Monthly*. Desk with a blotter and a rose bowl garnished with dried hydrangea heads. A cheque resting on the blotter, no doubt the reason Miss Helens had been reluctant to return to her office. She sat heavily in the headmistress's wing chair and put the cheque in a drawer.

There were two rush-seated chairs for parents, one with arms, one without: Daddy's chair and Mummy's chair. Deliberately, Stephanie pulled out Daddy's chair, sat sternly in it and went through the facts.

'Surely not,' Miss Helens said the minute Stephanie drew breath, eyes darting like fish around the room.

Stephanie suppressed cynicism; I must be an adult, I can rattle a headmistress. 'I am quite sure.'

'Little boys are always . . .' She was struggling through guilt to defiance, ritually moving her pen pot around her desk as if some magician had hidden the solution to the problem underneath it.

'Not to this extent. Max has severe injuries and the Carman boys have been picking on him for quite a while. I had suspected it before.'

'Dr Carman has already spoken to me, he assures me he will deal with the situation.'

'I am glad to hear that, although I'm sorry to say that wasn't the impression I got from the other Dr Carman half an hour ago.'

'Max is such a quiet boy,' Miss Helens advanced in her defence. 'This business with his father . . . and your only child. Only children do find social interaction more difficult . . .'

Stephanie felt a power surge; from the glow of rage in her heart, a charge of energy running through her veins, a murderous lucidity shedding from her mind. 'I hadn't noticed Max having difficulty with social interaction, Miss Helens. Not that Stewart and I ever taught him to regard beating up other children as a proper way of reacting to anything. So is what you're saying that because my husband isn't home Max ought to expect violence from other children? Or that a quiet child deserves to be attacked by the noisy ones?'

First blood to Stephanie.

'Good heavens, no, of course not. Mrs Sands, you're—'

'I was hoping you would at least agree that this is not a desirable situation to have in the school.'

'Of course I agree with that, Mrs Sands. Of course . . .'

'So, what action do you intend to take, Miss Helens? Max is in your care for seven hours a day. I'd like to be able to go to work and be confident that he is safe here.' Aaach! Wrong. Never mention work. A mother's work should be of no consequence, definitely not a reason for anything. Did the Virgin Mary work? Absolutely not.

'Yes. Your work, Mrs Sands. I do understand.' *I doubt it.* 'Although,' Miss Helens pressed on quickly, sensing that her adversary had stumbled, 'I would suggest that Max stay away from school for a week. To get over things. And then we do sometimes call upon an excellent child psychologist, very very skilled with the little ones—'

'Just a minute. Just a minute.' I will not shout. I will not yell. I will get hold of this. I will. I will get this under control. Icy dignity, grave concern, regretful intervention. I will be calm and rational and as polite as I can be. I will. 'I would have thought . . .' Her voice was scratchy. Air, I need air. She gulped the close atmosphere, getting a whiff of chemically simulated lily-of-the-valley. Diorissimo. How could we have chosen a school where the headmistress dabs on a scent fit only for Sandra Dee? My God, the woman even had a handkerchief. Miss Helens was patting at the corners of her mouth with a dainty wad of white cotton embroidered with edelweiss.

'I would have thought,' Stephanie managed the second time, 'that the proper thing to do would be to . . .' No, no, never say punish. Punishment is not a concept recognised here, this is PC heaven, we are too wholesome to punish anybody. '*Sanction* the children who have been the aggressors, perhaps by suspending them. It would certainly help Max to get over things, to know he could come to school for a week and be in no danger of being beaten up.'

'Max was not beaten up,' snapped Miss Helens, demanding recognition for the exemplary patience with which she was handling this distressing conversation.

'What would you call it then? Jon Carman stomped on him hard enough so you can see Nike written on his back in the bruises.'

'Semantics . . .' The queenly wave of the hand, dismissing a trivial annoyance. 'You see all sorts of things in a school, you have no idea what children can do.'

'And I can't imagine why Max would need to see a psychologist. I don't feel he's the one with the problem.'

'Now really, Mrs Sands. I was only trying to help. I can't have my families falling out like this. Dr Carman – both of them – are great supporters of the school and I can't possibly think of sending their boys home or suggesting to them that they need any kind of . . . treatment.'

'You didn't have any problem with suggesting that to me.' Icy dignity. Obviously the clear forty-eight woman-hours put into running the cake stall counted for nothing against the thirty couple-seconds it took to write a cheque.

'I don't think we can make any more progress with this, Mrs Sands. Not this morning.' Miss Helens heaved herself out of the wing chair, dragging off half the slip-cover. 'You're upset, it's perfectly natural, mothers especially are always upset when something happens to their children. And I'm sure the Carman boys are upset about what's happened. I know their father is certainly concerned. If you will leave this to my experience, I will speak to all the children today and remind them of all the things we believe in: good manners, consideration for others, good behaviour in general. We can move Max to another class, the top class. I was about to suggest that in any case because he's so advanced. I'm sure that will take care of the problem. Now I must get back to running the school.'

We are so busy in Westwick. It's so demanding, keeping the wheel of the ideal life turning, creating the ideal community. So we can't carry passengers or slow down for the weak or waste our precious time on needy people and their problems. They make their own problems, the needy. The kindest thing to do is just leave them alone to find that out for themselves.

As Stephanie was leaving, the children streamed out of the side door into the playground. She dawdled to watch out for Max, who came almost last with Sweetheart ahead of him. Ben Carman at once swaggered over and started pulling at the splint on Max's arm, but the junior teacher ordered him indoors. With his eyes sulkily averted, Jon was moping around the edge of the playground, kicking at nothing, raising puffs of dust. Ben appeared between the gingham curtains, making faces.

This is not the picture of Westwick life that Stephanie had imagined.

'Maybe you need a mirror by the door.' With muscular sweeps of her entire arm, as if scooping out Miss Helen's entrails, Gemma stirred her pot of fusilli. 'To reflect trouble away, you know.'

'Did that work for you?' Rod Fuller extended his legs and rested his crossed feet on the edge of Gemma's kitchen table. His feet were a little small for his build and very high at the arches. They always put Stephanie in mind of the statues of the Indian god Shiva, the dancing deity, balanced on one delicately cantilevered foot and high-kicking with the other.

'Well . . . at least once I had the mirror up we didn't get any *more* trouble.'

'On top of the barrow-load we had already,' Topaz explained, without taking her eyes off her screen. 'The plants are still dying.'

'Well, at least they're not letting your father out of jail.'

'Yet.'

'If I put a mirror up in the boat, will my tendon get better?'

'OK. I hear you, unbelievers. Rod, are you making salad there or what?'

'I'm making salad.' He winced histrionically in getting up, limped across to the worktop and grabbed the lettuce. 'I've got it cracked, anyway. I've trained the classes to work to my voice, so I can just stand up front and yell at them instead of jumping around the full sixty minutes. I miss you, you know.' This was to Stephanie, who had not taken the Bunbuster for months. 'You're one of those who always follows good. Now I've only got Catwoman left and a couple of new spods who're willing but they're s-o-o slow.' He threw garlic into the salad bowl and leaned around Gemma's backside to reach for the oil.

'Time,' sighed Stephanie, wondering where in the world she had found all those golden narcissistic hours.

'You'll come back to me,' he promised, his hands ripping the lettuces faster than their eyes could follow. 'They all come back to me in the end. And you never ogled, you know. That doctor, she does that.'

Gemma held out a spoonful of pasta for tasting. 'Al dente?'

'Al! We were kids together in Palermo. I hear he's a made man now.'

'Mamma mia, listen to him. Listen to my boy, e speaka mafiosa like-a goodfella.' Gemma hauled the pan of pasta to the sink and tipped it into the drainer.

The humour of the oppressed. When all you can do is laugh, you laugh. If there's nothing to laugh about, you laugh. Especially then, you laugh. The Irish, the Jews, the blacks, the single parents. Stephanie laughed. At least she was only one of the foregoing.

'Kids,' bellowed Gemma into the garden where Molly, Max and Sweetheart were supposed to be watering the vegetables but were actually watering each other, 'time to eat.'

'You've got a million tomatoes,' Sweetheart announced,

dragging in a brimming basket with Max's help. 'Look at this one, it's as big as a melon.'

'As big as a football,' suggested Max.

'As big as a pumpkin,' countered Sweetheart.

'As big as a big tomato,' said Flora flatly, dealing out forks around the table.

'Isn't this just like The Witches of Eastwick?' Rod took the tomato basket from his daughter and lifted it on to the dresser. 'The three of us keeping company here with all this fruitfulness.'

'You know what always gets me about that movie? Michelle Pfeiffer was supposed to have four children and you never even saw them, you never even heard their names.' Stephanie started putting out glasses but held a particularly smeary specimen against the light and wondered if Gemma would be insulted if she washed them.

'And the Cher character was meant to be fat. And nobody ever pointed out that the whole reason the witches were always getting together for spaghetti dinners was they were single mothers and nobody ever asked them out and pasta was all they could afford.' Gemma took hold of the tomato basket, carried it to the fridge, and poured the fruit of her soil into the salad drawer.

'I wonder why things don't grow so well at Gaia.' There was relief in thinking about another woman's problems. Stephanie surveyed the luxuriant vegetation in Gemma's garden, where red rose petals littered the shaggy grass and late nasturtiums snaked over what might once have been intended as a border. It was nothing like the diseased wasteland to which her business was sinking. In the steamy warmth of autumn every fungus known to mycology was breeding in the beds at Gaia, giving the *coup de grâce* to plants which seemed to have lost their grip on growth from the day they arrived.

Hanging out with Gemma, there had been plenty of opportunity to witness the process. Trays of patio lovelies would arrive from the growers in full lush leaf and brilliant bud. Within a week the leaves would begin to yellow and the buds shrivel and die; within a month the entire consignment would be reduced to withered stems. They were watered, they were sheltered, they were cossetted with foliar feeds and dosed with fungicide, and still they died, even the muscular modern hybrids, which normally grew so vigorously they looked like a vegetable world domination conspiracy. Topaz had started arguing that if her mother couldn't sell the place she should retain the greenhouse for floristry and decor plants and turn the outdoor space into a commuter car park with shuttle buses into the city.

'Please – what are a few sick plants compared to what Max has been through?' Gemma retorted in a voice intended to be too low for the rest of the gathering to hear, energetically slopping the fusilli into a dish so that twenty of them escaped over the side straight away. 'Or you, since the kidnap. Or Rodolfo here, recently bereaved and looking at the end of his career. OK, so his Achilles isn't actually busted, but his legs are his fortune right now. You know what I mean.' She turned back to the stove for a second pot and dolloped rich red sauce into the dish.

'You're so untidy,' Topaz complained, wiping down

the table with neat sweeps of a sponge. There was an oilcloth cover over the surface, white, printed with fluffy-topped red carrots which looked ridiculously suggestive.

'You're so anal,' Molly retorted, dripping in through the garden doors.

'Don't use words you don't understand,' said Topaz. 'And go and get out of that wet T-shirt and put on something dry before you come to dinner.'

'When I have a minute I'll come down to Gaia with my soil test kit,' Stephanie promised, passing down the loaded plates while Gemma served out her dish. 'It has to be a chemical imbalance. You've no problem in the greenhouse. It's not like nothing grows, is it? You can keep mint, eucalyptus . . .'

'Camellias.' Gemma nodded. 'Lady of the camellias, that's me. The only class plant I can get along with. The rest are just jumped-up weeds.'

There was a concentrated outbreak of stabbing, sucking, scraping, slurping and swallowing at the children's end of the table. The heaped plates were cleared of pasta, refilled with lettuce and cleared again before Gemma had finished grating the parmesan.

'Why do four children eat fifty times faster than one?' asked Rod, frowning at them. Molly burped.

'Daddy, can we go outside again?' replied his daughter, rolling her eyes around in exactly the cute way her mother used to do.

When the adults were alone they put Stephanie's problems at the top of the agenda.

'So the Carman woman denies everything?' Gemma put the steaming coffee pot before them.

'Totally. Boys will be boys, that's her line.'

'Unbelievable.' Rod poured himself a fresh glass of wine, scrupulously topping up the other two glasses first. With a meal, it was OK. At Gemma's, it was OK, because she had this exquisitely tactful way of managing the amount of booze available so he never drank too much and never even knew what was happening, although it happened all the same. He had allowed himself one bender after his wife's death, sent Sweetheart to sleep over with Molly and destroyed a couple of bottles of vodka; since then he'd been on wine-with-dinner only, but it was hard.

'How could she do this to Max?'

'Your child's just another weakness to them,' Gemma assured her. 'It's like they know there's a limit to what you'll do because of Max, so they push it even further. Rachel knows you won't scratch her eyes out and pull her hair because you're a good mommy, you don't do that naughty stuff.'

'Money, that's what this is about,' Stephanie declared, wondering if she was going to become as bitter as Gemma before long. 'The cheque was on her desk. Josh Carman just bought her off. Stewart would never have let them get away with it. He's got this way of just standing there being decent and people don't pull strokes on him. God, I wish he was here.'

'Believe me, Stephanie, if Stewart was here you wouldn't be having this hassle. They're picking on you because you're a woman without a man, and Max is a child without a father. So they think they can get away with it, all of them, even Miss Helens.' Gemma sat heavily back in her chair; it creaked with her weight. 'It's primitive. You've got no male to fight for you, so you're automatically a victim. That's what this is about.'

'But that's just animal,' Rod protested, thinking that Ms Arty T-shirt, with her soft, soft eyes and her long, long legs, did indeed at times have the air of a nubile doe antelope at the water-hole.

'Yes it is,' Gemma confirmed, picking up the coffee and beginning to pour. 'Nice, clean, leafy Westwick, exclusive Maple Grove – bullshit. It's a jungle out there. I bet you've had half your friend's husbands slavering round your door already. Go on – deny it if you can.'

Stephanie coloured and shook her head. 'How did you know?'

'Because the same thing happens to every single woman in a suburb. The husbands wheel around like vultures, the wives treat you like a pariah dog, like it was your fault their sex lives are so lousy the guys are permanently in rut. Excuse me, every single person. This is an equal opportunity phenomenon. Rod gets hit on just the same.' And she got up and went to open another bottle of wine, reckoning the occasion demanded it.

'Go on, tell about Allie Parsons.'

'There's nothing to tell,' he asserted, a shadow of disgust clouding his fine, broad forehead. 'I've been training her, if you can call it that, almost five months now and she never lets up. If they made steel shorts I'd wear 'em. She's even offered to fix me a job on her show.'

'Meanwhile, I'm getting harassment off the husband.' The cork popped indignantly and Gemma brought the bottle to the table. 'He gives me this fantastic contract supplying decor plants for his office and then it's a dozen oysters for lunch, the sticky paw on my leg and the big smooch in the taxi.'

'He's so pathetic, Ted.' Stephanie didn't realise she was smiling. In her grey mood, she had accepted a degree of responsibility for the pass in the garden; it was a relief to discover she had not been the only woman to arouse lust in Ted Parsons' despised loins.

'You too, huh?' Gemma refilled her glass. 'Yeah, he is pathetic. I can feel sorry for him if I let myself get that soft. Married to the witch-queen. Aren't those kids tragic? She should be prosecuted for child abuse, she really should. And spouse abuse. And they're always in the gossip magazines. "Allie Parsons of *Family First* with her lovely husband and her lovely family in their lovely home in Westwick . . ." Not that I read gossip magazines, of course.'

'Of course you don't.'

'Did we say you did? You just see them at the hairdresser, that's all.'

'Topaz brings them home for me from Magno. This is what my daughter thinks of me.'

It was after midnight when Stephanie unsteadily extracted her sleeping son from the back of the Cherokee in New Farm Rise, struggled upstairs carrying him and slid him into bed without waking him. The bruise on his back was now showing its full colours. Soon he was going to be too heavy for her to manage. Stewart was stronger, of course, but Stewart was gone.

She went downstairs and drank some water, feeling helpless. Stephanie never took her good life for granted.

She was always conscious of what she had left behind: shame, anxiety, being poor, and guilty pretence, the companions of her own childhood. Stewart had been her passport to safety. Now the passport had been revoked, she was being stripped of her privileges and pushed down again to raise her own child in the appropriate condition of misery. They weren't good enough to live good lives, not good enough for Westwick. She could leave, or she could stay. Staying meant she'd have to tough it out, work her ass off without getting paid for it, fight everybody when they picked on Max and the only joy would be a bitch session round at Gemma's place. No choice, really.

She walked around the house, enjoying the quiet and the order, feeling the emptiness. There was a fat moon shining and no blinds were drawn. Moonlight silvered the lawn and cast deep shadows behind their furniture. It's just a house, she told herself. Just a shell. Someone else can live here. I want someone to take care of us. I *need* someone to take care of us, I can't do it by myself. I'll call my mother in the morning.

CHAPTER 15

A Garden to Every House

'Chester?'

'Ted.' Like a toad gulping a fly, the BSD swallowed down the name, as if he were expecting the call, which paranoided Ted somewhat, because he had been counting surprise among his weapons. In the background the roar of the 31 could be heard above the crackle of the line; Chester was on his way to the airport.

'Chester, I need a meeting. ASAP. About the Sun Wharf sale.'

'I thought that was going through.'

'I think it would pay us to take a different approach.'

'How so?'

'It's complex. That's why I need a meeting.'

'Call my office.'

In the normal way, Chester's office ran his diary and his schedule was set in stone. Since Ted was asking to override the BSD's preordained course it was necessary to get Chester to call his office and sanction an emergency reschedule. Then Ted's PA – he employed only one – could call Chester's junior PA, one of two, and fix things so that Ted and Adam could walk over to Grove House at 8 pm on Friday evening.

Satisfied, Ted cut off, spoke to his secretary, then, with a glorious shudder of guilt, keyed in the next number on his list. 'Is this the City Theatre Museum? Do you have a conservation department? A conservation officer? Excellent! Let me speak to her.'

Four hours later he was again feeling his way down the dusty steps of the underground theatre, playing his torch over the coy chorus girls on the walls. 'This is just the beginning,' he promised the museum official, a round-eyed woman with a choirboy haircut, deliciously receptive to Ted in the role of the prodigal plutocrat seduced from the path of profit by this cultural treasure trove.

'A-m-m-m-m-azing. This is just a-m-m-azing.' She was stammering with excitement. Ted found himself pretty excited also, in the fine, clean, buccaneering way he had not felt for years. Not felt, in fact, since he bought his first property in Westwick. But there was an added sizzle now, a spin on the deal, because instead of crassly cutting through the regulations which might obstruct him he had turned the process on its head. What he was about to do, with the innocent connivance of this dear woman who devoted her life to the extracting of the lingering smell of greasepaint from crates of ephemera and memorabilia and sweat-rotted costumes, was get the regulations to work for him. Doing wrong and doing right at the same time! Whichever way you sliced it! The Jesuitical sophistication of the whole thing charmed him utterly.

Four days later he leaned over the labour-intensive patina of the Pikes' Jacobean-style oak dining table and laid a folder of drawings before Chester.

'The problem, quite simply, is that we won't get the price we need for Sun Wharf. The picture's changed. As of today, there is a preservation order on the site.' Chester's eyes bulged, the toad enraged. He opened his mouth to speak and Ted pretended not to see. 'Part of the site. Grade one. Applied for last year. I opposed it on Tudor's behalf, naturally. Got it kicked back to a sub-committee. But it was granted yesterday. They speeded things up when they saw we'd started work.' The joy of a paperless office, as the conservation officer had agreed, was that documents didn't exactly have dates any more. You could create them in time whenever you liked.

'It was a goddam sweatshop. Who the fuck wants to preserve that?' Chester looked as if he might even be able to excrete venom through his pores. A red flush of rage was rising up his neck, behind his ears, across his temples. He was almost shining with anger. To his right, Adam DeSouza shifted on his hams, his mind running on placatory suggestions.

'Nobody. The order applies to a music hall.'

'What music hall, for Christ's sake?'

'Originally, it occupied the centre of the site. The factory building was erected over and around it, concealing it totally. It was boarded up around nineteen-nineteen, in perfect condition. Absolutely untouched. Architectural gem. Body calling themselves Theatre Conservation Trust found it when they were willed a trunkload of old programmes and realised the building hadn't been demolished.' Imaginative details, his speciality. Ted glowed with proper pride.

Chester, who handled theatre programmes rarely, with disdain, and only as an expected element of corporate entertainment, departed from the project in spirit at this point, followed a few seconds later by Adam, who had been to a play once in his life, knew they were used for propaganda by so-called intelligentsia and was grateful that Belinda at least was as averse to the experience as he was.

'How much are we going to be short?' Adam enquired, uncapping his pen to take down evidence for the prosecution.

'I want to propose a creative alternative.' Ted felt he was cruising. 'I admit my initial reaction, like yours, was one of dismay. Then, when I looked at the new parameters, I realised that this could actually work to our advantage.' He felt like a conjurer, plucking the rabbit triumph from the black hat disaster. Chester and Adam were open-mouthed, hearing him. He had them, they would buy. He had not been to the theatre since the early days of his marriage but when he was working on Sun Wharf, he would go every week, and take his daughters when they were old enough. Yes, that was a click of Chester's back teeth at the word creative, but it was just a mannerism the BSD had, part of his dominance display, not indicative of an actual attitude. 'Basically, I propose we develop the site ourselves. Twenty-seven loft-style apartments, retaining the auditorium as the circulation area. It's not a costly option at all. Or a long job. We can have them all sold by the time Oak Hill's in phase two.

Double our original forecast figure at current prices. I've talked to the bank, they'll back us.'

He sensed hesitation. Chester had lidded his eyes and tented his fingertips. Adam was waiting on Chester. The drawings would clinch it, nobody could resist the drawings. Ted reached out and unfurled the folder, revealing an artist's impression of the pocket auditorium transformed into an atrium floored in blond limestone and garnished with palms, the gilded breasts of the nymphs glowing in the luminance shed by a new glass dome, the proscenium leading to the reception area for the integral swimming pool and fitness centre.

'Can I look at your figures?' Adam's fat cheeks were pleasantly creased but his eyes were elusive. Magnanimously, Ted handed him a sheaf of costings.

'We can also apply for a grant from the National Heritage Fund. Because this is a unique building and the quality of the decorative work is extremely high, we could go in with the backing of people like the City Theatre Museum. Perhaps twenty-five per cent of the total investment.'

'As much as that.' Adam ran his eyes down the figures, pretending scrutiny.

'It's a unique project. We can write our own ticket.'

'In essence, you're talking about a restoration job.' Adam, Ted knew, found more charm in the new than the old. It went with his immigrant insecurity, the idea that whatever was there already was just filling space until it could be torn down and the site colonised by something new. He had needed some convincing from Belinda to stay in Westwick at all, and still remarked uneasily on the inconvenience of having to live in a building which was not absolutely yours because someone else had lived there before.

'I thought the loft thing had peaked,' said Chester sourly.

'Projects like this, finished to a high standard, aimed at young professionals, singles, couples, *gay* couples even, two-income, high earning, high-geared lifestyles, are fetching better and better prices.' Ted handed out a reprint from a trade journal. There would be time enough to convince them that this was the right direction for Tudor Homes. The economics of it all might do the job for him. 'And when we come to Strankley Ridge,' triumphantly, Ted put the cherry on the cake, 'allowing two years for the inquiry to report, we will find ourselves in a substantially improved position. So our original scheme, which you recall was for a seven-acre development, could even be doubled in size.'

'Well, I think that covers all the angles.' Chester saw no point in wasting any more time. He rocked himself out of the massive carver chair, slipped down to his feet and walked around the table to dismiss them. 'Leave it with me, Ted. Good work. Interesting scheme, very. Very creative.'

At 5 am the next morning, the telephone rang in the DeSouzas' house.

'Adam – Chester.'

'Chester.' The murmur of the VIP lounge was behind the BSD's voice. He was at the airport.

'Parsons. Time we lost him.'

'Absolutely.'

'What's the best way?'

Anticipating the conversation, Adam had looked through the essential documents on his return from Grove House the previous evening.

'Some caution required. He knows where a few bodies are buried.'

'Surely.'

'I'd vote for a lifeboat manoeuvre. Ringfence this Sun Wharf thing, let him get in it up to his neck then cut him loose.'

'Excellent. How long?'

'Six months.'

'What'll it cost?'

'Maybe nothing. The man's not a total fool but he's emotional. I'll keep my eye on him.'

'Do that.'

Damon Parsons walked along the 31 in the night, facing the oncoming traffic, pretending to shoot out the head-lights of every car that passed: p-tchoww! p-tchoww! p-tchoww-eeee! Tonight he was going for tyres. Offside front tyres. When he got one, the car was going to spin out of control across all the lanes, cannon into the central barrier, bounce off it, slew across the fast lane and then maybe a container truck would hit the rear of it with an incredible smash and there'd be glass and metal all over and the speed of the truck would take it into a skid right out across the road and it would carry on skidding maybe fifty yards and other cars would hit it and maybe a

Porsche would come down the fast lane and the driver would lose control and hit the first car and the Porsche would flip up in the air right over it and crash down beyond and all its windows would burst out. And he would be first on the scene. This could really happen. I was on the police video.

His T-shirt rippled in the slipstream. One car after another whipped up a steady wind. He stopped and held out the shirt to see the wind made by the cars blowing the edges. When he stopped walking he swayed around. He was not very drunk but the rough grass of the roadside was difficult to walk on.

The cars kept coming, howling past one after another after another. The lights shone in his eyes, flash, flash, flash. Damon climbed up on the overpass that took traffic down into Helford and squatted like an ape in the girders. The overpass was as rickety as a helter-skelter. It was supposed to have been a temporary structure but it had been standing for seventeen years. Now the cars were running above him: da-boom da-boom, da-boom da-boom, da-boom da-boom. There were vehicles as far as the eye could see in both directions, a dragon of white light roaring out of the darkness before him, behind a snake of red lights crawling into the orange glow of the city night sky.

He lay down on the narrow cold metal and pretended a high-velocity rifle with an infra-red sight. They were accurate to half a mile. With one of those he could get a tyre half a mile out there, out past Acorn Junction near the 46 interchange. If he got a tyre right there on the 46 interchange maybe a tall truck would pile into the crash

and topple right over the edge of the approach road and
land on its roof and crush a car underneath, and the
windscreens would burst out and then more cars would
run into that heap of metal. But half-a-mile away he
probably wouldn't be first on the scene.

He thought about finding a rock and dropping it on a
car below. If you dropped it just right you could get a
windscreen but there wouldn't necessarily be a crash
because people could just push out the windscreen and
keep driving. It was cold. His arms were cold, the girder
was cold underneath him. He climbed down.

Along the river it was quiet. Quietness was intolerable
to him. In the absence of noise his thoughts got too
active and they wriggled around like maggots in a tin
and then started crawling everywhere. The more they
crawled around the stronger they got. They let things
into his mind, things which frightened him, questions
that did not have answers, or if they did the answers
were too big for him to grasp. Damon could not entertain concepts like what would happen to him, what
could happen to him, what he wanted to happen to him.
He just did not know. His mind was too shallow, those
things could not be packed into it.

In re-hab they asked him those kind of questions,
which is why he didn't like being in re-hab. Those people
were supposed to be so smart, but he couldn't make them
understand that he didn't understand. Every day almost,
somebody would sit there with him with that eyebally
look they all had and ask him something he couldn't
answer and he would sit there saying, 'I don't know, I
don't know,' but they never really got that he wasn't

hiding anything or avoiding anything or covering up anything; there wasn't anything to hide or avoid or dissemble. He just didn't know.

In re-hab they forbade you to drink alcohol but he was cool with that. Other people talked about wanting a drink but Damon never wanted a drink. He didn't like the smell of drink or the taste of drink; Coke was better, so something in Coke was what he liked to drink best. He never felt he wanted to sink a beer and smack his lips and wipe his mouth like sheep-shearers in the ads on TV, although he did those things because people seemed to like him doing them, it made them laugh.

Drink was like music, or lights or the noise of people talking. It filled up his head so his thoughts couldn't run around and that was good. The best thing of all for making thoughts behave was to do something scary, because then it was like the light was actually inside his brain making the thoughts lie down and be totally still, as if they were all dead. Running across the road, right across the 31, all six lanes of it, was scary, but Dad didn't like him to do that. Recently, Damon had worked out that there had to be something you could do which would be so totally scary that the thoughts would actually die, they would lie down and never ever move again.

There was very little water in the river, but it was running fast and the surface of it was crinkled in the light from the cars on the 31. He jumped over the embankment wall and down on to the stones of the dry margin of the riverbed. The stones crunched under his boots. He picked up some pebbles and threw them into the water to make more noise, but the splashes sounded lonely so he stopped doing that and went back to the road and turned away from the embankment up a side street which would probably lead up to the sound and movement of the Broadway.

The street he chose was the right one because his girl was walking down it. She was walking quickly on the other side of the street, so he hurried up and crossed the road to be with her. It was a few weeks since he had seen her last, he was afraid that she had been taken away. Under a street light he saw that she was more beautiful than ever. He could say that to her, it was the sort of thing boys said to their girls. He started turning the words over in his brain, making sure they would come out right. You are more beautiful than ever.

'You are more beautiful than ever.' There, they'd come out perfectly. She was still walking fast, maybe she was even walking faster. She didn't understand. Maybe she hadn't heard. Damon was half-running, trying to keep up with her. She couldn't have heard him properly. He had to stop her and make her stand still so she could hear him say it again. He put out his hand to take hold of her arm.

I will go like Josephine going to Malmaison, Stephanie promised herself, with grace and dignity because what I'm doing is for the best. Anyway, this is not a retreat, we are not running away. This is the best thing for Max, which is all that really matters. I thought it was the best thing for my son to bring him here but now the best thing is to move out. I can't manage by myself, I'm not clever enough to make the money we need, or strong enough to stand up to the whole neighbourhood. Gemma's right, there's a natural law operating here and I can't fight it.

'What a pretty garden. I'm sure we'll have your house rented in no time,' vowed the senior negotiator from Grove Estates gallantly, trotting from room to room with a clipboard, trailing her bitter atmosphere of great personal tragedy. Stephanie almost regretted having called her in, but there were only two agents in town and it was bad business not to compare quotes at least.

'Very popular street, neutral decor, good entertaining space, eat-in kitchen, well-arranged family rooms, nice big garden – we've got half a dozen companies looking for houses like this,' assured the man from Greenwoods on the Broadway, grinning like a fox while he measured the rooms with his electronic gauge. 'We'll need to see the deeds and the mortgage document if there is a mortgage document. Just a formality, proof of ownership. I'd recommend getting as much of your own stuff out of the way as you can before we bring people round. If a place looks empty people can imagine themselves living there more easily.'

I haven't time to be sad, Stephanie told herself, going back to her desk as soon as he left. Ridiculous to sit here shivering with misery because another family is going to live in your house, For a while, just for a while. Six months. And if Stewart is released tomorrow, then what? You'll have rented out his home.

Stewart would understand that she and Max had suffered also. She reached for a new green crayon. In the past few months she had used up one or even two green crayons a week, drawing in her special symbols for vegetation, little scribbled green circles for plants, big ones for trees.

The doorbell rang. She ignored it. She was not expecting anyone, it would be a Jehovah's witness or a scared-looking foreign teenager claiming to sell dishcloths for the blind. The bell rang again, a fierce sharp shrill that was somehow characteristic. Peering out from behind Max's curtains she saw the dark length of the Channel Ten limousine across the street and Allie standing on her front path looking up at the windows with a petulant frown.

'Stephanie! Darling! I've only just heard. Poor little Max! Those dreadful Carman boys! Chalice can't stand them, I can't tell you what they tried to put down her dress. I had to come!'

Stephanie found her arms full of Cellophane, tangerine gerberas, ultramarine delphiniums and chameleon-green bells of Ireland, all etiolated and greenhouse grown, lashed into a bouquet and decorated with Pot Pourri's loudest pink ribbon. 'How lovely,' she said, bemused by the high colour and high charge of emotion which swept them both through the house. 'You shouldn't have.'

'Of course I should. You deserve them. More than deserve them. Isn't that the extraordinary thing about tragedy, it's never just one thing? First Stewart and then this. One terrible ordeal after another. Let me hug you, I have to hug you.'

An explosion, a bomb of emotion it was, going off at Stephanie's front door, throwing all her feelings, so recently rearranged in functional little stacks, up to the sky in chaos and blowing the two of them clean through the house and out on to the terrace, where Allie's skeletal arms laced themselves around Stephanie's strong round ones and squeezed like a giant nutcracker. Then she hauled off to arm's length, and squeezed Stephanie's elbows with her little paws, and glared into her clear green eyes. 'Tell me,' she urged, 'how are you coping? How is Max coping?'

'Fine. Max seems to be fine.' Stephanie put down the bouquet.

'Stop this, Stephanie, you must stop this. Please, this is your friend asking. Don't say fine to me. You don't have to pretend, I know what you must be going through.'

I don't think so. To play for time while the dust settled Stephanie chattered on about Max, noting the film of boredom rising over Allie's bright eyes the longer she talked.

'But what about *you*, darling?' she pleaded. 'How are you coping with all this?'

'I'm not,' Stephanie said shortly. 'I'm leaving. I'm taking Max away from the whole sick thing. We're going to stay with my mother and I'll rent the house out.'

'But you can't do that! You love this house!' When excited, Allie had a way of poking her nose forward and rolling up her eyes which made her look like a small pig calling for food. 'You can't hand this house over to strangers. Why, it's you! It's you and Stewart You can't!'

'I can't have Max stomped to mush by the Carman
oys while Miss Helens stands by and waits to be bought
ff and the rest of you run around trading gossip about
s.'

'Stephanie!' The hand pressed to the heart again, the
ig round eyes turned up under reproachful brows,
nother steal from Princess Diana. 'I hope you don't
hink that *I* . . .'

The fairy dust wasn't working. Allie trailed through
Westwick like a comet, a ball of flaming media gas with
trailing tail of glamour, hurtling light years above their
ull terrestrial lives. It had been as if she shed fairy dust
n all their eyes, making people see her as something
antastic, a kind of Superbeing, a phenomenon. For some
eason, she now appeared to Stephanie just as an over-
ager, over-expressive, over-made-up little female. Her
ody seemed not to fill the seams of her coral-pink suit,
t flapped around her ribs; her spirit seemed not to fill
er face, either. Her grimaces and gestures were over-
fesize but empty.

'Of course not.' Was that the truth? Stephanie knew
er instincts were good. Her instincts said that Allie
nust at least have been as involved as any of them in
landering her. In fact, her instincts pointed out that
Allie was an opinion-former, a pack leader, the first to
peak on most topics. Quite possibly she had started the
vhole thing. Impossible to put that together with this
reature pleading friendship. Stephanie's logic fuse blew
f she tried it.

'I'm your friend, Stephanie. I'd never hear a word
gainst you, honestly. People say things but I don't take

any notice. I mean, Rachel – I'd never go to her, woul[
you? Be one of her patients, I mean. She's alway.
mouthing off, I couldn't trust her. That's what happen.
in situations like this, isn't it? That's what makes bully
ing such an issue today. It's a whole-community kind o
thing. You find out who you can trust, who's really ther.
for you . . .'

She babbled on, probing Stephanie's defences, feeling
about for soft spots. Stephanie let herself murmur occasional assents to keep the flow going. She felt confused.
She felt tired, in the same way she had done after she go
the news about Stewart, muffled in pain, emotionally
deleted.

What did Allie want from her? She had cast herself a.
a friend. Was it the price of this friendship that Stephani.
should disclose her emotions exclusively to a woman
whose profession amounted to mass-marketing human
feelings? This was still Westwick, there was no friendship here, she had seen that demonstrated beyond doubt.
Relationships here were expedient, necessary, profitable –
or nothing. 'Allie,' she broke in at last, 'are you stil
asking me to talk about this on your show?'

'It would make things so much better for you,' was th.
eager response. 'You have no idea, no idea. TV is only
thing people respect in this world, I promise you. I
you've been on TV, they treat you right. It's that simple
I mean, I wish it wasn't, I'm not saying this is right o:
anything. But can you imagine how Miss Helens woul[
be if she thought I'd be coming down with a video jour
nalist to film her fucking climbing frame?'

Fool. Fool you were to think this bitch could hav.

had anything else on her mind. Fool to think that anything as useless and sentimental as friendship could exist in this world. 'Go away,' Stephanie said sadly. 'Just go away, Allie. Leave me alone. You know how I feel about this, can't you just stop hassling me?'

'You're upset. I'm trying to help you, you know that.' That touch on the arm again, slimy with insincerity. 'Don't worry, I'll go, Steph. Of course I will, I'm sorry it was the wrong time.'

'No it wasn't,' was the weary reply. 'It was the wrong question and I'm the wrong person. You're a piece of work, Allie. You really are. How can you come over to my house thinking you can take advantage of me because our son's been bullied at school?'

'I'm just trying to help you,' she protested, as Stephanie advanced and began to shoo her out of the house like a chicken. 'You're upset, darling, or you'd see that. I just want to do what I can . . . I mean, the only point of a privileged position like I have is helping your friends, isn't it?'

Allie was still mugging sympathy on the front path when the phone rang, giving Stephanie perfect cause to shut the door in her face.

'Mrs Sands.' It was the vulpine young man from Greenwoods and there was a wholly different kind of energy in his voice. 'I wonder if you'd have the time to stop by our office? Something's come up on your property which I'd like to talk to you about.'

'What? What's come up? What do you mean, come up?'

'If you could stop by I could show you what I mean.'

'You mean it's too heavy to talk about on the telephone?' A drench of pure panic chilled her. What in the world could be that serious?

'Well . . .'

'OK.' There was half an hour before she had to leave for school. 'I'm on my way.'

Fifteen minutes later she wove her way through the yammering negotiators and the icy air-conditioning of Greenwoods' offices and found herself in another windowless, coffin-like interview room with another boy trying to do a man's job, this time with rather more sensitivity.

'What it is,' he began, holding some papers to his chest to hide them from her, 'is we have a routine procedure here with all our properties, just checking if there are any planning applications affecting the area at all. Now in this case, when we went through to the planning office, this is what came up.' Such tact, making it seem as if whatever disaster this might be had manifested spontaneously, without being any person's actual fault.

He put down the papers and turned the top page towards her. She recognised a map of Westwick. Each house plot appeared as a rectangle fronting its road. His finger traced the Broadway, then New Farm Rise. From the north, two thick black lines had been drawn through the grid of homes, slicing across the top of New Farm Rise. Every plot which fell between the thick black lines was crossed through.

The houses were numbered. 'You see,' he said. 'Here you are.' And there was her home, with a black cross through it.

'But what is it?' she asked, ready to burst into tears. He put a box of tissues by her elbow, freshly opened, pink. Amazing how considerate people could be when your relationship was only commercial.

'It's the route of the access road for the Oak Hill Business Park. Work is scheduled to begin early next year, so you would be hearing from the Department of Transport any day now. Basically, what it is, Mrs Sands — your house is scheduled for demolition.'

CHAPTER 16

Cozy Comfort

A high wind barged around Westwick, a bad-tempered blast of heavy air which threatened thunder and ripped the first dead leaves off the trees. As Stephanie drove to Gemma's house, she registered the noise of a police siren with the low-grade curiosity of a Westwick citizen confident that whatever crime might be in progress could not be happening here, but she turned into Alder Reach she found its calm ruptured. The blue light oscillated over the blank lawns and glared into the windows of the Lieberman house. This household, the beacon proclaimed, could lay no claim to discretion; this household had partaken in illegal activity, it had waived all rights to privacy.

'It's my sister,' Topaz warned, letting them in. With portentous solemnity she suggested, 'You might want to send Max up to play with the girls in Molly's room.'

All eyes were focused on Flora, who sat at the end of the sofa, folded over her knees with her hands over her eyes and her hair tumbling over her hands as if she could shut out the world. A police officer – Stephanie ecognised WPC Clegg's skewered coiffure – perched in he chair opposite with an open notebook.

At the opposite end of the sofa was Gemma, unnaturally still with her arms folded around her bosom and her ands in fists. 'Hi, Steph. Don't even think about excuses ot to be here, we need our friends right now,' was her reeting and she pointed towards the kitchen area where od was walking about in short, fierce paces, ineffectully tending a saucepan.

'What exactly did he do?' WPC Clegg was saying.

The curtain of Flora's hair twitched and she whisered, 'He grabbed me.'

'Grabbed you?'

'Uhhhh . . .' A long strangled breath.

'When you say he grabbed you, exactly where—'

'Is this necessary right now?' Gemma gave the officer er full-freeze eye contact. 'You can see she's upset.'

'There've been some severe injuries caused, we need to stablish the facts.'

'Surely the most important fact is that this man has een stalking my sister for months,' suggested Topaz, ith the air of a poker player putting down a strong and.

Gemma's face drained white and she leaped two cushons towards Flora, but was stilled by a glare from her ldest daughter.

'So what you're saying is that you know this young nan?' countered WPC Clegg, speaking as if Damon arsons were every girl's dream bridegroom and peering ideways at Flora, trying to make eye contact through the rotective screen of hair.

'Oh, please,' sniped Topaz. 'Millions of people "know
Damon Parsons. He's the son of a national celebrity, hi
mother's on TV. She gives interviews to the press abou
her problems with him. He's always causing trouble.'

'We are concerned with what actually took place, no
what people read in the newspapers,' the officer returned
primly smoothing the top page of her notebook.

'And Damon Parsons is well known in the neigh
bourhood,' Topaz continued unhesitatingly, 'where he
can be seen most days walking around like a crazy person
throwing stones at cars and where we all attended th
same school until he was suspended last year for disrup
tive behaviour, abusing alcohol and violence.'

'That's as may be,' the officer responded doggedly
'I'm only concerned with this incident which as far as we
are concerned is about an alleged assault. Severe injurie
have been caused to the young man. Obviously if ther
was provocation we need to establish its nature.'

'What do you mean, provocation? My sister didn'
attack this man.'

'If you don't mind, may I continue?'

Stephanie had never seen Topaz angry before -
annoyed, perhaps, when her mother irritated her, bu
generally Topaz did not waste effort on emotion. Still b
nature, she was now as immobile as marble, her slende
hands and feet both folded neatly together, lethally inert
Her blink rate was elevated and there was a neon glow o
indignation her eyes.

'So when he grabbed you, where exactly did his hand
touch you?' WPC Clegg repositioned her pen over he
notebook.

Flora suddenly threw back her hair, revealing a wet red face. 'First he grabbed my hair,' she said with angry sarcasm, picking out a handful and offering it to her inquisitor. 'This bit about here, I think.'

'I can understand that you are upset about this,' the officer snapped back, 'but it would help if we could all keep calm and just recall the events.'

'Oh, right,' Flora agreed with anger. 'Right. Well, I think the next thing was I turned around and pulled my hair away from him and started running away. Then he grabbed my shoulder and then my arm.' As she held out her left arm, the torn seams of her T-shirt parted; underneath, there were already red welts on her pale skin. 'And I pulled away from him and ran away. Then he ran after me and grabbed my arm again, and my clothes, which got torn, and then he grabbed my breast.' Defiantly, she pushed out her chest, letting the torn clothing fall away. Between breast and shoulder were two long scratches. 'And then,' she pulled up her chin and twisted her neck to the right, pointing at another angry abrasion with her fingertips, 'he went for my neck. He was holding me too tight for me to get away, so I decided to kick him. I can't kick very well, I'm really worst in the class at kicking. He was still holding my neck and ripping at my clothes. When I kicked the second time I got it right and then he ran off.'

Gemma opened her arms and her daughter fell into them.

'And I heard him yelling and I saw the whole thing from the house,' Topaz added.

'So it was you who decided to call us?' The officer

made it sound as if this was quite the most foolish course of action anyone could possibly have taken.

'Yes,' Topaz confirmed, dangerously obedient. 'I decided to call the police when he went for her neck.'

'So when you say you're the worst in the class at kicking . . .' Now WPC Clegg put on an earnest air of enquiry, but her eyes were full of guile. 'What class would that be, exactly?'

'Martial arts. Judo and stuff,' said Flora. 'I took it up because he was harassing me and I was afraid.'

'You know that if you're a brown belt or above you have a legal obligation to register with the police?' Censorious, closing the notebook as if further discussion was going to be futile.

'Brown belt!' The words came out between a snarl and a sob. 'In your dreams. I was crap,' Flora pulled away the ripped front pocket of her overalls with a disgusted gesture. 'I've only done six lessons. I won't even take grade one until next year.'

'Perhaps you're better than you think you are,' WPC Clegg suggested, tenacious still although visibly disappointed. 'The injuries are severe. There may be broken bones. We are awaiting medical reports.' She looked around the room as if for inspiration and her eye came to rest on Rod, who was folding and refolding a kitchen towel, the fig leaf covering the deficient masculinity which had allowed a female in his protection to be attacked. 'And when this was happening, you were . . . Mr, uh . . .?'

'I was coming over,' he said, with regret. 'I got here just before you did. My name's Fuller. Rod Fuller.'

'So you live here?' The question was delivered with thunderous absence of judgement: an immoral household, an absolute invitation to incident but we, the authorities, having no business with morality, will take no position on *that*.

'No,' Rod's voice was richly level. 'I live on the houseboat *Dawn Treader*, The Moorings, Riverview Drive. With my daughter Courtenay, who is upstairs. I'm just a friend of Mrs Lieberman. We know each other through our children.'

'Was anyone with you at home?'

'No one apart from her. I was on the telephone. I was talking to my agent.'

'What kind of agent would that be?' WPC Clegg knew she had paddled up the wrong creek but was intent on finding something to justify the voyage.

'I'm an actor.' Rod muffled the word, having increasingly less and less experience of his profession and memories which sadness and wine had faded a great deal.

'An actor.' An artistic so-called profession, notorious for irregular living but we, the authorities, having no business with morality, will take no position on that either. WPC Clegg turned back to Gemma. 'And you were . . .'

'Right there cooking,' was the defiant answer, daring the officer to suggest that a mother should be anywhere other than at hearth and home.

'You're not writing anything,' Topaz observed.

The officer decided the pursuit had gone on long enough and it was time for the kill. She shut her notebook. 'The man you say attacked you, Miss Lieberman, has severe injuries. He's lost some teeth and may have a broken nose or a broken jaw. The doctor is with him at this point in time. I understand his family are reluctant to get involved in any case against you because of the publicity—'

'That figures,' Gemma sniffed. 'Allie Parsons, the nation's top young mother, invites readers to her lovely home to talk about why her son's a rapist. I mean, it's not really tasteful, is it?'

'They are very gravely distressed but they have some sympathy for the young lady and what I would suggest in this situation . . .'

At this moment the telephone rang, and Topaz, who was nearest to a receiver, answered. 'This is the worst possible time,' she hissed furiously. '*The worst possible time.*'

'In these circumstances,' WPC Clegg continued, smiling at Gemma with extreme menace, 'given that there are two possible chargeable offences here, and that your daughter fortunately is not really hurt, or at least is not as severely injured as the young man, the best course might be for us to allow the two families to resolve this matter . . .'

'Why yes,' said Topaz to the telephone with toxic sweetness, 'there is one thing you can do, Ted. You can tell this . . . woman . . . from the police that if she gets as far as offering my mother a bribe on your behalf my mother will probably kill her. That would be a real help. I'm going to pass you over to her and you can do it right now.'

'Topaz!' Gemma freed an arm to make suppressing

gestures at her daughter. 'That's enough! You've no business . . .' But WPC Clegg had jumped to her heavily-shod feet and she was pink with what seemed to be outrage.

'Since you – ah – you – you're already in communication . . .' She was having difficulty mastering some inappropriate emotion. 'I don't think there's anything more to be done here at this point in our investigation and I'll . . . I'll be in touch as soon as . . . ah . . . as soon as we have the medical reports. From our point of view, you understand, if you were able to come to an arrangement between yourselves we would not pursue any charges and they would not remain on our files. And if . . . if, Miss Lieberman,' – this was condescendingly to Flora – 'if in the meantime you feel in need of counselling at all, I am authorised to give you this number, which is the rape crisis and victim support helpline here in Helford.' She put a card on the table and sidled rapidly to the door. Rod threw down the tea towel and showed her out with excessively courtly politeness.

There was a moment of silence. Gemma picked up the telephone. 'Just fuck off,' she said, cut the line and handed the receiver to Topaz who replaced it quietly.

'Hey, Flora.' Had Topaz been a physical person she might at this point have given her sister a hug. As it was she reached out one hand in Flora's direction as if to impart approval by stirring the air. 'You knocked his teeth out. Good going.'

'Yeah,' ventured Rod, tortured because he had arrived on the scene too late to do the job himself. 'Good going.'

The victim seemed restored by this praise, while

Gemma was annoyed. She was also annoyed with herself for having told Ted to fuck off when she had heard enough talk from him to know that he was only concerned about them. There was something truly manly in trying to make contact through such a firestorm of female emotion. And hanging in to take care of Damon, as much as he could, when many men just abandoned a child who turned out less than perfect. Pitiable as he was, Ted had that kind of benighted decency. He reminded her of his own dog. She ruffled Flora's hair, then got up from the sofa and made for the stove, ignoring her eldest child.

'She *was* going to fix the pay-off,' Topaz insisted mulishly.

'I know. Topaz, you were right – OK? Happy now? I do know. I just don't want to believe it.' She took possession of her saucepans again, taking the cloth from Rod to lift lids and peer at the contents. 'What is it with trouble, it always comes at dinner time? You know my father used to say that? "Why can't we ever sit down to a meal in peace?" he used to say.'

'Why don't you want to believe it?' Topaz was implacable. 'You hate Allie Parsons. You said she was the worst mother since Medea.'

'For Christ's sake, first-born child, you were supposed to fulfil my dreams, not run over them with a tank. Look, it's not about Allie Parsons. Like I care about some plastic dolly on the TV. It's this, it's – the Westwick thing. That dream. Nice people, nice neighbourhood, trees on the streets, where you girls were going to grow up with good schools and straight teeth, all healthy and strong and beautiful. That's why we came here. I don't want it to be crap, but it is crap, isn't it?'

'You know it's crap,' Rod felt able to come out from behind the kitchen table. 'Anybody gets trouble in a nice neighbourhood, the nice neighbours just ignore them until they go away – aren't we all the living proof of that? When have any of those nice people ever supported you or me, or Steph or any of us?'

Stephanie had judged her moment. 'Speaking of trouble . . .'

Now Gemma was crashing pans in her cupboards, those already in use having been judged inadequate. 'Oh God. Not you too. I'm gonna haveta smash that mirror, I know it. C'mon Steph, spill – what happened to you today?' Shoving back her hair, she dragged out a cast-iron casserole and threw it on to the stove, followed by its clanging lid.

'I decided I couldn't stand it any more, I decided my mother was right, I decided I'd rent out the house and move in with her until Stewart's home, so I went down to Greenwoods on the Broadway and discovered I couldn't rent the house because there's a road going to be built to the Oak Hill Business Park right through our house, and any day now the Transport Department are going to drop me a line to let me know before they knock it down.'

There was a silence. Flora twisted her hair into knots, looking encouraged that she was not the only sufferer in the room. 'They can't do that,' Topaz spoke first.

'My poor baby.' Gemma froze in the act of decanting arrabiata sauce. 'My poor baby. That is unbelievable.'

Stephanie, still standing next to Rod, sensed a movement, turned towards him and found herself embraced.
His arms were warm and hard, his shirt smelt faintly of
mildew, as clothes kept on boats often do. She had not
had a man's arms around her since the day Stewart left,
nearly six months ago. He had not put his arms round a
woman since he held Mairi-Sui's limp form for the last
time. It was a shockingly good feeling, so they pulled
apart fractionally to avoid full body contact, telling
themselves they were still lightheaded from trauma.

'They can't do that,' Topaz said again. 'There must be
some kind of consultation procedure . . .'

'Oh yeah. Like the one we just saw? Consultation on
how good your case is to be considered a human being,
how much you'll take for your innocence, exactly what
it's worth to you to look in the mirror in the morning
and like what you see. Topaz, you are so naive . . .'
Gemma reached for her largest wooden spoon, the one as
long as a forearm.

'The plans for Oak Hill were all properly approved,'
Stephanie sighed. Rod squeezed her shoulders and set
her free. 'We monitored the whole process at the Old
Westwick Society. I don't even remember a new road in
the scheme. A road would be the Transport Department's
show, it doesn't need the same kind of consent but they'll
have to go through a consultation process on the route.
You could be right, Topaz, if enough people protested it
could be thrown out. But right now it's all the same to
us, because I can't in good faith sign any rental contracts
when I know that up at the Transport Department there's
a big black cross through the house. The guy at

Greenwoods wouldn't wear it anyway. He said all I'd get was the nastiest kind of tenant offering me a rock-bottom rent and probably intending to squat the property anyway.'

'This is supposed to be a democracy . . .' insisted Topaz.

'Hah!' interjected her mother. 'This is a *suburb*, my girl. No politics. No right or wrong, no ethics, no morality, nothing liable to cause thought, no, no, no, Mamma don't allow no thought-provokin' round here. This is a profit-making system, it's self-regulating. Whatever doesn't add value is out.' Animated with anger again, Gemma splashed her sauce into the pot and ripped open a packet of spaghetti which she dumped in the boiling water and stirred impatiently, her momentary tenderness for Ted vanishing in the steam. 'And it was mostly created, I might point out, by that sleazebag who had the nerve to call up just now, who you, my darling daughter, have been trying to sell me as your ideal stepdaddy for the past six months. Ted fucking Parsons. I bet you've still got that stupid letter of his.'

'It wasn't stupid, it was a beautiful letter. You can't blame him—'

'Watch me. Listen, you like Ted so much, you shack up with him, give us all a break.' In accusation, Gemma pointed with the giant spoon. 'Ted Parsons, director of the Oak Hill Development Trust, trasher of our friend's fortunes, whose idea of a neighbourhood is any place where you can jack the price of property up more than twice the national average. A family to him is just what you need to live in a neighbourhood, like your passport.

If you said a neighbourhood was a place where people who shared the same values got together to raise families he'd ask you how much you were talking about.'

'He's the only person who was ever decent to Damon,' Topaz protested weakly.

'Yeah, well just at this moment I'd call that an error of judgment, Topaz.'

'I'm going to change my clothes,' said Flora suddenly, heaving herself to her feet. 'Shall I tell the little ones they can come down now?'

'Yeah, we can eat in ten minutes.' Gemma stirred her brew, defiantly planted on sturdy legs, her free hand supporting her waist, her hair falling in her eyes. Topaz sulked, unmoving. Stephanie and Rod hunted for knives and forks. 'Fucking Ted Parsons,' Gemma muttered again, banging a spoon on the edge of a saucepan, full of uncrystallised fury. Then she turned and advanced on her silent daughter. 'Who needs Jack Nicholson?' she demanded. 'I don't need to call up the devil to get some respect around here. I can trash this fucking neighbourhood all by myself. So, Topaz, now you can go and get that beautiful letter which you so thoughtfully picked out of the garbage for me.'

The man of steel taught himself never to show emotion. As a prisoner in Siberia, when the man of steel was punished with ninety lashes he read a book all the time throughout the flogging. Topaz looked at her mother with a blank face. 'All right,' she said.

It was past midnight. The children were asleep upstairs and Rod was opening another bottle of Chateau Mr

Singh. 'What we most hated about living in town was the car exhausts spewing out just at the height of a child's face in a buggy, so Sweetheart got gassed every time we crossed the road with her.'

'What did it for us was when somebody stole Max's buggy right from outside our door, while I was getting out my front door key.' Stephanie still winced at the memory. 'What kind of people would do something like that?'

'The usual kind.' Gemma pushed her glass over for a refill. 'The standard variety selfish ignorant murdering shithead. Common or garden *Homo sapiens*. Fools we were to think we could get away from them.'

Rod poured generously and fell back into his chair. 'We never thought, Mairi and I. Never knew what we were getting into. We just wanted to live on a boat because we thought it'd be cool and there's no schools near the city marina. *Dawn Treader* was the first boat we found in a place a kid could have a life and we could still get to auditions. So we sold up and bought her. That was our dream.'

Gemma caught Stephanie's eye with the look which said: the man is talking, talking like expressing, we have to let this run. 'Three months it lasted. We got Sweetheart into The Magpies, Mairi used to take her on her bicycle up Riverview Drive. She loved it, you know, the little baby seat. And Mairi. Caring for the planet, all that shit. She wouldn't learn to drive even. Then this truck got her right on the Broadway, right outside Catchpoles. No witnesses.' He looked down at his hands, lying symmetrically on his thighs like the hands of a pharaoh's statue, and it seemed that he politely swallowed a belch although the convulsion might have been emotional in origin. 'I always thought it was bizarre she called it The Magpies. Birds of ill omen, aren't they?'

To the faraway drone of the traffic on the 31 a bigger noise was added, a jet overhead, straying from the flight-path. Matters had been arranged so that air traffic was routed over Helford, where the citizens cowered behind their double glazed windows in fear of falling lumps of frozen excreta and environmental health officers staunchly maintained that the showers of coarse black dust which also fell from the sky must be occasioned by defective domestic boilers. In summer, when the airport seethed with holiday-makers day and night and planes almost grazed wingtips in the congested sky, aircraft were directed to circle over the river and occasionally roared over Westwick.

The wing lights moved steadily between the stars, the thunder of the engines engulfed them like a giant's heart-beat, drowning all other noises until it faded. The women stayed quiet, hoping in vain for more, but all Rod did was sigh and scrub his fingers in his hair at the back of his neck. He had impossible hair, short, dark, slick, bratpack hair which grew just right and fell just right and got cut just right by the same boy at The Snipper on the Broadway who had once turned out Stephanie with ringlets and a french pleat for the Berkman & Sands Christmas dinner.

'Bizarre.' Gemma twisted her glass by the stem, watching the paler meniscus on the ruby liquid tilt around the bowl. 'At least it's plural, so we get two for joy and counting. I guess she didn't know. Let's face it, she doesn't know much. When I told them Mr Lieberman had a bi-polar disorder she told the rest of the teachers the girls had congenitally deformed teeth. Next thing I knew I had that Carman woman creeping round me for weeks saying it was wonderful what orthodontic surgeons could do nowadays and why didn't I bring them all to her clinic? Now what I think's bizarre,' – she turned to Stephanie, just in time to blow away the fresh cloud of despair creeping over her – 'is how all these women go glass-eyed when you talk to them about plants. Have you ever noticed that?'

'Uh-huh. They look at you like you're an alien visitor and your interpreter circuits have blown.'

'They're actually threatened that you can grow things. Isn't that weird? They all live here for the gardens and the trees and stuff and they can't make anything grow. I mean, I should talk . . .'

'I'm going to test your soil,' Stephanie responded unexpectedly. The offer had been earning interest in her conscience for some time.

'Ah – I tested it, it's acid. What can I tell you?'

'Yeah, well obviously it's acid.' Through the insulating blanket of alcohol, Stephanie groped for the explanation. 'I mean test for minerals. You must have some imbalance somewhere, nothing else would make stuff die the way it has. There's a lab I used to use when I did commercial schemes, they'll do a full chemical breakdown. I'll do it tomorrow.'

'I do hate everything dying around me,' Gemma admitted fretfully.

'You should see how things die around Allie Parsons.'
Spiteful, that was actually spiteful, Stephanie congratulated herself. Good going.

'I bet it's a dump . . .'

'With that poor dog . . .' Rod nodded, remembering Moron's longing eyes.

'Will you cut that out? You sound like Topaz.'

Stephanie put her hand on her heart, mimicking Allie.
'True confessions, guys. The Parsons' garden was the start of it all. I owe them everything . . .'

Right back then, the first time she set foot in Westwick, she had sensed some geomantic flaw in the region. She took away from that first visit a passion to live here and the obscure sense that her love for plants transgressed some unwritten local statute. Her first private commission had been the Parsons' garden, and that same threatened shadow had come over Allie's face as soon as she showed the drawings.

It had begun in the name of friendship. 'I know – you must come over and tell me how to make the back yard into something,' Allie had decreed, and under cover of progressing their relationship she and Stewart had come to No 6 Church Vale on a rich June evening, Stephanie still in the first flush of pregnancy, nimble in new flat shoes, hopefully sweeping a loose print dress around her imperceptibly expanded belly.

At the front of the Parsons' house then was a parched lawn, and at the centre of it an old yew tree stood dying, rust-brown branches dragging the ground, ripped apart by the weight of its own growth. They passed through the house, retaining an impression of dark beams and white space, watched over by New England wooden decoy birds with scimitar beaks and gimlet eyes.

The back yard was the most desolate domestic enclosure Stephanie had ever seen. The terrace was tinged grey-green with grime and algae, and curtained along one wall with a glaucous large-leafed ivy. Withered stems in holes at oppressively regular intervals at the paving showed that roses and honeysuckles had been intended; the ammoniacal whiff of dog's urine explained their failure to thrive. When she knew the household better, she understood that Moron passed day and night out there, kept tethered by a leash looped over the clothes line like a guard dog in a builder's yard rather than a beloved domestic pet.

There had been some attempt to finish off this homestead with livestock. After more scorched grass, at the end of the yard sagged a decaying fence, beyond which were rabbit hutches, shingled miniature pavilions with windows, the most elaborate rodent housing money could have bought. Investigating, Stephanie found one unoccupied and in the other a terrified Netherland doe; it seemed to have given birth recently; a number of dead foetal rabbits were visible here and there in the saturated hay.

Leaning wearily over the whole scene was the amputated trunk of another ancient tree, a die-hard sycamore, sawn off ten feet from the ground, with new shoots bristling from its peeling bark like the last wisps of hair on a balding scalp. Beneath this, some reproduction French wirework furniture was arranged, and here

Stephanie sat with her client and friend-to-be, delicately soliciting her requirements. 'Oh, I just want it to be beautiful, you *know*,' was the most direction she could get.

Ted she remembered also, the same Ted who even then must have been sitting in his office with the planning application for Oak Hill. Had he been the one who drew that map full of crosses, condemning herself and her family to financial hara kiri? Her first impression of the husband was that he drooped like a parched vine beside his radiant wife. He had a handsome face but a scoured complexion and a pained look as if his head ached all the time.

'I think we just met the man who resurrected Maple Grove,' Stewart said as they drove back to the city. 'He was telling me a story of seeing some actress who lived here years ago when the place was run down, and getting in with the end of a short lease that he sold his car to buy.'

How cramped and dusty and unnatural their city life had seemed after the pale space of the Parsons' house, how meanly artificial the balcony where Stephanie had her lavender balls in pots and a yucca struggled to breathe in the fumes rising from the Thai Garden restaurant below.

'Those trees,' she sighed, looking over a vista of ten thousand living units and nothing vegetable rooted in the earth. 'Do you think they were in the original planting scheme for the estate?'

Stewart went to look at his books and found a biography of Tudor Wilde. 'Maple Grove was a garden before they built on it. I thought I remembered that – most of the land which Wilde developed was the park belonging to one of the big houses he had demolished, and the orchard belonging to his own father-in-law. The other house was owned by the founder of some botanical society. Wilde drew the street plan around the trees.'

She peered at the page over his shoulder. '"The arboretum planted by C E Crisp, President of the National Horticultural Society, with thirty-five different rare species of tree." So – that poor old yew could have been two hundred years old.'

'They're a size, aren't they, those trees. What are they, thirty feet? Fifty? You don't often see a tree that size.'

'I wonder if there was a ginkgo. They always had a ginkgo, when they planted an arboretum. The oldest tree we know.' For a while they said nothing further, turning the pages together, scanning the old photographs of working horses pulling carts down Church Vale, barges loading at Helford Wharves, and Wilde himself in a frock coat posed with his building gang in bowler hats and waistcoats. 'Would you like to live somewhere like that?' Stewart asked her finally, in the emphatically matter-of-fact tone he reserved for questions on which he had extremely strong opinions.

'We couldn't possibly afford it.' She tried to keep this as a statement, but it veered towards a question.

'Not now. Maybe in a few years. See how things go, eh?'

As things went, it was a year later when Allie called her to say a house was for sale in New Farm Rise at an unexpectedly low price. A family moving abroad, she had hinted; Stephanie recalled the conversation in the bitter clarity of hindsight. By then she had transformed the Parsons' back yard with a ravishing if slightly vulgar all-white planting scheme and dog-proof containers for a rank of spiral box trees, each one costing, as Allie put it, enough for a pair of new tits. Allie at least spent the money with enthusiasm, after falling into a wary silence over the drawings and giving Stephanie the outfoxed look which pledged revenge for an offence unspecified.

The scheme lasted less than a season. The box trees, never watered, immediately died. Tactfully, Stephanie sympathised and said nothing when Allie had the dead topiary replaced by common laurels. When the right moment came, she suggested a maintenance contract, thus inviting Derek and Dave into her life. They reported that Mrs Parsons screamed at her children a great deal and was never around on pay day. By then the Parsons were neighbours, and Stephanie considered that spreading gossip was bad for the community, so she received that information and chose not to transmit it further.

In this parish of distinguished horticultural connections, she had expected to find kindred souls. Naturally the people who chose to live in leafy Westwick would have a special empathy with the vegetable kingdom. Instead she found only women like Allie and Belinda, quite oblivious of the ugliness of their own gardens and superstitiously envious of the beauty of hers. They rolled uneasy eyes over her rose arbour and her homage-to-Sissinghurst silver border and were emphatically silent. Stephanie saw that it was correct to admire material possessions, for the boys to envy Josh Carman's Mercedes, the girls to sigh over Lauren Pike's Coalport dinner service, but there was a problem with her garden, which was a creation not a purchase.

'You can't create around here,' Gemma proposed, spreading out her hands flat on the table top. 'That's another thing that Mamma don't allow. No politics, no ethics, no creation.'

'What are you going to do with that letter?' asked Rod, pointing at the fruit basket where Gemma had tucked the missive between the fingers of a bunch of bananas.

'What do you think I'm going to do with it? Frame it? I'm sending it to his wife, aren't I? The Madonna of Morning TV, the mother of our neighbourhood rapist and the wife of another. She likes reading her viewers' letters out on air, doesn't she? She likes a nice human tragedy for breakfast, doesn't she? She should thank me.' And so should Ted, she added mentally, because the truth will make him free.

CHAPTER 17

Regular Dances

In the mind of Allie Parsons, such as it was, what was said had no importance. Thus she might babble sentimentally of friendship to Stephanie and the other wives of Westwick regardless of the fact that she did not consider them to be her friends. Her concept of friendship did not extend to people who were merely useful, only to those who were actually powerful. Most of her conversation included such adjustments of meaning. Obviously, the purpose of talking was to get what you wanted. What you actually said was irrelevant, the result was what counted. Obviously, therefore, it was right to say whatever was necessary for people to give you what you wanted, regardless of whether what you said would pass any kind of reality check.

Allie considered that she had been right to invite the Sands to buy their doomed house in New Farm Rise because Ted was going to cut Stewart in on the Oak Hill deal and make them very rich, definitely rich enough to join them in Maple Grove. Getting the Sands to buy the house had saved the rest of the New Farm area from waking up to their impending danger. It had been a nasty moment when the house went up for sale; Ted had talked about delaying the Oak Hill planning application until the sale was completed, at which Chester had seen red. Then Allie had saved the day by fixing up the whole deal quickly and privately. Besides, she needed Stephanie.

To Allie, Stephanie was an invaluable resource: she had whatever it was the Channel Ten viewers thought a woman ought to have, some rare essence of femininity. Allie lacked this, and so needed her. Tying her in had been tricky because the woman was obtusely immune to media glamour, although in the end a perfect sucker for the Westwick thing.

Allie considered she was right to live in Westwick, because the whole place stank of family values and added the ideal backdrop to her life to date. She was right to have married Ted, whose earnings had underwritten her TV breakthrough and who, with the children, completed the middle ground of her career picture. She felt she was right to be looking beyond Westwick, marriage and family now, to the primetime, mainstream, big-bucks phase to come. She was also right to anticipate the colossal cash fallout of the Oak Hill development because frankly it was the only real benefit of the marriage with Ted which was left to be garnered. Or so she had evaluated him, until she opened the thickish envelope exuberantly addressed in green marker with 'Personal and Confidential' underlined twice.

'It's OK,' her secretary assured her with a little embarrassment. 'I made security put it through X-ray. I wouldn't have bothered you with it but it was hand-delivered, so maybe it could be someone you know?'

Westwick being a closed world, a Shangri-La sealed from the outside behind a mountainous range of money, none of the women there whom Allie idly termed friends ever realised that a two-tier value system was in operation. In Stephanie's case, she was further blinded by her pure heart. For dear friends Allie would be witty and taking, she sent flowers, she dashed off charming notes of thanks, had her secretary enter their birthdays in the diary, entertained prodigally in restaurants and showered down the bounty of *Family First* freebies. For people called friends in Westwick she broke promises, forgot dates, never showed at parties and sent each a bottle of Magno fragranced bath oil at Christmas. All with the assumption that they would appreciate that they deserved no better.

You had lunch with dear friends, and to the others you said, 'we must have lunch.' You might even make the lunch date, but then you broke it. It was the way of the world, the others accepted it. 'Just locals. Local people,' Allie dismissed them. 'They won't mind. People you have to know, you know? Not really important but you have to know them so you might as well get along.'

Allie Parsons considered that a friend, a real friend, a *dear* friend, was essentially a person who could advance her career. Thus The Boss was a dear friend, and Chester Pike was a dear friend of Ted's. Stephanie was not a dear friend, especially since her husband had fallen out with Ted. The DeSouzas were not dear friends, but merited exceptional treatment while Ted and Adam were associates. And John

Redfern, editor of *Hey!* (Your Number One for Celebrity Gossip – Real People, Real Heartbreak, Real Homes), was a dear friend also, and after she read the contents of the envelope, she telephoned him.

'John, darling . . .' she snuffled enticingly down the phone. 'Can you do lunch? I so need to talk to a friend. I can't tell you the dreadful thing that's happened.'

For such a promising prospect, John Redfern immediately made himself available. They met at the first and most dignified of the city's shrines to a celebrity chef, a place to which socialites herded to toast their divorces, a breathless rotunda where triple tablecloths flounced to the floor and carved gothic rood-screens, plundered from old churches, concealed the bench where waiters made sure the tottering little pagodas of food were not actually so precarious that they collapsed before the moment of presentation.

'He's been having an affair,' Allie confided as soon as the orders were placed.

'Your husband.' Redfern had forgotten the name. It happened with husbands all the time. Besides, everybody knew Parsons was bonking The Boss and women's sense of ownership was curious when it came to men.

'Ted. I'm distraught,' she announced, pertly poised on the edge of her chair, the rolling turquoise eyes running a third celebrity check on the other diners. Important to know you were in a first-XI venue. Very important to judge the moment a restaurant started to slide and move on. Those little signs, rubbernecks, musos, people paying in cash, men romancing their afternoon pussy. She noted Tina Brown and relaxed.

343

'Of course, poor lamb.' John was completing his own assessment of the clientele. Three bankers on the house table. The chef must be branching out. 'How did you find out?'

'This.' She pulled the letter from her bag and dropped it in front of him. 'In the studio mail. I mean, she sent it, of course. The other woman. This has destroyed my life.' John was in delight, he was bouncing in his chair; the sample dialogue was going great.

'You know her?' He picked up the letter with a decent show of distaste and scanned the lines, thinking how truly pathetic heterosexuals could be, how pitifully vulnerable in these degrading attacks of erotomania, how absurdly unable to cast their sexual relationships in the proper recreational mould.

'Not really. Her kids were at school with Damon.'

'Uh huh. And what's she like?'

'Gross. I mean, really fat, you know. Messy. And obvious. The kind men like, tits everywhere.'

'Attractive?'

'John, she's *fat*.'

'Right, right. So – and does she do anything?'

'Some ridiculous poxy run-down garden place in Westwick.'

'How many kids?'

'Oh, I don't know.' Her memory suggested a picture of Gemma mountainous at the centre of a mob of snot-nosed filthy infants. 'A lot.'

John was seeing a blurred newsprint picture next to a 24-point headline; the protocol for photographing the mistress in these stories was something dishevelled and unposed, possibly indicative of the fatal charms but fundamentally unflattering. There would be plenty of time for the fully styled portraits if the romance ever came to anything. Right now the proper thing would be something rather rough-hewn featuring breasts, flowers and some cheeky-grinning spawn of sin who might perhaps clean up into decent Norman Rockwell types. 'Good,' he confirmed. 'Good. So what do you want to do?'

'I'm heartbroken,' Allie told him with emphasis. 'I'm devastated.' Few women had ever looked less devastated. She was as bright as laser, as up as a name in lights, as trim as a tender off Saint Tropez. Her suit was in zingy tamarillo, of the new one-button, super-short style. Whatever surgical procedure had taken place over the summer had given her the cheekbones she had never had before. 'It was such a shock,' she continued. 'I thought we had the ideal marriage. Ted was a wonderful husband, a great father. I thought we loved each other.'

The waiter bustled over with garnished plates. The staff were swathed from waist to floor in tight spotless white aprons which revealed a tantalising triangle of bum cleft at the rear and caused them to walk geisha-like with many tiny steps, delicately wiggling the pelvis.

'Why don't you forgive him?' John suggested.

'Isn't that a bit . . . fragrant?' she asked. 'I don't want to be put in the box with all those politicians' wives and Kennedy women. I can't be a role model for the women of the twenty-first century if I just kind of wallow around forgiving all the time. I hate that, that downtrodden "Stand By Your Man" thing, it's sort of demeaning, don't you think?'

'Family values,' he proposed. 'People love 'em, don't ask me why.'

'Yes, they do, don't they?' Her plump lips, glistening with balm, corrugated in perplexity. The *Family First* audiences actually went 'aah' over family values, like they did over kittens or puppies.

'How would it work out, a divorce?'

'Oh, OK, I suppose.' Her little forehead, nerves paralysed with cattle virus to preserve the carefree serenity of youth, registered nothing, but the eyes triangled as she thought of the riches of Oak Hill. 'Men are so devious, aren't they? I made him put everything in joint names of course but they always find ways to hide things. Besides, I don't want a divorce; I want our lovely life back. I want things to be like they were. I love Ted, after all, and I'm sure he loves me.'

'So this woman, would she talk, d'ya think?'

'Her?' Allie demanded indignantly, affronted that even crumbs of public attention might be gathered up by her antagonist. 'Why should she?'

'Well, she sent you that letter. She's looking for trouble, isn't she?'

'Not that kind of trouble . . .'

'If her place is run down she'd be grateful for the cash. Some PR smartie gets hold of her, she could rake it in.'

This was not at all the scenario Allie had envisaged. The notion that some ungroomed flesh-mountain might command the tabloids, and on top be handsomely paid for it, pained her deeply. A paparazzi stakeout down on Alder Reach was a dire blasphemy against the natural order of the world. As the waiter removed their plates she gazed into the middle-distance in aggrieved silence, forcing some water into her eyes, letting her lips quiver. It was possible to see the effect in a chip of the mirror set artfully behind the carved tracery of the rood-screen.

Another course was flourished before them, pats of fish like white baby's palms balanced on little hills of pulped vegetable with rills of sauce dribbled around and two chives crossed on top.

'What I'm thinking,' Redfern hastened to bring comfort, 'is that you should keep control of this. Nobody else knows about this woman, right?' He tented his fingers. Analysis, that was what was going on here, just analysis.

'Nobody who counts,' she confirmed, recalling that of late she had seen Stephanie Sands in the shadow of the flesh-mountain, sinking to her own level indeed.

'Well then,' – he drew his chair closer and leaned over his poised stack of food, indicating that none should earwig on the master plan – 'the way to do this, it seems to me, is for *you* to leave him . . .'

'Leave Ted?' She recoiled, wondering how the audience would take the news. 'Isn't that a bit . . . radical?'

'Sure, sure. But that's who you are, isn't it? You're assertive, in control, a shit-kicking woman of the nineties. Your husband strays – you don't collapse in a heap. You move out. Move out to a secret address. Issue a statement through somebody – your agent, if you like – that you're deeply wounded by this discovery, you love your husband but you need time to think, yeah?'

'Y-e-s-s,' Allie assented, beginning to get the picture in focus.

'We keep it low key, maybe a couple of paras down-column in the TV news. No names, no pack-drill. Let the tabloids run with it if they choose, it'll take 'em a day to get the name, minimum. Meanwhile hubby comes crawling around on the forgiveness trip and, in due time, you move back. That's where we come in – the double spread, overcoming the troubles in your marriage, more together than ever. When's your show airing again?'

'A month.'

'Perfect. Can you get the bedroom redecorated?'

'F-a-a-a-b,' Allie said slowly, mentally running through the timing. She reached over and pinched his hand between her fingers, the furthest she could go in conveying affection. 'Utterly f-a-a-a-b. John, I love you. You are a dear friend.'

'I'm going to leave you,' Allie informed Ted at 9.10 am the next morning. 'You've been having an affair and I can't stand to be under the same roof a minute longer.'

The denial was on the tip of Ted's tongue but he bit down on it. She was leaving him. Why spoil a good thing?

'I've read that disgusting letter you wrote,'

'What letter?' he asked, knowing full well but not daring to believe it.

'The letter you wrote that Lieberman bitch,' she snapped, groping for the correctly wounded tone. 'Or are there several women you've been pestering with love letters?'

'No, just the one,' he confirmed in haste, trying for a hang-dog look. If, heaven knew how, Gemma ever got the idea that he had even looked at another woman this bounty would be wasted. He was no cliché, no pussy-whipped harasser trying to escape from his suburban sex desert, but a man of rare taste and intellect paying loyally for a youthful error of judgment, viz, his marriage. Gemma must understand that, or she would never have let his letter reach his wife. Hope, there was hope at last.

'Don't try to find me. I need time to think.' Allie swept out of the door to the car where the driver had already stowed her bag.

He stared joyfully at the closed door. There is a God, he thought, smacking right fist into left palm. Then he jumped into the Discovery and sped away to Sun Wharf. An Audi Quattro had shunted an old Ford halfway in on the 31, which was the end of the joyous impulse to tear down the road to freedom, but he had Ultimate Opera II in the CD player and he picked out tracks 2, 10, 17, 23 and 29, all the Mozart, plus the Rossini, 21, and tapped his fingers happily on the windowsill. In the circumstances, his progress was exceptional, because his ear-to-ear grin spooked the other drivers who changed lanes to get away from the maniac. Normal drivers never smiled in a tailback on the 31.

'What am I going to do?' Miss Helens demanded of her empty playground at 3.30 pm. 'Mrs Parson hasn't called, we haven't any instructions . . .'

'What a shame.' Stephanie had lingered to savour the

moment. Max and Sweetheart were playing vertical hop-scotch, a game Rod's daughter had recently invented involving a bean bag and a climbable object, in this case the frame. Chalice Parsons was sitting on the playground bench, white-faced and trembling. She was ripping the hem of her dress to rags for extra emphasis.

'I need to close the school for the afternoon,' Miss Helens protested. 'I have a doctor's appointment.'

'Oh dear. That is a problem,' Stephanie agreed with her sweetest smile.

'I've got this number for Mrs Parsons but there's no answer.'

'She must be out.'

Chalice began keening like an Arab widow.

'And there's no answer from Mr Parsons either.'

'He must be at work.'

'We called his mobile.'

A struggle took place in Stephanie's heart. One faction held that it would be most excruciatingly embarrassing for Allie and Ted if, when they had wronged her so gravely, she returned good for evil by sheltering Chalice until they returned home. The opposing faction moved that Ted and Allie were so morally deficient that they would feel very little if any embarrassment in those cir-cumstances, and that taking Chalice home with her would in addition oblige Miss Helens, to whom she also owed no favours. The opposition also accused her of inverted masochism in even considering helping out here. She allowed it to prevail.

'We must be going,' she said cheerfully, 'Come on kids, into the car.'

Miss Helens abandoned all pride and followed them to the pavement. 'Mrs Sands,' she begged, 'I know you sometimes take the Parsons girls. *Would* you . . .'

'How could I possibly expose Max and Courtenay to . . .' and she indicated Chalice, now screaming from the prone position on the ground, 'such a disruptive influence, especially when they've both been so recently traumatised?' Stephanie watched while Max attentively handed Sweetheart into his infant seat and buckled her safety belt with chivalrous care. She moved a few steps back towards The Magpies' lych gate, out of the children's ear-shot. 'And, of course, Max has had his problems here as well, hasn't he? Mr Fuller and I both feel our children need special care right now. We really must put them first.'

She had played the ultimate trump, the right of a parent to put the needs of her own child above any other consideration. Miss Helens coloured magenta, twitched ingratiatingly, muttered assurances and began sidling crabwise away from the Cherokee. Chalice's ululations were piercing, the noise echoed weirdly along the empty street. Stephanie sighed. 'I can't bear her being so upset,' she admitted at last. 'Chalice! Come on, you can come with us.'

Three hours later, at home, she got a call from Ted, in the lather of embarrassment which usually covered a Westwick husband when he was required to do something more than pay for one of his children. She listened, idly wondering how many words he would use before being obliged to say 'sorry'. Or if, in fact, he would be able to avoid the hardest word altogether. Which is what he did.

'I do apologise, Stephanie,' he granted with excessive graciousness. 'I do hope we haven't put you out. I had no idea this had happened until I got the school's message. Cherish is still at St Nicholas's. Allie must have had some misunderstanding with the help. I'll be back for them as soon as I can. You're not going out, are you?'

'Where would I go, Ted?' she asked without remorse. 'I schedule my meetings in school time.'

'Well – uh – I'll be right over as soon as I can. Hope the traffic isn't too bad.'

Waiting, she screwed up her nerves. A confrontation was necessary, avoiding it would do more damage in the end. She was learning the interesting principle of vengeance, that an evil deed must be paid for, otherwise the evil of it would actually increase. She went upstairs to Stewart's desk, and took out the letter left with his will.

'Stay a minute, Ted,' she invited him, when he arrived 90 minutes later, flustered and irritable but still giving off the vinous aroma of a good lunch.

'Oh no, I wouldn't trouble you . . .' Chalice, comatose in front of the television, showed no sign of helping him make a quick getaway.

'Perhaps you already have,' Stephanie responded, indicating a seat at the end of the table and moving a stack of plant brochures so she could look at him directly but keep a physical barrier between them.

'I don't understand . . .'

'*I* didn't understand, Ted, when I found that Stewart

had written me this sweet letter in case anything ever happened to him. Now something has happened to him, of course I read it.' She passed him the page. 'What I didn't understand was the bit about our house – see, down at the end there?'

'It's a very good letter.' Ted was wishing he had Stewart's way with words. 'There's still no news, I suppose—'

'This house, Ted. Our home.'

'Oh,' he said, feeling suddenly shivery with dread. 'That.'

'This, really. Our home.' She gestured around, making him look at the children sprawled in the playroom and their food warming in the oven and the full richness of the late summer garden with the rose petals unfolding in the sun. 'Which because you're all so vile to us, now that my husband isn't around, I decided I wanted to rent out. You can guess what I discovered.'

'The new access road to Oak Hill?' She expected him to bluster and weasel and patronisingly tell her she didn't understand, but he was squaring up his shoulders, apparently getting ready to take responsibility. 'I'm sorry people are behaving badly,' he added. 'I hope you don't mean me—'

'I think I do mean you, Ted. Of course, not only you,'

Thank God, Ted congratulated the deity, she is not going to cry. Or at least, she doesn't look as if she is going to cry right now. He would have figured Stephanie as the teary type. He was relieved for a moment. 'But I've always been very fond of you, you know that . . .'

'How could I doubt it?' She froze him with a straight

look. 'But not fond enough to let me know that my home was going to be demolished.'

'Oh no,' he said at once, 'not necessarily. It was only an option. You understand, it's out of my hands. We're only concerned with the site itself. The Transport Department had three different routes under consideration . . .'

'I think they've made up their minds now, Ted. This is the way they want to go. We're going to lose our home. I can't even rent it right now.'

'But there'll be consultation . . .'

'You know what that means.'

'But I thought you approved of Oak Hill. When we were talking about it at the Old Westwick Society, that ridiculous man going on about the Nature Triangle – you kept out of it all.'

'If I'd known my house was going to be knocked down, I'd have felt differently. You set me up, Ted. You set us up. Or Allie did. That's why this house was so cheap, wasn't it? Because you knew this was going to happen.'

'No, look,' he writhed around in his chair and crossed his long legs as if to squeeze out the discomfort of his guilt. 'That's not how it was. I promise you, word of honour.' She sneered. The sweet woman actually sneered. Maybe she was going to yell instead of crying. 'Look,' he pressed on with anxiety. 'I had a word with your husband, with Stewart. We had a deal. The idea was he would come in on Oak Hill with us, his firm would be the consulting architects, they'd have done very well . . . it didn't work out like that. He changed his mind.'

'Why?' Stephanie felt outmanoeuvred. Worse, she felt

betrayed. How dare Stewart cut some secret deal with Ted and treat her like a little Lucille Ball wife and tell her nothing? Her impulsion fizzled out, confusion crushed her.

'I don't know.' The effort of telling that lie actually shot Ted off his chair to stand up and walk around the room. 'I didn't set you up, Stephanie. I promise I didn't. It would have been a great deal for Stewart, but it went wrong. And I had no idea the Transport people would do this. Look – I'll make some calls in the morning, I'll see what I can do. I promise. I'll get back to you on it. Promise. It wasn't a set-up. That wasn't how it was, you mustn't think that.'

'Whatever,' she said, helpless and deflated. He scooped Chalice into his arms and rushed for the door as fast as decently possible. 'Damn,' Stephanie said aloud. 'I never asked him how things were at home.'

The witches convened again that evening, and, while the pots were boiling and the children dispersed about their entertainments, they examined the omens.

'Nobody picked up Chalice from The Magpies,' Stephanie suggested. 'I took her back with us, and Ted came around to fetch her, but I was so mad about the house business I forgot to ask about anything else.'

'Figures,' ruled Gemma, chopping onions. 'If ever Allie does car pool she forgets, and if her help does it she forgets to tell the help to pick up. The poor kid's always weeping in a heap at going-home time.'

'I came down Church Vale but the house was just normal. No photographers or anything. I brought some anchovies and ham and stuff,' Rod extracted a packet from the inside pocket of his Levi jacket. 'I thought *alla putanesca* might be appropriate.'

'I don't shake *my* ass for a living,' Gemma observed.

Stephanie was impatient for action and suspicious of her new friend's propensity for chaos. 'Do you think she got the letter?'

'Sure she got the letter. She'll react, trust me. How do I do this?' This was to Rod, about the array of new ingredients before her. 'Why don't you take over? Will the kids eat it?'

'Sweetheart eats it.' He installed himself at the chopping board, trying not to appear masterful in another cook's domain.

'Well, Flora could stand to lose the weight and Molly never wants to eat and I swear Topaz lives on human blood anyway . . . what about Max?'

'He'll be fine. Where did you send it, the letter?'

'Nowhere. I sent it nowhere. I *took* it, in an envelope, marked personal and confidential, right up to Channel Ten studios. I did not send it to the house because Ted gets up first and could throw it away. Though if I'd given him the chance my money would be on him having it presented to her on a velvet cushion. He'd adore her to leave him; you know how husbands are, always hoping fate will do their evil deeds so they can stand back and get what they want and not be guilty at the same time. And I checked that she is in the studio every day now, even though the show isn't airing yet. Now do you trust me?'

'Maybe it's just in a bag with her fan mail.' Rod moved to the sink and ran the taps. He had bought the best anchovies in Parsley & Thyme, the salted anchovies from Collioure which cost one tenth of a private client per six servings, and needed rinsing thoroughly and picking over for tiny bones, although the women would laugh if he asked for tweezers for the job.

'Hah! Don't tell me she gets fan mail. Two sackfuls of death threats a day, maybe.' With a ferocious pop, Gemma pulled the cork on a bottle of Chateau Mr Singh.

'She says she does,' sighed Stephanie, 'but I'm sure her secretary would show her anything like that. Did you copy the letter?'

'Copy it?' Gemma, startled in the act of filling glasses, splashed another libation on her table. 'Why would I copy it, disgusting thing?'

'We'll just have to wait on.' Rod drained a jar of capers, the dearest little piquant pearls, Italian, another tenth of a private client per six servings.

At the far end of the room the door swung open and Topaz, returning from her evening shift filling shelves, rattled her bicycle into the room and out through the garden doors to its home in the shed. She returned with a newspaper, bright-eyed and pink-cheeked.

'I don't suppose any of you bought any media today.' She marched to the table, clutching the newspaper to her chest.

'What is it? Give it here, give it to me, let me see it. Topaz! Don't tease your mother, give!' Snatching the paper from Topaz's unresisting hands, Gemma spread it on the table, careless of the detritus of onion skins, car

357

keys, school timetables, telephone messages, deadly horticultural chemicals, reminders from the dentist, peppermints, flyers from pizza parlours and redundant Wonderbra padding which had somehow colonised the space since Topaz liberated it at breakfast.

The paper was the *Daily Post*, a once up-market tabloid proud of its reputation as the favourite reading of the wives of men who took the quality broadsheets, and morally time-warped in the era when such a gender division obtained. The present editor had nailed family values to his masthead and abandoned news-related items of more than 500 words, except in the theoretical case of an international disaster causing over 1,000 deaths in a country with a pronounceable name. The remaining acreage of newsprint was given over to gossip.

Gemma read the women's section, the gossip column and the Feng-Shui-your-car supplement. Stephanie read the front page, the rest of the news and the features. Rod read the health section, the showbiz pages and the sport. Finding nothing, they swapped pages and read each other's.

'Topaz,' growled Gemma, 'if this is a wind-up . . .'

'When did I ever?' her daughter demanded, indignant.

'Well, quite. So where is it?'

With contemptuous economy of movement, Topaz took the showbiz diary from her mother and indicated a small paragraph at the bottom, headlined 'TV Star's Marriage Agony'.

Allie Parsons, the nation's favourite breakfast dish, is reported to be in hiding at a secret address following a

row with her husband of eighteen years, ~~~~ ty tycoon
Edward J Parsons. 'Yes, Allie's marriag~~~~it a
rough patch,' confirmed a friend, 'but Allie ~~~~oted to
her children, Damon, 17, Cherish, 8 and Ch~~~~5
and we're all really hoping that she and Edward ~~~~
be able to work things out.' Family First, Allie's ~~~~
rated TV show, starts its new season in three weeks'
time and the smart money says that the new look
planned for the programme will no way run to a
divorced host appearing in dark glasses.

'Edward J Parsons,' snorted Gemma, tossing the page
away crossly so it planed off the table's edge and fluttered
to the floor. This was not the feature she had pictured;
she had imagined a tale of shame, failure and paparazzi
harassment, pictures of *Allie* running tearfully into
Channel Ten, of Ted dour and ambushed on his doorstep.
Truth to tell, the possibility of a hundred lenses poking
relentlessly at her own bedroom curtains had also been
considered.

'She's got a new picture.' Rod came around the table
to see the image the right way up. 'That's why we didn't
spot it. God, she looks about nineteen.'

'Devoted to her children,' sniffed Stephanie. 'Devoted
to them like she's devoted to her hairdresser. Actually,
less so. I bet she never forgets her fuckwit hairdresser.'

'Stephanie. That's swearing. I swear I never heard you
swear before. My God, what is this woman doing to us
all?' In her disappointment Gemma seemed physically
deflated by 20 pounds and a cup-size.

Topaz watched and waited. Rod found himself looking

at Steph__ __th covert fascination, watching the palest,
most a__ __e flush of embarrassment steal over her
cheeks __ __n he smelled his onions catching, shook off
his e__ __tment and went back to the stove.

'__ __e back here,' Gemma comma__ded him.

'__ __y?' Tomatoes, anchovie__ __pers, chilli, herbs,
p__er, taste, stir . . .

'You know why, tough guy. That leg's giving on you.'

'D'ya think it is? Really?' Bland h__ was groping for
bland, unconcerned, innocent, nothing wrong, but they
were hard to catch at that moment. They all knew him
too well.

'You know it is.' Gemma was pitiless, earthing her
annoyance with the Parsons' house. 'You're staggering
around like Quasimodo. It's been gipping you for weeks,
you've been covering up.'

'Fuck you.' Cornered, he deployed the foxy grin. No
woman within range of the foxy grin ever survived but it
ricocheted off Gemma's armoured heart and hit
Stephanie, who got the feeling of spiders waltzing
around the backs of her knees and found she had to sit
down immediately.

'Please, oh please,' Gemma taunted. He threw the tea
towel at her. 'You shouldn't work through pain, Rodolfo,
you know that.'

'What choice do I have? I could get cortisone shots,
but they'd only mask the symptoms. We have to eat.
Shaking my ass is all I can get paid for on a regular
basis.'

He turned back to his sauce to hide his red face in the
steam of cooking, and there was an embarrassed silence.

Topaz decided it was time to try the business of giving history a push. 'Wasn't the Parsons woman offering you a job?' She spoke with total lack of emphasis, as if commenting on a much-repeated wildlife documentary. Oh look, the penguins of the Antarctic standing with their eggs on their feet.

'No, Topaz, she was coming on to me. People say anything when they're coming on to you. You're seventeen, you should have found that out by now.' He limped over and picked up the fallen tea towel. 'I'm sorry, that was mean. I take it back.'

'I think it was quite fair,' Topaz told him, sounding objectively curious. 'In general, I'd say that you were right. Of course. But it does happen that people actually give other people jobs from sexual motives, doesn't it?'

'Topaz,' Gemma intervened, reflating to her real dimensions with indignation. 'Shut up. Just shut up.'

There are many kinds of insomnia, and Stephanie, who had slept like a proverbial baby except in the days when Max was sleeping like a true baby, was discovering them one after the other.

When the news of Stewart first broke, she had been wakeful and wired, thrumming with tension, twitching at every sound that might in the eagerness of her imagination be the first note of a telephone ring. The cure for this was nurturing activity, and she had gone out into the garden and watered her *Souvenir de la Malmaison* at 3 am.

Once the shock was over, and anxieties had blossomed instantly in her mind like flowers in the desert, lurid and luxuriant, she had woken in the darkness with a churning brain and a pain in the pit of her stomach. Work was good for this, and she had sat at her desk doing drawings until dawn, with a mug of hot milk to soothe her guts.

Then came the grey despair, the urge to look out of windows without seeing anything, to drift from room to room by starlight, picking things up for no reason, putting them down again, floating around the garden, stroking and holding leaves as if for a transfusion of fresh DNA, pure new life uninfected with sorrow. This was a mood which responded to nothing at first. Going to Rachel Carman for sleeping pills was out of the question and it was too hot to try a slug of brandy in the milk.

It took a supreme effort of will to take Max back to his own bed when he blundered into hers in the night. Sitting on the floor beside him was a comfort, but she refused to use her child that way. Eventually she regressed intellectually and started reading her old books, the adventurous tales she had gulped down as a schoolgirl and ignored in embarrassment ever since, bodice-ripping romances and the tattered old biography of Josephine which had seeded the fantasies that sustained her until Stewart.

For a week or so the charm of an attack on Westwick in general, and Allie Parsons in particular, had been so powerful that she had slept the night through, but now that a new rule of disappointment had commenced she could not sleep at all. After an uncomfortable hour of wadding her pillow this way and that, she got up, put on leggings and a T-shirt, and decided to tidy the house. Specifically, Stewart's desk, where one of the crates from his office still sat reproachfully waiting to be unloaded.

On the bookshelf, she made space for the manuals and handbooks and resource directories. Twelve copies of the Architectural Association quarterly, up to spring of that year, went next to them. His number three camera (one and two were with him) found a corner of a bottom drawer. Three mysterious add-ons to the computer went beside it. A box of back-up discs fitted into the top drawer, beside the equivalent archive for their household records.

That was it, the job was done. She took the crate to the garage. Inmaculada had been at work: the kitchen was spotless, the sitting room plumped and smoothed, the sun room was empty, the play room awaited Max in perfect order. Her office was clean, and the baskets of paper were half empty and squarely aligned, which was the best they ever got. In the darkness outside, an owl winged silently over the treetops. She picked a pencil off the floor and put it back in the pot. She was brilliantly conscious, vividly awake. It might have been Monday morning.

For distraction, she went back to Stewart's desk, fired up the computer and pulled out the box of back-ups. If there was evidence of that 'deal' with Ted, she would find it. He had researched that wretched trip to Russia, perhaps there were notes, she would like to read his notes. She flicked through the disks; they were arranged in date order from the middle of the previous year. The last disk but two was labelled *Oak Hill* in what struck her eye as angry black pen.

The disk contained three documents. The first was a technical report from a surveying firm whose name she did not know. It was very long and she decided to pass over it. The second and third were only short E-mails. She went into a note to Marcus and as soon as it was on the screen a bolt of lightning shot up Stephanie's spine. From the first scattering of words on which her eye fixed at random she sensed her husband writing in a tone that was hardly his, awkward, stiff phrases dragged out of a mind in pain.

It seems to me important to make our positions clear on this. In my view, developing this site without a pro-gramme of bio-remediation should not be an option for us. I can understand that the cost of that kind of programme, when the contamination is now at a level where nobody should be on the site without protective clothing, is not something the client is happy with, but I myself would not be willing to go forward with this project on any other basis. I'm hoping we can resolve this, Marcus, but I am looking squarely at the end of Berkman & Sands if we can't.

Go forward. Not an option. Stewart despised jargon. *Nobody should be on the site without protective clothing.* What? She stared at the screen in stillness and silence for ten minutes, then copied the document, quit it and called up the report. After she had digested its conclusions, she made herself some notes.

Dawn came, and then morning. Belinda was doing car pool. The post came, bringing the results of the soil analysis from Gaia; it showed astonishingly high levels of heavy metals in the soil, which was by then what she had expected. The report prepared for Stewart had found the same thing at Oak Hill. Rainwater running off Oak Hill would leech into the soil at Gaia.

When Max was off to school Stephanie telephoned Mrs Funk. 'Can I come over and talk to you?'

'Of course, you poor woman, any time.'

'I want to ask you about Westwick when you first moved here. In about half an hour?'

'Why not? Erich and I will be glad of the company.'

As she put the telephone down it rang again. 'Capelli, Mrs Sands, Foreign Office liaison.' Correct as always, but he sounded like a different man this morning, eager and breathless.

'I'm just on my way out,' she told him, unthinkingly.

'Just to let you know that we've had news in this morning of some really positive developments. The negotiator has at last achieved a meeting with the group holding your husband and managed to get some idea of what their demands are. It's really excellent news, Mrs Sands. I knew you'd want to know immediately.'

'Yes, of course. Thank you.' She rang off, not knowing what else to say. *Excellent news.* Her heart was suddenly jumping in her chest like an excited child. Stewart's coming home, this nightmare will be over, we'll be a couple and nobody will ever push me around again. She felt her old self-confidence, close enough to sieze and put on again like magical armour. She hesitated, turned back from the door, went out into the garden and sat on a bench. Stewart would make everything all right when he was home, surely. No need to fight any more.

Unexpectedly, she felt a faint regret. My goodness, she marvelled, I seem to have a taste for fighting all of a sudden. I really want to take this on. And suppose Stewart comes home only to find I've lost our home in the meantime? Some hero's return that will be. She got to her feet again and set off to see Mrs Funk.

CHAPTER 18

Tennis Courts

'Kids.' Ted Parsons surveyed his family around the fourteen-seater farmhouse table. Chalice was twisting her forelock into ropes and sucking her thumb. Her technique involved swallowing half her grimy blue-white hand while rubbing her nose red with her free fingers. Cherish was rocking in her chair and kicking the table leg. Damon, half his face still obscured by bandages, sat with his mouth flopped open and his elbows on his knees, his left heel vibrating against the floor tiles. They could have posed for a sculpture, The Three Neurotic Monkeys.

'Kids,' he started again, 'your mother has moved out because she's cross with me. She's going to be away for a while . . .'

The girls eyes went large. Chalice sat up straight and took her fist out of her mouth, trailing a thread of spit.

'Was it because I had a fidt widt Flora?' Damon asked, spluttering through his injured nose.

'No, it wasn't because of anything you did, any of you. It was because of me.'

'Flora hidt me, she hidt me. I fell over,' his son protested.

'It's OK, son.' Ted tried for a resonant, right-thinking, King-of-the-Hill tone but it came out plain pompous. 'This has nothing to do with you.'

'It's you.' Cherish crashed her chair down on all four legs and pointed at Chalice. 'You're a little bitch and you can't keep a dress on five minutes without messing it. She always said so. An evil dirty little bitch.'

'Well, you're a little hoo-er,' Chalice replied complacently, her thumb returning to her cheek. 'You're a filthy ugly little hoo-er and you're no good and nobody could stand to be in the same house with you one minute, so there.'

'Stop this! Girls!' In their childish sneers he heard the ghastly echo of Allie in a rage, the morning fit which she worked up most days on emerging from her dressing room. It seemed that she needed some surge of bad feeling to shoot her out of the house and into the studio. She would spew insults at all of them, spraying them with invective like a commando blazing away with a Kalashnikov on her progress out to her car. If he had been offered a fairy wish at that moment, it would be to have that memory erased and his daughters' minds filled with nothing but multiplication tables and scenarios for Barbie and Ken. Not until the girls had grown old enough to mimic Allie did he realise how severely limited Damon's comprehension was; of all the barbs and taunts directed at him by his mother he had never retained anything more than the notion that he was at times a bad boy.

'It's me,' Ted assured his children, unable to keep the pride out of his voice. 'She's cross with me.'

'You've had an effer,' Chalice accused her father, round-eyed and thrilled that the world of soap opera was finally merging with her own.

'Affair, stupid,' Cherish corrected her. 'You're such a baby, you don't know anything.'

'No, I haven't,' he told them, mystified at their immediate disappointment. He considered asking them how exactly, in the mind of precocious, under-nurtured five-and eight-year-olds, an affair might be defined but decided that this can of worms did not bear opening. 'But your mother thinks I have, which is why she's cross.'

'If you had an affair in true life,' Cherish fixed him in a cunning stare, 'would she go away and never come back?'

'Of course not,' he blustered, groping for the right way through the jungle of inadmissible possibilities which had suddenly opened up in front of him. 'She's your mother, she loves you . . .'

'That is bullshit,' Cherish said sweetly. 'She hates us, she always says she hates us.'

'Especially me,' Damon added. 'She said I spoiled her life for her all the time, she said I was a disaster and she wished I'd never been born.'

Ted found himself all out of appropriate platitudes. Denial was impossible, he had heard his wife say these things daily. He had allowed her to chase him out of his family, taken refuge in neutrality while she had wielded maternal *force majeure* and annexed them to the monstrous caravan of her public life. With his own flesh and blood, he was in alien territory.

The help, at present a timid relative of Lauren's Pike's Filipina, took care of their physical needs, put what they recognised as food on the table, picked up their clothes and washed them and provided a legally adult presence between the four walls of their home. It was dawning on him that whatever else they required for healthy growth was now his responsibility.

Somewhere on the misty outskirts of his mind, he had imagined another woman intervening, Gemma breasting the storms of his household like a figurehead, gathering up his personal huddled mass in her generous arms. Vain hope. This was down to him, three human disasters which had occurred while he ran around in his car saying he was about the business of making money when he was really just getting out of his house. Now, he recognised, he had to take charge and the first day of his command had not been creditable – the embarrassment of collecting Cherish from the darkened after-hours school and Chalice from Stephanie's house the previous evening had been searing. The guilt of Stephanie's accusation was still making him jumpy. At least he had the telephone number of Damon's psychiatrist. And he had made that call to the Transport office. And he would learn. His children turned their faces towards him with hope brightening their eyes.

'You could get us a stepmother,' Cherish suggested, as if proposing a new toy. 'Could you get one who was on TV? It's cool being on TV if you don't get too stressed. I think Mummy let herself get stressed too much.'

'Do I have to go back to re-hab? They said last time we had gone as far as we could go and I had to find

something else.' The plea was delivered with as much
coherence as Damon could command.

'We'll just have to get along as best we can and see
what happens,' he told them.

On his way to work in the Discovery, his phone rang as
he was approaching the tail of the vehicle snake backing
up from the city end of the 31. It was his wife.

'I'm in the Soho Hotel,' she informed him as if
imparting news of the gravest moment. 'You have to
come and see me this afternoon around three.'

'Why?' he demanded in a taunting tone. It was as if he
had run away, not her, and was now able to caper around
the edge of her universe, too nimble for her to take a
swing at him.

'God knows why you think you deserve any explanation.'

'Of course I don't,' he agreed readily. 'I've got a heavy
day, Allie, I can't just drop everything and run over to
wherever you are.'

'It's vital to keep the story running.'

'What story?'

'I must have been mad to think you'd be capable of
understanding. Look, Ted, the story's no business of yours.
Just come up here at three. You know the address?'

'Allie, if you've got another stupid press thing going
on, I'm happy to be out of it. Anyway I'm at Sun Wharf
all day.' The traffic eased forward a little more briskly, so
he cut the line and let the Discovery surge up to 20 mph.
Disobliging Allie, disobeying Allie, talking back to
Allie – the hit was better than any drug he'd ever wondered about taking, definitely better than whatever

whisky could offer. He was intoxicated, he saw himself in his wing mirror smiling a silly stoned smile.

Of course, she knew where bodies were buried. Having a wifely 50-per-cent slice of everything he'd done in the past 18 years, she knew more than was advisable about projects undertaken by Tudor Homes and the Oak Hill Development Trust. Being himself spatchocked over the marriage on skewers of money, and in partnership with men whose only agenda was financial, it had not occurred to Ted that his wife might reckon her imperatives differently.

The 31 proper had ceased now, officially he was on a road which had a name. It ran, six lanes wide, straight to the heart of the city, between the traffic-soiled facades of crumbling nineteenth-century townhouses, caged by iron railings, glared over by hoardings, here and there decorated by a struggling municipal planting of shrubs which served to sieve the wind of cigarette packets and fast food containers.

The phone rang again. He answered optimistically, waiting for good news on Sun Wharf, which, due to the over-elaborate way Chester and Adam had decided to do things, with a separate development company and all that entailed, was not progressing as fast as he wanted.

'Ted, don't play games.' Allie again, in Joan Crawford mode. He wanted to giggle. He imagined her in the kind of vulgar negligee which she considered the proper dishabille for a woman of her status in the hours between waking and dressing for the studio, perched over the telephone like a vulture in broderie-anglaise and pink ribbon bows.

'You're the game-player,' he told her magnanimously. 'Whatever this media scam is—'

'Ted,' her tone was ominously patient, 'it's quite simple. If you want Oak Hill to go ahead, and all of us to make a killing, you will do what I say. If you want a major scandal, keep right on as you are. Got it?'

'If Oak Hill stalls we all lose.' He had to stop himself singing the words. This conversation had been running on a loop tape in his imagination for the past 24 hours. 'Especially you. And that won't sit too well with the *Family First* image, will it?'

'I'm the only one who can stall Oak Hill,' she announced in a voice fit for Queen Elizabeth defying the Spanish Armada. 'So you can just get back in line, Ted.'

'I have to tell you, dear, that Stephanie Sands may not be your best friend any more. Nor the great supporter of Oak Hill she's been up to now. She put me on the spot about it yesterday. She was pretty mad, I can tell you – they're going to be running the road through their house, you know. I'd watch out for her, if I were you.'

'Don't be stupid,' his wife answered, now severely bored. 'She's nothing. Just nothing.'

'She practically runs the Old Westwick Society,' he returned, thinking as he said it that this was hardly a threat his wife would recognise. A hiss of amusement came over the line.

'Oh wow, that's really scary. Don't be more of a dork than nature made you, Ted. If Oak Hill stalls I've left you anyway because I was so devastated to discover how you had misled me, etcetera, etcetera. You will stand trial for fraud. I get the kids and fifty per cent of everything else anyway. I'm being lunched by the Daily Courier today, I can get to work right away if that's really what you want.'

'I dare you,' he chortled, swinging out of lane into a handy space opened up by a turning bus. 'Think about it. If I go down, I'll take you with me.'

There was a sigh, a small, irritated exhalation suitable for mourning laddered hosiery, and she rang off.

The regeneration of the east of the city was a triumph of greed over humanity. In their eagerness to realise their rake-offs from raising the maximum number of saleable units of property, the city fathers had overlooked the fact that people would pass their lives in these units, that they would need to eat, drink, play, be ill, get educated, enjoy themselves, look out of the window and travel back and forth.

There was housing, most of it of luxury standard; there were offices and marble atria. They rose in a pit of post-industrial slurry. At this time there was not much else east of the centre, no shops, schools, hospitals, restaurants, bars, cafés, cinemas, theatres, galleries, parks or vistas except those decayed and wretched facilities serving the indigenous slum-dwellers who were unable to take the hint and relocate themselves.

Water, the river and the old docks let into it, occupied inconvenient tracts of territory, making the land too swampy to build tunnels. A thousand-year-old forest had been felled to site a new road bridge, but that was still work in progress. A tinny little railway, of Disneyland proportion but without the charm, carried passengers too lowly to use cars. The rest of those who had business to go east resigned themselves to sit in traffic jams in the concrete canyons which cut through the business district with nothing to do but gawp up at the cranes deliberating over the landscape, the skeletal dinosaurs of a new Neolithic age.

Ted had some new toys: an in-car fax and a new stereo plus Trafficmaster facility which automatically cut in reports from the traffic helicopter patrolling the skies. He was longing for an excuse to use the fax, and the Trafficmaster had a knack of cutting in at the most exquisite moments in his brand new disc, Great Opera Love Duets No I. He passed time in traffic reading the manual for clues on how to disable it.

His phone rang again as Faust was entreating Marguerite not to break his heart. Punching the stereo volume button with his right hand, he had the phone in his left to pick up the call and, since the traffic chose that moment to break into a crawl, steered with his left elbow. In which ungainly pose a voice barked, 'Ted. Chester.'

'Chester! Good to—'

'Ted, your wife's been on.' Failure to control a wife, a major corporate misdemeanour. He could hear the BSD's annoyance over the fizzle and echo and tremor of the line, which suggested that he might be in flight at that very moment.

'I'm sor—'

'Do what she wants, Ted. We can't risk any exposure on this.'

'But there's no—'

'Just do it, Ted. Whatever it is will keep her quiet. You get me?'

The line hissed violently for a second then cut. Ted was momentarily blinded by frustration. The dented rear end of an old Nissan loomed too large ahead and he stamped on the brake so hard his tyres squealed and the Discovery rocked on its mighty suspension like a storm-lashed dinghy.

His mood of boyish defiance deflated, leaving him with the familiar dreary chafes of marital bondage. Around him the day greyed, the scummy pools lost their sparkle, the majesty of the cranes evaporated and such occasional architectural felicities as had already been constructed ceased to seem brave and brilliant and appeared merely bizarre.

The new stereo incorporated a route planner. With the manual balanced on the top of the dashboard, he succeeded in asking it for a route to the Soho Hotel from Sun Wharf. It suggested a perfectly logical itinerary smack through at least two of the most notorious gridlocks in the city, estimated journey time, from Ted's experience, seventy-five minutes minimum rather than the short half hour optimistically offered by the device's programming. He would have maybe forty minutes to go round the site with Yuris, then have to get back in the car. The echo of Chester snarled in his ear. The wing mirror told him he no longer smiled.

The tide in the affairs of men was about to turn. Allie could sense it. For a week, travelling to the Channel Ten studios from her hotel suite and back again, she had been looking at low water and no movement. She left Ted on a Wednesday; the *Daily Post* paragraph appeared on Thursday. On Friday, she got Ted into line and John called from *Hey!* and suggested a date for the photo shoot. She spent the weekend at a new spa whose management were delighted to pick up her tab, checked into this hot new townhouse hotel in most fashionable residential street in the city and talked productively to the owner about making over the master bedroom at Church Vale with a wrought-iron four-poster and red velvet swags. In the new series of *Family First*, they would feature the spa's new Stressbust Weekend programme, and consult the hotelier for tips on interior decoration. They might even do some interviews in the suite itself.

On Monday, Allie asked herself what kind of bedroom Barbara Walters might have and charged her secretary to find out. The *Courier* carried a photograph of her contrite husband calling on her at her secret hideaway in a desperate attempt to patch up their marriage. And on Tuesday, with the two producers, she interviewed eleven potential new co-hosts for the show, four fresh from university, three actors, two established faces from cable, a reporter from a Gaelic language news agency and a kid with waist-length dreadlocks recommended by The Boss's Edinburgh contact.

At first things did not go well. She somewhat favoured the last of the students, powerfully cute but capable of spelling media as *midea*, which irrationally enraged the senior producer. The others were respectively stoned, too slow and too tall; she felt a man over six foot made her look unnecessarily inauthoritative. The actors had hideous degrees of attitude and one of them had chosen to become blond, the cable kids had acne and looked too much like what they were, the Gael could not master comprehensible diction in any other language and nobody seriously expected them to hire the dreadlock kid although he half-heartedly hinted that he had been thinking of a crop.

It was as the interviewing triumvirate sat slumped in front of their lunchtime sandwiches that Allie felt the first tremor in the ether. Her secretary brought in her messages and there at the top of the list was the name Stephanie Sands.

'That prissy little thing.' She turned the paper over, hardly believing what she read. 'If she's calling me here about the car pool I'll . . . did she say what it was about?' Even in the furthest reaches of her consciousness the possibility that this weak-minded woman might have a vengeful purpose in calling did not exist. The fact that she actually had induced the Sands family to buy a house now scheduled for demolition had not been entered in her memory. At the time when Ted was fretting that the untimely sale in New Farm Rise might put the whole neighbourhood on the alert, the final route of the fatal road was undecided. A little subliminal sophistry and the conclusion of events, now so dire for Stephanie, Stewart and Max, had never quite registered in her mind, even when emphasised by her husband.

'She said you would know,' her secretary replied. He was new for the new season, and very efficient in a brittle, campy way. 'I didn't like to press her; she sounded, you know, kind of confidential.'

'Confidential. Well now. Get her back for me, there's a dear.

'Stephanie, darling,' she cooed in expectation, straining triumphantly back in her chair. 'So good to hear from you.'

And then, in that silly, breathy voice Stephanie had, she heard, 'Allie, darling, I feel so bad.'

'Darling, no – why? You've nothing to feel bad about . . .'

'Oh but I do. I've been so selfish and thoughtless and—'

'Enough! I won't hear another word. Why, you're the sweetest woman that ever lived, everyone says so.' Yes, it was happening, she was right, she'd been right all along and now she had her. Allie rolled her eyes around to make contact with the three men in the room. 'But having your husband kidnapped – why, that's just so stressful.' The men froze like statues, awaiting the next words.

'I feel I've been so pathetic, you know. You've been wanting me to come on your show, which is really such an *honour*, I mean anyone would be just so pleased, so *complimented*, to be asked to do something like that, and there I was, I just couldn't find the courage . . .'

'Darling, I *know*. I know. That's just the kind of person you are, you're terribly sensitive . . .'

'But that's no excuse. I mean, it must have been so embarrassing for you.'

'For me? Please, I'm not the important one here. It's you, darling, and how you feel, and how poor little Max feels. I mean, this is a terrible time for you. That's what's important. That's the only thing that could possibly be important.' For the benefit of her silent audience, Allie mimed vomiting into the hotel wastebasket.

The half-hushed voice prattled on. 'It's all just come to me today. You know, I think I must be adjusting to everything, to the kidnap and everything, because I'm starting to be able to get things in perspective now and I just feel so terrible about the way I acted to you and, well, I'm just calling you now to say that if you still want me on *Family First* of course I'll do it, and I am so, so sorry I couldn't say this to you before, and I do hope you can understand . . .'

'Darling, of course I understand, of course. Now are you really sure, because I know how much you're feeling about this . . .'

There was a noise over the line which Allie interpreted as a strangled sob. She gave the room a thumbs-up sign.

'I'm sure if you're sure,' Stephanie assured her.

'Let me come and see you right away.' Allie jumped to her feet as if she were going to run out of the door directly and drive immediately over to Westwick. 'You can be on the first programme of our new series. Look, let me come tonight, yes? We can talk about it then, woman to woman.'

'Get a contract drawn,' she commanded the producers in general as soon as Stephanie rang off. 'I'll take it with me. Let's nail her down right now. I don't want the silly bitch changing her mind on me.'

Among the yellow leaves and burgundy-red fruits of the crab tree, the thrush was asleep, having stuffed himself with snails in anticipation of the winter. Westwick was enjoying a few days of Indian summer. The gardens were being allowed to grow away to perdition. Even at midday the rich sunlight penetrated the thinning leaves and caressed the warm turf. The leaves were turning gold in the heat. The seed heads of the arums had burst, flaunting their orange berries in the soft air. The red vine tendrils overreached decency, probing everywhere for access. Japanese anemones, white as moonlight, shone at the back of the border.

'Now it's your turn.' Sitting on her terrace, Stephanie handed the telephone to Rod. He looked at her as if she were giving him a dead rat. 'Go on.'

'But what are you going to do when you get in the studio?' Visually, the man was not made to express concern. His normal physical state was blatantly relaxed; Rod never fidgeted, he had no twitches, frowns or nervous mannerisms. By nature, his body fell comfortably into whatever posture was appropriate for the moment. Even the way he talked spoke of repose, plain sentences simply delivered without hesitation. This outer calm had now been replaced with a nervous tension so strong that his shoulders were paralysed with it and his hands were shaking. His face was lined with anxiety. Apprehensively, he took hold of the apparatus and stared at the keypad.

'Its not what I'm going to do, it's what we're going to do. I don't know yet,' she told him. 'I need more material. I need the surveyors Stewart used to go on record. But I do know that the only place Allie Parsons is vulnerable is in her own element. If we're on screen, we can fight her. If we aren't, we can't even touch her. It'll just be like we're in some parallel universe.'

'But what if she says no?'

'She says no.' Stephanie shrugged. 'No harm done. But if she says yes – which she will – we can nail her hide to the barn door, hang her husband out to dry with the Environment Department and you'll still have a new career.'

'But I want my old career,' he sighed, smiling to apologise for his weakness, subconsciously rubbing his tendon. The ache of it was getting comforting, like the hurt of a scab.

'But does it want you?' she demanded, amazed at the force of her own will.

'No,' he agreed, 'it does not. Not with a busted ankle. And the career I had before that I can't have while Sweetheart's little.'

'Well then,' Stephanie prodded him unyieldingly. 'Make the call. Just hit the redial button.'

'But suppose I can't do that job? I've never done TV stuff, I can't write scripts . . .'

'You think the guys she has doing this job can write scripts? I've been there, I've been in that office, I know they're idiots. For God's sake, I did that job in my little way. How difficult can it be?'

'But you're intelligent . . .'

'You're intelligent. For Christ's sake, Rod. The researchers write the scripts. Now dial.'

He sucked in a deep breath and she watched his chest

swell and the top stud of his shirt strain against the flesh. He stretched out his arms and pulled his shoulders around to release their stiffness and she watched the sinews in his neck flicker in the light. The tips of his eyelashes were actually infinitesimally curled, so the sun caught in them and his eyes had a starred look.

The charge in the air between them hung like latent lightning. They looked steadfastly at the ground. Stephanie had not met plain physical attraction before. The passion she had with Stewart was woven into their relationship and embroidered with romance. When they made love, they strengthened their feelings, nurtured their son, solved their problems, renewed their hopes and blessed their home. She missed that, she longed for that.

Passion that was self-seeded, out of place but undeniable, was a new feeling. In the last few months, Stephanie had experienced many new feelings. She was coming around to the idea. That morning, Mr Capelli had reported the most thrilling development yet: the kidnappers had allowed Stewart to send her a message. Again, it had been an E-mail, a little miracle of printed words suddenly materialising from the computer's mysterious depths. It did not say much, just simple words like love and patience. She had read it over and over, printed it out. The end of her ordeal was becoming possible, she was allowing herself to dream of it. But the end of something else was approaching with it, some dimension of her liberty.

Staring at the ground, she saw a weed in a crack between the stones and leaned down to pull it up. At the same moment Rod suddenly got to his feet. For a split second her cheek was half an inch from his thigh, so close she could feel the blood heat glow through his jeans. Then he stepped back and she felt a hand heavy and warm on her shoulder.

'You're so patient,' was all he said. Then he took the telephone away across the lawn and she made herself busy nipping the last dead heads off her roses and tuned her ears away from the conversation. Patient, for Heaven's sake. She found she didn't want to be patient. Her time was running out.

Five minutes later she heard him cut the line. He came towards her, holding out the phone. 'All done,' he said with a sigh. 'I'm going in for an interview tomorrow. God knows what I'm going to say.'

She kissed him. It seemed like the right thing to do.

CHAPTER 19

Only Twenty Minutes from the City Centre

'*I am very loyal to my wife,*' *says Edward,* '*and looking back I can say that every year I've been with her I've loved her more. Allie is such a giving person, everything she does she puts in a hundred per cent.*' John Redfern paused at his keyboard and took another slug of coffee. For inspiration, he peered over the row of slides on the light box on the next desk. The boss shot, the one that was going to end up over a whole page, showed Allie Parsons in a white suit seated precisely on the end of a bed which was draped in red velvet. She leaned marginally towards her husband, who stood beside her. His right hand and her left were clasped.

It was hard to figure out why Edward the husband wasn't handsome; he was tall, lean, clean-cut, but there was just no spirit in him. He looked at the camera as if he were about to be shot. Maybe he was closet. Didn't people say that after midnight the difference between a gay man and a straight man was about a couple of beers?

'. . . and it can be hard to live with a woman who has that kind of commitment. It's hard sometimes to share Allie with three million fans. But in the future I'm going to try harder to do that.'

'I've told Ted he has to understand the role my work plays in my life,' says Allie, who's preparing for the new series of Family First *due to air next week.* 'It's the most important thing to me, next to my marriage and our three beautiful children. I feel a deep sense of responsibility to the show and to our wonderful audiences. They deserve to see the best of me, and that's what I'm pledged to give them. It was easy for me to forgive Ted because I understand how stressful it can be for the people who love me. But now we're back together, we're happier than ever.'

Redfern re-read the interview and considered it a masterpiece. He tapped out some headlines – *Sexy secrets that make Allie Parsons' marriage work. Family First star forgives her straying husband. I understand what drove him into another woman's arms. Allie Parsons invites us into her lovely home to speak frankly of the problems in her marriage.*

He put through a call to his star at the studio. 'I'm saying this is your home, is that OK?'

'F-a-a-b, darling,' she assured him. 'God, I wish it *was* my home. I swear, as soon as I'm out of daytime I'll move into a hotel for good. So much stress, running a big house, I can't cope with it.'

An extraordinary meeting of the Old Westwick Society took place at the house of Mrs S Sands, who acted as chair in the absence of Mrs Pike and kindly made her dining room available to the delegates, although on this occasion the delectable cakes for which they had been so grateful in the past were not forthcoming and hospitality was limited to coffee and biscuits.

No apology for absence was received from Mrs Pike, nor from Mr E Parsons, or Dr R Carman or Dr J Carman, because the Secretary had not advised them of the meeting. 'In the circumstances, which I'll get on to in a minute,' Stephanie announced, 'I felt it inadvisable to tell them.'

'Yes, and what are these circumstances, may we ask?' Mrs Funk prompted her, her sunken face eager under the brim of a green felt cloche hat with a curled feather which tickled her cheek. Mrs Funk knew what was to come and she was spoiling for action. She was gripping her umbrella as Joan of Arc gripped her sword.

There was an encouraging degree of shock. The faces turned attentively to her said that if this nice Mrs Sands was being underhanded, there must be a direly good reason.

Stephanie reviewed her troops. Next to Mrs Funk was Jemima Thorogood from the Maple Grove Society, a spare, androgynous figure often seen proceeding about Westwick on her traditional black bicycle with its wicker basket tied to the handlebars with leather straps. Next to her cowered two new town-planning students, recently enrolled in West Helford College. Rod and Topaz were beside them, serene and serious. The delegate of the Oak Hill Nature Triangle was reassembling his broken ballpoint with inky fingers, while the chair of his environmental sub-committee picked bobbles off the sleeve of his sweatshirt. Penelope Salmon, another Maple Grove goodwife, sat expectantly upright, fingering her pearls, next to timid Sonia Purkelli. Mr Singh from the Grove Parade Trader's Association was squaring off the copies of last meeting's minutes. Major Lloyd-Richards, the treasurer, young for an ex-officer, with a private income just big enough to keep a roof over his head and vodka in his freezer, floated gently on the afterglow of his 6 pm pick-me-up. Mrs Funk and her husband huddled beside him.

It was evening and the still-spotless calico blinds shut out the twilight. The company sat nervously around the table, occasionally looking up at the flip chart installed beside Stephanie with discomfort in their faces. As a battalion of warriors, they were not impressive. How sad, Stephanie observed to herself, that the job of looking after this community was deemed so dull and worthless that it should fall to people with nothing else to do with their lives.

'Thank you, Clara. First of all, I'd like to introduce two new members: Topaz Lieberman from the Alder Grove Residents' Association and Rod Fuller from the Westwick Basin Society.' She tried not to blush. These two bodies, with membership of five and two souls respectively, had been created over *penne all'amatriciana* the night before. Topaz assured her that this was legitimate political strategy. The rest of the table was nodding to the newcomers, no questions asked.

Nothing for it, time to plunge in. 'Over the past couple of years we've watched the progress of the plans for the Oak Hill Business Park make their way through the due planning processes and reach the stage they are at now, where permission has been granted for the development and work has begun on the site,' she began.

'And bulldozers come down our Broadway at seven am in the morning,' Mrs Funk added righteously.

'What we didn't appreciate is that a new road is going to be built . . .' Stephanie turned to the flip chart and unrolled the first page, the map of Westwick. 'Down to the Oak Hill Business Park from the Forty-six up here, cutting through New Farm Rise. As things stand at the moment, it will run through this house.'

They gasped. 'You poor woman,' moaned Mrs Funk. 'That dear little boy.'

'In total,' Stephanie went on, trying to look as elegantly martyred as she could, 'one hundred and thirteen houses in the New Farm region are scheduled for demolition. I've seen the plans myself at the Department of Transport.'

'They can't do that!' vowed Penelope Salmon.

'Actually, they can,' Topaz informed her. 'If this were a private development, like the Business Park itself, the council would be legally obliged to consult the community, although not to listen to what we say. But a road is a government thing, it's the Department's business; their strategy for consultation will be to send us all a form with a choice-of-routes option for the road and we get to tick a box for the one we prefer. There's no box for no road. Then there's a public inquiry; almost all public inquiries are lost.'

Topaz was acquiring an almost effortless air of authority. As people around the table took in what she was saying, Stephanie felt the level of anger in the room rise considerably. 'The fact is,' she confirmed, 'they can put it where they like. And I'm afraid that's not the worst of it.' She savoured her moment. 'I have discovered that the permission for the development has been improperly granted. Improperly because the site was formerly occupied by a power station, which was demolished twelve years ago.'

She sensed confusion in her audience. There was a certain miasma of hopelessness emanating from the older people, expecially from Jemima Thorogood, a distinct suggestion in their deepening apathy that this was all by the by.

'I remember it when we first came here,' Mrs Funk announced, 'so does my husband. Chimneys with smoke coming out high in the sky. Making electricity for all the west side of the city.'

'I found out that the permission had been wrongly granted when I was putting away some of my husband's things from his office,' Stephanie went on, making a shameless grab for sympathy for her abandoned state. There was some guilty restlessness. 'The Development Trust asked his firm to consult on the buildings to be put on the site. The reason they did not do so is that the ground is polluted. The chemicals left behind by the power station are toxic. Highly toxic. A programme of what is called bio-remediation needs to be carried out to clean up the ground before anything else is built there. You'll recall from the plans we saw that no such programme is proposed and the developers haven't acknowledged the need to clean up the site at all. In fact, if you read their documents carefully, you'll see that they've gone to some lengths to cover up the problem.'

'What do you mean by toxic exactly?' The earnest question came from the Nature Triangle.

'She means poisoned!' declared Mrs Funk, half rising to her feet. 'Don't you know English? Toxic is poisoned! The ground there is full of poisons, enough to kill us all.'

'Surely not,' remonstrated the Major under his breath.

'I have here the chemical survey commissioned by my husband from the country's leading experts in this field.' Stephanie pointed to the pile of paper in the centre of the table. She leaned on the word husband. It rang in people's ears; husband seemed to compel their attention much more effectively than the facts of disaster. After months alone, Stephanie was beyond cynicism. *Whatever gets the job done*, pledged her inner voice. 'As an architect, my husband needed a detailed technical analysis, but I think we can all understand the conclusions. And I myself, as a landscape architect, did a soil test on some land near Oak Hill. The pollutants discovered were lead, cadmium, mercury, copper, zinc and boron.'

'Ah!' cried the man from the Nature Triangle. 'Copper! That explains everything. The red ghost moth is always found in areas where the soil is rich in copper.'

'Isn't zinc supposed to be good for you?' asked Sonia Purkelli. 'I thought it was a really important trace mineral that we all needed for fighting stress.'

Topaz smoothly nudged the meeting back on track. 'In small quantities, as I'm sure we're all aware, these heavy metals occur naturally. The trouble with Oak Hill is that they're present in huge quantities and in poisonous compounds. That report says the site's so toxic that nobody should even go on it without a full protective suit, a face mask and breathing equipment.'

'Good God,' exclaimed Penelope Salmon.

Timidly, people took copies of the report and began turning pages as if the papers themselves were shedding carcinogens into the atmosphere.

'To show you how this could affect the whole of Westwick, I've done some diagrams based on those in my husband's report.' Triumphantly, Stephanie unfurled the next page of her flip chart. Excellent invention, giving every new sub-heading a theatrical flourish. 'With some help from Topaz on the graphics,' she added hastily. 'You see that Oak Hill is – well, a hill, so it's higher ground than most of the area. What's happening is that the pollutants are getting washed down in rainwater through the drains, into the little river Hel here, which feeds the city water treatment plant in Helford, and then into the main river and down to the city. You may have noticed some of the willows along Riverview Drive looking a bit sick?'

'Why yes,' Jemima Thorogood agreed, 'they're yellow all year round.'

'And at the Gaia Garden Centre,' – Stephanie turned a new page, showing them a vertical section of the land between the river and Oak Hill – 'I found that the chemicals are at toxic levels in the soil and in the water as well. The drains and the water pipes in Westwick date from when the area was built up eighty years ago, they're in pretty poor shape. It's possible, for instance, that when the drains flood in times of heavy rain, polluted water leaks into all the basements of the shops on Grove Parade.'

'And the trucks,' prompted Mrs Funk with indignation. 'The trucks driving down our Broadway.'

'That's another thing. The soil being dug out of Oak Hill for the foundations of the buildings is being transported in ordinary open trucks to an infill site out somewhere on the Thirty-four. That soil is such a considerable bio-hazard that it can't legally be taken through a residential area.'

'Well, they must stop it at once,' said Sonia Purkelli, colouring at her own boldness.

'Isn't the soil going out to somewhere near Whitbridge?' ventured one of the students. 'Near where the demonstration is on Strankley Ridge?'

'I didn't know that,' Stephanie continued, 'but it would be quite likely. You see, the Oak Hill Development Trust is made up of local businessmen – that's part of the reason the planning committee were so dumb, they've dealt with some of these guys for years, they're all in it together. Ted Parsons is one of the directors.'

'And he was always such a friend to Erich and me,' Mrs Funk lamented.

'And that's his wife on TV talking about baby milk and everything,' Mr Singh marvelled, hoping to distract the meeting from the issue of flooding on the Parade. It was true that every time rain fell in quantity the Kwality Korner Store, as well as Catchpole & Forge, Parsley & Thyme, Bon Ton, Grove Estates, Pot Pourri and the Bundles Baby Boutique, experienced about six inches of floodwater in the basement, for which only Pot Pourri was grateful since it saved the assistants having to water the plants. Mr Singh was forced to store his dried foods on upper shelves. If the water was bringing in chemicals which were so bad that they could not be driven past people's houses and labourers needed masks and oxygen to dig them up, what might it have done to his biscuits and his rice and his apples?

'And Chester Pike of Magno supermarkets is also a director, which is why I did not invite his wife to this meeting although she is our chair.' The idea of marginalising Lauren Pike was delicious. 'The third director is Adam DeSouza, one of their associates, a lawyer who works for Pike. Magno are planning the biggest supermarket in the country at a site near Whitbridge, which is probably where the waste from Oak Hill is going.'

'A conspiracy!' declared Mrs Funk. 'A conspiracy to poison the whole country!'

'I really think,' Topaz interjected, 'that isn't too dramatic a description.'

'We must do something,' the Nature Triangle demanded, smiting the table with his fist. 'Make a protest.'

'A petition!' Penelope Salmon proposed. 'We can all sign it.'

'We must protest,' Jemima Thorogood insisted, all of a sudden looking remarkably rejuvenated by enthusiasm. 'We should have a demonstration. With banners and placards and chanting. Up and down the Broadway. I organised them for nuclear disarmament.'

'You didn't do too well, then,' observed the Major.

'Yes,' Stephanie agreed sweetly, 'we must protest. But if we march down the Broadway, the only people who will take any notice are the *Helford and Westwick Courier*, and if we send in a petition with a thousand signatures the council can still ignore us. Now, what I would like to propose is something really ambitious. For a start, I think we should target Channel Ten.'

'The TV won't cover this kind of issue,' declared Nature Triangle sourly. 'We've tried to interest them before, they don't want to know.'

Rod cleared his throat and found the voice he'd been saving for King Lear by the time he got back to his real job. 'Maybe I should introduce myself now,' he suggested.

The oyster bar was crammed to the gills, men in suits and women in suits shoulder to shoulder, throwing down champagne from silver tankards and pulling the legs off the new season's crabs. The room was panelled in mahogany and lit by twinkling cut-glass chandeliers. The floor in the basement bar was of reclaimed flagstones sprinkled with sawdust. Upstairs there were thick beige carpets and little mahogany-stalled booths around each table. The tablecloths were thick and white, the curtains dark brown brocade, deeply fringed. The walls were decorated with a collection of maritime paintings, quite famous although the canvases were restored to within an inch of their lives and gleamed slick with varnish by the light of the chandeliers.

The table Ted and Adam preferred was below a large canvas of a storm-tossed frigate. The brass plate proclaimed its title, *The Wreck of HMS Redoubtable off Newfoundland, 1792*. It was a stirring composition full of flying spray, broken spars, billowing sails and monstrous waves, and as Ted did not believe in omens he liked it because it was the most exciting picture in the whole restaurant, full of movement whereas the others were meticulous ship portraits and rather static. The artist had even included a couple of lost sailors plunging to their watery graves from the high gunwales, and a few luckier souls gesticulating in a tiny lifeboat.

Ted admired the lighting, the subdued glow of the ground glass mantle lamps, the pretty sparkle of the chandeliers, the little rainbows generated by the cut glass panels topping the mahogany screens between tables. The optimism of the past week had evaporated the day he came home and found Allie there again, ready to arraign him for another ridiculous photo shoot, but something sturdier had taken its place. She had left him once, he reasoned, she would do it again. All he had to do was give her a good reason.

'Bevelled edges,' he informed Adam enthusiastically, forking into the luscious creaminess of his *coquilles St Jacques*. 'The edge of the glass panel is cut at an angle, giving a continuous prism which multiplies and refracts the light. We've got the same thing in the old doors at Sun Wharf. I was thinking of the same effect in some of the internal doors in the apartments. Won't cost much. Buyers just love that kind of little touch.'

Adam contemplated him coldly over the rim of an

oyster shell, marvelling that the man could waste his energy on anything as irrelevant as the tastes of his market. Adam did not see the future occupants of Sun Wharf, or the future workers at Oak Hill, as having much claim to humanity. They were the means by which the development companies acquired cash, no more. Whether they liked twinkly glass doors was of no importance.

'Sun Wharf keeping you busy?' he enquired.

'Busy enough,' Ted responded. Never, ever, admit you had too much to do. Rule 1. He was learning the corporate moves pretty fast.

'Things settled down at home?'

Rule 2: Never, ever, admit to domestic problems. 'Fine, fine. It was all done for the newspapers, you know. The old media game. They all have to play it.'

'We were thinking, Ted, perhaps you needed to be able to focus more. With so much going on, Sun Wharf and so on.'

See Rule 1 above. 'Hey, not me. This is my business, Adam. It's all meat and drink to me. This is what I love about it, going on site, getting my shoes muddy, talking to the man on the JCB . . .'

Adam sighed and discarded his last shell. At one point, earlier in the year, Ted had suggested they ask for their orders separately rather than in the French style of one huge ice platter studded with oysters to share. For an uncomfortable week Adam had suspected that Parsons might be able to get back the iron in his soul and the steel in his spine, pull something out and check his slide into outer darkness. Then he saw that there was no significance in the change, that his lunch companion had never noticed him creaming off the best oysters but for some reason wanted the liberty to order a different dish once in a while, like today's nursery food on a half-shell. Adam found this typical of the man's self-indulgent individualism; he just was not a team player.

A waiter took away their plates. 'Ted.' Adam swept imaginary crumbs from the cloth with the side of his thick hand. 'I'll get to the point. Chester wants you out of Oak Hill.'

'Chester can go fuck himself,' Ted retorted instantly. 'It's my project.' But he felt stabbed, fatally. He felt his confidence bleeding away through the puncture to his ego. His spine ran cold and his stomach squeezed around a gout of acid. He could easily have vomited, the warm white blend of sauce and mashed potato from the *St Jacques* rose in his throat but he held it down. 'It's my show,' he said again.

'Was your show. You've lost the BSD's confidence, Ted. This Sun Wharf thing, he doesn't see it.'

'Sure he sees it, he was all for it . . .'

'He's prepared to let you go on with it if that's what you want to do, but you've got to get out of Oak Hill. We'll refinance. At this stage there'll be no problem with that.'

'No, no problem at all,' Ted agreed with bitterness. 'Now that I've found the site, and cleared the titles and piloted the project through all its potential hazards, now it's a copper-bottomed, five-star, 22-carat, money-making proposition, I should think new investors'll be beating down the doors.'

'You can leave the rest of your stake in, so you'll

certainly see some of your money back with a good return, I think. But we'd like you to resign. Quietly, no need to draw attention to it. You've enough on your plate of your own.'

'Peace with honour,' sneered Ted. The waiter reappeared with two halves of a bifurcated lobster on beds of flouncing lettuce. The beast's long feelers trailed dramatically from the plates. 'Fuck both of you. I won't do it.'

'You ought to do it, Ted,' Adam seemed perfectly calm. There was no crack in his normal ingratiating superciliousness. He spoke with condescension which was irritated but not without tenderness, as if advising a wounded woman to accept her divorce settlement because her husband was never going to come back to her. The little lobster fork, almost invisible in his big hand, moved rhythmically between the shell and his mouth, conveying the succulent flesh to be eaten. 'We can go through the motions and vote you off the board, but who wants that kind of hassle?'

'Do you really know what I've put into Oak Hill?' Ted demanded. 'Have you any understanding? All the years I've been in Westwick – what – twenty? twenty-one? all those relationships I've built up, the trust, the give and take, with people who were nothing but junior assistant surveyors when we first met, who're now chairs of this and officers of that. The guys who actually made it happen for us; they trusted me, I trusted them. We'd been doing business twenty years. You'd have got nowhere without me, nowhere. I brought the project to you, I found the site . . .'

'Nobody denies any of that, Ted. Your contribution is

of paramount importance, crucial, of course. But it's over. We have to move on, you have to move on. Chester wants us to get into the Whitbridge development and you've dragged your feet. That might be called a mistake.'

'Does he want to pull out of Tudor Homes too?' The scenario now in view was disturbing. This was no time for Tudor to suffer a capital amputation.

'Not at this stage.' Adam was as emollient as ever but the menace in his words was unmistakable. 'I get the feeling for some reason your heart just isn't in the Whitbridge thing. No sense trying to make water run uphill, is there? Chester's been talking to some people, he may go forward with them.'

'What people? Belgrave? Harrier?'

'I don't know what's in his mind for the future, Ted. But here we are, at the parting of the ways.' The lobster shell was empty. He put down his fork, reached into his briefcase which lay on the velvet banquette next to him and took out an envelope. 'I drafted something for you. All you have to do is sign.'

'I need to think,' Ted insisted, hoping from the depth of his heart that there was some way of turning this situation around.

'Ted,' Adam urged, 'there's nothing to think about. You have no choices here. If you make us throw you off the board there's nowhere to hide, we'll get more attention than we need, people will start sniffing around and the whole thing can go down the pan. You were always the one who was so concerned about the media, for God's sake. So this is it, this is the end of the road. We're being more than fair. Just sign the thing.'

As he finished speaking, his eye fell on Ted's untouched plate, on the juicy pink and white chunks of lobster tail dished into the rosy shell. There was acquisitiveness in his look. Ted had a strong urge to seize the crustacean by its long trailing whisker, whirl it around his head and throw it through the etched glass window into the street. Instead, he read through his resignation letter to the board of the Oak Hill Development Trust and signed it.

CHAPTER 20

Scientific, Literary and Political Subjects

'Uh – I have an idea,' Rod informed the *Family First* team.

'Great,' responded the senior producer, who turned towards his new star presenter with a full-on earnest expression designed to eradicate any possible perception of sarcasm. 'Let's hear it.'

'It's kind of a consumer thing. I mean, I don't know if it's quite what *Family First* needs now that you're going in this new direction and everything . . .' He devoted hours to finding this character, the bear of little brain. He needed to be a naive, unthreatening figure whom everyone would dismiss and nobody suspect, the hot media equivalent of Clark Kent. In a group which he immediately discovered to be composed of paranoid careerists, this was hard. Most of them would suspect their own grandmothers of trying to outflank them and saw the rest of humanity as positively after their jobs. Making it worse, he was aware of a new energy in himself, the flame kindled by Stephanie and leaping higher every day as he explored this new role. If I can do this, he was asking himself, chewing up the opposition, what else can I do?

He went for sentimental, honest and caring, which in this company added up to stupid. He found himself some glasses, thin-rimmed large-lensed speccy things which would have been hot in the eighties, and dropped them frequently. He talked about his daughter all the time. He was polite and fetched people coffee. He wore plaid shirts in pastel colours. Unless he was on camera, he mumbled. It was a challenge, sustaining the role throughout a working day, but so far the audience were with him. Maria, the junior researcher, was listening now like a Titian Madonna, with her head on one side and a saintly expression of patience. The guys were expressing manly forbearance.

'Consumer issue! How f-a-a-bulous!' Allie encouraged him, considering it dreamy that her new find should be so thick as to dig himself voluntarily into a ratings grave-yard. He'd hardly been on the team two weeks and already Rod Fuller was bidding for whatever was worthy, earnest and an instant switch-off. She had successfully shunted him towards this feature on the supermarket of the future, made naturally with the co-operation of Magno. Wardrobe had found him a Norwegian sweater fuzzily hand-knitted in iceberg blue and glacier grey; it was scratchy, heavy as a greatcoat and much too hot but the dear boy, eager to please, was gamely wearing it draped over his shoulders.

'What it is,' – he looked down at his notes; still ter-rified of fluffing the delivery, he had written himself a

script – 'is a look at the business of supermarket diver-
sification . . .'

He had argued with Stephanie about how much Allie
knew about Oak Hill and its problems. On his last visit
to Church Vale to train her, he'd let the name come into
the conversation, and got no reaction.

'She doesn't know, she has no idea,' she assured him.

'I know she's dumb, but nobody could be that dumb,'
he argued.

'When Stewart passed on the project, I didn't know,
did I?' she rejoined with pain. The fact that her husband
hadn't confided in her still stung. It spoiled her fantasies
of joyful homecoming, she imagined herself flying into
his arms, then hauling off and demanding, 'But why
didn't you tell me . . .?' Mr Capelli was promising positive news any day now, but at that moment Stewart
would have got a mixed reception back home.

'Allie never talks to her husband, she's probably got
no idea what goes on with his business. But she is tied
into everything financially, she told me that one day,
hinting she'd be well off if they split, you know? So I'm
going to propose a dummy feature and we can film all we
want under cover of that.'

'You'll never get away with it.' Stephanie found it
delightful to tease him, now he was popping at the seams
with confidence.

'She's been talking to me about a report on the supermarket of the future. I'm going to go right along with
that, which gets me out to Oak Hill with a camera. If she
reacts – fine, we can reframe the story and I'll have to do
some secret interviewing. If she doesn't, I can go out

with a reporter, you can bring your surveyors out to be interviewed, we'll make exactly what'll be screened, and she'll never know. I'll make a dummy report on the supermarkets as well. Then I'll fix it so she sees the film before transmission, not the producer. And I'll show her the dummy.'

The level of energy around the table was falling fast. Maria appeared transfigured. The guys were nodding slowly. Allie, however, was reacting right along with the rest. Nearly six months of close physical contact with her on a regular basis had at least taught him to read her reactions.

'Which means – uh – branching out into credit cards, financial services, mortgages, medical services, even crèches and day care. Destination shopping, with all kinds of attractions planned around the supermarket, parks, cinemas, play areas . . .'

'So what's the actual story, do you think?' The senior producer spoke in the excessively gentle tones mothers use to persuade their infants to put the second brick on the first.

'Well – ah – is it in the customer's interest, will it give these commercial giants strangleholds on our lives, what about the traditional shopkeepers, what about the reliance on the car, the development of car culture . . . you know the government estimates a growth in the number of cars on the road by over a hundred per cent by the year two thousand and twenty-five – I mean, do we really want that? Twice as many cars as there are now?' He felt the interest around the table sinking.

'Yes, we get all that,' coaxed the producer, sensing a destination for this rambling argument, 'but how do you suggest we make it mean something to our audience?'

'We can just find some place they're building a new supermarket and ask the people who live there what they think about it. There's a new Magno going up somewhere near here!' Allie exclaimed. 'It'll be as f-a-a-b as our sad fish story. I must say, I think that was the triumph of the last series.' Rod appeared delighted to have the burden of explanation taken from him. The rest of the team, sensing another thinly disguised commercial for Magno, drifted from indifference to profound boredom.

'You're sure? How far have you looked into this?'

'I – uh – did quite a bit of research, actually.' Rod had an impressive stack of files in front of him and he made as if to open one. 'I've got the plans for the new complex Allie talked about and a retail industry analysis here going back five years, and a land-use survey done after a big hypermarket was opened outside Lyons which is supposed to be the real cutting-edge stuff. We can get some really great graphics out of it. Here's a copy.' He held it up for the table to see.

The senior producer nodded, impressed. For once Allie Parsons had dragged in a Himbo with half a brain. Allie herself was impressed. 'Rod, that is so great,' she cooed. 'Can you get it done for the first show? It'll just go really well with our kidnap wife. But not too negative, yes? Keep it upbeat. Maria, why don't you work on it with him?'

Maria scowled.

'Who're the developers of this shopping complex?'

he senior researcher enquired, resentful that the Himbo
night alienate her affections.

Rod eyeballed him with utter sincerity. 'It's a consor-
ium. The major backer is Belgrave, probably our biggest
ommercial property group. It's a Magno supermarket.
We like them, don't we?'

'It's not really a *sexy* idea, is it?' The senior researcher
melt blood. 'Won't it take years for all this to actually
mpact people's lives? Not very immediate, really. It's
ll a bit . . . faceless, to me.'

'Can you find a face for it? Like someone who actually
nas a supermarket mortgage? It's kind of a rule we have
on the show, every idea has to have a face.' The senior
oroducer was tapping his teeth with his pen, a sign of
apid thought.

'Ah – well . . .' Shit. He hadn't thought of that. Rod
crubbed his fingers through his hair in alarm.

'Oh, for Heaven's sake,' Allie interjected, 'he'll find
he people. You can't get gossip into a consumer feature,
t just doesn't happen.'

'People need gossip,' the senior producer ruled. 'Now
hey all live in suburbs and nobody knows their neigh-
oours, they just like to gossip about celebrities instead.
'll let it go this time because it's a good story, but in
uture I don't want any more ideas that we can't get a face
or.' And so the senior producer gave Rod his blessing,
dding, 'And go easy on the graphics. Big zap factor
with graphics.'

On Strankley Ridge the hawthorn hedges were blood red with berries. The cornfields were bare stubble waiting for the plough, and seagulls, foraging inland away from the autumn storms, walked proprietorially between the bare stalks. The sky was clear bird's-egg blue and drops of the heavy morning dew were still sparkling on the ground when Gemma turned the Lada off the 34 through a gap in the hedge before the dragon sculpture and rattled over the rutted ground towards the stone circle.

A minibus was parked in a patch of gravel to the right of the field entrance, and a squad of uniformed security men sat in it, staying out of the wind which thrashed the bushes and thrummed in the car's aerial. Gemma turned to the left, where two Volkswagen campers and a lopsided Citroën 2CV stood in the meagre shelter of the hedge. The force of the wind blew the grass blades horizontally over the ground like waterweed in a current.

Topaz got out of the Lada, her dainty feet loose in Flora's boots, her trim legs clad in black trousers, buttoning up her high-collared black jacket against the wind. Even as a world leader, Stalin knew the value of dressing in military style, claiming the authority of a uniform. Gemma, thinking the trousers looked impossibly clean, strode forward vigorously and splashed them with mud. 'Hey!' protested her daughter.

'Camouflage,' her mother growled. The wind tore her hair out of its braid and whipped it around her head. She put up both hands to hold it out of her watering eyes and see their way.

Their path was plain. In less troubled times it would
have led from the Visitor Centre, a larch-lap hut with a
plan of the site outside it, to the stone circle. The tractor
had ruled Strankley Ridge for decades, the fields were
vast and treeless, stretching past the horizon over the
hilltops, and the hedges were few and neglected. The
megaliths, mossy grey stones the height of a group of
ten-year-old children, stood demurely in a ring of fine
turf at the centre of a vast ploughed field, protected by an
outer circle of earthworks, leaning towards each other as
whispering three-thousand-year-old jokes.

The protesters had made camp right around the circle,
pitching tents of every possible shape, size, ethnic deriva-
tion and viability in a random sprawl on the bare earth.
There were few muddy patches; the weather had been dry
and the good brown soil, speckled with chalky stones had
been beaten into a maze of paths.

Flapping from two thin poles was a white banner,
once probably a sheet, with *New Green Army HQ* lettered
on it in an appropriate shade of emerald. From the power
inlet to the Visor Centre ran a heavy-duty insulated cable
looped on crazed posts and guarded by hand-painted
lightning signs with the words *Fuckin' Lethal, Hands Off*
on a signboard below.

A faint whiff of wood smoke blended into the gale and
a skewbald horse stood patiently with its back to the
wind, its tail blown between its legs. A couple of dogs
ran crazily about but few people were evident. Topaz led
the way around the guy ropes and between tent poles
over to a man with an Inca wool hat tied under his goatee
who was trying to weight the front flap of his igloo tent

with a stone where the wind had torn the peg out of th
ground.

'We're looking for Crusty,' she shouted.

'Nwah?' he answered, pulling aside one of his ear
flaps.

'Crusty,' Gemma bellowed, making a tunnel with he
hands to get the words out audibly.

'Yurt.' And he pointed to a black tent pitched close t
the biggest of the standing stones. A stove pipe poke
from its apex, and wisps of smoke could be seen tearin
from it.

There was no door to knock on, so Topaz yelled
'Hello, there!' into the teeth of the wind. Three or fou
voices made optimistic sounds from within, so sh
boldly pulled aside the entry flap and they ducked int
the tent.

Out of the wind, the snugness and stillness of th
interior stunned them for a moment. At its highes
point, the yurt was big enough to stand up in, althoug
the sides sloped down to a height of about five feet. B
the glow of a light bulb masked by some shreds of bati
they saw Crusty, looking exactly as he did on the TV
news, with his bouncy six-inch dreadlocks hanging ove
his cherubic round eyes and his little black waistcoa
buttoned over his boyish chest, kneeling by a cylindrica
black stove and peeking into a hissing kettle.

'Nice in here,' he observed, with his puckish smile
'Have a seat. Would you care for tea?'

'Great,' said Gemma, hitting the floor next to a long
haired woman who sat cross-legged at the side of th
tent, pessimistically examining mugs for cleanliness.

'Why not?' Topaz answered, trying not to sound surprised. She registered a couple more people reclining at a breathable distance from the heat of the stove. Various piles of sleeping bags, pillows, cushions and carpet fragments lay about the interior and a tin trunk in the centre of the space stood as a table. In one corner an open laptop balanced on a pile of clothes. She selected a piece of old shag-pile carpet near her mother to sit upon. The trousers were tight and made it difficult to cross her legs properly so she sat to one side.

'Yurt's the warmest place in the whole camp,' Crusty continued with pride. 'Even when it snows we're nice and cosy in here.'

'It certainly is warm,' Topaz agreed.

'We're burning sheep-shit,' he informed them. 'Stove's meant to burn yak-dung, that's what they use in the Himalayas. Not a lot of yaks around Whitbridge, of course, but there's plenty of sheep. Hundreds of them, actually. So we have a shit-picking party every now and then, getting our fuel in before the winter. There's a long-range web-site on the weather says its going to be dreadful this year.'

He made tea in a new-looking brown pot, covering it with a flap of sleeping bag to keep in the heat.

'I brought you some home-grown,' Gemma offered, pulling a well-filled plastic bag out of her coat pocket and putting it on the table.

'Great.' Graciously, he picked up the bag, rustled the contents, sniffed them and handed it to the long-haired woman. 'I don't smoke myself but I might nibble occasionally. We can put it with our stash. Thanks.'

411

'Nettle tea?' Gemma enquired hopefully.

'Oh no. Disgusting, nettle tea. Have you ever tried it? No, this is from Harrods. Breakfast blend. From our well-wishers. Other well-wishers. My mother, actually.' The tea was poured, and lump sugar in a box and a carton of long-life milk passed with the mugs. 'So,' Crusty blew thoughtfully on his beverage, 'did you have a reason for your visit? Or were you just coming to take a peek at an eco-warrior resting on his sword, as it were?'

'We want you to help us,' Topaz began boldly. The Man of Steel was famous for getting straight to the point.

'If I can be of help,' Crusty assented. It was always said of him that his manners were lovely. He also spoke well, with many hints of a first-class education. Cleaned up, he would have made a promising junior diplomat.

'We are facing an environmental catastrophe.'

'Isn't everybody?' muttered the long-haired woman.

'Where?' Crusty took a thoughtful sip.

'Westwick.'

There was no response. 'You know, west of the city on the Thirty-one, near the airport?' Topaz prompted. Her ears and nose, frozen outside, were now smarting with returning circulation and probably scarlet.

'I know Westwick,' agreed the eco-warrior. Crusty was giving nothing away. He stared meditatively at the roof of the yurt, sipping his tea from time to time.

'Rich, isn't it?' asked the long-haired woman. 'Another posh suburb.'

Crusty kept his gaze fixed on the top of the stove's

himney. 'Of course, one might argue that every suburb is an environmental catastrophe.'

There was some nodding around the edge of the tent and Topaz was encouraged. In plain but graphic terms, she outlined the potential scale of the Oak Hill disaster. If they're allowed to go ahead with it, hundreds of homes will be destroyed and ten thousand workers will be living in a toxic environment,' she concluded. In the soft, warm enclosure of the tent, with the faint howl of the wind outside, the splendid oration she had composed sounded rather muted.

After a pause, in which he finished his tea and replaced his mug tidily on the brass tray on the trunk top, Crusty addressed the empty space above their heads. 'Strange,' he remarked in a weary tone, 'isn't it, that although lots of people may well worry about the great global issues of our time – climate change, air pollution, fossil fuels – people don't seem motivated to protest until some disaster is actually in their back yard. A disaster which may well be related, of course. But nobody wants to look at the big picture. Perhaps they just can't understand it. Having their house knocked down, well, that they can understand.'

The acolytes gazed into their mugs and murmured agreement. It seemed the green knight intended to refuse the quest.

'The whole history of the green movement is of growth from the bottom up.' Topaz argued with marvellous fluency; she planned a thesis on the affair when it was over, and had the background section already completed. 'Grass-roots, single-issue protests like ours drawing in the mainstream, multi-issue environmental organisations who have embraced the potential of local movements and play a vital role in their success.'

'The New Green Army is not exactly mainstream,' Crusty corrected her with a hint of pained offence on his grimy face. 'Maybe you should talk to Greenpeace.'

'They don't get involved locally. Their thing is national action. You must know that.' Gallantly, Crusty inclined his head, acknowledging the hit. 'Anyway, I think that compromise is essential with a multi-issue organisation, and the absolute refusal to compromise is the most effective weapon in political conflict.'

'Not in my back yard.' Crusty now smiled like a mischievous cherub. 'That's all you're saying, actually.'

'My back yard is your back yard,' Topaz countered 'We're all on this planet together.'

'But some of us have bigger back yards than others. Some of us have enough money to pick out our own choice portion of planet and fence it in.' Crusty reached into his waistcoat pocket and produced an old silver watch, which he opened to read the time. 'And then we tell the rest of the world to fuck off. We seem to be able to forget that we're still on the same planet as other people.'

Topaz swallowed, desperately searching her memory for another good Bolshevik argument. Then Gemma, who held that it was a mother's duty to give her children the freedom to screw up big time when they insisted on bucking the energy of the universe, and who had been deeply absorbed in braiding her hair again, finally spoke up.

'Look, Crusty,' she said, 'we want to hijack a TV show.'

'Ah!' exclaimed the eco-warrior, immediately putting away his watch with enthusiasm. 'Why didn't you say so in the first place? Are we talking primetime here? Nationwide or what?'

As a physical entity, Chester Pike lived in a permanently impaired state. Flying to St Louis at least twice a week left most of his biological systems deranged. He was dehydrated, constipated and temporally disoriented. Josh Carman had supplied him with a whole shelf of drugs to regulate his sleep, his heart and his bowels, drain his legs of oedema and his sinuses of mucus and when necessary, for he was intent upon replacing Lauren within eighteen months and Chester was nothing if not goal-oriented, to supply more blood into his penis which for some years had been acting as if it didn't know quite which day of the week it was. Far from the BSD of legend, the organ remained small and wobbly. In this, Chester's penis was in tune with the rest of his corporeal being. His mind, however, was still up to reading the state on whatever electronic mechanism might be his companion, whatever car he was in or whatever desk he sat behind. And his instinct, buried though it was under the accumulated abuse of a lifetime and unaccustomed as it was to being heard, still had a voice.

Chester's instinct told him to drop by Oak Hill. On a some morning, when his driver collected him from

Grove House, he was being driven out of Westwick to
the Magno Southeast Building, which sprawled across
several acres in an industrial park twenty miles down
the 31 beyond the airport. Ted Parsons, sadly for he had
in some measure liked the man, was history. The contractors clearing the Oak Hill site had been informed
Adam DeSouza had found a new project manager, starting the following week. For seven days, no one was
minding the store. Chester disliked these situations; in
his experience, when you gave destiny a flash of white
underbelly like that, the great cosmic predator could
never resist.

'Turn off here,' he ordered his driver through the limousine's telephone. 'I want to take a look at our little
project.'

He did not register Stephanie in her Cherokee, driving
Stewart's surveyor colleague away from his clandestine
interview, and she, thrilled in the process of her strategy
working out, did not register Chester's limousine, which
in any case had dark windows.

As soon as the chain-link fence topped with razor
wire came in view, and inside the site Chester saw a
Channel Ten van painted searing blue and green, and a
young woman with a camera and a man in a suit standing beside it, he knew he had been right.

Oak Hill was no longer a wasteland; vast excavations
had taken place, and diggers were still working in them,
scooping out the gravelly sub-soil and raining it into
waiting trucks. Above their roar sounded the pounding
of jack-hammers driving the first piles into the earth, and
at the far end of the territory the first crane had been

erected and was ponderously transporting girders to their last resting place. A two-storey stack of Portakabins housed the site offices, and their outer wall was faced with the signboards of architects, engineers, contractors and the Oak Hill Development Trust itself, appropriately embellished with an acorn and a leaf.

Chester made his driver stop by the Channel Ten van. 'What's going on here?' he demanded, running down his window.

'Good morning, sir,' replied Rod Fuller, preparing to squat submissively by the vehicle door. Chester opted to get out and stand face-to-face, and Rod, catching sight of the documents scattered on the back seat and having retained some subliminal memory of the face of the husband of Butter-Wouldn't-Melt-In-It, MD of Magno Southeast and sometime member of The Cedars although he had made it through the gym just the once, knew how to react.

'Rod Fuller,' he extended his hand, 'from *Family First*, Channel Ten Television. And this is Maria D'Amico, our researcher. We're making a short documentary feature on the supermarket of the future and we're just getting some shots here of the place where the new Magno store will be opening next year.'

'My name's Pike,' muttered Chester uneasily.

'I know,' blushed Rod. 'I recognised you.'

Ever bufonious, Chester's swelled a little around the thorax. They shook hands. 'Allie Parsons,' he said, 'she's on *Family First*, isn't she?'

'Our star,' Rod confirmed proudly. 'We're back on the air the day after tomorrow. I've been in touch with your public relations people about this, of course. They've been most helpful.'

'She's a neighbour of mine around here,' Chester made a proprietorial gesture towards the rest of Westwick outside the metal mesh.

'Oh, you *know* her then.' Rod was finding fresh irony in the ability of people to digest whatever quantity of gush he cared to extrude.

'Clever woman,' Chester announced. 'Done well.'

'Indeed she has,' Rod agreed.

'Well . . .' Chester considered calling at the site office, but felt unequal to the task of talking to men who actually got their hands dirty. 'Splendid. Glad we've been able to help. Look forward to seeing...'

'We'll send you a tape, sir,' Rod promised, courteously closing the door of the limousine as Chester sank back into his seat. Dark clouds blew over the sky as they watched the great black vehicle glide away over the mud and disappear in the direction of the Broadway.

'Why d'you come over all creepy when a guy with a limo shows up?' The problem called Maria shifted the camera to her shoulder, ready for action. 'And what was that survey stuff all about? He wasn't talking supermarkets.'

'Ah – he's in a feature I'm putting up on sick buildings,' Rod assured her. 'I just needed a building-site for a background and this seemed a good opportunity. The limo guy's Chester Pike of Magno. I just wanted him to go away. You know how civilians are about objectivity, they just don't get it. He knows The Boss, for a start, as well as Allie. If he gets the idea we're doing anything investigative they'll pull the plug on us.'

'Why do I get the feeling you don't want anyone to know what this report's supposed to be about? Especially not Allie?'

Maria was chewing gum cheerfully but her eyes were sharp. Having noted the dynamics of her relationship with Allie, Rod decided to take a chance. First he deployed the foxy grin. 'What's your opinion of Allie?'

'Piece of work, since you're asking.'

'If her career took a new direction, would you feel a sense of loss?'

'Are you kidding me? Listen, I'm the only woman researcher this show has ever had. She's not exactly a sister. The best thing that could happen to me right now is her career could take a new direction and mine could keep right on going.'

'How would that work out?'

'Well, my contract's a year, and it's with the show, so even if the show was axed . . .'

'You'd be OK.'

'I'd be OK. Look, you want to tell me more, can we do it at lunch? This thing's heavy and it's going to rain any minute.'

They went to the Wilde At Heart and he told her almost everything.

All the way out to the office, Chester Pike sent faxes. He wrote: WHY WAS A CHANNEL TEN REPORTER FROM FAMILY FIRST OUT AT OAK HILL TODAY? GET BACK TO ME SOONEST. He faxed this to Adam, to Allie, to Magno's publicity director and, on a last irrational impulse, to Ted. Adam spoke to the site foreman and, in reply, Chester got three memos citing a feature on the supermarket of the future. From Ted's office he got a note from his assistant to say Mr Parsons was at Sun Wharf all day.

Even as, in a Channel Ten edit suite, Rod and Maria screened their dummy feature for Allie, Ted Parsons stopped by the Oak Hill site the next evening with a half-bottle of schnapps. Yuris, now employed as foreman on this far less skilled but far more lucrative job, liked a shot or two at the end of the day; it gave him the energy to get cleaned up and hit a few bars. Ted talked to him for quite a while about the questions the TV crew had been asking and the directions in which they'd pointed their camera.

Ted's instinct had been talking to him ever since his wife had hired her personal trainer as co-host on her show. He connected Rod to Stephanie, Stephanie to her husband, her husband to the damning report on the site, and all of them to Gemma, a subject in which he remained highly interested. When he got home from Oak Hill, still glowing with schnapps, Ted dialled Gemma Lieberman's number one more time, and Topaz picked up.

'Your mother wouldn't by any chance be part of some media conspiracy, would she?' he asked, feeling ridiculous. The arctic silence at the end of the telephone banished the feeling immediately.

'Don't be ridiculous,' Topaz ordered.

'Because I happen to know that Chester Pike of Magno has been sniffing around a certain Channel Ten TV crew and asking questions about why they were out at Oak Hill.'

'We could ask you some questions about Oak Hill,' was the vitriolic response.

'It's not my show any more,' Ted said, feeling sad and happy simultaneously. 'They threw me out last week. But that's not why I called. I just called to warn you, if you needed warning, which of course you may not. I do care for your mother, you know. I wish her success, I really do. Give her my love, will you, Topaz? Goodbye now.'

CHAPTER 21

Peace Assured

Rain fell in Westwick with regret. Drops fell lightly but intently from a pale pewter sky, bringing down the first serious fall of leaves of the season and inviting the community to contemplate the inevitable succession of life, death and rebirth.

The rain falling through the cherry trees on New Farm Rise made the empty street glisten. It chuckled into the gutters and streamed through the drains and caused Stephanie Sands to adopt a completely untypical expression of cynicism as she belted her son into the back of the Cherokee at 5.30 am.

Max removed his cute yellow sou'wester and placed it gravely on the seat beside him.

'You will need it later,' she told him.

'It's weird,' he replied with sleepy confidence.

'You have to walk to school today, remember?'

'Uh.'

'If it's still raining, you'll get wet.'

'Uh.'

'Your hat will keep the rain off.'

'Can we go now?'

The air was humid and warm. The earth, even the sour, poisoned, paved-over earth of Westwick, smelled fecund. It was the season for the *pousse d'automne*, the most crucial growth period of the year when plants silently and invisibly reached their roots further down into the ground and reasserted their hold on life.

Mildew had tipped the shoots of the *Souvenir de la Malmaison* with its deathly white dust. The leaves were wrinkled, brown-edged and falling early; her rose was sick. Stephanie did not even consider that she could be out back spraying and mulching when the rain stopped; today she was taking a more radical attitude to cultivating her garden.

Half a mile away in Maple Grove the rain dripped relentlessly through the mighty branches of the old trees. At the corner of Church Vale and Grove End a front door opened and Moron stomped unhappily down the front path. After him came his master.

Ted Parsons pulled the hood of his sweatshirt firmly around his face and tied the drawstring under his chin. The raindrops stung his bare hands as he opened the gate in his picket fence and stepped into the street. Under the half-naked trees the downpour was less vigorous. With Moron following at a sullen trot, he jogged forward towards the church, picking his feet up over the fallen leaves.

Lately, Ted had taken to interviewing himself. Ted

Parsons, the godfather of Maple Grove, talks about the legacy of Jackson Kerr. 'What first brought you to Westwick?' he would ask himself, the imaginary microphone alert for his reply.

'Harrier Homes,' he would reply. 'I owe it all to Harrier Homes.'

There was a joke about Harrier Homes: which is the odd one out – AIDS, herpes, gonorrhoea and a Harrier Home? The answer is gonorrhoea, because you can get rid of it. A Harrier Home would typically be bought new by a dewy-eyed couple, upwardly mobile from the working classes, who knew no better than to be reassured by its impressive portfolio of guarantees and design awards. In twenty years, when their children were grown, the guarantees would have expired, the awards would be forgotten, the paint would have peeled, the plaster would be cracking off the walls and the foundations shifting like Irish dancers; the Harrier Home would be as worthless as a dwelling could be.

After twenty-five years the couple approaching retirement would discover that the major investment of their lifetimes had been a turkey and resign themselves to rejoining the disadvantaged. They would cut their losses and sell, usually to another developer, who boarded up the property and waited until the majority of the estate was derelict before buying out the obstinate few resolved to die there and sending in the diggers. Harrier Homes extended the principle of built-in obsolescence to bricks and mortar. After thirty years, it was cheaper to knock them down than fix them up. Ted had been brought up in a Harrier Home, watching his father dedicate his meagre leisure hours to painting warped timbers and filling cracks in the walls which eternally reopened.

At the church, man and dog swung smoothly along the Broadway, heading for Alder Reach. It was many months since Ted had considered any other route. There was no sign of life at the Kwality Korner Store. It was 5.56 am.

At Alder Reach the Lieberman house blazed with light. In the kitchen, the cat scooted in through the cat flap and left a trail of muddy pawprints on the floor from the kitchen to the stairs. Topaz, careful of her charcoal worsted interview suit, removed them with a mop.

'Fucking weather,' Gemma announced. She was moving her wind chimes into the fame and public life quadrant of her house, which fell over the fireplace in what had once been the sitting room. 'Have you got an umbrella, Flora?'

'Why can't I come?' Flora demanded. 'I can easily ride over after I've dropped the little ones off. It's not fair.'

'No, it isn't,' her mother agreed, 'but it's the way it has to be. Molly's too young. Somebody has to make sure all the children get up and get dressed and get their breakfast and get to school and get to grow up and get a life. Normally, that's my job. Today I have to save the world, so I am delegating the job to you. You should be honoured.'

'Huh,' her daughter replied. 'I don't see you getting much honour for it.'

Approaching the Lieberman house, Ted decided that running with his hood up looked wussy. With a little difficulty he untied the drawstring and let the hood fall. He ran his fingers through his hair, so it would slick back aerodynamically instead of getting plastered allways to his skull. Rain trickled down his neck and tickled his backbone. Behind him, Moron plodded onwards with his head down and his tail hanging, water running in rivulets off his coat.

Ted saw the lights at the Lieberman house from way off, and the Sands girl's Jeep, and the Sands girl herself with her little boy in a yellow raincoat going into the house. Lest anyone should think he had a particular reason to be on Alder Reach, Ted chose to run on the opposite side of the road to the Lieberman house. He kept his head up and facing forwards, trying to peek into the illuminated windows as he passed, but saw nothing except the hazy, sulking shape of Flora on the window seat.

In Maple Grove, Allie Parsons looked in her dressing-room mirror and saw a woman in her prime. Her complexion was smooth, pink and glowing – laser treatment every year from now on; it worked and it solved that problem of what to do in the summer. No more puffiness around the eyes, either, thanks to the new radionics diet analysis which said she needed more magnesium and selenium but could eat all the yeast and dairy products she liked.

You're irresistible, she told her reflection. It's God's own truth, you always get what you want. You wanted Rod Fuller, and you've got him, and what an absolute trophy the dear boy is turning out to be. You wanted Stephanie Sands sobbing on the sofa, and in three hours' time that's just what you'll have. You want a primetime show – lunch with The Boss tomorrow, his invitation. It speaks for itself. Irresistible. Congratulations, my dear, you *are* a star. She reached for her sunscreen. Very important to protect the new skin. Pale as Gwyneth Paltrow, that was the look for now.

On the 31, the snake of city-bound vehicles glowed by the light of half a million headlamps; half a million windscreen wipers plied across a quarter of a million windscreens. In the back of a viridian Volkswagen camper sprinkled with painted five-petalled daisies, with the name *New Green Army* stencilled on its sides, the windows were steamy.

'OK,' demanded Crusty merrily, 'who prayed for rain?'

'We did,' answered fourteen robust voices.

'Well just because it worked this time, don't you shamans start thinking you're anything special, OK?'

After more than an hour of crawling forwards at a

speed slower than walking pace, the camper reached the Helford interchange, where it turned off and took the road for the river frontage and the Channel Ten studios. A second camper followed it, and a seriously overloaded Citroën 2CV, and a further procession of rusted, dented vehicles reconceived in colours well beyond the scope of the manufacturer's paint chart.

Along the river, Ted crossed to take shelter under the willows, then crossed back because the trees were already almost leafless and their huge roots breaking up the path made the paving slabs lie crazily; he didn't want to turn an ankle. Ten years ago, of course, he'd have jumped over the cracked slabs with joy, glorying in his strength and agility. Suddenly it had become amazingly easy to twist a foot.

'So Harrier Homes brought you to Westwick, Mr Parsons?'

'Yes, indeed. My first job in the property business. I was a surveyor for Harrier Homes.'

In those days, Harrier Homes had three designs: the Adam, the Washington and the Smythson. The Adam had pillars at either side of the door, the Washington had a pillared porch over the door and the Smythson had no pillars but long windows with broken pediments over them.

Now, as in those days, Harrier were the most successful residential builders in the country. Their target market were the young couples culturally unprepared for property ownership, whose parents had been production-line workers or machine operators or labourers, living careful, hard lives in rented homes. The young found themselves living differently; with clean hands they filled out credit applications for personal computers and named occupations in customer service and client care.

When the first of their 1.8 children arrived, they turned their attention to the full-page advertisements for Harrier Homes. Trees on the streets meant security to them, pillars meant class and property itself meant wealth, part of the arcane process of acquiring advantage in life, that trick which their parents had never mastered but which they were sure would come to them easily with a little practice and changing times.

At twenty-one, Ted Parsons would have been relieved to get any job at all and when Harrier Homes accepted him he could hardly believe his luck.

'Well done, son,' his father blessed him, 'I'm pleased you've found an outfit to take you on.'

'Well done, dear,' his mother concurred, with the tilt of her head and the rueful smile she usually deployed on hearing news of a death.

'Their stock dropped a couple of points last week,' commented his sister, freshly married to a market analyst. Unlike his sister, Ted had done badly at school and at that point in his life shared his family's relief that he was not unemployable. Having the close horizon of his youth, all other considerations were unclear to him.

In a detestable little two-tone Ford he scampered around the fringes of the city looking for sites. He scanned town plans and zoning laws and, anxious to impress and be promoted, he read widely on megatrends and demographic prophecy. Being lonely much of the time, he would talk to anyone in a bar or a café, and learned at least as much from those conversations as from his professional studies. One day he went to a place called Fuller's Eyot at Helford, where the roofless shell of a once-elegant riverside villa stood beside a rotting warehouse, the dismal sight reflected in the scummy surface of the water.

From a distance, Fuller's Eyot was tempting. The following year a new bridge was to be built and the 31 upgraded from four lanes to six. By accident, rather than transport planning – a question which the city fathers were reluctant to address least they lost their official cars – the little orbital railway connected Helford directly to the heart of the business district in twenty minutes. The Helford Picture House had just become a shopping precinct and thanks to a major settlement by Polish immigrants in the forties there were junior and senior Roman Catholic schools of good reputation. In the neighbouring area of Westwick, he noted a synagogue, sports fields and a little park with a lake and a pseudo-Parisian bandstand, much decayed but still charming.

Ted drew up a list of pros and cons and made only one entry on the negative side. The river was still tidal at Helford and, geographically speaking, about a third of the area, including Fuller's Eyot, was below sea level. At spring tides ducks paddled above the sagging jetties. Another decade of global warming and the site would go the way of Bangladesh. 'Pity.' He shook his head, regretfully and crossed the list through. 'And people have lived there for hundreds of years.' The report damning the site as prone to flooding and uninsurable was already dictated when he left the office on Friday night.

The rain pocked the calm surface of the river and bounced off the flat roof of a houseboat. As he passed, a male figure appeared on the deck, followed by a child. They wore matching blue cagoules and scurried down the gangplank with their heads down, making for an old Toyota. Ted had never realised that people actually lived with children on those things. Surely it was a dangerous place to bring up a child?

At 6.57 am the security camera on the 31 recorded the breakdown of a Land Rover with a horsebox behind it. The vehicle was in the slow lane. Police cars arrived at the scene within five minutes, and directed the traffic around the obstruction while awaiting a tow truck.

The driver of the Land Rover and her companion went around to the doors of the horsebox. What happened next was not clear to the camera. What it recorded was a horse suddenly loose on the highway, and the two women running after it with outspread arms. The homeless youth who had been sitting out of the rain in the girders under the overpass jumped down to help them, but their efforts to restrain the animal only seemed to put it in the mood to party. Soon it was cantering up and down the hard shoulder, throwing bucks energetically to either side, out of control.

The police activated the speed warning signs, which flashed HAZARD AHEAD – DEAD SLOW over both eastbound and westbound lanes of the 31, to the annoyance of the eastbound drivers who had already been at a standstill for a quarter of an hour. A police helicopter with a searchlight was called up, and hovered over the scene tracking the horse, to its considerable alarm. The horse put its head down and galloped towards the Acorn Junction.

Chester Pike's driver carried two suitcases out to the car waiting on the gravel carriageway drive of Grove House. When the man was out of earshot Chester turned to his wife, who had lately taken to sleeping in full make-up and getting up early to restore her face and hair before seeing him off in a lace-edged yellow satin peignoir. Lauren had also started talking about taking a holiday together without the children. Chester was not a sensitive man, but in this matter also his instinct was prompting him to action.

'Goodbye, dear,' he said, kissing her on the forehead while keeping hold of his briefcase.

'Why all the luggage?' Lauren asked, holding him at arm's length, looking at him with uncomfortable directness.

He licked his lips before replying, 'I'm not sure how long I'll be away this time.'

'Why not?' she pressed him. She was trying to hold both his hands but the briefcase allowed her only the left. Now he took his fingers, clammy from his morning shower, out of her grasp.

'There's a lot happening in St Louis,' he answered.

'My sense,' Lauren informed him briskly, 'is that things have been happening in St Louis for quite a while and that it's time you sat down and told me about them.'

'I can't,' he responded with a degree of triumph, 'the flight's at eight ten and we're running late already.'

'I think I deserve to know, Chester.'

'We'll talk when I get back,' he promised her, turning towards the door.

'You're not coming back,' she pointed out.

'I did not say that,' he insisted from the doorstep. 'Take care of yourself. I'll see you soon.'

There seemed little point in waving him off. There seemed little point in the silk peignoir, which she found extremely impractical because it swirled around her legs at every step. Lauren took off the redundant garment and put it on the breakfast bar in the kitchen, the place where she left any clothes she intended to pass on to the housekeeper. Then she went upstairs to change into her street clothes. She was doing morning car pool.

'So, Mr Parsons, if you decided not to recommend Helford to Harrier Homes – what happened?'

Ted was steaming up Riverview Drive, feeling warm and strong and powerful. Maybe he ran better without the weight of Oak Hill on his conscience. Now he was free of the project, it was taking on a doomed look. He had been accustomed, in his career, to seeing expert advice disproved by time, but the way young Sands had reacted to the Oak Hill job had always stuck in his memory. Until he got free of the problem, he had not realised quite how much it had weighed him down.

'Looking back, it was almost like destiny,' he told the imaginary microphone. After closing the file on Fuller's Eyot, a series of serendipitous events typical of the life of a man of twenty-four in the city brought him to a party given by an absolute stranger on a baking summer night, from which he found himself going home with a tall, deep-bosomed, snake-haired beauty, who wore red sandals with four-inch spike heels. Ted woke on his first day in Westwick on a mattress on the floor of a studio in Maple Grove, saw blue sky through green leaves and the beauty naked on a wicker lounger on her verandah, and began to dream.

Ted never gave up his dreams without a fight. In a few years, after he chose a breathless girl with unravelling clothes named Alexandra Azarian to be his dream, this became a source of much misery to him. Back then his persistence was an asset.

The beauty threw him out of the house as soon as he was fully conscious. By temperament Ted was tranquil to a fault, but nothing summoned up his blood as powerfully as rejection. In a daze he rambled through the neighbourhood, goggling at the ancient trees and the Dutch gables, basking in the rosy afternoon sun reflected from the mellow brick walls. The deep peace of Maple Grove restored him. He sensed dignity, exclusivity, stability, a potential of a wholly different order to the crass margins of Harrier Homes. Like a bomb, the recognition that Maple Grove could be everything that Harrier Homes were not crashed through the branches and fell on his head.

Since his car was still in the city he took a train, which was headed the wrong way. Rolling out of Helford, he decided to look at Fuller's Eyot again and on Monday recalled his dictaphone tape and set to work.

Meetings with the river authority and the city environment department and the government environment department took place. Ted read international reports on global warming and consulted professors of geography. Having discovered more than he cared to know about the state of the planet, he lunched underwriters, seeking their opinion on the flood barrier planned in ten years time down river to the east, between the city and the sea.

He concluded that while the world would warm and the sea would rise, the river would also fall and the flood barrier would stand effectively against freak tides and high winds. He predicted that for the next thirty years, Fuller's Eyot would be drier than it had ever been since the first barge tied up there in 1753. This prediction, correct so far, was never shared with the owners of the site, who were relieved to sell to Harrier Homes for what they considered a very reasonable price.

Fuller's Eyot became an estate of new homes named The Willows, and Ted used his end-of-year bonus to buy the end of a lease on the lower half of a house in Church Vale. The next year, he used his bonus to buy the freehold of the house, and helped the upstairs tenants, Mr and Mrs Funk, to buy a brand new ground-floor apartment in a retirement development with a warden just off the Broadway. Mrs Funk came to look on him as a son, and he came to look on her as the living archive of the area because in her rambling conversation he found out every material fact about his neighbours; who was dying, who wanted to move south to be near their children, whose investments had been unwise and who owned the cat's cradle of leases and sub-leases into which most of Tudor Wilde's houses had been divided.

In five years Ted was in business for himself, turning over his first million, about to sell the restored Grove House to Chester, and married with a son. He never saw the beauty again, but he looked out for her every night as he drove home, until Gemma Lieberman came into his life.

'My God, we're only just in time,' marvelled Gemma from the back of the Cherokee as Stephanie swung it past the front of the Channel Ten building, where fifty people stood huddled under umbrellas near the queue sign. 'It's not even seven-thirty yet. Crusty wasn't due till eight.'

'Crusty's over there,' Rod observed, pointing to the VW camper pulling into the roadside. 'This is just the regular audience.'

'Don't these people have lives?'

'I don't think so.' Rod waved his car-park pass at the security officer who raised the barrier and directed Stephanie to a bay with Rod's name painted on it.

'My, you're grand,' Gemma observed, descending from the vehicle with a flounce of her skirts. She had picked a trailing dress of grape-coloured crinkle fabric with a matching embroidered jacket in which to make her screen debut.

'I think my agent felt undervalued. They just gave me whatever he asked. He had to hold out for something. Did we bring umbrellas?'

'God, no . . .' said Gemma, at the same time as Topaz answered, 'Of course,' and pulled a neatly furled parasol from under their seat.

'We'll see you guys later,' Stephanie promised.

Rod signed her in as a guest of *Family First* at the reception desk, where Allie's secretary had already left her name. They went up to his office. Rod changed into his new suit, a splendidly tailored, pin-striped, single-vented, double-breasted affair which endowed him, he felt, with only slightly less authority than the Pope on his Vatican balcony. He reassured Stephanie that his report was safe on a cassette in the inner pocket, and in addition he had mailed copies of it to both the Environment Minister and the Planning Director of Helford & Westwick Council, to arrive that morning.

With jangling nerves and nothing to do for at least an hour, they went up to the canteen for coffee and sat watching the rain sluicing down the window panes. Some die-hard ducks were paddling across the river, swept out into midstream by the yellow foaming effluent from the storm drain which carried the River Hel into the main channel.

Rod ran his fingers down Stephanie's forearm where the faint freckling of summer was fading to white. The damp air had made her hair frizz in a manner he found adorable and she found annoying. Apart from that difference, they were thinking the same thoughts.

'I know we can't ever do that again,' he said, taking hold of her hand, 'but I'm really glad we did it.'

'Yes.' There was nothing to say for a while. Then Stephanie remembered how soft the grass had been under her bare skin. 'I wish I knew what seed they planted,' she said. 'If I ever have a lawn again, I'd like to use it. You have to think of all sorts of things for a lawn, the shade and the drainage and the traffic on it. Making love on it isn't a standard check. But important, really.'

'Will you ever have a lawn again?'

'I don't think so. I'll talk to Stewart when he gets back, but I was the one who wanted to live in Westwick, he's not so concerned.'

'He's definitely OK, then?'

'Yes,' she assured him, touchingly certain. 'They let him send another E-mail yesterday. The Foreign Office say the negotiations are almost over. Not long now.'

In Riverview Drive, Lauren Pike picked up Ben and Jon Carman. Because her son Felix refused to sit within arm's reach of either of the Carman twins, she made Ben sit in the front seat beside her and belted Jon into one of the dickey seats at back of her new seven-seater Mercedes, leaving Felix to share the back seat with Chalice Parsons.

It never occurred to her that she could run a smaller car if the boys did not fight. She also confiscated a toy pistol from Jon.

In Church Grove, Chalice Parsons had made the mistake of trying to hug her mother as part of a bid to be let off school because of the rain. As a result, she had the red imprint of Allie's hand across her cheek, and was made to wait indoors until it had subsided. 'Hurry up, dear,' Lauren chided her. 'We're late.'

No sooner had they turned into the Broadway than it mysteriously filled with vehicles which immediately ground to a halt. Outside Pot Pourri, Marcia was lowering the awning to keep the rain off her stock. Mr Singh had opened up the Kwality Korner Store. A van delivering some of the new season's stock to Bon Ton was too big for the parking bay and slowed the traffic down still more. The boys craned out of the windows to see Sky High's traffic report helicopter bank over Westwick on it way to join the police chopper hovering over the Acorn Junction.

Lauren found herself short of breath. She turned up the air conditioning and reached for her handbag to find her Ventolin. The inhaler did not seem to be there.

'Felix,' she said, handing the bag back to her son, 'you're a clever boy. See if you can find my puffer in my bag now, be a dear.'

A mile further down the Broadway, Ted Parsons made another break with the tradition of the past years and slipped four discs of an entire opera into his CD player. He had decided to graduate to Wagner.

The Rhine maidens were interrupted by the Travelmaster. 'An incident on the Thirty-one at Westwick has fouled up traffic for at least five miles eastbound into the city,' the artificial voice informed him, 'and the westbound lane is also affected. The tailbacks are running down the Forty-six now and all vehicles are advised to avoid the area if at all possible. That's the Thirty-one eastbound at Westwick. All vehicles avoid the area.'

'There's been an incident out on the Thirty-one,' Allie's driver informed her, holding his umbrella reverentially over her head as she inserted herself into the back seat of her car. 'It sounds pretty serious. I don't know what you want me to do . . .'

'If it's bad on the Broadway, cut along Willow Gardens,' she ordered him. 'We can take that little road which runs under the bridge. I can't be late this morning. It's the first show of the new series. I've got a new co-host, poor lamb he's so-o-o nervous, I must, *must* be there early so I can give him confidence.'

CHAPTER 22

A Green Location

Damon didn't mind the rain. For once, he could ignore the cars. The horse was what enthralled him. It had jumped, actually jumped, nimbly picking up all four of its huge flat hooves and flying into the air, jumping over the crash barrier at the central reservation of the Acorn Junction, and now it was eating the weeds as if it this were a field and it was just grazing peacefully on long green grass.

'Don't go near him,' the long-haired woman warned Damon. 'He's dangerous, he'll kick you. Stay away.' But Damon wasn't afraid. The horse was watching him, he could see the white of its eye rolling as he walked towards him. The horse knew he was his friend. They hadn't looked after him; he was very dirty, with mud in his shaggy coat and tangles in his mane. From an old leather head-collar hung a plaited rope of orange plastic twine. He was big, as big as the biggest horse they had at the animal facility at the re-hab place, and brown and white.

'Stay away,' the other woman yelled. 'You'll frighten

him out into the cars. You stupid fucker, stop where you
are.'

The horse shook its mane and carried on cropping the
weeds. 'You shouldn't be here,' Damon informed him.
'This is a dangerous place. You wouldn't believe the
wrecks I've seen out here.'

The horse snorted, as if inviting him to astonish it,
and raised its head. A hank of vegetation hung from its
mouth and it carried on chewing. 'They're not good for
you,' Damon told him. 'They'll give you a bad stomach.
You should eat hay and stuff, good food. Somebody
should take care of you. You're a mess. Here, I've got
something you can eat.'

Earlier in the day he had bought a sandwich at the
Acorn Service Station. He had been eating it when he
saw the horse running up the road, and half of it was still
in its plastic wrapping in his coat pocket. Damon
dragged the packet out.

The horse appeared well acquainted with plastic sandwich packs. Eagerly, it stepped forward and snatched the
snack from Damon's outstretched palm. The wrapping
fell to the ground, and while the horse was snuffling at it
Damon found it was easy to walk around the animal and
get hold of the rope from his head-collar.

This wretched piece of harness immediately disinte-
grated. Damon was an excellent knot-tier. While the
horse returned to eating the weeds, he unravelled the
orange twine, cut a length with his Swiss Army knife,
and mended the head-collar. The horse never even
realised it had been caught.

It was the best thing Damon had ever done in his life.

He felt marvellous, and even better when the first police-
man to arrive at the scene called him a hero and said he
could have a ride in the helicopter one day. The women
who owned the horse, however, were not at all grateful,
and called him nasty names. But Damon was used to
that.

'This is the big one,' yelled Sky High, the traffic reporter
on City Southeast News. 'This is the super SNAFU, the
road to hell, the ultimate gridlock, the biggest traffic
jam I have ever seen in my entire life!'

Below the bank of monitor screens, the crowd shuffling slowly through the reception hall at Channel Ten,
raised a noise somewhat like a cheer. The security men,
noting that they were an unusually lively bunch and
unusually ill-dressed, adopted stern expressions and
paced along the blue rope barrier intended to cordon the
public a safe distance away from the station's staff.

'Yes!' Sky High continued, yelling over the roar of
her helicopter. 'It's our old friend the Thirty-one at Acorn
Junction near Westwick, and it's a nightmare! Nothing
is moving down there, nothing at all, nothing for five
miles in every direction. Do not, repeat, do not even
think of getting on the Thirty-one eastbound or westbound until this incident is over.'

'Another wet Monday in Westwick,' observed Jemima
Thorogood, shaking out her umbrella as she made it
inside the Channel Ten doors.

'The police have told us that the cause of the snarl up

is a horse! A horse running along the edge of the road! Everything has come to a complete stop down there! All vehicles are advised to give this one a miss – I'm talking about the Thirty-one at good old Acorn Junction.'

Another cheer, less ragged this time, rose from the queue. 'Look, do be quiet, please,' Crusty cautioned them. 'Remember we've got something to hide, eh?' Under their coats, the New Green Army were carrying dozens of banners proclaiming PEOPLE NOT PROFITS, NO MORE ROADS and THEY SHALL NOT PASS. They had smoke bombs, firecrackers and bags of flour in their pockets. Somebody had brought along a rabbit's foot for luck, a live foot, with the rest of the live rabbit still attached.

'Mum.' Topaz, who had been following the radio reports on her Walkman, took out one of the ear-pieces and turned to her mother. 'I forgot to tell you. Ted called last night. He said to tell you he'd heard that guy from Magno Supermarkets had been out at Oak Hill asking about Rod and the TV crew.'

'Now you tell me.' Had it not been for Topaz bullying her so much about Ted, and the fact that she was about to bring the man's empire crashing about his ears, Gemma would have allowed herself to feel touched. As it was, she snuffled and pretended offence for her daughter's benefit, while sensing a degree of unreasonable warmth towards him stealing around her heart. Trying to keep her mind on the day's enterprise didn't help. She felt like the sorcerer's apprentice, standing beside the eco rabble which she had raised to avenge the wrongs done to her family. Her spell had worked too well, the process was out of control.

'He calls quite a lot, you know, but I never tell you because you always say you don't want to know. Especially since what happened to Flora.'

'Don't make this my fault,' her mother warned. 'What else did he say?'

'He sent his love.'

'No, I mean anything worthwhile.'

'No. He said Oak Hill wasn't his show any more, that they'd fired him.'

'Oh, good,' responded Gemma incautiously.

'He's got some idea we're doing something, I think. But he didn't say anything. I thought it was pretty nice of him really. Won't he lose a lot of money?'

'Yup,' agreed Gemma, feeling confused. He had called, he cared, he had been fired, he was still a sleaze anyway. She had spent days organising this disaster to hurt him and now he was going to escape, and she was pleased about that. Gemma was not a morning person, she felt the hour was too early for all this. She decided to concentrate on the new threat to their success. 'Crusty, what can they do, the people at Magno? There's nothing they can do, is there? Even if they suss us.'

'Never fear,' Crusty reassured her. He was behind them in the queue with a knitted hat pulled down to hide his dreadlocks. It was not much of a disguise but it was enough. Few people ever realised that off-camera he was definitely below-average height for a man, but then, Topaz recalled, so was Stalin, who had to wear built-up boots and stand on a special podium for Lenin's funeral. 'If they sussed what was going on they could get an injunction, but then they'd have to deliver it.'

He gestured at the TV screen, now showing pictures of six lanes of stationary traffic petrified in the action of entering and leaving the Acorn Junction. 'You have to deliver an injunction by hand. Medieval, really. No fax, no E-mail. The actual document has to be taken from the judge who signs it, and handed over. Can't see anyone getting through unless they were on a bicycle. As long as that Parsons woman is out there in that lot, we've got nothing to worry about.'

'News just coming in – don't give up, down there on the Thirty-one!' Sky High was back on the screen, chattering excitedly into her headset. 'The horse causing the incident has been caught. They've rounded him up and they're bringing him in. That's the Thirty-one at Westwick, stationary in both directions right now because of an incident caused by a horse straying on the road. Hope is at hand, drivers, the horse has been caught. Our friends over there in the police are telling us things will be moving normally again in forty minutes. OK, that's it from me, Sky High at City Southeast News, signing off at nine-twenty.'

'Blow it,' observed Crusty with annoyance. 'That horse is the flyest animal that ever lived. None of us can *ever* catch him.'

'Don't like the look of this,' Allie's driver told her, heading down Willow Gardens as fast as he dared. Since the last occasion he took this route the municipality had elected to install speed humps and half-barriers in the road, so progress was a tedious matter of waiting at every obstruction to negotiate a right of way with the steady stream of cars, driven by men with desperation on their faces, which passed them in the opposite direction. 'Look's like it's blocked up ahead somewhere.'

'It can't be blocked,' retorted his passenger. 'Why should it be blocked?' She pretended not to see her husband in his Discovery bumping disconsolately past her, but felt the first shiver of panic in consequence. Whatever else could justly be said about Ted, he knew the back-doubles in Westwick better than any driver alive, and if he had despaired of this route, something was seriously wrong.

At the bottom of the road they saw through the streaming rain a line of red-and-white-painted iron posts and a metal gate barring the route under the bridge. The posts carried a bright new sign which read: EMERGENCY ACCESS ONLY – ROAD CLOSED.

'Shit,' Allie said, bold faced. 'Shit, shit, shit.'

The driver did not like guttermouthed women. He felt that they were claiming an unfair advantage for their gender in using language which decency would restrain a normal man from employing in the same circumstances.

'You could walk,' he suggested. 'It's only ten, maybe fifteen minutes from here along the towpath. I can give you the umbrella.'

'Don't be ridiculous,' she snarled. 'There has to be some way to get there. I'm on air in forty minutes. It's the first show of the new series. I *must* get there. There's no alternative. What does it mean, emergency access?'

'Only the police, fire service and ambulances. They get a key which unlocks the gate.'

'Well, this is an emergency. Call the police.'

'I can't do that – I'd be prosecuted. I'd lose my licence.'

Allie hissed through her teeth as if facing unreasonable defiance. 'Don't be stupid. Don't you understand? I *have* to get there in time for *Family First*. You're being paid to get me there, for fuck's sake.' The name of the programme could work like a magic spell, but not this time.

The driver took off his cap and smoothed down his hair to give his brain a better look at the problem. 'I can call the studio and tell them what's going on,' he offered ungraciously. 'Traffic report says things'll start moving soon. We can wait it out on the Broadway or try going west around Oak Hill, over the Forty-six and then cutting across the Thirty-one at Acorn Junction. That's all I can think of.'

'How the hell long will that take?'

'On a normal day, less than twenty minutes,' he offered, knowing full well that this morning was far from normal and that every other escape route would be clogged by this time.

'Well then.' She threw herself angrily back in the seat. 'What are you waiting for? And for fuck's sake, *hurry*.'

'She's held up.' In the *Family First* gallery, where the vision mixer was checking that the first frames of Rod's so-called supermarket feature were cued up and ready to roll, the senior producer was moved by the scale of the emergency to half-rise in his chair. 'Allie's held up, everybody. Change the running order. Rod, I'm going to come to you first. We'll go with supermarkets, then the makeover, then we'll hope Allie gets to the studio in time to finish up with the interview.'

'Fine.' In the half-darkness at the back of the gallery, Rod tried to tranquillise himself with breathing exercises. Tension in his neck would rob his voice of resonance. He started relaxing his face muscles one at a time. At the desk in front of him sat Maria. Under the desk top, she was pouring two fingers of vodka into a styrofoam cup from a bottle hidden in her handbag. Doing this, her professional gloss vanished and she looked pathetically young, like a schoolgirl passing a note around the class. It had not occurred to Rod that she might also be feeling the heat. 'You OK?' he asked her.

'I will be,' she muttered covertly, winking over the rim of the cup. 'Butterflies in the guts, that's all. Have a belt?'

'No, thanks.' It was such a little deal to say no that ten minutes had passed and he was down in the studio when he realised he had done it.

'Allie's been delayed, everybody,' announced the director's voice over the PA. 'We're starting with Rod and his film report, hoping she'll get here by the break.'

'I knew it,' muttered the Tarot reader, standing beside Stephanie in the windowless holding tank furnished with stained seating units and a flatulent coffee machine which served the show as a green room. 'I knew it. First card I turned up this morning was The Wall.'

'What does that mean?' asked Stephanie, feeling as if her make-up would crack if she showed too much animation.

'Destruction,' the woman informed her, digging a cigarette out of her handbag. 'Unexpected events, chaos, laying waste, irrevocable changes. It's not a bad card, we should not look at any of the cards as bad in themselves. We are the masters of our own fate. Good can come out of bad. Something in your life is destroyed, it makes way for something better. But most people don't like to get The Wall.'

'No,' murmured Stephanie, watching Rod on the monitor. Looking several million dollars in his glorious new suit, he was listening to someone talking through his ear-piece. His face was radiant with satisfaction, as if the most beautiful woman in the world were whispering endearments to him.

'Is he new?' asked the Tarot reader. 'I don't remember seeing him before. He certainly is cute.'

'Yes,' Stephanie agreed.

'Can we smoke in here?' The woman had the cigarette in her lips and her lighter poised.

'I'm sure you can. I don't mind,' Stephanie told her.

'You're very calm.' The lighter clicked and she exhaled a stream of smoke. 'Aren't you nervous? You don't look nervous?'

'I ought to be nervous.' Stephanie looked down at her knees as if they belonged to another woman. In a mirror, she saw herself sitting in a corner of the worn seating unit, looking quite regally relaxed. The terror of public exposure which she used to feel at the mere idea of television was absent. Other things had grown in its place: a sturdy courage, a trust in life. Curiously, she turned her head and tried to examine her profile – was it there, the poise of the Empress Josephine? Chaos, waste, irrevocable change – for six months she had been eating that stuff for breakfast. She felt like the master of her fate.

Lauren Pike could hear herself wheezing. They were still on the Broadway, fifty yards from the turning for The Magpies. She had sanctioned the use of the Gameboy, passed out crayons and paper, confiscated a crossbow from Ben Carman, played a tape of musical multiplication tables and still the children were squabbling.

Chester was leaving her. He had abandoned them, her children would be fatherless and she herself was being hurled from the heavenly security of being a wife to the deep, dark hell of being a lone woman. She would be victimised and despised now as she had victimised and despised other women, and so would Felix. No one would invite her, her friends would pass her by with 'we must have lunch', she would be pushed off the tennis ladder, supplanted at the Victim Support Scheme. On the fringes of the community, she who had once enjoyed every privilege as her right would be condemned to beg for scraps of attention.

They were late for school. She was going to be late for her morning game. Lauren Pike could not breathe. She knew now where her Ventolin was, in the pocket of that stupid silk robe in her kitchen. Her head was swimming, her vision was clouding, she could not get air into her lungs. Her breath seared her throat like smoke. Her chest felt as if it were being crushed between iron weights.

Lauren realised that she was gasping like a landed fish. She had suffered from asthma for nine years – it had developed shortly after she and Chester had moved into Grove House. There had been a few close calls; without her inhaler an attack could be fatal. Her last priority was not to die in front of the children. She engaged the handbrake, shoved open her car door, got out and collapsed on the grass at the roadside.

Ben Carman watched with interest. 'Hey,' he called to his fellow passengers, 'Felix, your mother is drunk.'

'No she isn't,' was the pained reply, 'she's got asthma.'

'She's getting wet,' observed Chalice with distaste.

It occurred to Ben that this might be an occasion on which the use of the car phone would be perfectly justified. He unfastened his seat belt and called home.

'Mom,' he announced, 'I'm on Felix's Mummy's car phone.'

'Well, get off it right now and quit running up our bill,' Rachel ordered him, angry because neither she nor Josh had this particular piece of equipment in their cars. 'Those calls are expensive, you idiot.' And she cut the line.

Felix was his mother's son, with an unerring instinct for right behaviour. Using all his superior weight, he wrenched the phone from Ben, retreated to the back seat with it and hit the number 9.

'My mummy is having an affsma attack,' he informed the emergency operator.

'OK, dear, now where are you?' she asked him.

'I'm in our Mercedes,' he replied proudly, kicking Ben away as he scrambled towards him between the front seats.

'I mean, what road are you on. The name of the road, dear . . .'

'We're on our way to school,' Felix explained, struggling to get away from Ben's fists.

Jon Carman unbuckled himself and hit Felix in the face with the Gameboy. Chalice screamed. People were getting out of their cars and gathering around Lauren Pike, who was shaking all over on the grass, her first and last involuntary movement.

Behind the Mercedes was a van which had delivered roses to Pot Pourri, and behind that was the car carrying the raging Allie Parsons.

Westwick had not, at that time, been designed to accommodate helicopters with ease. The neighbourhood had an inconvenient number of trees. The police officers who arrived on motorbikes were relieved to be dealing with a life-threatening emergency instead of a quarter of a million cases of road rage; they cleared the entire width of the Broadway for the helicopter ambulance from Helford Hospital to set down. Ted Parsons, grateful for his massive tyres and four-wheel drive, ran the Discovery out of the way up a grass verge, opened an umbrella and got out to watch the helicopter fly in at 9.57 a.m.

The rain had doubled its force. It beat on the helicopter's cockpit and streamed off the jackets of the paramedics as they leaned over Lauren trying to resuscitate her.

Allie watched the helicopter descend with dawning hope. 'I can't stand this, I'm going to see what's going on,' she declared, jumping out of the car. The driver did not feel moved to produce his umbrella. She stepped into the gutter and water filled her dainty slingbacks. As she picked her way through the gathering crowd with all the elegance she could manage, the rain made her mascara run into inky smudges under her eyes. It flattened her prettily blow-waved hair into lank strands across her forehead and stained her sugar-pink jacket to puce. The semiology of Allie Parsons' jackets could have supported a doctoral thesis. She picked red for politics and pink for social issues, darker shades for major celebrities and paler for ordinary people, larger buttons and smaller buttons likewise. Stephanie, being social and lightweight, had merited sugar pink with one tiny pearl button at the waist, which popped off as Allie shoved her way towards the scene of the action.

'I know her!' she shouted to the paramedics. 'She's my friend! My dear, dear friend! Let me through! Please, please, let me through!'

Hesitantly, the crowd drew aside and allowed her to kneel at the feet of the victim.

Ted identified his wife struggling dementedly through the on-lookers and decided he should be on hand in case intervention was necessary.

'Lauren!' squealed Allie, confirming her status. 'Lauren! Oh my God! She has asthma! Is she dying?'

Lauren Pike was only technically alive. They were injecting her heart with adrenaline as Allie knelt beside her but in a few minutes it was clear that she was not going to respond. Around her nose and mouth her skin, evenly tanned toffee-colour from daily tennis, turned a deathly blue-white. The urgency of the group gathered around the body drained away. Somebody picked Lauren's handbag, a little leather purse, off the grass where it had fallen and put it beside her. With proper respect, the paramedics lifted the body on to a stretcher, arranged the limbs tidily, laid a blanket over them and fastened the straps.

Allie seized one of Lauren's feet. 'Oh my God,' she wailed. 'Oh my God. I can't believe this. Lauren! Oh my God. Where are you taking her?'

The police kept the crowd back as the stretcher was raised and carried it towards the helicopter.

'Where are you going?' Allie demanded, stumbling alongside. 'She's dead, isn't she? Where are you taking her? Are you going back to Helford Hospital?'

'Alex!' Ted stepped forward and put his arm around his wife's shoulders. 'Calm down. There's nothing—'

'Fuck off!' She hit his hand away. 'She's our friend and she's . . . don't you feel anything?'

'She'll be at Helford Hospital. That's the procedure,' a paramedic confirmed, thinking he was dealing with a woman distraught with grief.

Blessed hope flowered in Allie's heart. Here was the way out. From the hospital she could taxi to the studio in three minutes. 'Let me come!' she begged the man, getting as far away from Ted as possible. 'She's my friend! I

455

can't bear to see her alone like this! I can't leave her, I can't! Please . . .'

They were about to help her into the cockpit when a police officer carrying a child ran forward through the driving rain.

'Mummy!' screamed Chalice, now purple in the face after an extended period of hysterics. 'Mummy! Mummy!' And she struggled furiously in his grasp, holding out her arms in supplication.

'This is your daughter?' the officer asked.

'Oh yes,' Allie answered dismissively, making no effort to take Chalice from the officer. 'Don't worry about her, she'll be fine. They're on their way to school. My husband's right there, for God's sake, he can take them.'

The faces around her disagreed. They said that a child's place was with its mother, and a mother's place was with her child, definitely not in an air ambulance carrying a dead person to her penultimate resting place. But Ted stepped forward to claim his screaming daughter and Allie inched closer to the helicopter.

'Look,' Allie pleaded, suddenly collected. 'You have to take me. I'm Allie Parsons from *Family First*. Channel Ten, you know? I'm due on air right now, right now, right this minute. It's a live show, you know. First show of the new series. A new co-host, new to TV. I've been caught in this appalling traffic . . .'

The officer, the pilot and the paramedics never saw daytime TV, nor were they regular readers of *Hey!* magazine. They saw before them a skinny woman with running make-up, stupid shoes and an unpleasantly demanding manner, a child in ear-splitting distress who claimed that this was her mother and a man looking wretched and helpless. Their instinct was that this was a spoiled sensation-seeking bitch, quite possibly a nutter, and both child and husband were seriously unhappy. And the traffic was backed up for miles around.

'Best get away, boys,' the police officer ordered, nodding to the pilot and beckoning a comrade to deal with Allie. 'Stand back, please. Let them take off. You can follow on to the hospital by road. Stand back, please.' Allie was hanging on to the side of the helicopter with both hands. Preparing to detach her, an officer put his hands over hers and used the most powerful argument he could think of. 'What about your car, madam? You can't leave your car, can you?'

Allie pretended to have been persuaded, and nodded her head. The office released her hands. When she was free she leaped for the open door of the air ambulance as the runners left the ground. The nearest paramedic decided it was safest now to pull her aboard.

CHAPTER 23

Good Gravelly Sub-soil

This was what TV was all about: seizing the time, pushing your advantage, getting your story. In the air ambulance, Allie crouched beside the stretcher bearing the body of Lauren Pike to Helford Hospital and felt the adrenaline surge through her veins.

'Look,' she explained to the team of two paramedics, one male, one female, who were looking at her with distaste, 'I'm sorry about all that back there. I know I shouldn't have jumped. I was just – distraught. Distraught with grief, you know? But it was wrong of me. I apologise, I'm sorry.'

'Take it easy,' suggested the woman guardedly.

'Yes,' Allie agreed, glancing at the body with lash-trembling tenderness. 'She was such a dear, dear friend to me. So dear. A wonderful woman, you can't imagine . . . or, perhaps you can. Doing such wonderful work, I mean. I mean, you do too. Wonderful work.'

The paramedics caught each other's eyes, looked down and said nothing.

'So dedicated. You must be so dedicated to do this

job,' Allie pressed on, confident of her victory. 'I've often thought we should do something on *Family First* about people like you. You know, the stress, the drama, the personal fulfilment of being a paramedic. It's so important. Society just wouldn't function without people like you.'

Nobody spoke. The engine roared, the storm lashed the craft as it flew over Acorn Junction; on the ground below, half a million vehicle lights gleaming blearily through the sheeting rain. The helicopter banked to head for the hospital. Allie checked her watch. It was 10.12 am. Not much time left.

'Look, I'm much better now,' she pressed on. 'I'm really quite all right. It's been a terrible morning, with the traffic and everything. This . . . terrible tragedy . . . was just the end. I'm late for the studio, you know. I should have been on air at ten, but it's all right, they had a film report they can fill in with. Our show goes out live. What I was wondering was . . . the studio has a heli-pad, you know. You could just put down and let me out. It wouldn't take a minute. I mean, there's no hurry now, is there?'

There was a pause while the two paramedics believed their ears. 'We can't do that,' said the man at last, speaking awkwardly because his mouth was stiff with amazement.

'Yes, you *could*,' wheedled Allie, as much as a woman can wheedle when shouting over a throbbing engine. 'It's the Channel Ten building, just over there.' She gestured out into the storm. 'You could just drop me off and fly back to the hospital. Easy.'

'I'm not hearing this,' he muttered, appealing to his colleague for help.

'Take it easy,' the woman suggested again. People did awful things when they were grieving.

'But how can I?' Allie's eyes were wide. 'I have to be on air right now. Right now. Four million viewers. How can I let them down?'

'What about your friend here?' the woman suggested, gently.

'She wouldn't mind,' Allie assured them. 'If she were here now – I mean, here and alive now – she'd say, 'Go on, Allie. You go on. You can't be late.' She was so understanding. She hated anyone to be unprofessional.'

'Yeah,' said the man, shifting his position uneasily. 'Well.'

'So you'll do it?' Allie persisted. 'Just tell you friend the pilot? Or shall I tell him? I can go . . .' She half-stood, but the woman pulled her firmly down.

'Stay here,' she ordered. 'Sit down now. Everything's OK. You've had a shock . . .'

'But I'm over that now and I must—'

'No!' It was dawning on the woman that this was less than a case of emotional trauma and more a display of epic selfishness. 'Sit down now, please, madam.'

Sulkily, Allie subsided. Her next idea was to try bribery, but her money was in her briefcase and that was still on the ground in the back of the studio car. She sniffed. Her eye fell on Lauren's purse, respectfully tucked under one of the straps holding the blanket over the body.

Allie sniffed again, more loudly, and reached for the

purse. 'Tissues,' she muttered. With her fingertips, she opened the purse, which fortunately did contain a small pack of tissues. Under cover of dabbing her eyes and patting her nose, Allie investigated further, looking for cash. Instead she found Jon Carman's toy pistol.

She crushed the tissue and let it fall, then took hold of the toy, clamped one finger over the maker's trademark and sat as far away from the paramedics as she could in the hope they would not would notice that her weapon was made of plastic.

'All right,' she snapped. 'This is a gun. Now tell the pilot to drop me at Channel Ten.'

The paramedics cursed under their breath. Operating procedures were quite clear: in the event of a threat of attack with a firearm – any threat whatsoever – they should send a coded message to air-traffic control in West Helford but obey the attacker's instructions and do everything possible not to endanger life. The man slowly got to his feet and moved forwards towards the pilot.

'Quicker!' ordered Allie, twitching the gun. 'I must be there by half-past.'

'Welcome back to a new series of *Family First*.' Rod stood squarely in front of Camera One. 'I'm your new host, Rod Fuller, and I'm standing in for Allie Parsons, who's been unavoidably delayed on her way to the studio. I'd like to introduce you to our first guest, Stephanie Sands, an ordinary *housewife* whose life was shattered earlier this year by a *disaster* beyond her worst nightmares . . .'

Stephanie sat on the sofa and smiled at him trustingly. Success was a few seconds away. The glow around them was not lighting but the euphoria of victory.

In the gallery, the vision mixer's finger lay feather-light on the cue button for the taped report. The senior producer frowned intently at the screen, marvelling at the rapport the new Himbo had with the camera. In the audience, the New Green Army hugged their banners closer to their chests. The rabbit struggled, and its bearer was so rapt in the proceedings that he put the animal down, and it sat for a while by his feet, getting its bearings.

Rod turned back to Camera One and deployed the foxy grin. Around the country, three million woman stopped whatever they were doing and sat down to watch, feeling as if spiders were waltzing around the backs of their knees. 'But first,' he continued winningly, 'a report on something which increasingly affects all our lives . . .'

The helicopter set down at Channel Ten at 10.22 am, a good ten minutes before the handful of available police officers from Helford Station ran into the precinct. An anti-terrorist squad was on its way in another helicopter from the centre of the city, but they also arrived long after the small pink figure tottered frantically on its high heels across the tarmac and into the building. From force of habit, Allie made her entrance through the front reception hall, where the head of the queue for the next show stood thankfully in the dry, watching the monitors above them.

'Shit!' muttered Allie, seeing multiple pictures of Rod standing in front of the excavations at Oak Hill. The sound from the monitors had been muted, so she paid no attention to what he was saying. 'Shithead! What's he doing in a suit, for fuck's sake!'

Seeing a filthy, demented, dishevelled woman swearing violently in front of the reception desk, and the three receptionists shooting anxious glances in his direction, a security officer approached her.

'Can we help you, madam?' he enquired, allowing his mass in its blue and green uniform to loom menacingly over her head.

'For fuck's sake,' she said again, 'call up to make-up and tell them to get ready. And wardrobe, they gotta find me something to wear. Anything, anything. I'll take over after the break. Hurry!'

'Are you sure you're in the right place, madam?'

'No, I'm not in the right place, you fuckwit. I should be up there!' And she pointed at the monitors, almost jumping out of her shoes with rage.

'Madam, we're going to have to ask you to leave . . .'

'Are you out of your mind?' For the first time, Allie focused on the man in front of her, her eyes now indigo with urgency. 'Don't you realise who I am? I'm Allie Parsons and that's my show . . .'

The security officer was about to escort her to the door when a grey-faced child detached itself from the queue and ran with flapping unlaced trainers over to Allie, carrying a McDonald's bag and a pencil. These the child held mutely under her nose. Recalling the gracious behaviour that her public deserved, Allie smiled on the brat and leaned on the reception desk to autograph the bag with due ceremony, returning it with an affectionate chuck under the grimy chin. The child ran away.

'It's her,' one of the receptionists whispered to the security officer. 'She's been held up in traffic today. She must have walked. But it is her.'

'Of course, Mrs Parsons,' the guard intoned, saluting as he stood courteously aside. 'I do beg your pardon, I should have known it was you. I'll have someone call the studio straight away. Straight away. I do beg . . .' Without wasting time to abuse him any further, Allie sped into the elevator hall and took the express to the studio.

As the doors closed on her, the first police officers ran into the building.

'Later this week, we'll be offering the Oak Hill Development Trust the opportunity to explain *why they* want to build a business park where ten thousand people will come to work every day on a piece of land which is *so poisoned* that nobody should even be walking on it without a mask and protective clothing,' Rod leaned into the camera confidently, making up the words as he spoke and quite intoxicated by his own fluency. 'And we hope that the Helford and Westwick Council planning office will be able to tell us just *why* they gave permission for this development. And today on *Family First*, after the break, I'll be talking to Stephanie Sands . . .' – From Camera Two came a shot of Stephanie, smiling serenely in her new hound's-tooth check suit from Bon Ton, poised on the sofa – 'who has just found out that *her house* is going to be *knocked down* to make way for a road to the development. How's *that* for your ultimate suburban nightmare? So stay with us now, we'll be back *very soon* . . .'

An eruption of cheering and applause from the audience greeted the *Family First* logo, something colourful featuring flowers and a rising sun, which flashed on to the screen before the commercials rolled. The rabbit, lolloping purposefully down one of the aisles, froze in alarm.

'Isn't that our kidnap wife?' demanded the senior producer of no one in particular.

'What it is . . .' Maria got up and came over to sit on the arm of the director's chair next to him. She was perfecting the earnest yet pouting manner, Meryl Streep does Betty Boop, for those little moments when a woman just has to front up to trouble and argue that black is white. 'We did start with her as a kidnap wife, I know. But it turns out her husband's going to be released now. Only he's coming home to find his house is going to be demolished, you see? It's even better, isn't it? I mean, it was two tragedies for the price of one kind of thing. How could we turn it down?'

'How indeed.' The senior producer ruffled what was left of his hair with the end of a pen, looking perplexed but intrigued. 'Oak Hill Development Trust, yeah? Isn't Allie tied into that somehow. That husband . . .'

'He's resigned,' the senior researcher put in gallantly. 'It was on the financial news last week.'

Maria looked squarely at the producers. 'This was such a great story . . .'

'Great story!' The senior researcher, scenting freedom, backed her all the way.

'You mean, this was Allie's tip?' The senior producer suddenly seemed downcast.

'No!' Maria insisted, 'No – she – ah – well –'

'She doesn't know?'

'Well, not exactly . . .'

The senior producer weighed the value of his star against the value of the show, and found that Allie lost. She'd be fired, but so would they. On the other hand, another season of having his nuts vaporised by that over-active Barbie doll might have been too much. He might just walk away with enough career to save.

A telephone warbled on the console and the vision mixer answered it. 'No kidding!' she squeaked. 'No kidding! They want you . . .' and she handed the producer the telephone. He listened attentively, rolling his eyes.

'Right,' he said. 'Right, right, I got ya. Right.' And he hung up. 'People,' he announced, suddenly full of the joy of incident, 'there's an emergency. Right here. A real one. Some woman hijacked a helicopter and ran into the building just now. She's armed and dangerous. Because we're transmitting, security are going to cordon us off. Rest of the building's being evacuated. Of course, Alamo rules apply – anyone who wants to leave now . . .' He looked around the room, but nobody moved. The rush of live breaking news was making all eyes sparkle. The idea of giving the audience the same chance to avoid being shot was not considered.

'OK. Better speak to the studio.' He reached for a switch. 'Rod?'

Rod heard the voice of the senior producer buzzing in his ear-piece. 'Emergency situation in the building, some woman with a gun – security are on the case, nothing to worry about, just carry on, OK?'

'Sure,' Rod agreed, uneasy. Excitement was making the man talk at twice his usual speed.

'Oh – and – uh, great report, Rod, great, great . . . next time, if you have to reschedule a film like that, remember to check with the gallery here that everyone's up to speed with the transmission schedule, OK?'

'Yeah, sure, OK.' Standing in the middle of the set, Rod looked over the heads of the audience in the vague direction of the gallery, which was invisible at the far back of the auditorium. Since his microphone carried his voice, all he had to do was speak into the air like Moses chatting to God on Mount Ararat. The rush of being on camera was wearing off. Where, he asked himself, was the barrage of outrage and complaint for which he had rehearsed. They had both been fully prepared for Stephanie's half of the programme to be summarily axed. 'You're really OK with this?' he ventured.

'Yeah, yeah. Absolutely,' the senior producer reassured him, a chuckle in his voice. 'But thank God Allie's been caught up in traffic, eh?'

'*Why, may I ask?*' Had it been possible for him to turn into a pillar of salt, the senior producer would have done so. As it was he shuddered momentarily, turned around and faced his star. Allie stood in the doorway, stripping off her wet jacket and kicking off her ruined shoes while a make-up artist behind her combed back her hair. 'Gel,' she ordered, 'no time for anything else. Slick it back. Then the face. Hurry.'

'Thank God you're safe,' he blustered. 'There's a maniac on the loose in the building. With a gun. Didn't you see the security . . .'

'Network's coming to us in ninety,' announced the vision mixer, preparing to begin transmission again. A wardrobe assistant appeared with a green jacket, apologising.

'It'll have to do,' Allie told her, twitching her arms down the jacket sleeves with reptilian speed. 'I'll sit behind the worktop. Tell the floor. I'm coming down.'

'Allie's doing the interview behind the desk, everybody. Move Stephanie over now. Coming to us in one minute.'

Stephanie, having heard nothing of this, only saw the floor manager convulse into action and leap towards her. 'I'm going to have to move you,' he announced, snatching the microphone from her lapel. Obediently she got up from the sofa and followed him to the tiled worktop usually reserved for mixing the Cake of the Week where she struggled on to a high stool and looked around for Rod. A sound man appeared to help her re-fix the microphone.

Rod had not moved from the sofa area. He was listening intently to his ear-piece, an expression of tragedy settling on his face. He shook his head, looked over at Stephanie, mimed something unguessable and waved crossed fingers. The sound man scurried over and detached his mike. Immediately he ran over to Stephanie.

'God, I got my worst marks for mime,' he hissed in her ear. 'What I meant was, the bitch is back. It's over to you. Break a leg, sweetheart!' A strong warm hand squeezed her thigh and then he was gone, back in the twilight zone beyond the studio lights.

'Ladies and Gentlemen!' The floor manager was capering out in front of the audience. 'Our star presenter, award-winning hostess of *Family First* – Allie Parsons! Put your hands together everybody . . .' He waved his arms, trying to conjure applause. The illuminated signs under the monitor screens facing the audience flashed the word 'Applause'. A few biddable souls clapped. Allie appeared at the back of the seating, scampered down the aisle waving left and right to the silent audience, and tripped over the rabbit.

People laughed. In the gallery, Maria laughed so severely that she got hiccups. At the edge of the set, Rod laughed from the depth of his diaphragm, the sound of Jove chuckling over a thunderbolt. Stephanie laughed so heartily that the last shred of fear in her heart evaporated. The rabbit's owner, with an air of deep injury, struggled out of his seat and recaptured the animal.

The floor manager helped Allie to a stool on the far side of the counter, where her wet pink skirt, ruined hose and bare feet were concealed. The make-up artist combed her hair again. Somebody shoved two coffee cups in front of them. The audience subsided to titters. The red light on Camera Three flashed.

'Welcome *back*,' gushed Allie, almost falsetto with relief that she had triumphed over every foe to reach her goal. 'Welcome back to *Family First*. I'm Allie Parsons. I'm sorry I wasn't here for the first half of our programme, but well, I'm here now and isn't this cosy?' She pulled a cup towards her and pretended to sip coffee. 'Just like home! Only for my guest here, Stephanie Sands, home hasn't been so sweet lately, has it Stephanie?'

The light on Camera Three died. The operator dragged Camera Two closer to Stephanie and the light shone red. Allie mugged encouragement at her. Out in the audience, she saw Gemma give her a thumbs-up. 'No,' Stephanie agreed. 'Ever since I found out that our house was going to be demolished to make way for a road to the new business park, things have been just about as bad as they could be.'

'*Huh?*' Allie almost dropped the cup, slopping coffee on the worktop.

'My house is going to be demolished,' Stephanie repeated, suddenly feeling as if champagne were running in her veins instead of blood. There was a warm patch on her thigh where Rod had touched her. She caught Allie's gaze, noting that the true colour of the eyes was a dismal muddy grey. 'You know, the house which you picked out for me, Allie. For me, and my husband and our baby. Because you were my friend, you said, you picked this house for us. And now it's going to be knocked down so they can build a road to the new business park. At Oak Hill.' In her mind's ear, Stephanie heard four million people gasp in outrage.

Allie was white with surprise and making a strange gurgling sound. As if trying to call a waiter, she was waving at the gallery while she was out of shot. The light on Camera Three suddenly shone again.

'Get ready,' muttered Crusty to the eco-warrior next to him in the audience. 'Get ready,' he warned Gemma. 'About a minute now. Pass it on.'

'Stephanie,' Allie broke in with relief, 'I'm going to have to stop you right there. We're having a little technical problem—'

'No you aren't,' Stephanie told her, standing up and leaning over the counter. 'The problem you're going to have, Allie, is that you were a director of this Oak Hill Business Park, so you're not just a lousy excuse for a friend, you're also responsible . . .' From the corner of her eye she saw a banner appear in the audience. GREED KILLS, it read. Jemima Thorogood was holding it up with both hands, waving it from side to side. She saw more people standing up, unwrapping their coats and pulling out their hidden weapons – 'Responsible, in fact, for trying to poison at least ten thousand people . . .'

Allie jumped off her stool and ran out to the front of the spotlit stage. With malicious attentiveness, the operator in charge of Camera Three swung around and followed her. 'Cut!' she shouted, waving with both arms to the impervious gallery. 'Cut it! Cut it now! This woman's crazy! Get security . . .' A paint ball exploded by her feet and she jumped. A string of lighted firecrackers sailed through the air and landed behind her. Allie saw herself on a monitor, a lank-haired, paint-spattered, gesticulating scarecrow, and she screamed.

As Stephanie recoiled from the firecrackers she found Rod beside her, scooping her protectively to his side. 'Brava!' he whispered, ducking to dodge a flour bomb. 'Now let's get the hell out of here.'

Eco-warriors waving banners were climbing over the seats and jumping on the stage. 'Forward!' shouted Crusty, tearing off his hat and tossing it into the crowd. A dog had appeared from somewhere, barking in ecstacy. People at the back were throwing toilet rolls. Topaz jumped on one of the sofas, waving the flag of the New Green Army.

'Rock and *roll*,' muttered the senior producer in the gallery happily. 'We can stay with this a minute or two. Grass-roots reaction. All good television, I think.'

CHAPTER 24

The Most Approved Sanitary Arrangements

The riot in the Channel Ten studios, when local campaigners protesting against plans to develop a toxic site in Westwick were joined by the mercenaries of the New Green Army under their famous leader, Crusty, was blessed a thousand times by the compilers of the midday, six-o'clock and evening news bulletins, who had live footage to engage their audiences, and by all the newspaper editors, who slapped a large picture of Crusty on their front pages. Crusty had one arm around Clara Funk, who held a placard insisting PEOPLE FIRST.

An inquiry into the Oak Hill Development Trust was immediately ordered by the environment department, and by Sunday the supplements had geared up to crucify Helford & Westwick Council, with Chester Pike and Adam DeSouza nailed up each side as the accompanying thieves. Ted Parsons was highlighted as the heroic whistle-blower who had resigned his directorship and left his wife rather than see profits put above public health.

Stephanie stayed in bed that Sunday morning. She felt oddly fragile. Max, of course, said nothing, but padded to the kitchen to make her coffee and bring it up on a tray with a bowl of Crunchy Nut Cornflakes and a red leaf from the garden. Whereupon she found herself crying. The day had been the day she had dreamed of for six whole months, the day Mr Capelli called from the Foreign Office to announce that the negotiations were over and Stewart was coming home. She had been bursting into tears at odd moments ever since; tears of joy, she told herself, knowing that there were other emotions involved as well. Fear, for instance, and a little shame for having fallen short of perfect fidelity, and sadness for the bold, independent self she feared she would now have to put in a basket and file away. But mostly joy. Joy for Stewart, and for herself and her son, alone and undefended no more.

Stewart Sands, who was awarded a copy of the *Sunday Post* by the first secretary of the Embassy in Moscow before boarding his Aeroflot flight home, looked at the picture of Crusty and discovered it meant less to him than if it had been an alien from another universe. The world to which he was returning seemed bizarre.

Stephanie and Max were there to meet him at the airport. Stephanie thought he looked thinner, warier and calmer. Stewart thought that his wife had somehow regained the enchanting something which had captivated him the first moment he saw her. It was a bewitching, thrilling, indefinable quality, the vital essence of her, which he thought he must have overlooked for a few years in all the hurly-burly of young parenthood. He felt he might be able to make sense of the world again.

Stephanie knew that her husband had overlooked nothing. She had lost herself for a while in Westwick, allowed her spirit to follow a chimera, the seductive dream of an ideal life which had no existence at all except in the minds of people who felt their lives were less than ideal and sought to buy their way into perfection. As soon as she sensed that her husband had reoriented himself, she told him she wanted to move back into the city.

Allie Parsons was arrested for obstructing the emergency services in doing their duty. She was released without charge, but betrayed to the media by an indignant police officer and slimed in the tabloids over her connection with the now notorious Oak Hill Trust. Sacked by Channel Ten, she moved to Los Angeles to make a new career, lost ten years from her age and married a plastic surgeon.

The senior producer of *Family First* seized on Rod Fuller and ensured that he followed his sensational debut with a tri-partite documentary on urban renewal which won them the Prix Italia. Rod then found himself propelled to Channel Ten's flagship news programme. Maria d'Amico took over *Family First*. Eighteen months later Rod and Maria got married, with Sweetheart as a still-dubious bridesmaid. In their pre-nuptial agreement they pledged never to court the curse of *Hey!* magazine by allowing it into their lovely home.

Topaz Lieberman decamped to Strankley Ridge to be with Crusty, but after a winter of boiling water to wash

clothes and trying in vain to stop the eco-warriors treading mud into the yurt she moved back to her family,
arguing that a presence in the city was essential for the
next phase of the revolution. Damon Parsons also joined
the New Green Army. The horse was soon an unrecog-
nisably well-turned-out animal, the brown parts of its
coat glowing like new chestnuts and its mane neatly
pulled to a length of nine inches. To ensure the Army's
self-sufficiency, widen their skill resources, keep the horse
shod and enjoy hammering things, Damon signed on for
a vocational degree in blacksmithing at Whitbridge
University.

Harrier Homes took over the remains of Tudor Homes
and allowed Ted to resign with dignity and a pay-off
which he considered perfectly reasonable. He moved in
with Gemma and they were robustly happy, although
the cat terrorised Moron and Ted found that the pain of
living in a botched modernisation was like having a
tooth abscess.

When the Sun Wharf project was completed they
moved into an apartment there with their five girls, and
argued about the roof-terrace, which Gemma wanted to
plant as a urban jungle and Ted saw in more formal
terms. She called him boring. He called her unreasonable. She called him controlling. He called her
impractical. She stuffed a handful of manure down the
neck of his shirt. Flora demanded silence for the comple-
tion of her project on Psychotherapy and the Practice of
Martial Arts.

The manure was not as well rotted as it should have
been. Ted took a lengthy shower, was encouraged to find

that the plumbing functioned perfectly and retired to his own territory, his study, where he unpacked the sad crate of his personal things from his office at Tudor Homes. Jackson Kerr's advertisement for the second phase of Maple Grove houses was dusty but unscathed.

'*Maple Grove*,' it proclaimed in lettering with fanciful serifs such as was used in story-book illustrations:

The Healthiest Place in the World – annual death rate under 6 per thousand.
Only 20 minutes from the City Centre
Close to Westwick Green station.
The Estate is built on Gravelly Soil and has the most approved Sanitary Arrangements.
Cozy Comfort
A Green Location

About 500 houses on the Estate, all in the picturesque Dutch Farm style of Architecture.
A Garden to every House
Hot and cold water to every House
Good cheap Day Schools on the estate
Peace assured by the Vigilance Committee

Also: St Nicholas's Church
A Club for Ladies and Gentlemen
General Stores and Provisioners
Tennis Courts
Masquerades every month
Regular Dances
A School of Art

The Tudor Theatre
A Ladies' Discussion Society
A Natural History Society
Weekly lectures on Scientific, Literary and
    Political subjects

Several new houses now available at reasonable prices.

These attractions were listed around a picture of a woman dressed very much like the milkmaids in the nursery rhyme books of the period, with a spotless long apron tied around her tiny waist and a pretty white cap pulled low over her hair, although a few curling wisps escaped to frame her little upturned nose. Two smiling infants crowded at her skirts, the boy dangling a wooden soldier, the girl cradling a doll, both gazing adoringly up at their mamma, and behind this Madonna-like tableau billowed a garden of flowering shrubs and a tree-crowned hillside. The actual houses, Ted noticed for the first time, were not pictured at all.

He took it out to the living room, intending to find a place for it on the brand new, freshly plastered, papered and painted wall which had never been pierced by a picture pin before.

'Look at this,' he suggested to his newly extended family.

'Oh, that's *so* pretty,' Molly sighed.

'It's *so* bullshit,' her mother retorted.

'But it is a really pretty picture,' said Flora.

'It's old,' sniffed Chalice.

'It can't be old, its Princess Di,' protested Cherish.

'No, it's old,' Ted told them. 'It was the original advertisement for Maple Grove, printed in a newspaper before our house in Church Vale was even built. It must be – oh – seventy years old at least. Where shall we hang it?' He was happy that he was getting the hang of hands-on parenting at last.

'Nowhere,' ruled Topaz. 'It belongs in a museum.'

In a few more years, Whitbridge swallowed up Ambleford, and the stone circle at Strankley Ridge was allowed to decorate the central reservation of a new traffic interchange. A leisure consortium took fibreglass casts of the standing stones and made them part of a new theme park, The Stone Age Experience.

Westwick did not change. Westwick never really changed. New families moved in and barbecued together in summer. The thrush in the flowering crab in New Farm Rise built a nest every year and successfully launched its young into the sky. The Oak Hill site was dedicated to an experimental green-tech project exploring the ability of trees to absorb soil pollutants. Groves of willow, poplar and alder were planted, with the intention of felling them in due time to enable the land to be profitably utilised.

Read on to enjoy the tantalising first chapter of

Sunset

The new novel by
CELIA BRAYFIELD

Available in its entirety as a Little, Brown hardback

CHAPTER 1

Beach Bar

Only certain people come here. The sign at the end of the row of white concrete buildings says 'Placido's Beach Bar', with a kinked arrow below to tell you to walk around the back of the buildings to get there. The sign is old and hard to read, the street looks like the streets where people get shot in spaghetti westerns. Square white buildings turn blind walls to the space. It's empty and it promises to lead nowhere.

There is no beach here. This is the rocky end of the bay; the bar overlooks long ridges of black rocks which lie in jumbled spines like dinosaurs' backbones between the land to the sea. However, the sign is not a joke. In spirit, Placido's is a beach bar. *The* beach bar. Once you've been there, the only beach bar.

The beach at La Quemada is the other way, a shining field of wet sand running maybe two kilometres to the black cliffs. The sea is always rough, the waves are huge. At low tide, because there is almost no slope on the beach, the sea boils over itself halfway to the skyline, angry and silent. When the tide rises the waves come racing in over the sand faster than you can run. Boys are drowned every year. With the strong wind from the north, storming down from Africa, Quemada is a great surf beach, but deadly to the innocent. There is never a lifeguard, nobody bothers much running up flags. The island lets people take their chances. I used to think this was callous; Stella thinks it's how the Spanish death thing works out; they give people a decent opportunity to get killed.

The wet sand is silvery. At the back of the bay, beyond the reach of the sea, it becomes yellow and rises to a stretch of low, shifting dunes. Nothing has taken root here, no grasses, none of the glaucous plants holding down the soil farther inland. Hippies have made wind-breaks out of small rocks, semicircular half-huts. They play house in them, huddle up over a joint, build a little fire and leave scorched hearthstones; the ash is soon blown away.

When the tide is in and the sun shines, the air below the cliffs is full of sea spray and you can watch the rain-bows all day, little arcs forming and fading and reforming until the light fades. The cliffs are vast, a wall of rock a thousand feet high, curving round to make a colossal basin which the sea fills with water vapour. The waves roar; you have to shout into the noise. But the beach is not this way and Placido doesn't want passing trade. He wants the people who trust their dreams. We are the ones who will follow the faded sign pointing in the wrong direction down a street fit to die in, because we have faith that what we seek will be there at the end. So far in my life, I have absolutely believed that what I wanted was there at the end. Now it seems possible that I was wrong.

The street ends at the bar. Streets on this island used to be mostly like this one, pointless strips of sandy earth around the buildings, scattered with small black pebbles. There are no footprints, no tyre tracks, no paw marks, no dog turds, no litter, no flies. The wind erases everything, sweeping whatever is unwanted out into the ocean. There is no need for paving because there is never mud, because there is never rain, except when there is. But when all the rain collected in the idiotically primitive device which I sometimes tend at the Instituto de Geografía is added up, the annual fall in Los Alcazares isn't usually more than an inch.

With the wind and the sun and the dust, people stay indoors if they can and keep their shutters closed, so the streets are empty. Not that Quemada would have much street life. When I first came here the whole place was maybe six houses, plus the boat house, and the bar.

Stella brought me here. She taught me to find these little waterholes of pleasure in the desert of my life. Placido's was the best of them. Now I come here and she doesn't. I brought Matthew here. It ought to be a place for lovers, but not many come. Perhaps lovers are too anxious for their perfect moments, too unsure of each other to take the chance and follow the sign, and so paradoxically they miss the peak experience which they're looking for. Instead they find something pleasant but mediocre; they turn the other way, to the new restaurant on the hill, a smart place with white sun umbrellas over the tables, but nothing compared to Placido's.

Stella doesn't come to Quemada at all now. The island has no more pleasures to offer her. She is bored with them all, especially since I brought Matthew along. She wouldn't come here with him, so I've come here, but I don't like having my dream faded and blemished and compromised by these pathetic moves.

The door is usually open and the curtain of plastic straps in truly horrible colours, brown, orange, green, cream, hides the interior. There is a stone floor and a Formica-topped bar and a poster of the fish of the tropical Atlantic as an aid to ordering. Maybe there's a man or two men sitting at one of the little plastic tables, smoking. From time to time – you learn never to expect normal sights at Placido's – a bowl of octopus salad or a platter of tortillas may sit on the counter. The door behind the bar is open sometimes; you get a glimpse of black rocks and sea.

You go through this room to the terrace, which is a small area of gravel fenced in to the height of the table tops by screens of split bamboo and shaded by a roof of the same flimsy material. However, people mostly come here in the late afternoon, when the sun is no longer cruel. The tables are wooden, the legs painted green. 'This is very Zen,' was Matthew's comment. It is all very plain, very essential. There's very little wind because the cliffs cut it out. So you sit down.

It feels like the beauty begins then, but of course the beauty had no beginning, you just begin to be with it. The rocks run out to the sea, the waves break over the rocks and the sun sets. Stella says the island has the most beautiful sunsets in the world, and she has spent a lot of time in her life checking out the contenders, so I believe her. On the south side of the island you see the sun fall out of sight behind the mountains, making them look harder and denser as the light fades. Here on the north side the sun sinks right into the sea, slowly, slowly, passing through layers of sky vapour, slow-motion fireworks, violet, orange, pink, red. The last rays blaze up from the sea, tinting the underside of the dark clouds with fire, gilding the waves.

The sunset takes about two hours from the time the sky gets the first wisps of rose. This is an island full of wonders, but the sunset from here is the greatest of them, and Placido's terrace is the best place to see it. Sometimes people applaud when the last slice of flame disappears into the sea. Placido despises that; he slams the door behind the bar and starts yelling at his boys to fetch up more beers from the fridge and get more fish cleaned.

Beauty and pain, what a mix; they make each other worse. Pain makes beauty unbearable; beauty turns the knife in your wound. These last weeks I have chosen to drive around all the ugly roads on the island because I'm feeling enough pain already. I took the fast road from Torrenueva, and the road along the neon strip through Playa Los Angeles, and the airport road out to Ubrique and the road to Santesteban del Campo which runs by the water park and the derelict greenhouses flapping dirty plastic in the wind. Now I take my seat, the best seat, the one at the end corner table where you get the ultimate experience, where there will be nothing between me and the rocks and the water and the sunset, wondering why I want to torture myself, what kinky geophysical S & M session this is going to be. There is a mackerel sky and the sea is milky slate.

This was Matthew's idea. He chose this for us. 'Let's meet at Placido's,' he said, as if he were saying nothing important. 'We've got to talk. I'd like to get away.' He thinks if he chooses my favourite place to tell me, I won't cry so much when he tells me he's leaving. He is thoughtful, even if he gets it wrong sometimes.

I am no good with love. It's new to me, I don't know about it. What are the essential properties of love? Should it make me happy? Should it give me pain? What's happy, anyway? I don't know. Stella used to straighten me out over this kind of thing, but I can't ask Stella now.

That used to be my line: 'We've got to talk.' Weasel phrase. I know what I meant when I used it, which was: 'Bad news, you're not going to like this.' I never actually wanted to talk to Conal, or hear what he had to say; I just wanted to act out civilised behaviour, to look as if I was doing the kind of thing that a thoughtful, responsible, intelligent wife would do with her husband for it to seem as if I was behaving decently. I wouldn't sink to his level. Acting well was my only revenge.

That was my personal delusion, because everyone else around me was too wrapped up in their own things to notice I was alive. I decided, when I was very young, around the time my son was born, that if I was going to be cheated over love I would not retaliate. I would still act the way people should, the way good people acted, the way people who loved, people who went to restaurants together, people who lived in white-walled apartments with shelves full of books acted. Then I met Stella, someone who was already living my delusion, including the love, the white walls and the books; my life became a *folie à deux*.

My husband and my son had my body, but Stella had custody of my soul, until Matthew arrived. Matthew did decent behaviour big time; that was why I believed in him. But Matthew, I discover, is a great faker. He has a gift for it and most of his life he has faked for a living. 'We've got to talk.' I do not like that. All the same, I can't resist the sunset, so I'm here early, when the only other people are two Swedish boys by the door, lingering with a couple of brandies, picking their teeth at long intervals, their conversation like drops falling in a pool, just audible over the grumbling surf.

They found Stella's husband dead a week ago. His car had run off the road that winds down from their villa through the vineyards and crashed into a valley. This happened at night. It is pretty easy to run a car off many of the island's roads at night, because the tarmac is black and the lava rocks are black and the district governments are not bothered about painting white lines along the roadsides, let alone putting up crash barriers. That cult of death again. Somebody told me that the island has the worst road-accident rate in Spain; that would be quite an achievement, if it's true. People are also not bothered about verifying facts here.

It is true that Stella's husband is dead. I went with her to the hospital to make the formal identification. She didn't ask me to; she wouldn't have done that. I knew she wanted someone along and for choice she would have picked a man, most likely Matthew, so I moved in. It was her kind of action, so perhaps she saw it coming. 'Oh my God! You're not going by yourself! No, no, darling, you can't possibly. Heavens, what kind of a friend would I be if I let you walk into a morgue by yourself? Don't even think about it. Listen, I'll drive you, we'll go in my car . . .' So I went with her, another spot on my dream, the pox of deceit rotting it away from inside.

He was a mess, although I have seen worse. His face was split open like a cracked melon, the nose and mouth were mush, one of the eyes was not exactly in its socket. The gashed skin was white like raw pork rind. The nurses had washed him and tidied him a little. The dead must be buried within forty-eight hours here, one of those exotic hot-country customs Stella finds so exciting. That we both find exciting.

His hair was wet and someone had combed it to the side. Tom had hair like a lion's mane; it stood up from his forehead in dark brown tufts, beyond combing. Stella reached over and tried to make it lie right, a tender gesture with her stiff suntanned hand. 'Poor dear, he must have been so unhappy.' She was yelping into a tissue; Stella was not made to weep. 'I should have been there for him.'

Later in the day, when we went back to their villa, her mood changed. 'Stupid, stupid, stupid,' she said over and over again when she was in one of the bathrooms and thought I couldn't hear. 'Why are men so fucking, *fucking* stupid?'

All this was not in the morgue, because the island doesn't rate that kind of amenity. He was in a little room at the back of the hospital and one of the doctors had signed a death certificate. Here on Los Alcazares we have only eighty thousand inhabitants, plus a hundred thousand tourists a week, which means that a morgue and a post-mortem are luxuries for which we do not qualify. If a full autopsy has to be done, the body can be sent on one of the police boats to the regional capital on Gran Canaria. Nobody bothers much about foreigners, even though most of the population weren't born here. And in this case the cause of death was pretty obvious.

I ordered a beer. Placido only keeps Cervesa Tres Reyes. The man has a lot of focus; he's a *conejero*, Canarian homeboy. He has travelled; once he went to Vallodolid to visit his wife's family. Because he serves Americans and Germans and Belgians he sees no reason to keep their native beers. We all admired this, Stella, Tom and I, and later Matthew. We all liked to think of ourselves as such absolute folk, although Stella was the only one whose life produced evidence of this. Now my lover is coming to tell me that Stella has him, absolutely.

Los Alcazares gets television from a satellite in seven languages. Telephone calls go by satellite; you can get a lot of echo or you can get a completely clean line to the mainland, as if you were calling the house next door. The newspapers come from Stockholm, Geneva, Paris, Frankfurt and London at least a day late. People are on the Net, but the wonders of the world-wide web seem puny next to the miracles you can see out of the window, and besides, there's really only one way to find out what you need to know here. Los Alcazares lives by word of mouth; it's one of the many medieval aspects of island life. To get information, you go to a bar and ask. What you are told may or may not be true, but after a few weeks here the truth itself starts to become unimportant.

I had been here two weeks when someone told Professor Emilio Izquierdo Menendez, director of the Instituto and of a joint project with the Canarian Oceanography Foundation, that there was a woman geography teacher on the island who had good Spanish. It was to be presumed that I needed a job, because most foreigners who come here need work pretty urgently. Milo did the proper thing and sent Eva, his assistant, to find Stella and ask for an introduction. On the island, people do not make calls or send letters; they know each other, by sight at least, and they talk. Stella brought Eva to the bar by her office where we were meeting in the evening, and very shortly I had a desk at the Instituto.

Now when I am not scrambling out to the sea level monitors along the north coast, I'm making a new translation of the journals of the Cura Don Agustin Perez Rosario, the parish priest of Yesto, one of the few literate people who were able to witness the creation of Los Alcazares as it is today. When Milo's survey is completed, I will also translate the whole report, thereby, he hopes, helping to get it published in *Nature* magazine and discussed across all America, so that the United Nations will put up some money for his next project.

Yesto now is hardly even a village, just a junction on the road to Puerto de la Frontera where the road to the national park joins the main highway. There is a bar like an aircraft hangar for the coach parties, the old church standing between two dying palms and a stupendous stretch of dual carriageway built with EEC investment and landscaped with hundreds of scarlet canna lilies. In 1793, however, Yesto was a market town nestling in wheat fields and vineyards, the centre of the most fertile region of Los Alcazares.

This is how the Cura Rosario recorded the first signs of trouble.

September 20, 1793
To Almonte to give thanks for the vintage. There has been rain this year, the harvest is good and there was much celebration. One would imagine that in this cruel climate the grapes would wither on the vines, but God has given these people such ingenuity that the farmers first dig for each vine a hollow in the earth to catch the dew and shelter the young plant from the wind. A cactus is rooted first at the bottom of the hole, and the vine grafted on to its stem, so that the succulent plant can nourish the vine with its moisture. The wine has a smoky taste; they would not think much of it in Santiago, but here one can get used to it. As I was coming home at midday, a white rain, like a fall of snow, came down so thickly that my mule became Balaam's ass because he could not see his path and refused to walk on, though I beat him with a thorn branch until it split in pieces.

My life has been very corny. Fate saves all the worst clichés for me. The way I met Matthew was so corny, I should have refused to believe it. I would be ashamed of it if things had not turned out so gloriously.

The whole event is like a video stored in the archive of my memory which I can get out and run any time. While I'm waiting for him I run it over and over for myself. I can run it in slow motion and pause the best moments. Here I am at the bus stop in very heavy rain, jumping back as the bus pulls up and sends a wave of gutter water towards my feet. It's evening in winter and the lights of the bus glow out into the dark street. If I look carefully, I can see the blurred dark shape of Matthew's jacket just inside the window. I'm not feeling anything much – I didn't use my feelings then; they were hung up in a cupboard waiting for the right occasion. Maybe I'm tired at the end of the day, and I have that sad, cramped sensation that going home used to give me.

The bus stops, the doors crash open, I fold my umbrella, get on, pay the fare and take the nearest seat, on the benches that run lengthways along the vehicle. I'm carrying a bag of work, twenty-seven essays by eight-year-olds on How Rivers Begin. I put the wet umbrella on my left and keep the work on the seat on my right; then I look up and my whole life goes off in my face like a bomb.

I always pause this moment. In real life when you pause a video it's not very satisfactory. There is a tendency for the picture to shake, and it's like that with my memory of this. I can't quite make out the details. All that's really clear are Matthew's eyes, with that laser look he gets when his feelings erupt, and the eyebrows drawn flat, each black hair etched against his skin, dragged from vertical to diagonal. I can also see the raindrops on his black leather jacket. And his lips: he had a few days' growth of beard, which made them stand out bare, like they were getting ready to kiss. What's most clear is something invisible, the charge there was between us, the hissing lightning of affinity.

Next I see us thrown back in our seats by the explosion. That really happened; it's not my memory editing in comic-strip effects. I recoil and he recoils, and his foot shoots out and knocks my umbrella over, and he snaps forward and picks it up, and then we get the first line of dialogue: 'I'm sorry.' A Cary Grant moment. Corny or what?

Then comes the funny part. Matthew has to think of a way to start a conversation. He looks at the umbrella, which is the most boring piece of haberdashery ever made and no help at all. He looks at the bag, which is an anonymous black nylon thing, and closed, so no clues there. He dare not look at me in case the lightning strikes again and knocks him over – he told me afterwards he actually felt the force was that strong, that he would be thrown right across the bus if our eyes made the connection again. I'm looking at the floor myself, knowing that he's struggling with all this, understanding it all absolutely with that instant transference that's part of our thing, feeling as powerful as Cleopatra at least, another new sensation. In the end he just laughs, and shrugs because there is no natural entry to our love affair, and manages to look at me with half-closed eyes, and says, 'Are you getting off at Custom House Walk?'

'No,' I say, 'my stop is out at Green Lanes.'

'Why don't you get off at Custom House Walk,' he says, 'then we can have a drink together.'

I had to say yes. Saying no would have been like trying to make the world turn backwards. I put my right hand over my left to hide my wedding ring and found he was watching me. 'Too late,' he said.

Maybe because my life as an adult had begun with such disgrace I had tried to compensate ever after. All my life was maintained at high standards, everything I did was policed by my conscience. I never had any desire to be bad in any way, but I was out of practice with surprises. Random strikes from the great joker in the sky were not in the programme. So saying yes does not feel sinful at all, but completely correct. Only the very feeble voice of reason says that no good can come of what we are doing.

So here is Matthew handing me down from the bus. He has a special manner for these somewhat wussy acts of chivalry, a habit of quarter-turning away from the woman so that he can be polite and macho at the same time. Matthew has a natural aptitude for inspiring romance and when I remember this, it makes me think of a highwayman gallantly handing down his victim from her coach. And here we are going into the cheesy little bar in Custom House Walk, the kind of place that has wooden wine box lids nailed up and hundreds of yellowing business cards pinned to the walls. We have two glasses of their Rioja – already, please note, the Spanish motif. It's half an hour before we admit that it tastes like turpentine. We don't say much but we laugh excessively. And at the end of it, Matthew takes someone else's card off the wall and writes his number on it with the waitress's pen, and says, 'I'd like you to call me. Please.'

I can't remember exactly how I was getting through life then. It wasn't dreaming of meeting a handsome stranger; I have the impression of a state of existential patience. I know I didn't dream actively; that was something I let go of when my marriage began. When I say I followed a dream in coming here, I mean the sort of vision that burns dimly in your mind, the little votive light to the person you know you are at heart, which gutters feebly in the huge dark cathedral of who you have to be to get by. I cherished that flame but I did not pursue it, and if Matthew had not been on the bus I would have kept the flame for nothing; it would have died when I died and nobody would have known it existed. That is now a frightening thought. It makes me feel I was standing next to death, as if a truck came along instead of the bus, and hit the person standing next to me at the bus stop, and killed them. It could have been me.

Here is a story that tells you about Stella. Her villa, like all the old houses on the island, was built with an underground water cistern called an *aljibe*. The roofs of the house, which has three identical wings around a square courtyard with the external wall making the fourth side, slope to a system of gutters, to funnel the dew and rain into the *aljibe*, where it can be stored with as little loss from evaporation as possible. It's an excellent system, invented by the Arabs, and even now that the island's water comes from the desalination plants, the water truck will pipe its costly load directly into the *aljibe* where one exists.

About a third of Stella's courtyard is taken up with the shallow dome of the cistern, which has a little hatch at ground level to allow for cleaning. One day she discovered that the hatch was broken. 'Tom!' she shouted, tottering into the living room on her ridiculous sandals, 'Tom! We must get this fixed at once. We can't have a hole in the *aljibe*. Some child will fall in and drown and poison our water. You must call the builders, Tom. Tom!'

Tom came in from out back where he was washing his paintbrushes or something, smiling because he loved to serve her, and said, 'Some child will fall in and poison our water? What child is this, Stella?'

'Any *child*,' she insisted, sagging against the door frame with her cheek to the wood. In the presence of any significant male, Stella went into Marilyn mode. 'It'll be a nuisance, Tom. Can't you make them fix it?'

'Sure,' he said. 'Does it have to be today?'

'To-om! It's a *hole* in our *aljibe*.'

'Of course.' He looked at his watch, because although he had been two years on the island at that time, he still needed to remind himself of Spanish working hours. Tom adapted slowly, which was one of the things Stella had against him.

So she sighed, 'Aren't you going to call them, Tom?'

'Sure, sure.' You could almost hear the wheels going round in his head while he worked out how to make the request in Spanish. Tom was not a linguist, either, which also counted against him with Stella, who disdained contact with manual workers. Then he sloped across the room to the telephone, rummaged for the number in their book with his big, square-ended fingers and made the call. While he was speaking, Stella, who by this time would tell anyone who would still listen that Tom was no longer the man she had married, that island life had ruined him, that he had degenerated to a shadow of the glorious hero she had taken for her third husband, tripped across the marble floor and hugged his free arm. Her method of doing that was to apply her whole body to the arm, rising on tiptoe so his hand fetched up in the region of her crotch. She disengaged herself exactly at the moment he finished the call, and tripped out into the courtyard again, throwing an idle, 'Well done, darling,' over her shoulder.

This episode is typical of Stella in four ways. First, she is compulsively seductive: she plays any exchange with a man as an erotic encounter in miniature. Second, she believes that men are here to serve her. She believes this so completely that it's true, her men all adore making themselves her slaves. Of these two features of Stella's personality I was in awe for at least the first ten years of our friendship, without understanding that Stella's concept of service is not gender-specific, and that I had also been enslaved.

Third, let us observe the confusion between tragedy and nuisance. What to others may be a tragedy will impinge on Stella's life as a nuisance, but on the other hand to Stella a nuisance is actually a tragedy, because it derails her primary life activity, which is having fun.

Fourth, note the lack of proper concern for the notional child whose drowning would constitute such a nuisance. Stella actually proposed this scenario with a relish, her eyes flashed when she said, 'Some child will fall in and drown.' She regards children as a supreme nuisance, or indeed a supreme tragedy. She hates them.

Tom, unlucky fellow, had the gut feeling that there was some connection between marriage and children. It was one of those Maupassant-dark misunderstandings between the two of them; he had imagined that she wanted to get married in order at last to have a child, while she had just wanted a husband. This mismatch of life goals was beyond Tom's understanding. He was flummoxed by the role reversal; he came from a world where girls entrapped men to get children. For two years, since he got off the plane with a few grains of the wedding rice still in his hair, he had lurched uncomprehendingly after his brilliant wife, expecting her at any minute to stop flitting all night from bar to bar and stay home to decorate a nursery.

My story, of course, pushed the child button with Stella. 'That is one bum rap,' she pronounced. 'A life sentence. You poor, *poor* darling. Oh, I just can't believe something so cruel could have happened to you. I want to make it all up to you right now, I want to give you some real good times. My God, and you weren't even twenty. It's too mean, it really is.' So she saw me as disadvantaged, because of my child, and I saw her as disadvantaged, because she had no child. Now I no longer have a child, the equilibrium is out.